Marigold

and the

Marvelous Misfits

Becky Smeltzer-Lowe

Marigold and the Marvelous Misfits

by

Becky Smeltzer-Lowe

Cover Design: by Steve Smeltzer (ssmeltzer@comcast.net)

eBook Conversion/paperback format by: Word-2-Kindle

MARIGOLD AND THE MARVELOUS MISFITS

Dedicated to Lilly

Much appreciation is given to my editor, Janice Marie Hieber. Your attention to detail, your expertise, as well as your positive comments, kept my fingers tapping the keys. For Steve Smeltzer: artist, musican, and creative genius. Thanks for designing the cover and for being my brother.

I am so grateful to granddaughter and middle school student, Lilly Hutsell. Your encouragement and suggestions were insightful, as well as constructive. For my grandchildren, Evan and Olivia Weisenburger. Higher than the highest star; deeper than the deepest sea. For Andrew and Camille Stroh; Josephine, Eleanor, and Marie Hesler. I love all of you! ..

This book is the first in the Misfit series.

Chapter 1

"Oh, look! Here comes ug-ugly Freak G-Girl!" Marigold knew it was Billy Smith without even looking: Billy, with his fake stutter as he imitated her. Billy, as he encouraged the other kids around him to join in the cruel taunts. Billy and his cohorts from elementary school, now traveling together to middle school.

Marigold Stroop stumbled slowly to the bus stop that sunny August 19th in Freemont, Michigan. First day of sixth grade at Brentwood, first day of middle school, first time on a school bus. A lot of firsts. And she knew that she could have been a lot less anxious, her heartbeat would of been a normal thump, thump, thump, instead of a pounding bama-bama-bama (like some crazy alien was about to charge out of her chest), if only she could have talked right, been wearing a regular pair of jeans, a nice T-shirt, and cute gym shoes. Nothing fancy, not even expensive.

Normal could have been great, but that wasn't going to happen--not with her mother, a self-proclaimed Miss Fashionista, in charge. The night before, Marigold had gone to bed under her sunset comforter, her head resting on a ruffled yellow pillowcase, when her mom tiptoed into her room. Tenderly, she'd placed a folded gold and orange flowered dress, orange socks, orange underwear, and yellow tennis shoes on the chair beside her bed. These were the clothes she was going to have to wear to school the next day? Marigold's large green eyes became even larger. What sixth grade girl dressed in those kinds of clothes?

Marigold pulled the comforter over her head and said in a muffled voice: "N-No, Mom, I c-can't wear those! Not c-cool! No sixth grade g-girl is going to wear clothes like those at Brentwood t-tomorrow!"

Marigold's mom, smelling like roses from her job as a florist at Greta's Garden, uncovered her daughter's head. The daisy barrette above her yellow bangs bobbled, as she lowered herself onto her knees and stared into her daughter's eyes. "But you don't have to be like everyone else, do you?"

Marigold said, "Yeah, M-mom. Pretty m-much."

"No you doooo not." Marsha Stroop kissed Marigold on the forehead, before standing up with crackly knees and tippy-toeing from the room, taking the smell of roses with her.

So now Marigold was walking to the bus stop, eyes down, stepping in her stupid yellow sneakers over the big cracks in the sidewalk. That saying, Step on a crack, break your mother's back, sang in her head. It was a rhyme her mom had taught her many years earlier when they had walked, hand-in-hand, to the store. Marsha Stroop often told Marigold, "I break my back every day arranging flowers to make others smile, even though nobody ever sends me any. Do you know why I do that?"

And Marigold always said, "S-So you can put f-food on the table, a r-roof over our heads, clothes on our b-backs."

And Marsha Stroop would nod and make the daisy barrette above her bangs bounce. "Because?"

"Because you l-love me so much."

"Yes, I do. To the stars and back."

So Marigold wore the stupid clothes, dumb yellow shoes and flower hair clip--things she'd worn to elementary school. Add the new orange kitty book bag her mother had bought with her "very last dime". She smiled through gritted teeth and put on the clothes and shoes, slung on the book bag, but knew someday it was going to be different. It was going to be oh, so different.

With each step toward the bus stop, the smells of bacon and eggs wafting through open kitchen windows made Marigold want to throw up. Barf right there on that sidewalk, with huge cracks to who-knew-where (which her mother must never fall into). The closer she got, the words from the other kids increased in volume and tempo. She had heard them all before; they weren't new to her. The words were slimy venom spitting at her from very familiar lips.

"Here comes ug-ugly Sun-Sunshine Girl!"

"Freak!"

"Dw-Dweeb!"

Marigold adjusted the flower clip in her gold hair as she tried to think of something, anything—-another rhyme or a song or multiplication facts to fill up her mind, so she couldn't hear the kids. She tried to stop up the tears welling like pools in her eyes. Her breath was short, hot, and she felt dizzy. Was she going to pass out right here? She looked up and took deep breaths...because that always helped.

Staring up into the blue sky above her with its puffy white clouds, she imagined what it would be like to be a bird, soaring freely, no problems in the world. Oh, up there flying in the clouds would be so nice.

Then, at that very moment, a huge black bird (the largest bird Marigold had ever, ever seen) suddenly careened through the sky and made a circle directly above their heads. "What?" She stumbled, almost losing her balance in the process. What kind of crazy monster bird is that? And why aren't the kids at the bus stop watching it? But she knew their attention was focused on something else--her. Fourteen eyeballs taking her all in with her stupid yellow shoes, orange socks, and flowered dress, not to mention the absurd flower clip her mother had fastened in her hair before planting a slobbery kiss on her forehead. So far, they couldn't see the orange kitty book bag Marsha Stroop had bought with her "very last dime". They would though-soon enough. Then things were really going to get bad.

Without even looking, Marigold knew her mom was standing in their front yard watching her walk to the corner. Her mom did that every school day morning-rain or shine, snow or icy sleet, just like a mailman. Even when Marigold had walked to Harrisville Elementary the last six years of her life, only two blocks away, her mom had been a statue in their front yard-lips in a straight line, eyes intent, as she focused on her only child walking to school. Now, Marigold knew she was watching her walk to the bus stop. How embarrassing! Maybe that was okay kindergarten through second, maybe third--but fourth grade on up? Man, so uncool!

"I watch you walk away until I can't see your golden hair shining like the sunshine anymore," her mother often told her. Marigold had begun cringing when Marsha Stroop said that. When she was in the primary grades, okay, but now? Puh-lease. Her mother's "standing in the front yard" attire also embarrassed her. She always wore the same thing: a shabby yellow robe with orange fuzzy slippers and her hair in curlers. It was her outfit each morning, before she changed to go to her job at Greta's.

"You are my whole life," was another of her mom's favorite sayings, and even though it made Marigold wish her mom would get a life, she also knew her mother was her only friend and the only one who would have cared if she flew up into the blue sky with that huge, black bird and disappeared into the clouds forever.

Her arrival at the bus stop, where the other seven kids wore cool jeans, T-shirts, and name-brand shoes, brought more taunts and giggles. To Marigold, each unkind word, every whisper and cruel laugh, felt like a sharp nail pounding into her not-so-tough skin. She swallowed hard, chewed on a thumbnail, and spit it out.

The Plan she had been considering reentered her mind. She used to think about it once a month, then once a week. It seemed like she was considering The Plan daily now, and she had begun thinking of ways to do it. If she hadn't known her Plan might hurt her mom, she would have turned right around and done it today. But for now, she would keep putting one ugly yellow shoe in front of the other, as she stepped over every crack. Someday would be the right time, and when that came, that's when it would happen.

The bullying continued. Words like "Bird Puke, Canary, Flower Girl, Ugly Freak, St-St-Stutterer" were hammered out until the yellow school bus pulled up with a screech. Marigold chewed, then spit out another fingernail, trudged up the steps into the bus filled with many unfamiliar faces, and found a seat way in the back away from the other kids. She knew they didn't want to sit with her--and it went without saying, she sure didn't want to be close to them. Then, as the bus zoomed past her house, there was her robe-adorned mother waving crazily at her face in the open bus window.

"Have a good day, sweetie!" Marsha Stroop shouted.

That resulted in even more loud yells and laughter. Marigold tried to concentrate on a poster of smiling children stuck crookedly to the bus's ceiling. Didn't the bus driver hear them? Why didn't he say something?

Billy Smith, the boy from the bus stop who had caused Marigold great grief since kindergarten, turned around and shouted, "Hey Flower Freak, was that your mommy waving bye-bye?"

Marigold bit on a knuckle, tasted blood, and acted like she was ignoring him.

"D-Did she make sure you went p-poop this morning?" Billy's friend, Mike Botowski, chimed in with his stutter imitation..

"Then did she wipe your butt?" Billy laughed.

The whole bus rocked with merriment. Marigold forced her eyes to stay on that poster until the bus finally stopped with a loud screeeech in front of the school, and all the kids flew out, a swarm of wasps ready to attack some new, thin-skinned victim. When it was finally quiet, Marigold lowered her eyes and reached for her book bag.

The bus driver, some sweaty man with black, slicked back hair, had turned partway in his seat and was staring at her. He raised his chubby hands in the air and said, "Whats-a wrong with you? Aren't you gonna get off-a this bus and go into school?" Marigold hurried past this guy wearing a name tag that said "Mr. Carini" and through the open bus doors. She figured he was Italian since he looked like one of the chefs from Italy on TV and sounded like him, too. But those chefs on television? They were always laughing and friendly. The snarl on his lips, as she scurried by, said he thought she was a dweeb, too.

Marigold's sweaty hands took out her locker combination from her book bag, and she spun the dial. She took deep breaths in and out, in and out. After three tries, she finally got it open and put her afternoon social studies book away. Her homeroom was just on the other side of her locker, a fact that almost made her smile. Almost. Smiling probably wasn't going to be on her agenda today, but not having to walk through the throngs of kids to get to where she had to go was a good thing--a very good thing.

She ducked into Room 102 and plopped down in the back. Because this was her first day at Brentwood Middle School, she saw a lot of new faces--new faces above bodies wearing cool clothes and nice shoes. There were lots of unfamiliar sixth graders from different feeder schools, who were probably about to launch insulting comments in her direction. She bet these new kids were going to be "attackers", not "attackees", like her. She bit a cuticle, stared down at the scratched desk, and breathed in the smell of chalk, books, and stink from adolescent kids who hadn't showered recently. Marigold tried to ignore the whispers happening between huddled friends who giggled, and she bet they were staring in her direction.

She tried hard, really hard, to not look affected by what she knew was happening. She was the new dork to the new faces and the old dork to the old ones. If she ignored them, maybe (poof) they would disappear, or at least be quiet. But she knew in her nauseated gut that wasn't going to happen--never ever. And as for the future? Nothing was going to change. Why should it? It never had.

Mrs. Drebel, homeroom teacher manned with a wooden clipboard and fountain pen, raised her hand in the air, as if she thought that was going to get the kids to be quiet. Wrongo-Pongo. Her navy dress, with the stiff white collar, and those dark blue, rubber-soled shoes were probably carefully selected by her a week ago to show students she was professional and quite in control. Nobody had better mess with her. Good luck with that, Marigold thought.

The black framed eyeglasses, hanging on a lanyard around her skinny, wrinkled neck supported that "I want to be professional" appearance. Yep, she was Mrs. Drebel and in charge. Except she wasn't. The talkers paid no attention to her. The corners of her red slash of a mouth traveled downward on her white powdered face, and she stabbed the air with the fountain pen. Still, none of the yackers stifled it.

"Be quiet!" she yelled.

Nope. Wasn't going to happen.

She pounded her clipboard on a kid's desk in front of her. Nada.

"I'm warning you!" Evidence of huge tears were pooling in this teacher's eyes.

The roar of the crowd was deafening. Marigold shook her head and tented her sweaty fingers. Oh, brother. First day of school, and kids were out of control.

"Class, you must be quiet so I can take attendance!" She raised the sword-pen above her head and bounced on those shoes, like she was on a war horse heading into battle. "And if you don't? Detention tomorrow after school for the whole class!" She had screeched so loudly, she began to choke.

Well, that threat of detention worked, and the talkers hushed. She started again. When she was almost through the roster and coughed out, "Marigold Stroop?", the snorts and giggles began once more.

"H-here," Marigold said, but the teacher couldn't hear her above the din.

Mrs. Drebel looked over the top of her glasses, and her gray eyes scanned the room. "Class, shut the h-heck up ! Marigold Stroop? Are-you-here?" Her croaky voice was almost gone.

"Here!" Marigold said again, a little louder this time. She also raised her hand in the air.

Billy hollered: "She's r-r-right there!" He imitated her stutter, then stood up and pointed a dirty finger in Marigold's direction. "The one with the crazy clothes! Ha! Ha! Ha! Can't you s-s-see her? Well, if you can't, you must be blind, T-T-Teach!" Then all of his friends, of whom there were many, joined in the guffaws.

Marigold slunk down further into her chair, as Billy's big belly shook and wobbled from side to side. Why, she wondered, didn't anyone make fun of Billy but thought her clothes and the way she talked were so awful? A question she would never have an answer to, she figured, and The Plan began nibbling at her brain once again. That Plan was an ever-present visitor, who had set up residence in her mind, liked to remind her-often-that it was on the pad and ready to launch.

Luckily, since homeroom only lasted twenty minutes, the bell bonged announcing it was time for first period. Mrs. Drebel hadn't gotten past the letter "T" on her attendance roster. Even though this teacher held that writing weapon high into the air and shouted, "Be quiet!", "Sit your butts down!", and words no teacher (even frustrated ones) should ever, ever say, still the moving mountain of children occurred--almost mowing her over in the process.

As Marigold began through the door behind the rumbling onslaught, she saw the teacher slide down into her wooden chair and wipe her eyes with the back of her hands. If she wasn't in a hurry to get to her next class, Marigold would have told Mrs. Drebel she was sorry those kids had treated her so disrespectfully. Her heart hurt for this upset teacher, during homeroom, on the very first day of school.

Chapter 2

First period, math. Marigold didn't like math. No, more like Marigold hated, detested, and abhorred math. She would have rather swum through pond scum with her mouth and eyes wide open than journey to math class, even though she knew she had to go. It was one of those rules her mom had instilled- "You must graduate from high school, college, medical school, and make lots of money for us." The back row was calling her name, and so she headed there-back row, seat by the open window. That way she had a place to barf if math or the rude, wicked kids made her sick. Or she could escape. She analyzed the space and wondered if she would fit through it. Then she decided yes, she would. She plunked herself down and pretended she was interested in her math book, even if she wasn't.

"Hi!"some guy said, as he slid into the desk beside her.

Marigold ignored him. Why was this dude sitting beside her? Nobody ever sat beside her voluntarily, and nobody, but nobody, ever said, "Hi".

The next thing she knew, five fingers with five rings had jutted into her space and were dancing in front of her face.

"Hi?" the same low voice said.

Marigold continued staring into her math book.

"Hey, the least you can do is be lookin' at me, mon. You know, tryin' to be friendly. In Jamaica, kids are taught to be friendly--place I'm from."

She looked over and quickly sucked in some air. If she thought she was absurdly colorful, her brightness did not come close to this guy's red T-shirt; purple cargo pants; green, sparkling shoes; rings on each finger of his brown hands; black dreads with various colors of beads woven through them; and a wide smile with teeth that were oh, so pearly white. And that hand protruding in her direction? It now grabbed and shook her right, sweaty one up and down.

"Well, now, that's more like it," this guy said as he stretched out his purple legs and bright, green sparkling tennies. "Name's Jus, short for Justice Michael Jury--too long, I'm thinkin'. So I just go by Jus, mon."

Would you just be quiet or evaporate into space, Marigold wished. She wasn't used to anyone wanting to sit by her and talking in a friendly way, so what was up with this dude? Kids only wanted to say rude words to her and try to hurt her feelings. That's how it always had been, always would be, so why was this weirdo wanting to be nice? Maybe if she ignored him, he would just go away. (Poof)

But Jus wasn't about to go away. "So, what are you thinkin' about this new school, Marigold? Me? Well, it's just bein' a place where I put in my time, so someday I can be graduatin' from high school and do what I am really wantin' to do-be a fashion designer. Yeah, mon. This is just a cruisin' through place for me. Kinda like McDonalds, but without burgers and fries."

Well, now, Marigold couldn't have kept her eyes off him--even if she'd tried. He had a very cool, Jamaican accent and knew her name. How did he know her name? She had never seen Jus before in her life. She decided he had probably been in her homeroom and heard her name called, seen Billy point her out, but she hadn't noticed him. Because if she had ever seen this Justice Michael Jury (Jus for short), she sure would have remembered him. Yep, no doubt about that.

"I am likin' all your colors, mon," Jus rattled on. He ran his bejeweled fingers over his body. "I'm bein' colorful, too, as you probably noticed. Can ya imagine what people woulda said about me back in the sixties here in America, mon, when racism was alive and well? They woulda said I was the colorful colored boy!" Then Jus laughed loudly at his own joke. "No, wait--the queer, colorful, colored boy. Yeah, that kinda prejudice might have improved, bein' this is the twenty-first century, but the judgmental attitude, the bullyin', hasn't. Guess you, Marigold Stroop, are knowin' all about that, mon."

Marigold couldn't help but smile, probably the first smile she'd made at school for a very long time.

Still, she wondered how this guy knew her name? Now, first-and-last name. Homeroom? No, probably since she looked so weird, well, word got around. But she didn't look any weirder than he did; at least, she hoped not. And she might stutter, but he talked strangely, too. A cool kind of strange, though.

"We've been waitin' to meet ya, you know." He quickly looked around, and the dreads swirled like they were doing some kind of salsa dance around his head.

"M-Meet me?" Marigold asked. "And who is 'w-we'?"

But then Mr. Nicholson, the math teacher, started taking attendance.

"We'll be talkin' more at lunch, mon," Jus whispered. "Can't wait for ya to be meetin' the Misfits."

"M-Misfits?" Would "Misfits" mean they didn't "fit" someplace? Was it possible somebody else felt that way, too?

Marigold raised her hand when the teacher called her name and actually said, "H-Here" loudly enough for him to hear.

When the teacher said, "Justice Michael Jury", and Jus said, "I am goin' by Jus, mon," Mr. Nicholson only stared at him. No nod, no smile, just stared. Marigold looked around the room and felt a rush of relief, realizing Billy was not there. Without him to stir everyone up, there were only a few kids whispering and pointing in their direction. Hurtful but not causing great pain. No knife-like words stabbing into her thin skin, and she could sort of deal with that. Applying a Band Aid was always easier than wearing a cast. The fellow weirdo sitting beside her? Well, Jus didn't seem to even need a Band Aid.

"Let's begin with the beginning," Mr. Nicholson announced, then smirked like he thought he was some stand-up comedian. "Page three, math wizards. We are about to begin on a great adventure, a journey that will take us to a land where we can solve difficult equations. Isn't that exciting? Did you pack your bags?" He pointed to his forehead. "Your bag better be a carry-on! Ha!"

Marigold and Jus exchanged rolling eyes. Great adventure? Pack your bags? Carry-on? Really?

But Mr. Nicholson was all involved in his metaphor, as he continued tapping a finger on his forehead and swaying from side to side. "You must pack your attention, your organizational skills, your memory, and your hard work all up here. Plus, you must be in class, don't miss one day—unless, of course, you break out in a Hooley Booley rash that is highly contagious, and you will end up giving it to all of us!" He laughed so hard, he actually bent over at the waist, and Marigold wondered if he had packed any sanity up in that brain of his. Maybe his wasn't a carry-on; maybe he had checked his bag at the front door. Would he stand back up? Did he need the Heimlich Maneuver? Nope. He finally stood up.

Marigold and Jus both shook their heads. This teacher had already given her a headache, packed bags or no. She turned to page three and stared at math terms, but had a hard time concentrating on the words. The fact that Jus knew her name and how she'd been bullied, said they'd been "waitin' for" her, blew her away. Waaay crazy was when he said she was going to meet the Misfits at lunch. Huh? Well, all of that bunched together prevented her from focusing. Guess her bags weren't carry-ons, especially her attention one, and she doubted she would ever pack one. She had other things to think about right now.

Crazy Mr. Nicholson continued blabbing, and at one point even turned out the lights, jumped up on a table, and started shining his laser beam all around the room. What did he think they were? Cats? She loved cats but wasn't one. Marigold caught bits of some terms he was trying to explain, but she wasn't going to be able to say them back with their definitions, even if she'd tried, and she wasn't into trying.

At one point, she looked over at a picture Jus was doodling on his notebook paper. She guessed he couldn't concentrate either. He was sketching a black bird, with very long wings, soaring through the sky. A bird that reminded her of the one she had seen earlier that morning, as she'd walked to the bus stop. She chalked that up as coincidence. There was no way Jus could have known about that bird.

At long last, math ended, and it was on to second period, language arts. It was a subject she actually liked--or had liked in the past. She hoped this teacher wouldn't disappoint. Jus walked his over-six foot self beside her down the hall, but when she started to turn into Room 109, he said, "I am headin' down to science, mon. Room 115."

Marigold looked up at him. Way up. "Science? I don't have that till later."

"Yeah, science. Bet science's not gonna be helpin' me in my fashion goal, either." He chuckled and twisted his rings, did a little green-shoed dance.

Marigold actually felt a bit disappointed that he wasn't going into Room 109 with her, then wondered why she cared. "So where do you g-go third period?" She retrieved her schedule from the front pocket of her book bag, very glad Jus didn't make a rude comment about the kitty on the front.

Examining his schedule, he said: "Third is gym (yeck), fourth, language arts, then lunch. After lunch is art—-finally, and last period, social studies. How about you, mon?"

"Third's art, f-fourth is science, then lunch like you, s-sixth's gym-then social studies. Where d-do you have social studies?"

"Room 216, upstairs."

"M-me, too," she said with a grin. She was glad he hadn't looked at her strangely because of her stutter-— not even once.

Instead, he high-fived her. "Yay. We can be endin' the day together, mon."

She smiled and nodded, then wondered why she had already made such a connection with this guy. She always kept a big distance between herself and other kids, for fear she was going to get hurt, and also because nobody ever acted like they wanted to be her friend, anyway. It sounded weird, even to her, but it almost seemed like she was supposed to meet this guy named Justice Michael Jury, "Jus" for short.

"Sounds g-good." She hoisted her book bag up onto her back.

"But I'll be seein' ya at lunch, girlfriend. Look for the guy havin dreads and shiny rings!" He waved his fingers in the air and did another shuffle dance with his sparkly shoes.

Marigold realized they had arrived at her room, and Jus bent down to try and whisper in her ear (a difficult task). "Hey, mon, you are gonna be fine. Don't be lettin' the Droobs bring ya down. They're the idiots, not you."

Slowly, she walked into her class. Without Jus by her side, she could feel herself caving and considering The Plan once more. Still, she tried to remember Jus's words (after all, he was somehow surviving the cruelty, which she was certain he also faced). Plus, he seemed happy. At least he was laughing and had friends, the "Misfits". What had he told her? She was going to "be fine", and that "they're the idiots, not you"? So she took deep breaths and tried to relax, tried to ignore Billy already in the front row, and the Droobs (the name Jus had called them), joining force with giggles and chatter.

"Okay, let's begin class." Mrs. Toon, the teacher, had glistening black hair and wore a black dress.

Billy jumped out of his seat and flipped off the lights, then announced that the teacher didn't have to turn them back on, since Marigold's clothes were so bright, they would light up the whole room. Several classmates tittered. When he didn't seem to be getting all the attention he wanted, he jumped up and down in place and gestured with big sweeping motions that those gigglers were to laugh louder, which they did. Marigold felt her face getting warm and knew her blush was adding even more color to her already "bright" self.

Mrs. Toon clearly was not impressed. "You must sit down and be quiet," she commanded as she turned on the lights. "What is your name?"

"Mike. Gee, Teach, I was just trying to save energy! Aren't we supposed to be saving energy?" He hadn't sat down yet, and the laughter continued.

The teacher reached for a referral form. "Mike what?" Her pen was poised above the page.

"Mike Botowski." The laughter only increased in volume.

"His name is Billy! Billy Smith!" some kid beside Billy shouted.

Mrs. Toon scrawled her pen across the referral and stuck it out in Billy's direction.

Billy stopped mid-bounce. The laughter of the others settled down.

"What? What's that?" he feigned idiocy, which really wasn't too much of a pretend, Marigold thought.

The teacher strolled over and placed it in the middle of his desk. "Go."

"Where? Go where? Is your name really Looney Tunes? Are you a cartoon? My dad watches 'Looney Tunes' on that TV station for really old people-like you."

Mrs. Toon, still with complete composure, stated, "If you look at the top of the referral, I think you will be able to tell where you are to go. You can read, can't you Billy Smith?"

Billy picked up the form; his eyes scanned the page. Then he threw his arms into the air. "To the office? You are sending me to the office for trying to save energy? Really?"

"Really," she replied. "So glad you can read."

Well, now Billy pointed a finger at Mrs. Toon. "That's fine, just fine. But I'm telling the frickin' principal you don't care about saving energy, and he's going to fire you. You are going to lose your job, Mrs. Looney Tunes, very old cartoon lady."

That got Billy's supporters laughing again, as he exited the premises. He bowed first, though, before slamming the door behind him-with a huge bang.

Mrs. Toon's eyes perused the class, and she raised a stack of referrals into the air. "And as for Billy Smith's allies? I can give a form like this to each one of you, and you can join your grand leader down in the office. I'm sure he would love that." Like someone had raised a magic hush-wand, the laughter stopped, and the room became silent.

Now, I guess we can get started," Mrs Toon said. She took attendance and then said, "Your assignment for today is to write an essay entitled, 'The Kind of Person I Am'. I would put some thought into this, if I were you, and it is due at the end of the period." She glanced at the clock. "You have exactly forty-four minutes to write a thoughtful 'A Plus' paper."

There was a shuffling of notebooks and the sound of the popping open and clicking shut of metal-ringed binders. Marigold began writing:

THE KIND OF PERSON I AM

I am a regular person, and I want people to know I am normal inside. I wear bright orange and yellow clothes and stupid yellow shoes. I have a crazy flower clip in my hair. I stutter but I am a normal kid inside. I never want to hurt anybodys feelings. I am a person who loves animals a whole lot, especialy cats and dogs. But I hate my stupid book bag with a kitten on it since it's for a little kid. I am the kind of person who loves her mom. She is raising me all by herself. I never knew my dad. Mom doesn't make much money working in a flower shop so she can't aford many clothes. I am the kind of person who appresiates what Mom has bought me but I wish I had cool clothes. I am the kind of person who is normal inside even if I sometimes don't look like it on the outside or can't talk right. I love animals and my mom. I am somebody who never hurts anybodys feelings. I know how bad that can hurt.

When the bell rang, Marigold realized someone was looking over her shoulder. She hoped it wasn't a Droob, but when she glanced up, she saw it was the teacher. Mrs. Toon made a loud sniffle, reached down, and carefully picked up her essay.

"Marigold," Mrs. Toon said, as all the kids threw their papers on the front table and rushed out of the room, "let me assure you that your life is going to get better, so much better. You won't feel a victim much longer of the cruelty that, I believe, so many kids are capable of slinging at others. You will have friends. I promise you that. We have been waiting for you."

Then Mrs. Toon sashayed back to her desk, where she grabbed a tissue, and Marigold chewed her nail. Those words stating "waiting for you" sounded waaay familiar. Hadn't Jus told her that last period? What was going on?

"You had better get going, Marigold-on to your next class. Don't want a detention for being tardy from a Droob teacher. Tweet!"

Tweet? Marigold wondered if she was hearing things. "O-O-kay," she said, while she gathered up her belongings and started for the door.

Then, as she was leaving the room, Mrs. Toon said, "Stay strong, Marigold. Everything is going to get better soon. Keep your eyes up, look for the sunshine, the bird. Tweet! Don't let the dark clouds blur your vision."

Well, Marigold almost tripped over those yellow shoes. It had to be a coincidence again. First, Jus drawing a huge bird resembling the one she had seen on her way to the bus stop, and now Mrs. Toon telling her to keep looking up-just like what she had been doing-in order to survive. Then she'd added to "look for the sunshine, the bird"? Then a "Tweet"?

Chapter 3

Marigold shook her head and aimed her shoes to Room 105, art. She knew she needed to hurry, but as she was scurrying that way, Billy's best bud, Mike Botowski, stuck out his brand new Van shoe and tripped her. Down she went, and the book bag she was carrying in her arms went flying. A group of kids had gathered around, while Mike ripped the contents out of the bag, then started stomping all over it. Several kids cheered him on with, "Go! Go! Go! Go!"

"Look!" Mike shouted, when he kicked the book bag to the wall, "I'm kicking her little kitty cat! I'm gonna crush this cat so it can't breathe anymore! Aw, poor puddy tat is going to die!"

Marigold finally raised herself up and tried to gather the strewn books and papers. She had about given up, since Mike was now in the process of scattering all the wrinkled pages in different directions, when a girl with messy black hair, a black eye mask, and a black outfit stepped up to Mike and gave him a quick kick in the rear. Once he was down onto his stomach, she twisted his arms behind his back and said, "Go ahead, Marigold, get your things, dude." Then she glared at the surrounding group. "And the rest of you Droobs? Unless you want to end up like Mike, here, get your butts to class! Now!"

The others fled, as Mike whimpered, "Go get me help! Tell the office I was beat up! I'm hurt!"

Nobody seemed to be paying attention and just kept running the other way. When the bell rang announcing the beginning of third period, Super Girl in black stood up, releasing her hold on Mike.

Mike slowly inched upward with a moan and groan and ran his hands over his behind. He glared at this powerhouse in black and pointed a shaking finger. "You messed with the wrong guy. You are going to pay-big time!" Then he hobbled away.

Suddenly, with a whoosh, Mrs. Toon was standing there. Since Marigold had been re-stuffing her book bag, she hadn't noticed her approaching. "Here," the teacher said, handing the girl in black and Marigold each a pink slip. "These are passes to get you into your next class." She patted the girl in black on the shoulder. "Good work, Della. Mike was very deserving of what he got-and Marigold? Well, I think you have just met your second new friend. Tweet!"

Della nodded, with a slight smile at Marigold, and rushed down the hall.

"Thanks, D-Della." Marigold brushed herself and the book bag off. Her second new friend? Mrs. Toon somehow knew about a first new friend? Would that be Jus? She turned to thank Mrs. Toon, only to discover the teacher was no longer there. Marigold plodded to her next class, with a bloody knee and a very dirty book bag in tow.

At least it is art class, she told herself. Art is good. Art allows me to be creative, to use my imagination, to-to-and that was when she tooled into Room 136 and saw Mike Botowski, bent over at the teacher's desk, an anguished look on his face, while he complained about his injuries. Marigold could tell that's what he was doing, because he was pointing to his rear end, then at each arm. The teacher, Mr. Reynolds, was nodding his head and taking it all in.

Mike happened to turn and notice Marigold coming through the door, a pink pass in hand. "There she is!" he whined. "That's the girl who started it all! I was just walking down the hall, minding my own business, when she- (he pointed a finger) she tripped me and started pounding the sh-pounding the crap out of me. Some real tall girl in black, who looked like some kind of freaky Batgirl, joined in. They both took turns hitting me, twisting my arms! Here, see the bruises they gave me??" He stuck out his arms for Mr. Reynolds to see.

Marigold, all four foot eight inches of her, gently laid the pass on the teacher's desk and started for a table in the back. The blood from her knee had now begun trickling down her leg; she knew her hair was a total mess.

Then, just to add even more insanity to the bizarre bin, Billy stood up from a middle table and hollered, "Mike's right! Marigold went to Harrisville Elementary School with us, and she's always been a big trouble maker! She might look small, but she's real mean, and she gets kids to help her beat us up!"

Marigold slowly slid into her seat and tried to mop up the blood dripping down her leg with a tissue she took from her grimy book bag. She attempted to smooth down her hair and reattach the flower hair clip back where it had been, tried to ignore all the probing eyes aimed at her.

Stomp, stomp, stomp! Mr. Reynolds now stood his very tall frame beside Marigold, and she looked up into his frowning face. He cleared his throat. "Is this true? Did you instigate the altercation?"

Marigold didn't know what "instigate" or "altercation" meant, but she knew nothing Mike or Billy had said was true, so she just shook her head no and kept wiping away at the dripping blood that had now stained her orange sock and yellow shoe.

"Well," he continued, "I'll tell you one thing. If you are a troublemaker, like they say you are, you are in for a very long school year. And I will be watching you. You are mine." He pointed two fingers at his eyes, then at hers. After a stomp, stomp, stomp, he was back to the front of the room again. "Here, take this pass and go to the office," he said to Mike.

Finally, Marigold thought with a sniffle. Finally, that Droob will get what he deserves.

But Mr. Reynolds finished with, "Have the nurse look at those bruises on your arms. Maybe she'll put some ice on them. Not your butt, though."

Whaat? Why was he babying that creep who clearly "instigated" the whole "altercation", whatever that meant? Marigold continued dabbing at the blood.

"But before you leave, Mike, I am the football coach." He turned toward the class. "How many of you guys would be interested in playing football this year? How many macho men do I have in this room?"

Mike and Billy instantly had their arms waving in the air, before a couple of other guys joined in. Marigold wondered how in the world Mike was able to wave his arms, but needed to go to the office for ice?

"Good." Mr. Reynolds wore a big smile. Then, pointing at Mike, he said, "You go get those sore arms iced down, so you will be ready for football tryouts next week." He patted Mike on the back before holding the door wide open for him to leave.

Marigold checked her leg and saw the bleeding had almost stopped. Strange, she thought, how Mr. Reynolds was all about sending Mike to the office for ice, but he didn't care about her bleeding leg. Well, it was probably because he hadn't noticed, or she wouldn't make a good football player, all four feet-eight, puny inches of herself. Plus, she was a girl. Except, as Mike and Billy had lied about her meanness and her strength, she was amazed he hadn't signed her up for the football team, anyway.

"Today, I want you to sketch a picture of yourself doing the best thing you did on summer break. You need to take a long time, so it'll be good, and don't turn it in till the end of the period. Plus, don't bother me."

He pointed at a girl in the front row. "Hey, beautiful. Nice legs. You pass out the paper."

Then he nodded at Billy. "And you, future quarterback, you give everyone a pencil."

As the girl and Billy got materials off the teacher's desk and began distributing them to the kids in the class, Mr. Reynolds slid down in his chair and closed his eyes.

Nap time? Marigold wondered. As she asked herself which of her very unexciting events during the summer she would attempt to illustrate, Billy slapped a pencil on the table in front of her, then hissed, "You messed with the wrong guy, when you got Batgirl to be your attack dog, um, attack bat. Wrong guy, you frickin' freak." He formed his eyes into narrow slits. "You are going to pay—big time."

Marigold's hands were shaking so badly, she had a hard time holding onto her pencil. Finally, after taking a few deep breaths and trying to calm herself, she began drawing. Her favorite memory from this past summer?

First, she sketched some pin-point lines of grass on the bottom. Stems and leaves with flowers- roses, marigolds, and daisies-poked out of this grass. With a small sigh, she let the imaginary breeze in the trees she was sketching sweep her mind back to that warm summer day.

Between the two oak trees she had drawn, she penciled a line. There was a woman wearing a blowing, orange dress with a large basket beside her. She was hanging a dress on this line, and seated cross-legged on a blanket in the garden was a young girl, with blowing hair and a flower barrette clipped to the side of her head. The girl wore a smile, as she watched her mother at work. A bird flew through puffy clouds above their heads, and butterflies danced among the flowers.

She couldn't help but feel the calmness she had known that warm summer day, and so wished she could return right then to that time and place. She signed her name, Marigold Marsha Stroop, at the bottom of her creation. Next, came the refining of details, until the bell rang, and then she made her way to the front, carrying her book bag on her back and the drawing in front of herself.

As she placed her drawing carefully on the teacher's desk, a mean boy's voice she well-recognized came from behind and said, "Really? That's the most fun you had all summer? Not exactly Disney World, huh?" Then Billy slapped his drawing of a bunch of scribbling lines on top of hers.

Mr. Reynolds came over and looked at Billy's creation. He grinned. "What's this, Billy? An example of impressionistic art?"

Billy nodded enthusiastically. "You got it, Mr.-Mr-"

"Reynolds," the teacher said. "Coach Reynolds."

"Right. Mr. Reynolds-um, Coach Reynolds. This is what I saw when I was at the top of the ride, Space Mountain, in Disney World last July."

Mr. Reynolds held it up and squinted. "Yes. Looks crazy and violent. I can see that, Billy!"

Billy smiled and began to tromp out the door. "I knew you would, Mr. Reynolds-Coach." He gave the teacher a "thumbs-up".

Marigold felt some relief when she exited into the hall and no Billy or Mike (who had never returned to class) were in the hall waiting for her. She was tired of being afraid. That was when The Plan resurfaced. If she could do it, she would never have to deal with this bullying again. Never ever.

Tonight she was going to make The Plan happen, and there would be no going back.

Chapter 4

Ms. Henley stood smiling at the door to Room 116. "Good morning!" she exclaimed, and Marigold turned around to see if there was another kid behind her. "Good morning!" she said again, and that's when Marigold understood the teacher was addressing her.

Marigold said, "Good m-morning?" softly.

Ms. Henley gave her the once-over and asked, "So what happened to your knee?"

Marigold saw that the blood had begun to drip down her leg once more. "Umm-"

"Let me guess. You tried to grab a tiger by the tail, but he snagged you instead?"

Marigold grinned. "Yeah, that's what h-happened." She wondered what Ms. Henley would say if she told her the truth.

But Ms. Henley put her arm around Marigold's waist and led her into the room. "Here. Let's see how we can help you." At her desk, she pulled out a drawer and removed a container of sanitizing wipes. As she removed one, Marigold reached out a hand to receive it, but Ms. Henley, in her beautiful sky blue slacks, knelt down and began dabbing at the wound. She tossed back her long black hair.

"Does that hurt?" she asked.

"N-No--" Marigold said, disbelieving that this teacher was actually trying to help her.

"Well, good as new. Almost." She opened a small box on top of her desk, and then removed a Band Aid. Down, she went to apply the strip over the wound. Then up again. "Now, if you start having any problems, you just use this." After scribbling on a pink pass, she handed it to Marigold and said, "This pass is to use, if you need to see the nurse. You can use it any time today." Her tiny black eyes sparkled. "Why don't you just sit here in the front row? That way I can keep a look-out on you, okay?"

"B-But-I-usually-sit--"

"Just for today. Then be sure to see me after class, all right? Twitter!"

"Twitter?" Marigold nodded slowly, sat down in the designated seat, and kicked her ruined book bag under the desk. Why, oh why, did Ms. Henley want to see her after class? Her imagination knew no bounds, and she came up with all kinds of reasons-none that made her very anxious for the end of class to arrive.

Ms. Henley went over the syllabus for the first six week grading period. They would do several experiments at the back tables; there would be weekly quizzes, monthly tests, and every night some homework to complete. Scientific terms were important to know, as well as understanding certain concepts. If you failed a quiz, Ms. Henley would work with you after school, until you showed you understood the material, and then you could retake the quiz. There would be a Science Fair in the spring, and everyone should start thinking now about what project they would like to exhibit in the fair.

Marigold opened her book, as the teacher directed, and started reading the first chapter about climate change. The questions at the end were to be homework. At one point, she turned around and looked at the students sitting behind her. No Billy, no Mike--not that she could see anyway, and she exhaled.

There was a girl, who was covered with big brown splotches, seated next to her. She had seen people with large birthmarks; in fact, she had one on her leg, but this girl had them all over her face and arms. Her olive green T-shirt said, " Awesome Alien". She was wearing jeans, so Marigold didn't know if the spots continued onto her legs. She forced her eyes back down into her science book; she didn't want to stare at "Awesome Alien" girl, scribbling away in her notebook.

"Hi," this girl said, as she pushed her glasses up the bridge of her nose. "My name's Kate. I observed what happened to you in the hall. Indescribably detestable."

Marigold looked into Kate's big eyes located behind very large, black framed glasses. The thick lenses made her eyes look like huge, blue pools. She didn't know what 'detestable' meant but said, "Y-Yeah, a boy named Mike tr-tripped me. My name's M-Marigold. Marigold Stroop."

"I know you are Marigold Stroop. I assume when you observe me, you can understand why other students utter jokes frequently regarding my skin and my eyes. I'm astounded it wasn't me being assaulted and lying prone on the floor. It occurred frequently to me in elementary school. I attended Mason Elementary--"

"Oh, I went to H-Harrisville. That bully who tripped m-me? Mike? He went to Harrisville, t-too. He and another bully, B-Billy Smith, are BFFs. You need to stay a-away from them. Sorry you get b-bullied, too. How do you know m-me?"

But without a beat, Kate said, "Well, we certainly can empathize with each other." Kate removed her large glasses and cleaned the lenses on her T-shirt. "Tinea Versicolor, by the way."

"H-Huh?"

"My skin disease is called Tinea Versicolor. I call it TV for short, a bit of humor I am somewhat unaccustomed to using. I'm on the spectrum; I have autism."

"O-Oh..."

Ms. Henley strolled up. "Well, I'm glad you two have discovered each other. Have you already finished reading the first chapter?"

Marigold shook her head. "No...s-sorry-"

She began to resume reading, while Kate nodded enthusiastically. "I did complete the assignment; in fact, I read it twice--first a perusal-next a detailed reading. Here are the answers to the questions, too, if you'd like them." She shoved a piece of notebook paper covered with writing toward the teacher.

Ms. Henley took the sheet of white paper. Her eyes became almost a large as Kate's. "Really. Now, when did you have time to do all of this?"

"Just now."

"Just now?"

"I affirm your inquiry. The assignment on the board reached completion during this class period, approximately five minutes ago. Do you have any books on Einstein? I'd certainly relish doing further study regarding his Theory of Relativity."

Ms. Henley walked backwards and tossed the answers to the questions on her desk. "No, I don't have any books like that, but I'm sure you could find some in the library-." Then the bell rang.

Marigold tried to slip out among a group of kids, but Ms. Henley called her back. "Come here, Marigold. I have something to show you." With her hand on Marigold's shoulder, she steered her to a row of gray, metal cabinets in the back of the room.

What did Ms. Henley want to show her? The teacher took a small key from her pocket, unlocked the far left cabinet, and pulled out something large, wrapped in brown paper; then, she thrust it in Marigold's direction. Marigold caught and unwrapped the package. Out popped a bright red book bag!

"Every year, I make a stockpile of pencils, paper, rulers, T-shirts, shoes, etc., all kinds of stuff. This year, I found this book bag on clearance. Now, I noticed your book bag is a bit beat up. You don't have to take it, of course, but it's yours if you want it."

Marigold took in the sight of this brand new, bright red book bag like she had just discovered some precious treasure in an underground pirate's cavern. "Really? I c-can have this? I mean, I don't have any m-money to give you--"

Ms. Henley said, "No, dear child. It's totally free, and I'd really appreciate it if you could take it-free up some space in the cabinet, so I can have room for more stuff. Twitter!"

What was with the "Tweet" from Mrs. Toon and the "Twitter" from Ms. Henley? Marigold had no idea but quickly dumped out the materials from her mutilated kitty book bag and made the transfer into the new one. "Thank y-you! Thank you so m-much!" For the first time in a long time (except with Jus), she wore a smile from ear to ear. She slung the new book bag up onto her back, tossed the old one into the trash can, and really hoped her mom would understand.

"You are quite welcome. Oh, and I hate to say this, but your shoe is covered in blood--sock, too. No amount of scrubbing is going to wash that blood out, I fear."

Marigold lowered her eyes and saw Ms. Henley was right. "Yeah. I-I have other socks and my old gym shoes at h-home, though."

"Have you grown since last year? I mean, I don't know, but I do have some socks and shoes in here that just might fit you, since you are probably a bit bigger than you were in fifth grade."

Marigold watched her teacher happily rustling through-what looked like-a messy nest of newspapers, in the same cabinet. Finally, she pulled out some white crew socks and a pair of new, white Nikes. She handed them to Marigold, now speechless. "You might not like these plain, white shoes, though. Your yellow ones are so cute. And I do like those orange socks."

Marigold looked at the new shoes and socks, gently took them, and cradled them in her hands. "They're s-so cool. I l-love them." She could smell the new, leather shoes and fresh, cottony socks.

Ms. Henley nodded her head up and down eagerly. "Well, good. Do you think they'll fit?"

Marigold quickly sat down onto the brown tile, yanked off her old socks and shoes, and replaced them with the new ones. She jumped up, started walking around, and couldn't believe how comfortable the shoes felt-like she was walking on air. Is this how an astronaut felt walking in space? "P-Perfect fit! I l-love them! Thank y-you!"

"Well, good. They are yours, if you don't mind taking them, and giving me more room in this cabinet. Now, you must hurry. The cafeteria and new friends await your arrival! Twitter!"

Chapter 5

The hallway, crammed with kids, reminded Marigold of shopping on Black Friday. Her mom and she never shopped together on Black Friday, because they never had any money--terrific sales or not. But one morning, the day after Thanksgiving two years ago, Marigold ventured out at three a.m. For the first time ever, she was going to be able to buy her mom something.

She'd pedaled on her rickety, red bike across mounds of snow and ice to the mall, about two miles away. She had ten dollars crumpled in her coat pocket to hopefully find her mother a fantastic necklace or bracelet or earrings for Christmas, and she thought Macy's was just the place to find it.

She had earned the ten bucks shoveling many driveways, and after shoving her tiny self through just about a million searching, grabbing people, all aimed at the jewelry counter-while "Jingle Bells" played in the background, Marigold found a fake, sapphire bracelet on sale for $8.99. She'd grabbed it up, paid for it, and then pedaled herself home. Snowflakes danced overhead and covered her eyelashes with frozen, puffy clouds. It had been nice seeing her mom smile that Christmas morning, when she'd unwrapped the silver box containing the bracelet.

"There sh-she is!" Mike's attack voice, bellowing from behind, caused her sweet, Christmas memory to shatter like icicles falling to the ground in cold, splintering fragments. A crunching reality of where she was took its place.

Then Marigold felt someone walking on the backs of her new shoes. Before she knew what was happening, she had completely stepped out of the right one.

"Hey, I got it!" Mike again.

"Throw it!" Billy's voice sounded above the clamor of a zillion hungry middle-schoolers headed for the cafeteria.

"This ain't her shoe! It's a Nike!" Mike hollered.

Billy yelled, "Throw it, anyway!" His voice blasted from the crowd ahead of Marigold just before, swooooosh, her white shoe went flying overhead. She stumbled, trying to walk with one shoe on and one shoe off. The "off shoe" had landed who-knew-where.

Shoulder to shoulder, the crowd pushed and shoved, as they moved toward the smell of pizza and chicken nuggets. Marigold felt like a salmon must feel swimming upstream--a being shoved, shoeless, wanting-to-reach- its-destination salmon.

"Hey, keep it flying!" It was Mike's voice, now also from up ahead. Then, there went the soaring Nike into the air. Laughter and cheers careened off the green, cement walls.

That's when a large hand, with five ringed fingers, appeared above the bouncing heads to snatch that shoe; it looked like some eagle's talon, snagging a flying fish.

Marigold heard Billy holler, "Hey! Keep the shoe going!"

Then that low voice (which could only belong to a very colorful guy named Jus), shouted back, "You better be shuttin' your mouth unless you want to be flyin' through the air next!" Marigold didn't see the shoe take any more flights.

Once she stepped into the cafeteria, Jus's hand touched her back and guided her to a table in the rear. His other hand held the shoe. When they arrived at the table's green bench, he motioned for her to sit down, and then he knelt on the tiled floor. "Is this bein' your slipper, Cinderella?"

Marigold easily slid her foot, with the once-white sock, into that Nike shoe.

"Well, I'm guessin' it belongs to you, Princess Marigold. Fittin' like a glove-I mean, a slipper."

Mike and Billy charged up. "Hey, Yellow Girl, you didn't come to school wearing those shoes!" Billy announced this like he was some forensic scientist imparting important information to the FBI.

"Yeah, you ugly creep. You didn't come to school wearing those shoes!" Mike repeated his great leader's words.

"I already said that," Billy said.

"So what? You think I care?"

Billy stood within inches of his BFF and partner-in-crime. "Well, you oughta care!"

"Maybe you oughta just shut up!"

"Make me!"

Next, they were on the floor slamming punches, while kids in the cafeteria surrounded them with words like, "Hit him!", "Punch him!", "Smash his face!" Within seconds, Mr. Reynolds appeared and dove in, separating them in one fell swoop. With a wriggling boy under each of his muscular arms, he flipped them upright.

"What are you two future football pros doing?" he asked with a little smile.

"Oh, we were just--" Mike began.

"Playing around," Billy finished.

Mr. Reynolds put a hand on each of their shoulders. "Just a good thing I was assigned cafeteria duty today;

some other teachers aren't as understanding as I am. Just playing around, huh?"

Both boys nodded like bobble heads Marigold had seen on cars' dashboards.

"Well, good. I like tough guys--tough guys practicing for my football team. I was a little worried about your manliness in class today, Mike, when you said some weinie girl beat you up."

Mike quickly spit out, "Oh, I was only kidding, Coach Retters. No girl hurt me."

"Reynolds. I'm Coach Reynolds."

"Yeah, Coach. That's what I said. Coach Reynolds."

With that, the coach directed both boys to the food line. "Hey, go get some food. Eat lots of protein-it builds muscles." He displayed his muscles, two mounds protruding from beneath his rolled up shirt's sleeves, and marched after them. "Until you can buy guns, your body is your strongest weapon."

With all the interruptions, Marigold hadn't looked at the kids sitting at the table with her. Now, she realized she already knew three of them.

Jus stood up. "Let me be introducin' ya to the Misfits, Marigold."

Except for an Asian girl with her eyes closed and sitting cross-legged on top of the table, they all smiled in her direction. She wondered why they were smiling;

that name didn't sound too cool to her. "M-Misfits?" And what was with the girl on top of the table?

"Yeah, the Misfits. Well, you and I were already bein' acquainted, mon. Like ya know, my name is Justice Michael Jury-Jus for short. Next is Kathryn Rettinger, otherwise known as Kate. I think you were meetin' her last period." Kate nodded at her.

"In the hallway, Della Walters came kickin' and punchin' when Mike came at ya. Della is sittin' right next to Kate." Jus pointed in Della's direction, and Marigold knew there was no way to miss Batgirl, still wearing her mask.

"Now, Marigold, there are two others sittin' at the table ya don't know. They weren't bein' in any of your classes, or in the hall, because they are seventh and eighth graders. They got their schedules changed, so they could be havin' lunch with us, mon."

"The office was f-fine with that? Ch-changing their schedules for lunch?" Marigold didn't think any principal she'd known would say that was okay.

"Yes. Let's just say there is much understanding for you to acquire concerning us," Kate said. "We all met several years ago, but we have been anxiously awaiting your arrival. Timing was of the essence."

"O-Okay." Marigold wondered why Kate used such big words, and these Misfits? How did they know so much about her? Why had they wanted her to be a part of their group, and what did they mean about waiting for her? Yes, Kate, she knew she had much understanding to acquire. Or not.

"It will be quiiite all right," the beautiful Asian girl, in a green silk blouse with matching pants and sitting cross-legged on top of the table, said to her. This girl opened her eyes and pointed an index finger into the air, like she was making a point. "Really, it will beee. Actually, it will be better thaaan just 'all right'. You will be so much happier, you will soon forget about the Plaaan." Then this girl closed her eyes again, put her hands in a prayer position in front of her heart, and made an "ommmm" sound.

At that, Marigold stood up and started backing away. How did this very weird girl know about the Plan? Nobody knew about that-except for herself, and she sure hadn't told anyone. And what was with the closed eyes and the "ommmm"? Why was she sitting on top of the table? This was beyond craaazy.

"Hey, where are you goin'?" Jus asked. He jumped from his seat and put his hand on Marigold's shoulder. "Please don't be leavin'--"

"This is just w-weird," Marigold said, as she shook his hand off and turned to face him. "Everybody h-here is part of some group y-you call the Misfits, and you w-want me to sit with you? No way! That t-table of kids is the crazy cr-crate!"

"Oh, we don't want ya to just be sittin' with us, mon; we want ya to be part of us, part of the Misfits. We can't be whole, can't be doin' what we need to be doin' , without you, Marigold. We have been waitin' for you to arrive."

The others joined Jus with words like, "We need you", "C'mon girl", "Been waiting on youuu", etc., but Marigold turned away from the group she had decided was really, really off-the-chart nuts and began hurrying toward the front of the cafeteria and the food line.

Jogging in her cushioned Nikes, she tried to get away from those wacko Misfits, even stranger than she was, and that was saying a lot. But that's when the Asian girl yelled something that made her bouncing shoes stop mid-bounce, and come to a very abrupt stop. This caused some kid behind her to crash his tray into her back.

"S-Sorry," she said over her shoulder. "What did she s-say?"

Chapter 6

"What's wrong with you?" the kid yelled from behind. "You are a freaking idiot!" Marigold ignored him and turned completely around to peer back, with squinty eyes, at the Misfits' table. Had she really heard what she thought she had? And just when she thought she had definitely been hearing things, since nobody, but nobody, could know what that girl in green (now standing atop the table) had hollered, well, that's when the beautiful, Asian girl yelled it again.

"Don't you waaant some celery sticks filled with peanut butter, pickles, and chopped raaadishes?" Then to top it off, the girl started waving one in the air! How in the world could she know? Who had told her that was her favorite snack? The only other person who knew was her mother, and Marigold could guarantee Marsha Stroop hadn't told that girl, dressed in green silk, about her very favorite munchie.

She had never eaten them at school. Could you imagine how nuts the other kids would have thought she was, if she ate celery stuffed with peanut butter, pickles, and chopped radishes? Oh, brother! Talk about another reason for them to bully her! Only her mom and she knew about that snack.

But that Asian girl just kept waving the celery stick in the air. “I maaade them last night; chop, chop, chopped for a long tiiime so you could have your favorite snack today, Marigold Marsha Strooop!”

Thankfully, the other kids in the cafeteria were all involved in getting their food and didn’t appear to be paying attention to the crazy girl in green, standing on top of the table and yelling about her favorite snack. But Marigold had heard, and she aimed her bouncy, white shoes back to the table. She had to stop that girl’s shouting before the Droobs heard!

By the time Marigold got there, a pile of stuffed celery sticks had been placed on a napkin on the table, right before where she’d been sitting. After she sat back down, she couldn’t resist and began crunching down on the very delicious treat, so unbelievably yummy (in her estimation, anyway). The Asian girl resumed sitting on top of the table and humming, “Ommm.”.

“Well,” Jus began, “now that we are all bein’ here again, mon, let’s continue with the introductions. The girl who was makin’ ya the delicious snack, your very favorite, is Jade Chung. She’s a seventh grader.”

“Thanks, J-Jade.” Marigold started on a second stalk of stuffed celery.

"You are quiiite welcome," Jade replied. "Ommm."

With a green celery strand protruding through her lips, Marigold asked, "B-But how did you know about m-my favorite snack?"

"You are going to beee a Misfit; that's howww I knew."

"H-Huh? I-I don't understand--"

Jus, however, interrupted her. "And last, but not least, is eighth grader, Mo Domki." A boy wearing a turban on his head jumped up and gave Marigold a wave. "Nice to meet you!" he said, before spinning in a circle and sitting down.

"So there you are havin' it—-the Misfits, your new family: Mo Domki, Jade Chung, Della Walters, Kate Rettinger, me-Jus, and now, we are havin' you, Miss Marigold Marsha Stroop. Finally, there are bein' six of us kids. Lucky number six."

"But I-I still don't get it!" Marigold kept chomping away on celery.

"Don't understand? Well, here's somethin' you will be understandin'! Time to chow down, you crazy Misfits!" Jus wore a large smile when he drew out a plastic bag from his book bag, and the others followed suit. Marigold watched the bags being thrown around the table to each other in a somewhat organized pattern. When each bag came to her, she drew out a different food , threw it to the person on her right, and this continued until the bags stopped flying, and everyone started slamming down food.

In a pile in front of her, Marigold saw some very strange food: carrots with hummus, apple slices with peanut butter, large black olives, carrot slices and red onion chunks stuck on toothpicks, cucumber on rye bread, then more of her favorite-celery with peanut butter, pickles and chopped radishes. Marigold was blown away! She also felt bad, because she had nothing to contribute.

"Don't worrry," Jade said with a wink. "You can bring somethiiing tomorrow."

"But no more of your favorite snack!" Mo laughed. "Kind of gross!"

Mr. Reynolds appeared at the table. "Why am I not surprised where you decided to sit, Marigold? Weirdos, just like you." He pointed at the bags and leftover food. "Don't let me find one tiny bit of this rabbit food left on the table or on the floor. If I do, someone will get an office referral!" Then he turned on his heels and marched away.

Marigold tried to cram down her food and clean up her space. Nobody else seemed all that concerned, but when the bell rang, the table looked spic and span, and she didn't see as much as a crumb on the floor. As everyone stood to leave, Marigold got a good look at them: Jus was as she remembered-all colorful and flamboyant; Della, in her black outfit and mask, did look like Batgirl. Oh dear, Marigold thought, if Della doesn't want to get bullied, she needs to lose the mask, for sure. Kate was covered in brown spots, but to Marigold, they made her beautiful; Mo jogged around the table with the biggest feet she had ever seen on a kid; and when Jade shuffled out, hands in prayer position, she stared into space and hummed like she was no longer in the same time or place as everyone else.

Marigold felt like she had been transported to some strange land where the Misfits existed, a land where she had been invited to live, but where she wasn't so sure she wanted to reside. Was she really as different as they were? Then she thought about how she had been bullied for dressing weirdly and stuttering her whole life. And what was going on with Jade knowing all those secrets about her? Things nobody else-or practically nobody else-knew?

Jade turned around and scurried back in her green satin shoes to stand in front of Marigold. "It shall all be maaade clear, Marigold Marsha Strooop. Very soon, you will understaaand." Then she glided away, humming, "Ommm".

Marigold hurried to her locker to switch out her morning books for her social studies book and head toward the gym. Of course, her physical education clothes were bright yellow shorts with an orange shirt, and as she changed in the locker room, many other girls filled the echoing space with high pitched giggles. Even her underwear was orange flower-patterned, and there was no privacy. Well, she guessed she was providing cheap entertainment for those fellow sixth grade girls, who were putting on navy, black, and gray gym clothes around her. Normal colored clothes.

The thing that helped Marigold the most to survive the Droob cruelty-the separating of herself by focusing on the ceiling, a rhyme, the sky, a book-didn't really help her in this locker room. In this place, she had to focus on changing clothes, hanging stuff up, and she couldn't escape the mean words and laughter.

"Hey, girlfriend," some lovely girl, wearing black yoga pants and a long sleeved gray Nike "Just Do It" shirt, said loudly, "I happen to know a woman who does personal shopping for my mother and me. Want me to hook ya up?"

Then came the laughter, the laughter Marigold was so used to.

"Oh, Shreeva, she so needs it," another girl spoke up.

"I bet her mother could use that woman, too. From what I've seen, her mom lives in her robe-even wears it in the front yard!" Danielle Realm, a girl from Marigold's elementary school, giggled.

Another voice said, "OMG! Really?"

Danielle replied, "Really."

"Well, I'm so sure I can fix her mom up, too, but not sure she could afford it," Shreeva said. "Dumpster diving is so much cheaper."

Uncontrolled laughter ensued, until the unbelievable happened! Della charged in, black outfit with mask and all. "Sorry to be late, Marigold. Another fight to break up in the hall, dude."

After a flying somersault, she went into some martial art's position and faced the group of gaggles. "Really? You want to be mean to this girl? This girl, who is made up of more kindness than you, all put together, could find on the tips of your little, manicured fingernails?"

"Go ahead! Who is going to say the next rude thing?" Della made a few chops in the air. The group formed a tightly woven Droob knot and tripped over each other, while they stumbled from the locker room and into the gym.

When the only people left were Marigold and Della, the girl in black said, "Again, sorry I was late, dude. I was breaking up a fight, like I told you, and didn't get the message you needed me here till just a couple of minutes ago."

Marigold managed to speak. "M-Message? Who gave y-you the message?"

"Oh, I think you know who gave me the message, Marigold," Della said with a kick-kick. "But I'm off to protect the halls. You need to remember I got your back, dude." She did a series of flips to the door and was gone.

Marigold tried to stop shaking. Della was off to protect the halls? What kid got permission to protect the halls, instead of going to class? And somehow Batgirl knew she needed to show up in the locker room, because she had her back? Huh? Plus, Della said Marigold knew who gave her the message, and Marigold figured, yep, she just thought she did-"Ommmm".

Finally, Marigold managed to force her trembling legs into gear and walk from the locker room into the gymnasium. Gym class was okay, since Della had made her appearance, and Marigold made a small smile. She spent class jumping a jump rope in the corner, while the others played basketball, and the gym teacher, Miss Smith, let her. With each swing of the rope over her head and every hop, Marigold could not stop wondering about that crazy Della and the group called the Misfits.

Chapter 7

Last period, social studies. Marigold was running a bit behind, due to having to change clothes in the locker room, but thankfully, without drama. When she tore into the classroom, her eyes were peeled for Jus. There was no Jus, however. Maybe he is late, too, she thought as she ran toward the back of the crowded room and to two empty seats she spied. She lowered herself down in one by the window and threw her book bag onto the desk next to her, a place she reserved for Justice Michael Jury, Jus for short.

Then she saw Billy and Mike, side-by-side in the front, both laughing loudly and gesturing in her direction. She didn't care. Jus would be there soon and make everything okay, make her life better-at least her life here in this dungeon called middle school. But the bell rang, and no Jus appeared.

"Good afternoon," the teacher, Mrs. Johnson said. Her eyes looked tired and her smile was crooked, like she was trying to smile but her lips were too exhausted to form a perfect curve; the left side had already gone to bed while the right side was on its way. She was wearing a gray jacket, a high collared white blouse, a black skirt, black tights, and black heels. Wearing that outfit made Marigold wonder if Mrs. Johnson was trying way too hard to look boss-like. She reminded her of Mrs. Drebel.

True, the school was kinda-sorta air conditioned, but with the sun shining in the windows, that teacher had to be real hot. Her gray hair was in a tiny bun on top of her head, and her silver, round glasses had slid partway down her thin nose. Marigold felt sorry for her: old, sweaty, and probably stressed teaching middle-school students, during last period, on the first day of school.

Mrs. Johnson grabbed a clipboard from the podium in front and began taking attendance. When she came to "Justice Michael Jury" and nobody said, "Here", Marigold nervously chewed on a fingernail.

He wasn't in that classroom, for sure. Was he confused about his schedule? She hoped he was okay but wondered why she was worrying, being as he seemed to head up the Misfits-one weird group that she probably didn't want to be a part of. So why did she care about him? That's when Della, dressed in her Batgirl outfit, ran into the room and gave a wave in the teacher's direction.

"Sorry to interrupt Mrs. Johnson, but I have an important message to deliver, dude!" Della bolted toward Marigold and put a note on her desk. Then she was at Mrs. Johnson's side and whispered into her ear. After that, she was out the door.

"What?" Billy was out of his seat, jumping up and down in place. "That Geek Freak just gave Flower Girl a note! Why does Batgirl get to be out of class and delivering notes? That's not fair!"

"Be quiet, Billy," Mrs. Johnson said. "Della just told me Justice Jury is in trouble and in the office. Do you want to join him?" Her tired eyes peered at Billy, as she pushed her glasses up her nose and marked something on the clipboard. Billy lowered his bouncing self back down into his chair.

In the office? Marigold wondered why Jus would be in the office. She remembered the note Della had delivered, unfolded it, and read silently, "Dear Mairgold, Soryr I cant be with you ni class. I got in truobel for food undre the tabel. See yuo latre. Dont let the Droosb bothre yuo! Jus"

Well, Marigold wondered three things: One, why would Jus have gotten in trouble for food under the table, when she sure hadn't seen any? Two, who had sent him to the office? And three, why was Jus's spelling all messed up? He seemed so smart when he talked-but his spelling was awful!

There was actually one more thing she questioned.: What gave Mrs. Johnson the right to let the whole class know Jus had gotten into trouble and was in the office? Wasn't that against HIPAA or was HIPAA just for medical things? Whatever, Marigold didn't think it was right for Mrs. Johnson to share that info with the class. She felt bad for Jus, since he had gotten in trouble for something lame that she didn't think was even true (food under the table), and now when he walked into social studies class for the first time, everyone would believe he was a troublemaker. Just plain unfair.

Mrs. Johnson finished attendance, sank down into the big wooden chair behind her desk, and everyone started reading in their books. Marigold saw the assignment on the board and turned to that page. She began reading but had trouble concentrating, especially when Billy got up and walked behind her. He threw a folded piece of paper on her desk and mumbled, "Guess I can give you a note, too, you ugly idiot."

Mrs. Johnson, blankly gazing about, suddenly gave a quick blink and stood up. "Billy! You need to ask permission to leave your seat!"

"Sorry, Teach, just had to sharpen my pencil." Billy now went to the front and churned away at the pencil sharpener. "I didn't know where the sharpener was."

"My name is Mrs. Johnson, not 'Teach', and you need to sit down immediately."

Billy kept the churning going. "Sorry, Mrs. Teach," Billy said, turning to see just whom he was entertaining. Since lots of kids laughed uproariously, Billy's smile grew larger. Having kids think he was cool was really important to him, Marigold guessed.

The note on her desk was unopened, and Marigold told herself that's how it was going to stay. Hadn't Jus told her to ignore the Droobs? And Billy was King of the Droobs. In a split second, Mrs. Johnson pointed a finger at Billy's empty seat. "Sit--down--now!" He did.

Billy said, "What's the matter, Teach? Kids can't sharpen their pencils in here?"

"Marigold, bring that love note Billy wrote you up to me now!" she commanded.

Well, if the class had been laughing loudly before, that was mild in comparison to their current bellows. "Love note, love note," some sang.

Billy was up with a fist above his head. "It's not a love note! That's the last thing I would write her! Are you kidding me? Write that ugly thing a love note? You are craaa-zzzy!"

Again, "love note, love note" continued but at an even faster tempo. Marigold could have sworn the whole class, except for Billy, the teacher, and she had joined in the chant.

Mrs. Johnson pointed at her, which Marigold knew meant she was to bring up that note—-pronto! So she did and then ran back to her seat.

Mrs. Johnson quickly tore the note open and screamed, "Be quiet! Because I do not allow any note passing in my classes between students, I always read them aloud!"

Well, everyone became silent at that. Marigold sank down as low as she could go into her seat, closed her eyes, and pressed her sweaty palms together. Mrs. Johnson, now having a captive audience, read in a hoarse voice, "Dear Yellow Flower Girl, Because you are so ugly and stupid, nobody in this whole school cares about you. Nobody wants you here. Why don't you just kill-your-self?"

Mrs. Johnson looked shocked at what she had just read to the whole class. Marigold wondered why she should look surprised. This teacher believed in sharing personal things with everybody there; she had told the class Jus was in trouble and in the office. Why was she going to care about what she'd just read aloud? It probably didn't matter to Mrs. Johnson that she'd caused her a whole lot of pain piled on top of the whole lot of pain already there.

Mrs. Johnson started busily writing on a pink form and then waved it in front of Billy. "Here. To the office. Now. I hope I never see your face in this class again. You are a mean, mean boy."

Billy snatched the referral form quickly and snarled. "Sure! I'll go to the office, Teach, but you know what? You have no proof I wrote that! I didn't sign it! Maybe I was delivering it for-for-" His big blue eyes in his flushed face darted about. "For Mike!"

Mike was up. "Hey! I never wrote that!"

Billy continued, "Yeah, it was Mike! Or I could be delivering it for somebody else in this class. Nobody wants that Dweeb in here. Everybody would be happy if she died! Just ask them!"

The whole class was amazingly quiet, and Marigold attributed that to the fact that they didn't want a referral to the office, or because they all agreed. All of them want me dead, she thought. And again, the Plan, her Plan, took center stage in her mind. She knew she would never have to deal with these Droobs ever again, after she did what she had to do. And it had to happen tonight.

Now, Mrs. Johnson's eyes narrowed to skinny slits, and she growled, "Billy, you will go to the office-immediately. If you do not, I will call an administrator to escort you there."

Billy began stomping out the door, but not before he shouted, "Oh, I will go to the frickin' office, Mrs. Jackson, but my policeman dad will call his best friend, a lawyer. Yeah, that's right! A lawyer! And do you know what he is going to charge you with? Do you? That you made a false-a false-"

"Accusation?" Mrs. Johnson interrupted. "A false accusation? And my name is Mrs. Johnson, not Mrs. Jackson. Better get it right, if your dad's attorney is going to charge me with a false accusation. Good luck with that, by the way. Now, go to the office!" Mrs. Johnson removed her glasses, flipped them onto her desk, and rubbed her tired eyelids. Billy finally exited with a loud slam of the door. Marigold noticed the right side of this teacher's lips had now joined the left in going to bed. The class worked silently on the assignment, until the bell sounded the end of the school day.

After everyone had left, Marigold wiped away the tears streaming down her face, put her book into her book bag, and then stood up. Mrs. Johnson said, "Marigold, I am so sorry I read that out loud. So very, very sorry."

"R-R-Right." Marigold made her way into the loud hall and knew that the damage had already been done. Yes, Mrs. Johnson, you might not have begun the pain; it started a long time ago, but you sure made it worse. Much, much worse. At her locker, she wondered if she needed to take any books home with her. If I'm not going to be here at school tomorrow, why should I care about doing any homework tonight? she asked herself. But for some strange reason, she packed her books inside her book bag anyway. It was like something was telling her to do that, even if she didn't understand why.

As she started out toward the bus, Billy was racing ahead of her. Wasn't he supposed to be in the office? Well, his tearing up his referral and letting it fly into the wind answered that question.

Marigold managed to make it onto the bus just before it drove away. It was so packed, she couldn't tell if there was even a seat in the back. As it turned out, the bus started rocking and rolling so much, Marigold fell into a front seat right behind Mr. Carini.

She made sure she didn't look back into the crowd of kids sitting together, because she didn't want to see the Droobs making faces and pointing at her. Their loud laughter caused her enough stress. Finally, the bus driver stopped at her bus stop, and she rushed out the doors. She tore away to her house; her goal was to get away from all of those Droobs-as quickly as possible.

Thankfully, her house was close to the bus stop, but unfortunately, her mother (all decked out in an orange and red floral dress), stood in the front yard. She was waving her arms in the air and calling to her daughter, as if Marigold was just returning from a year-long sail at sea. Some kids from the bus stop had followed Marigold and started imitating Marsha Stroop's voice, screeching, "Marigold! Marigold, sweetie! How was your first day of middle school?"

Marigold stomped past her mother and bolted into the house-very quickly into the house. When her mother entered, Marigold exploded, "M-M-mother, what are you d-doing? I am s-so embarrassed! Didn't you hear those k-kids imitating you?" She stomped her foot.

Marsha's face dropped. "Well, yes, I did-but what do you care? Don't you know how much I love you? How much I miss you when you are gone all day?"

"Yes, I know you love me, miss m-me, but I'm in sixth grade n-now! I'm n-not your baby anymore!"

"Oh, but once a mother, always a mother! You will always be my baby Marigold Marsha Stroop." Then she walked over and threw her arms around her daughter. Marigold did not hug her back.

Marsha took a few steps backwards and gave Marigold the once-over. "I don't think my sweetie had a very good first day of middle school. Am I right?"

With rolling eyes, Marigold said, "Really, Mom? D-Did you hear those kids? Did you? Do you think I had a g-good first school of middle school?"

"Oh, you mean because some of the kids were rude?"

"Rude. R-rude? They were worse than rude, M-Mother."

"Well, can't you just tune them out? Pretend they aren't talking?"

Marigold stared in wonderment at her mom. Did she ever leave "La-La Land"? That's when Marsha's eyes settled on Marigold's shoes.

"What happened to your pretty yellow shoes, orange socks, and-and--" She walked behind her. "Your book bag, too? Where is your kitty book bag?"

"In the trash c-can. My book b-bag, socks, and yellow shoes are in a trash c-can at school."

"What? In a trash can? Didn't you like them? I picked them out special for you-spent my hard earned money." Marsha looked like she was going to cry.

"Well, Mother, those k-kids that you say I'm supposed to just ignore? T-Tune them out? One of those k-kids, named Mike, knocked me down in the hall and my bleeding knee got blood all o-over those yellow shoes and orange socks; then, he stomped on my b-book bag till it was ruined! It was kind of hard to t-tune out Mike, Mother."

Marigold's mom raised her hand to her mouth. "Marigold! That's horrid!"

"Y-Ya think?"

"Well, we need to do something about those bullies!" Her eyes traveled up and down her daughter. "How did you get all these new things?"

"I have a very n-nice science teacher named Ms. Henley and she h-has a cabinet full of things that she g-gives to kids. Things she b-buys on sale."

"And she gave you socks, shoes, and a new book bag?"

"Y-Yep."

"Well, we must pay her. The Stroops don't take charity from anybody."

"No, M-Mother. I already told her I d-didn't have any money to give her, and she said she didn't w-want anything-that I-I was helping her, by cleaning things out of h-her cabinet."

"But--" Marsha began.

"No 'b-but', Mom. She wanted me to h-have all this."

"Then I need to send her some beautiful flowers, and I must go over to school and report Mike to the principal. Nobody treats my baby like that."

Marigold held her hands in tight fists at her sides and tried to squeeze out the tension. "M-Mother, promise me you will not go over t-to school, and if you send flowers to Ms. H-Henley, and the other kids f-find out-oh, that w-would be awful. Plus, I-I have a Plan, and none of this is going to make any d-difference anyway."

Mrs. Stroop analyzed her daughter's face. "What do you mean, you have a plan? What kind of a plan do you have?"

"It doesn't m-matter, Mom. I just need to take a n-nap because I'm so tired." Marigold grabbed her book bag and began to walk toward her room.

"Okay, sweetie, but I'll get you up around six for the special dinner I'm making. I'm cooking your favorite meal to celebrate your very first day of middle school." Then she waltzed into the kitchen and started banging around pots and pans.

"You just don't g-get it," Marigold said to her bedroom walls. "Mom, you don't h-have a clue. Well, when I-I do my Plan, maybe then you'll g-get it." She removed her brand new shoes and placed them carefully by her bed.

Chapter 8

Marigold fell asleep and had a dream about flying through the sky on the back of a big black bird. She was happily gliding about, sweeping this way and that way, through white, puffy clouds when she heard her mom enter her room.

"Wake up, middle school girl! I have made you a very special dinner! Your favorite foods!"

As Marsha gently shook her, attempting to rouse her from sleep, Marigold opened her eyes. Marsha Stroop bent over and kissed her daughter's forehead. The strong smell of mums slammed her nostrils. Marigold's stomach was churning, and she wished she were still soaring through puffy, white clouds aboard that black bird and not thinking about supper. "I-I'm not very hungry. My stomach's n-not good--"

"Oh, but I slaved two hours to make you this supper--count'em, 'one, two', and it is going to make you feel so much better." She held up two fingers, as if to emphasize the "one, two".

Marigold only moaned, pulled the comforter over her head.

Marsha Stroop flipped the comforter off and began yanking on Marigold's right leg. "Listen up, buttercup, dinner is ready. Rise and shine!"

"R-right--"

Marsha pulled harder, and Marigold sat up.

"St-Stop, Mom!" She tumbled out of bed. "Quit it!"

"Then hurry to the table, sweetheart, before my fantastic dinner gets all cold and dried up." Marsha Stroop gestured toward the door.

"Oh, I-I can hardly wait," Marigold mumbled.

"What? Did you say you hope it's steak? Not steak."

Marigold followed her excited mother to the kitchen. "R-right. That's exactly what I s-said." She sat down into a chair at the table, as her mom opened the oven door and began covering every space available on the white, silk tablecloth with covered glass dishes. She lit a tall, red candle in the center.

"I hope you're hungry!" she said, proudly displaying various dishes: lasagna, broccoli in cheese sauce, homemade garlic bread, green bean casserole. Then, from the refrigerator, came a very large tossed salad, and she poured Marigold some almond milk. "And for dessert? Carrot cake!" Marsha finally sat down and started dishing up food for Marigold onto a bright red plate.

"M-Mother, stop! I c-can't eat all that!"

"Excuse me? Shouldn't you be saying, 'Thank you, Mother, for working your fingers to the bone making all my favorite foods?' Shouldn't you be appreciative?"

Marigold took a bite of warm bread. "Thank you, M-Mother, for all this food. I r-really appreciate it."

Marsha nodded. "You are so welcome. I hope it tastes good! I wanted my baby girl to have a celebration after her first, fantastic day of middle school."

Eating all the food on the red plate was going to be difficult, Marigold knew, but she smiled and began to chew and swallow, chew and swallow. She didn't think she could possibly put down any carrot cake, though. "D-Delicious," she mumbled to her very observant mom. She wanted to add, I'm not a baby and could have served myself. Also, hot dogs would have been just fine. She didn't say any of those things, though. She didn't want to sound unappreciative.

"Well, it looks like you were hungry." Marigold's mom stared at her daughter's empty plate.

Actually, Marigold felt like she was going to barf. "Mmmm. Yes, I was s-so hungry."

"What did the cafeteria serve for lunch today?"

"Didn't eat c-cafeteria food. Smelled like pizza and chicken n-nuggets."

"You didn't eat cafeteria food? Then what did you eat?"

"Let's s-see: apple slices with peanut butter, onions, c-carrots, olives, hummus, cucumber on r-rye bread, celery sticks with p-peanut butter, pickles, and r-radishes."

"Your favorite snack? Who fixed your favorite snack?"

"J-Jade."

Marsha furrowed her brow. "I don't understand. Who is Jade?"

"M-My new friend. She's Asian."

"And she knew that was your favorite snack? How did she know that?"

"D-Don't know." Marigold shrugged her shoulders.

"Hmm. So you just happened to sit at a table with Jade, your new friend, who somehow had prepared your favorite snack."

"Y-Yep. Everybody brought sn-snacks. All the M-Misfits."

"The who?"

"M-Misfits--Jus, K-Kate, Jade, Della, M-Mo, and now me. At least they want m-me to be p-part of their group."

Marsha now wore a big smile. "They do? They want to be your new little friends? I never knew you to have new little friends at school before, and on the first day of school you meet-" She began counting on her fingers--"Five? Five new friends? All in one day?"

"And I m-make six. Lucky number s-six."

"Lucky number six?"

"Y-Yes, they have been w-waiting on me."

Now, Marsha's brows had formed one bushy line above her eyes: a huge, pulsing caterpillar. "They have been waiting on you? What does that mean?"

Marigold stood up, started clearing the table and rinsing the dishes. "I don't know, M-Mother! Why would I-I understand that?" She threw her arms in the air. "They are a b-bunch of freaks, and I just want to g-go to bed!" She stomped to her bedroom.

"Well, goodnight, sweet girl! Get some sleep before you head out to your second, wonderful day of middle school with all your new little friends!" Marsha hollered.

Her only reply was Marigold's shutting her bedroom door.

Marigold jerked a suitcase out from under her bed and started unloading her clothes from the dresser drawers into it, before snapping the latches closed. This was the Plan, and she was going to make it happen. Her life sucked; and most of the kids at school wouldn't care if she didn't go there anymore. The words in Billy's note were true. She knew her mother would be so sad, but she was the only one who would be. Her mom would find somebody else to care about-maybe a puppy or a cat; she might even get a boyfriend.

Right now, her mother focused all her attention on her, so there wasn't room for anyone else. And the crazy Misfits? They would find a new, lucky number six. She put on her shoes.

Grabbing the suitcase's handle, Marigold raised it up. She was going to sneak out and disappear into the night. Didn't know where she was going. Didn't care. She began stepping quietly toward her window.

That's when there was a pound, and next, a really loud-kaboom-on her bedroom window. "What is th-that?!!" she gasped as she parted the curtains and looked outside. Was someone trying to break into their house?

The full moon hung like a giant, yellow, Japanese lantern in the sky, and in the light spilling down from it, stood Jus, Mo, Kate,and Jade bunched together. They were staring at her face inside the glass. Where was Della? She didn't have to wonder for long, because Della flew through the air, with a giant leap, and kicked the window hard! Marigold also didn't have to wonder what had made that loud kaboom anymore. As a result, a crack had begun snaking its way up her bedroom window's glass!

"No!" Della screamed, aiming another kick toward the window. "Put the suitcase down! Now!" Marigold dropped the suitcase.

Suddenly Marsha Stroop barged into her bedroom, and Marigold quickly pulled the curtains tightly closed-just in time.

"What was that?" she asked.

"Wh-What?" Marigold pressed her back against the closed curtains.

"That loud crash! What was it?"

"I d-don't know, didn't h-hear it."

Marsha Stroop's eyes had gone into squint mode. "Of course you heard it. Probably everyone on this street heard it. And why are you standing in front of the window? Why is that suitcase on the floor?"

Marigold shrugged her shoulders. "D-Don't know."

"You sure don't know a lot of things right now. Here, step away from the window. I want to look outside."

"There's n-nothing to see, Mom. I was just going to o-open the window to get some fresh air in h-here, and there is nothing to s-see."

By then, Marsha had yanked open the curtains and was sweeping her head from one side to the other. She stood there for a few minutes, staring out into the darkness like a ravenous owl searching for a rodent. Finally she closed the curtains, walked away, then turned and faced her daughter. Her arms were crossed over her chest, and she tapped her toe.

"You wanted fresh air?"

"Yes, M-Mom."

"You didn't hear a loud noise?"

"N-No Mother." Marigold crossed her fingers behind her back.

"And the suitcase...because?"

"I-I don't know." Double crossed fingers.

"You aren't going to leave me, are you? Leave me all alone?"

"N-No. Why are you asking m-me that?" Crossed toes, right foot.

"Because you were at the window with a suitcase beside you, your shoes on. I'm thinking you are going to run away and leave me all alone." She sat on Marigold's bed and put her head in her hands.

Marigold sat beside her. "N-No, Mother, I wasn't going to r-run away." Crossed toes, left foot.

Marsha Stroop raised her tear-filled eyes. "Because if you left me, I wouldn't have any reason to live anymore."

"No-No, I'm not going to r-run away tonight." Nothing left to cross.

"Well, good. Do you want me to open the window, so you can get some fresh air?"

"No, M-Mom. I'm g-good now."

Marsha kissed Marigold on top of the head. "Then I'm going to let you sleep."

She started out the door but suddenly stopped. "I still wonder what that loud noise was--. Guess we'll never know." She left the room and closed the door with a quiet click.

Only when Marigold could hear her mom clanging dishes around out in the kitchen, did she uncross everything and allow herself to walk over and ease the curtains apart. There the Misfits were again, but now Della stood as part of the group, instead of flying through the air. Marigold pushed the window open."What are you d-doing out there? Trying to g-get me in trouble?"

Della somersaulted over to the window. "No, trying to keep you here, dude. You can't run away."

Mo joined her in a flash. "You are one of us now! We need you, and believe it or not, you need us, too!" He began running in circles.

"I don't n-need you. I don't n-need anybody."

Jade was now beside Della. "Really? You don't neeeed anybody? So happy with your liiife that running away is the only answer to yourrr problems?"

"H-How did you know--?"

Next came Kate and Jus. Jus tossed his dreads. "Doesn't matter how Jade was knowin', mon. She just was knowin' and told all of us."

"It should now become apparent to you, through inductive reasoning, that Jade knows. She-just-knows," Kate said.

"But now you need to be comin' out here," Jus continued. Marigold noticed that they were all still wearing the clothes they had worn to school.

"I am n-not going outside. D-Do you know what time it is? It's l-late!"

Jade came within inches of Marigold's face and said, "Weee are not asking you; weee are telling you. Come-outsiiide-now."

"Well, I-I am telling you I am not going outside. I'm going to b-bed."

"Really? Really. You are still probably thinkin' about runnin' away, too, mon," Jus said.

Jade nodded. "Yes, sheee is-"

"Oh, don't be thinkin' that. Don't be makin' us force you to come out of your house, mon."

"I will tell m-my mother and she will make you l-leave." Marigold closed the window and headed to the living room, where she knew her mom was watching TV. Except her mom was conked out, snoring away, and no amount of shaking awakened her. A shuffle in the kitchen caused Marigold to quickly turn around, almost losing her balance in the process. Standing together, as a pack of wolves in the small kitchen, stood the Misfits.

"Good luck in making that happen, dude," Della said.

"Not going to happen!" Mo jumped up and down in place.

"What's 'not going to h-happen'?" Marigold asked.

"You aren't going to be successful in arousing her, Marigold," Kate said.

"Wh-Why?" Marigold began shaking her mom once more. "Mom! M-Mom! W-Wake up!"

But Marsha, wearing a smile, was happily sleeping away. With no results, Marigold turned and faced the Misfits. "How did you g-get in here?"

Jus said, "Back door. Not locked." Then the Misfits walked into the living room to join Marigold.

"Why can't I w-wake her up?" Marigold's voice had now increased in volume.

Jade stepped forward. "I was aaable to hypnotize her quite eeeasily, even from outside the house, since you are almost a Miiisfit.

"H-Huh?" Marigold put her feet in reverse.

"She won't waaake up until I give her permission. When weee get back, I'll snap my fingers, and she'll open her eyes. She won't have any idea why she just toook such a long nap. She also won't be able to figure out how it got to beee so late. Now, we are leeeaving. You meet us in the front yarrrd."

"You d-did what? You hypnotized h-her? How d-did you do that?" But the group had already left the living room and headed out. Because she guessed she didn't have a choice, Marigold walked through the door to join these Misfits in the moonlight.

Chapter 9

"Follow me." Jus made a waving motion with his long arm, while he walked behind Marigold's house and into an alley. Everyone followed his lead.

"Where are we g-going?" Marigold asked. She was second to the last, with Mo behind her, and when no one answered, she repeated her question. Still no one replied, so she shouted it, "W-Would somebody tell me where w-we are going?"

Jade, walking in front of her, turned around. "You will fiiind out soon enough." Then she turned about-face and continued to scoot forward.

In front of Jade was Kate, then Della, and finally Jus led the way.

The air was hot and stifling. It wrapped around Marigold with more warmth than her sunset comforter ever had. They traveled from one alley to the next, crunching on broken glass and pieces of sticks, stones, and probably broken animal bones.

Littering the ground was trash that had fallen out of garbage cans, and due to the empty beer cans and liquor bottles scattered about, Marigold had to step carefully. The smell of urine, beer, and rotting food filled her nose, so she took turns sucking in her breath, holding it; then finally, letting it out with a great spurt. Then she repeated: inhale, hold, spurt; inhale, hold, spurt.

Providing background music were crickets chirping in a unified chorus, telling anyone within hearing distance, that summer had not ended-certainly not yet. Crickets were alive and well; just ask them. Because the bright yellow moon was full, it was easy to see where to step and where not to step-a fact which Marigold thought was a good thing. A very good thing.

Finally, after at least a twenty minute walk, Jus stopped, and like a row of train cars chugging behind him, so did everyone else. Marigold looked around and realized she had absolutely no idea where they were. In front of them was an empty, weed-infested lot with one small, rusty, green shed dotting its center. Beyond that, overgrown fields swayed in the night. No houses, no cars, no people-only stretches of tall grass-waving hello at the night's sky. She shuddered, and it wasn't from the breeze just beginning to blow. Jus motioned everyone over into a circle.

Jade folded her hands and started the "Ommmmmm". She was soon joined by Jus, Kate, Mo, and Della. The hum continued, becoming louder and louder, until it drowned out the crickets' choir. Marigold joined the, "Ommmm," just because, like she had heard repeatedly from her mom, peer pressure was a powerful thing. She felt like adding to this humming, however, "You, ommm, are a bunch of crazies, ommm..."

Suddenly, Jus gave a signal by raising his arms, and the voices hushed. He said, "Marigold, you are about to be pledged into this group, the Misfits. But first, I need for you to be swearin' you will never repeat to anyone, not even your mother, what you are seein', hearin', or doin' tonight-or any times the Misfits are meetin'. Do you promise, mon?"

But instead of listening to her answer, Jus turned his back and looked up into the sky. Marigold thought that was probably a good thing; she wasn't so sure she wanted to be a part of this weird group. She wondered if he was afraid she would tell him, "no", and that is not what he wanted to hear. She also questioned if Jade knew what she was thinking, and had somehow signaled Jus not to wait for an answer.

Instead of waiting for a reply, Jus bent over, put his finger in the dirt, and then walked over to Marigold. She could feel him mark a big "M" on her forehead. An "M" for Marigold? she wondered.

He said, "Marigold, with this 'M' (standin' for Misfits), on your forehead, I am now pronouncin' ya a member with all the rights and privileges that come with bein' a part of this fantastic group. Are you havin' any questions?"

Marigold opened her mouth to shout, "I d-do not want to be a part of this cr-crazy group!" Again, however, Jus didn't give her that opportunity, since the moment she parted her lips, he said, "That is bein' good, mon."

Suddenly a cheer was shouted by Della, and she leaped up with a kick into the air. The rest joined her by yelling, clapping, and hugging Marigold--hugging her like she'd never been hugged before.

"Welcome, dude!"

"Welllcome.."

"We are so glad you're here!"

"We have been eagerly anticipating your arrival!"

"You are now bein' part of the Misfits, mon!"

All the shouts were fired at her; their voices-some great Marigold Celebration Fireworks- popping loudly in the night's silence. She swore she heard a loud "Caw" from above, but decided, nope. No way.

And even though she felt like it was really corny, she also knew (maybe for the first time in her whole life) that she belonged. Not like belonging to her mother, but belonging to a group. Maybe she belonged to a gooney group of crazies, but she belonged, and that made her feel really good inside.

Once the laughter and yelling had subsided, Jus went to the shed and placed his hand on the door handle. The door was so old and rusty, it took quite a bit of yanking, but with a slow scraping noise of metal against metal, he finally got it ajar about three feet,and motioned that they all were to go inside.

"What?" Marigold asked. "You h-have got to be kidding. There is n-no way all six of us can fit inside that sh-shed!"

But Marigold watched as first Jade went inside, then in went Mo, followed by Kate. Finally Della went, and Jus still motioned that she was to follow them.

"W-We can't all get inside there! We'll b-be squashed! Plus it's d-dark and spooky!"

But Jus just stood by the door and pointed toward the darkness. Marigold hesitantly walked over and peeked into the shed. It was empty!

"Wh-What? Where is everybody? They're g-gone!" Had the darkness swallowed them up? Marigold backed away. She had been right before-this group was way too crazy for her. Disappearing people, in an old shed, in the darkness? Huh uh. No way.

But Jus was quicker, and he wrapped his arm around Marigold's waist. Then he pulled her, ever so gently, and pushed her inside. "Trust me on this one, girlfriend. Just watch." He stepped in behind her and took a little flashlight from his pocket, shone it onto the shed's dirt floor, and illuminated a raised trapdoor at their feet. He motioned with the light, toward a large circular opening, the raised trapdoor had revealed in the ground.

"What?" She looked down into the black hole at their feet. "I'm s-supposed to jump down into that hole? Not g-going to happen."

"No, girl. Here, sit down." Jus pushed on her shoulders, forcing her into a seated position with her short legs dangling down into the opening. "Now, have fun!" He shoved her back, and she was off! Down and around, doing loop-de-loops on a very, very long slide. Finally, she shot out into a large space, lit with many, many candles, and landed on something soft.

Applause surrounded her, and the flickering candles, which illuminated the area, also lit up the smiling faces of the other Misfits. "You did it! You safely journeyed here to this underground sanctum, a hidden place where we, the Misfits, initiate our gatherings! Welcome to The Meeting Room!" Kate announced her arrival, once she had situated herself. Marigold placed her hands beneath her and realized that she was sitting on a very plush blanket, atop a hard, cool, dirt floor.

"You had better move over a bit, dude," Della said. She pulled Marigold toward her, just as Jus flew through the opening and plunked himself down, right where Marigold had been sitting.

"I love it!" Jus giggled. "Every time I am goin' down that slide, I think it's bein' more fun than the last time! More fun than Pete Starr's Amazing Anaconda Roller Coaster at the amusement park!"

Marigold felt goosebumps pop out on her arms, as she peered around. All the Misfits were seated on blankets on the cool, hard floor of what appeared to be a cavern. She had once visited a cave in southern Indiana on a field trip, and it reminded her of that. But a cave under a tiny shed in an empty field? A cave you got to by a long, twirly slide?

Wide-eyed, Marigold took in her surroundings. The walls were shiny dirt canvases displaying carefully drawn pictures of various animals and symbols; many-sized hand tracings had also placed themselves randomly across the surfaces. In addition to this artwork, streaks of color covering the walls glistened like beautiful rainbow-ribbons in the light from the candles.

Ping, pinga, ping. Narrow streams of water trickled down the smooth sides of this cave and made tinkling sounds, while they landed in tiny puddles on the ground. The ceiling was so far above their heads, it was hard for Marigold to make it out.

The smell of burning wax filled the place, and the number of candles was amazing! Some were huge and atop metal stands, some were medium sized and dotted indentations in the walls, and then there were the tiny votives perched like tiny birds in nests of dirt upon the ground. They twinkled and created a glow of late afternoon when the sun has begun its descent, and everything basks in a heavenly, golden beauty. Marigold started counting the candles but gave up after she reached "52". It was really cold down there, and she, only wearing her little dress, wished she would have worn warmer clothes.

"III'm on it, Marigold," Jade said. "It is chilly dowwwn here. By the way, there are exactly 103 caaandles." She wavered to a standing position and glided over to a wooden chest located a bit to the left of where they sat. There was a creeeeeaking sound, when she raised the lid and pulled out a piece of material. Then she slowly shuffled over to Marigold; the "ommmmm" sound she made echoed throughout the room. Once Jade stopped and held the shimmering golden material out at arm's length, Marigold discovered it was a fur-lined cape, and when Jade flipped it to the reverse side, she saw an embroidered initial "M" on the back. After motioning she was to stand up, Jade wrapped the silk cape around her and tied its long black ribbon beneath her chin. It reached to her ankles. “Welcome to the Miiisfits,” Jade said.

Marigold smiled for two reasons: one, she felt positively regal wearing this beautiful golden cape and two, she was so much warmer with it wrapped about her. She couldn’t help but wonder if Jade had said, “I’m on it, Marigold,” because she knew she was cold, and the cape would help make her warmer. Then that raised the question: How did Jade know she was cold? But by now, Marigold understood, Jade-just-knew, in the same way she had known about her favorite snack, about the Plan, when she’d needed help in the locker room, and even that she had been counting the candles. And thinking of candles? Who in here had lit all 103 of them? What a lot of candles to light! All these questions bounced about in her boggled brain.

“The Propriiietor,” Jade remarked. “The Propriiietor lit all the candles, Marigold. He liiives here.” She pointed toward a very tall ladder. “He uuuses that.”

“The Pr-Proprietor?” Marigold asked, then wondered why Jade was reading her thoughts and her thoughts alone. Why not the other Misfits’? Or did she read their thoughts, too, but just didn’t say them aloud? And who was The Proprietor? However, Jade didn’t answer those questions.

Jade's humming resumed, and like outside the shed, the others made the same sound. She walked around to the Misfits with the capes, and each took a turn standing up, before she wrapped the cape around them and tied the ribbon in a big bow under each chin. With one cape left, Jus walked over and put it on Jade. Finally, they all formed a circle and motioned for Marigold to join them. Once she found a place between Kate and Mo, she watched as they all put their palms together in front of their chests, then took a deep bow. Marigold did the same.

"The Organization of the Misfits will now be comin' to order," Jus announced, and each Misfit took the hand of the person beside him in the circle. He continued, as the members echoed his words in unison:

"For Right" ("For Right"),

"Not Might" ("Not Might"),

"For the greater good" ("For the greater good"),

"To all upon this planet earth" ("To all upon this planet earth"),

"And for all who have met on these hallowed grounds" ("And for all who have met on these hallowed grounds"),

"From Time Unknown" ("From Time Unknown")

"Until Time We Know" ("Until Time We Know").

Then, like synchronized sitters, everyone lowered themselves to sit cross-legged, on the blankets, sprinkled across the floor. Well, everyone except Jus, who perched himself atop a tall, gold stool. The room was hushed, without even any "Ommmmms". The only sound was the trickling water, slipping down the walls, and cascading into the ground's puddles.

Jus began, "Today is a very special day. This is the day we Misfits have been awaitin' for a long time. Today we are welcomin' a new friend into our group, and thank you, Marigold Stroop, for joinin' us, mon. The rest of us became aware of each other and our need to start becomin' part of this group several years ago. We were bein' called to come together in various ways: through word of mouth at different schools, out on the streets, in our deepest dreams. Through many methods, we were all led to be joinin' in this place, this underground sanctum, with The Proprietor. There were five new members who were comin' together and beginnin' the one thousand sixtieth year of the Misfits to be meetin' here, mon."

"One thousand s-sixtieth?" Marigold squeaked.

"Yes, Misfit groups, bein' known by many different names, have been meetin' here for one thousand sixty years. Of course, the shed and slide weren't always bein' there." Jus looked at the others for confirmation, and several nodded.

"Before then, members were just slidin' down through the hole by a rope, mon, or so I was told."

"B-But people weren't even alive one thousand s-sixty years ago," Marigold said. She shook her head and thought how nobody was pulling the wool over her eyes, a phrase her mom had taught her when she said not to believe everything people might tell her. And the Misfits? Well, they were telling her a whole lot of stuff that was probably untrue.

Kate gestured at the walls. "This is the year two-thousand and twenty-one. We have been keeping time 2,020 years A.D. Do you observe the ancient drawings? Are you actually negating the evidence in front of your eyes, proving that people were present and creating this type of cave artwork thousands and thousands of years ago? Major civilizations have been walking the earth at least 6,000 years."

Marigold shook her head. "N-Nope. Didn't h-happen. People haven't been on earth that l-long."

Mo started running in circles. "Oh, yes they have been, Marigold Marsha Stroop!"

"Huh uh. Not tr-true."

Kate ignored her. "Anyway, we needed at least six Misfits to supply the desired talents, or gifts, in order to carry out our purpose here on earth. Our base is our residency here in Freemont, Michigan."

"Our 'p-purpose'?" Marigold wondered what kind of purpose she was needed for. Nobody had ever needed her for anything, except for her mother, of course. And gifts? Well, she knew she didn't have any of those.

Jus nodded. "Yeah, our purpose, mon. 'For Right, not Might. For the Greater Good'."

"I don't understand." She wrapped the cape more tightly about herself and felt its soft lining warm her cool skin..

"We will be explaining everything to you!" Mo ran around in circles with his huge feet.

"Listen up, dude!" Della jumped up and did a kick-kick before sitting back down again. "You are about to hear all about the Misfits!"

Chapter 10

"Let's be startin' with each of the Misfits relatin' to you about themselves and explainin' why they are such an important part of this organization, mon. I think when we are bein' finished, you will start to understand your uniqueness and the importance you are playin' in our group," Jus said.

"O-Okay," Marigold said but thought, again, there was nothing special about her, and they had just made one big mistake in thinking she was going to add one 'unique' thing to this group.

"Who should be startin?" Jus asked.

Mo exclaimed, "I think you should, Jus!"

"You are our group leader, dude," Della said, chopping the air.

Jus slowly left his stool and stood in front of the group. The stones in his rings twinkled in the candlelight. "Well, mon, as you are knowin', my name is Jus--a shortened version of my real name, Justice." He ran his fingers through his dreads. "I have been bullied for as long as I can remember because of bein' black, dressin' wild, havin' dyslexia (reason I can't spell right), but mostly for bein' gay, mon. Even when

I was a little kid, I was playin' with dolls and would of rather had girls for friends, instead of boys. I loved drawin' beautiful gowns, you know, designin' them. It is so much fun thinkin' of ways to make lacey, lovely dresses. Maybe someday, a star will be wearin' one of my dresses to the Oscars! I want to be a fashion designer, like I was already tellin' ya. So it doesn't take a whole lot of figurin' out to understand why kids have been callin' me names, beatin' me up, and doin' all kinds of mean things to me."

Della stood and did a swift kick in the air. "And I'd like to kick em all in the butts, all in the butts! How could anybody be treating you mean, Jus?"

"Hey, I'm cool, mon. I got all you guys. Anyway, Marigold, the Misfits from the last group that met here were lookin' till they found me. They were all gettin' old and needed young blood-like what they'd been about eighty years ago. They told me I was gonna be a leader and started tellin' me what kind of kids I needed to find. You know, all of them had to be bullied, plus had to be havin' certain gifts-just like them. These old Misfits also introduced me to The Proprietor, who helped me in findin' all of you.."

There it was, that name again-The Proprietor. Marigold wondered who The Proprietor was. Probably something else they were just making up.

"There is also another leader, mon, who will be showin' up another day."

"Jus! Tell her what you have that the Misfits need!" Mo shouted.

"Well, The Proprietor said that even though kids bullied me for so many things-bein' black, dressin' crazy, bein' gay, havin' dyslexia-stuff that was makin' me weird in their eyes, well, I had somethin' special they didn't have. And because I was willin' to use my gift to make things 'Right', I was important to the Misfits." Jus sat back down on his gold stool.

"Staaand back up and tell her whaaat your gift is, Jus," Jade said.

Jus stood again and shuffled his green shoes. "The Proprietor said I am creative. And because of my creativity, I am able to be helpin' the Misfits when they have to come up with a different kind of solution to things. Maybe that's cause I can be thinkin' about things in a different way and developin' a plan."

Marigold nodded. "Y-Yes, I can sure see that you are very creative, e-even if I haven't known you for very long." That was something she knew was true.

Jus took a bow. "And I am thankin' ya for that, Miss Marigold Marsha Stroop. I'm also a heck of a decorator, if you are needin' ideas about wallpaperin' your bedroom or paintin' a bathroom," he said with a chuckle.

"And when did the Misfits ever have to wallpaper a bedroom or paint a bathroom?" Kate asked.

"Just some humor, Kate," Della said. "Only a joke, dude. Lighten up!" She sat back down.

"But you never are knowin', right, mon? Marigold might want to be sprucin' up her place," Jus giggled. "Now, let's see. How about you, Mo?"

Mo jumped up, when Jus sat back down on the stool. "I'm Mo! Mo Domki! I came from the Arabian Peninsula, where I was born. I am of the Muslim faith, and my mother wears a hijab,a scarf on her head! My father and I wear turbans! I have been bullied for as long as I can remember. We wear something on our heads as a show of respect to Allah, our God! It is law to cover your heads in some Muslim countries, but not in all of them. I am high energy!"

"I would be interested in knowing which Muslim countries do not make covering up one's head a requirement?" Kate asked.

"I really don't know, Kate. Google it!" Mo jumped up and down on his large feet.

Della giggled and made a short leap in the air, before sitting back down. "Google it, dude!"

"Hey, I was only inquiring," Kate said. "Other cultures pique my interest."

Mo didn't reply but continued talking to Marigold. "You know, after 9/11, anybody who looks like me often gets treated badly. In my faith, if you read and live your life by the Quran, the last thing we are supposed to do is hurt anyone else!" He rubbed the dark hair already growing on his face. "So being Muslim, having huge feet, wearing a turban, and talking fast makes me different; as a result, I get bullied! I don't drink caffeine, but man, I am highly excitable!"

"Tell her what you are suuuper good at," Jade said with a thumbs-up.

"Yeah, Mr. Cheetah Dude," Della said.

"Yeah, yeah. I'm getting to it! My gift? The thing I can do to help the Misfits?" He kicked out a large red gym shoe. "I am only five feet tall and scrawny, but I wear a size 14 shoe! And I'm fast--really fast! Being quick helps out when the Misfits want somebody to run like a flash! So if you need speed, well, that's me. I'm your guy! Yeah, do I look dumb to some kids because of my turban and huge feet? You bet! But can I put on the speed? Uh huh!" He wiggled his hips. "Movin' Mo, Movin' Mo! Now, you tell me which one is more important? Looking weird to the Droobs or being faster than you could ever, ever imagine?" He leaped into the air with his huge feet again.

"Being f-faster than you could ever, ever i-imagine,'" Marigold said.

"You got that straight!" Mo said, while he adjusted his turban and sat back down.

Jus was up. He scanned the group. "Well, let's see, mon. How about Kate?"

Kate stood. "Hi, Marigold. My real name is Kathryn Rettinger, but I go by Kate. Like Jus, I think Kathryn is much too lengthy--and proper. I grew up in this town and have had kids call me names like Moo Cow, Dalmatian, and Spot from the time I was old enough to socialize outside and play with them." She held out an arm and pointed to the splotches covering it. "I already told you the disease I have is called Tinea Versicolor, a rather lengthy name which means I have a disease caused by a fungus, for which there is currently no cure, and it causes spots to appear all over me. My mother has it, her mother had it, so it appears there is a genetic predisposition involved in acquiring this condition."

"Wow. Sorry, K-Kate, Marigold said. "That has to b-be so hard."

"As my mother would say, 'It is what it is'." She removed her large glasses and rubbed the lenses on her cape. After she had shoved them back onto her nose, she said, "The humidity in this place causes my lenses to fog. Added to my disease, I am also legally blind--the reason I wear these beautiful glasses with the extremely thick lenses. As you most likely observed, since the lenses are so thick because of major magnification properties, my eyes appear positively huge to anyone looking at me."

Marigold nodded.

"My vision loss is so great, no contact lenses would assist my ability to see; therefore, in addition to nicknames that are focused on my multitude of splotches, I am often taunted with 'Alien Girl', 'Bullfrog', and many more insulting names-due to my visual handicap. There are, however, others who are totally blind, so I consider myself fortunate in that aspect. I am also autistic and, at times, have difficulty with humor and socialization. I tend to strongly focus on certain things; currently, Albert Einstein.

"I do possess an asset which is beneficial to the Misfits: my level of intelligence. My intelligence quotient is quite high, and it is evidently a gift with which I was born. Some would consider me a genius, and I should feel proud; however, I believe my brain's functionality is just another way that I am able to help the Misfits bring right to a world which, at times, can be so very wrong. My intellectual ability is no greater than Jus's creativity or Mo's speed. No better than your or anyone's gift. My brain simply happens to work well."

"Right. Reading with comprehension and playing classical music on the piano at the age of three! Nothing fantastic about that!" Mo said.

While Kate sat down and resituated her large gold cape back about herself, Marigold dug the toe of her shoe into the dirt and wondered why in the world these Misfits wanted her. She wasn't creative at all, couldn't run fast, and was sure no brainiac. They'd made a mistake by choosing her; they picked the wrong girl. There was nothing she could do to help them-not one single thing. Her thoughts transferred to her packed suitcase at home, a suitcase she would use when she returned. The Misfits didn't need her.

Jade stood, without being called upon. "You are greatly neeeded here, Marigold. You just don't know whyyy yet." Then she placed her palms together, closed her eyes, and made the "Ommmm" sound. Finally, after about a minute, she said, "Hello, Marrrigold. My name is Jade Chung, and my parents immigrated to the United States from Chiiina." Her black hair and eyes shone in the candlelight, making a distinct contrast to her ivory skin. She continued, "I would imagine youuu already can figure out why I am bullied."

Marigold gave her a smile, since she already knew that answer.

"As youuu already know, I walk around with my hands in a prayer position in front of my chest, sometiiimes with my eyes closed, and I make a strange humming sound. I talk strangely liiike this, and kids make fun of me since I walk and talk weird. Buuut, I have great telepathic powers. That just means I can reeead Misfits' thoughts, without understanding why. I am also able to hypnotize peeeople within a certain proximity of a Misfit. My mother caaan hypnotize, and so can her mother; it muuust be inherited. I can also sometiiimes tell what's happening to a Misfit in another plaaace, what did happen, or foretell what's going tooo happen in the future.

"Sometiiimes my gift works for people who aren't Misfits, but not usually. I often live in another dimension; that's the reeeason for talking strangely and walking around with my eyes closed, as I listen tooo voices from somewhere else. The 'Ommm' sound I make? It helps meee connect to that other world. Because I have this gift, Jus found meee and explained how I could help the Misfits. This connection to another world only haaappens when the other universe cooperates and sends meee messages, but it doesn't happen all the tiiime. Oh, and I am able to move objects sometimes." Jade slowly lowered herself to a seated position once more and folded her hands, closed her eyes, and quietly hummed.

Marigold sure understood why people were going to make fun of beautiful Jade. It wasn't because of her looks, but her actions? Weirder than weird. She wondered what it would be like having Jade's gifts and thought it would be pretty awesome. Hearing words from another dimension? Hypnotizing people? Reading thoughts? Telling the future? Seeing the past? Moving objects? It was just a good thing that Jade was putting her gifts to good use. She imagined Jade living in America as some Russian spy. That would be crazy bad-for the United States, anyway.

"Della, I think it's bein' your turn," Jus said.

Della stood and made a kick in the air and a chop with her hand. She had actually removed her mask and, for the first time, Marigold could see how pretty her face was. She yelled, "Hey, Marigold! My name is Della, Della Walters. You can call me Dell for short, dude. Or Batgirl, cause I go by that, too. Well, I know you can probably tell why I get bullied. I mean, what kid dresses up like a a super hero and runs around all day like this? Sometimes I sleep in this outfit—in case I am needed during the night.

"When I was a little kid, I just loved all the super heroes in movies-Spiderman, Batman, Batgirl, Superman, Catwoman—you name them, I loved them. I used to get in trouble for living in my make-believe world and believing I really was a super hero. I mean, I didn't grow out of it, dude. To me, I wasn't only pretending; I actually thought I was one."

"Really? You kept b-believing even when you started g-getting older?" When Marigold was little, she used to believe she had an imaginary friend named Abby; she thought Abby walked with her and talked to her. But when she got to be about six, she knew Abby wasn't real. It was a sad time for her, since Abby had been her very best friend, and she didn't have any other close friends. Her mom had explained that when you started growing up, well, you began knowing what was real and what was just pretend.

"Yeah, dude. I never quit believing. Then, one day, my dad took me to a psychiatrist, and that doc diagnosed me with a mental illness called schizophrenia. That's why I believed I was somebody I really wasn't, and why I thought someone was telling me to fly off a roof or jump from a bridge. Good thing I never did! Cause if I had? Well, I probably wouldn't be here talking to you, dude.

"So now I have to take medicine, and that medicine helps me understand that I'm not really a super hero, and I'm just pretending to be one. Not as much fun, but safer, I guess. Thing is, though, I'm really strong-really, really strong, dude." At that, she made a giant leap into the air and came down kicking, chopping, and shouting: "Hi-yeeeeee!"

"Because the principal knows why I'm on meds, she told the secretary how I can be helping them out and feeling useful. The office or another teacher notifies me whenever there's a fight that I need to break up, or I have to protect somebody who needs help. Jade might contact me tele-tele-"

"Telepathically," Kate said.

"Yeah, dude. That word. Sometimes I just deliver messages to teachers or a Misfit."

Marigold nodded. "That's why y-you showed up in the locker room, helped me in the h-hall, carried that note to me in s-social studies, and told the teacher J-Jus was in the office?"

"Yeah, dude. That's why. Jade let me know you were needing my help in the locker room today. Why do the Misfits use me? Cause I am so strong, man, and can bash anyone in my way, your way, anybody's way. That's why I'm a Misfit." Della gave another chop, leap, and "Hi-yeeeee!" before landing onto the ground. Then she sat down.

Jus was back up. "So, mon, everyone here is bringin' different gifts to the Misfits. Mo's got speed, Della's bein' strong, Kate's havin' brains, Jade's freakin' telepathic, and they keep sayin' I'm creative. Now, Marigold, please be tellin' us about you."

Marigold shook her head and bit at a fingernail.

"Please stand up and relate to us about yourself. We already have been enlightened concerning much-why you were selected, but we need to hear your own, individual testimony," Kate said.

Marigold stood up, and Jus plunked himself back down onto his stool. She shuffled her feet and stared at the ground. "I-I don't know what to say—-I d-don't have any talents."

Jade came over and stood beside her. "Marigooold, just tell us about yourself. We will tell you what we seee as your gift, the way we know you can help the Miiisfits."

Marigold started, "Well, I-I am Marigold, Marigold Marsha Stroop. My m-mother is Marsha Stroop. She's a single mom, and I never knew my dad; he left when I was a b-baby. My m-mom works in a florist shop, and she really likes flowers, so that's why she n-named me Marigold and dresses m-me in weird, flowery dresses like she w-wears. S-So I always dress stupid, and I tell her I don't want to wear the clothes she buys for m-me, but she never listens. I-I am her whole life, and I don't want to hurt her feelings, so I w-wear the crazy clothes. She w-works so hard and cooks and cleans."

Mo interjected, "Hey, Marigold! Tell us about yourself, not your mom, okay?!!"

"Oh, r-right. Well, I get bullied because of the w-way I dress, and because I st-stutter. I l-like to draw; I love animals and w-wish I could rescue lots of them. S-Someday, I want to have an animal sanctuary where all unwanted animals can l-live. Animals are always n-nice to me. I w-want to be kind to everyone, because I know what it feels like to be treated m-mean.

"Someday, I want to be real r-rich and get my m-mom a beautiful house, a new c-car, and make sure she doesn't have to w-work so hard anymore. I-I don't want her to break her b-back to keep food on the table, clothes on our b-backs, and a r-roof over our heads. I want t-to take care of all unwanted animals and bullied kids, old p-people, the homeless, too. That's all about m-me, nothing special." Marigold sat down and started digging the toe of her shoe in the dirt again..

Immediately, Jus stood, walked over, and raised her back to a standing position. He said, "Misfits, this is bein' Marigold Marsha Stroop, the sixth member, who is havin' one of the greatest gifts of all."

Kate and Mo stood and began clapping. Della started punching the air with her fists. Jade remained quiet with her hands folded in front of her chest, with closed eyes, but she wore a smile.

"B-But I don't have any important gift. There's nothing I-I have that the Misfits need."

Jus shook his head. "Oh, but you do, mon. You are havin' the gift of empathy, Marigold."

"Em-Empathy?" she asked.

"Yeah, empathy, mon."

"What's th-that?"

Kate said, "Empathy is the ability to put yourself in another's position, and more importantly, to be able to care about that person. Your hard-working mother, whom you love, may push you to insanity due to the clothing she purchases and expects you to wear; however, you understand she loves you immensely and you only want the best for her.

"You care so much for abused and neglected animals, bullied children, older people, the homeless--members of society who are in great need of assistance. That's because you understand, you feel for the plights they are experiencing, and you wish you were equipped to make their lives better. You even care about those who are mean to you, I suspect, because you perceive they may be experiencing cruelty themselves, and that is the reason they strike out at you and others."

"Buuut," Jade said, "you must be certain that you also begiiin to care about yourself, Marigold."

Marigold stared back down at the ground. "I d-don't think I know how to do that. I-I don't see anything about me worth c-caring about."

In a flash, Mo jogged to her side, put his arm around her shoulders. "But we will be helping you work on that! I think once you see how cool the Misfits know you are, you will, too, Marigold Marsha Stroop!"

With a finger, Marigold stopped a tear slipping down her cheek.

"That makes you sad?" Mo asked.

"No," Jade interjected, "Marigold is overwhelmmmed with the kindness of your words, Mo. She is not used to hearing that she's cared about, that sheee has worth-- except by her mother, of course. Certainlyyy not by her peers."

Marigold nodded and wiped another tear away. "Thank you, M-Mo."

Jus said, "This is only the beginnin', Marigold. This is only the start of your seein' your awesomeness."

"I thiiink it's time, Jus. I think it's time for Marigold to meeet The Proprietor."

"I agree," Jus said. On his long legs, he loped over to a far wall and knocked on it. It made a deep hollow sound, and then to Marigold's astonishment, a door opened in the exact spot where Jus had been pounding. Everyone stood up.

Chapter 11

If Marigold felt surprised at the door's opening, it was nothing compared to the amazement she knew seeing who walked through it and, into the space, where they were gathered. A wee man, not more than four feet tall (well, his stooped back helped contribute to his lack of height), shuffled slowly out, and he rapidly blinked his eyes, seemingly, to adjust them to the light from the many candles. This was The Proprietor? He wore a beige burlap tunic and was barefoot, bald, very wrinkled, and turned his head from side to side, as he tottered forward with tiny steps.

Jus swept a long arm outward and said, "Marigold? This is bein' The Proprietor!" Jus announced the arrival of this shriveled up, bent over man like he was introducing some great king. As if to affirm his opinion, all the Misfits formed a circle about The Proprietor, folded their hands in front of themselves, and bowed deeply in this very old man's direction.

"Up with ye!" The Proprietor commanded and pointed a gnarled finger toward the ceiling. "I am not your king!" They stood up-straight. Immediately.

"Marigold, I would be likin' to introduce ya to the man who is the supreme-leader of the Misfits, The Proprietor!" Jus bowed even deeper.

The Proprietor scooted his bare feet over to Marigold and squinted up at her. Then he touched her face and ran his crooked fingers across her tear-stained cheek. Finally, stepping back a few steps, his face crinkled with a great smile. "Welcome, beautiful girl!," he exclaimed with a screeching voice. "We have been waiting for you!" There were those words about waiting for her again.

"Thank y-you," Marigold said.

"As the last group of Misfits informed me, you have been through much, but still you possess empathy. Great empathy. We have been watching you."

"Watching m-me? Who has been w-watching me?"

"Why, the Misfits, of course," he continued and raised that gnarled finger again. "That includes me, as well."

Marigold looked at the Misfits in the circle. "You have? When? How?"

"Let's just say we have our waaays," Jade said with a wink.

"It would be our great honor if you would be tellin' Marigold about yourself," Jus said.

The Proprietor nodded, and all of the Misfits sat back down. "Let's see. Where should I begin?" He cleared his throat, stretched his arms over his head, behind him, then out to his sides. It appeared like he was trying to work out many kinks, and Marigold thought the sound of all the crackles testified to that fact.

"Let me begin by saying I am currently 120 years old, and I began this journey as a Misfit, standing right where you are, over 100 years ago." His eyes rested on Marigold. "It has been a long, but a very rewarding journey." He cleared his squeaky voice once more.

"One h-hundred twenty years old?" Marigold asked, astounded.

"Yes, and I hope to live many more," he went on. "The Misfits, called by many different names, have been meeting here for centuries. One leader eventually assumes the new Proprietor's job, but only after The Proprietor has reached the age of 100 or older." He stomped his skinny little legs up and down.

Marigold blinked rapidly. She didn't know people could live to be 120, but she didn't believe most of what was occurring here tonight, anyway. She took in her surroundings: a door in this cave's wall that opened; a very, very old man in burlap who came out; 103 burning candles; gold capes; trickling water; all the artwork on this cavern's walls; and a long slide twisting around and around from an opening in a very old shed's floor. All of this was unbelievable! She pinched her arm to see if she was dreaming, but when it hurt, she knew she wasn't. Plus, they wanted her in their group? They had been waiting for her? She had some gift called "empathy"? Saying she had a gift was the most unbelievable of all.

"Our organizaaation is not ordinary, Marigold," Jade said.

The scrawny man aimed his watery, blue eyes up at Marigold. "No, we are certainly not ordinary. We have important and very essential tasks to perform in order to make this world a better place. Because of that, we have been given many years upon this earth," The Proprietor squeaked, his voice now almost gone. "My gift is sensitivity." Then he scuttled back to the door, jerked it open, and disappeared.

Jus stood and said, "I believe it is bein' time to start home, even though I wish I could be stayin' here forever. Marigold, I'm thinkin' you might be surprised at the way we are leavin' this place, too, mon."

"I m-might?"

"Yeah! Real surprised!" Mo said.

Jade smiled. "No, I know sheee will be."

After removing their capes, and Jade's putting them away into the chest, Jus led them to the wall opposite of where The Proprietor had emerged. He pressed a button and voila! Another door opened. "Be seein' ya at the top!" he said, when Mo entered the dark space. The door closed, and there was a whooshing sound. After a pause, the whooshing sounded again. After a bit, the door opened, but no Mo was in sight.

"Wh-What?" Marigold asked. "Wh-Where is Mo?" Of course, there was no reply.

Each Misfit took a turn stepping into the opening and disappearing! Marigold began trembling as, one-at-a-time, Kate, then Della, and finally Jade stepped inside the space, and Jus closed the door. After each entry, there was a whooshing sound, a pause, then another whooshing again. When Jus opened the door, that Misfit had disappeared!

"I am n-not going inside there," Marigold said, pointing a shaking finger at the opening, after everyone (except Jus and she), had done the disappearing act.

"Really, mon? You want to be stayin' here till our next meetin'? Might be gettin' kind of hungry, except I guess The Proprietor could hook ya up—the Timmers are bein' great chefs. Must be healthy food, since he's lived to be 120 years old and doesn't show any signs of leavin' this world."

Timmers? she wondered. He held the door open for her, and because Marigold didn't think she had a choice in the matter-probably couldn't climb up that twirly-whirly slide to return the opposite way and didn't want to stay here-she stepped into the dark hole. Jus closed the door, and with another whoosh, up, up, and away she zipped! After mere seconds, whatever thing she was in came to an abrupt stop, and the door opened.

She stepped out into the shed! The Misfits were talking outside, and although very dizzy, she somehow stumbled from the old, metal building and into the moonlight. The others stood there laughing, high-fiving each other, and having a good old time. Once they saw Marigold had arrived, they greeted her happily, and Mo gave her a fist bump. Within a few seconds, Jus entered the scene and moseyed over to all the Misfits standing together.

"How was that for an elevator ride, mon?" Jus asked Marigold.

"An elevator r-ride? Really? That was the f-fastest elevator ride I've ever b-been on!"

Mo chuckled. "Fast, all right! Zip! Zip! Zip!" He jumped up and down.

"More than a z-zip. It must travel at the speed of l-light!" Marigold said. She was still trying to regain her balance on very unsteady feet.

Kate interjected, "You are stating a hyperbole, Marigold, since the speed of light is 186,000 miles per second and I can guarantee you, although fast, the elevator certainly didn't travel that swiftly."

Mo smiled. "Guess you could google it!" Marigold and everyone, even Kate, laughed.

Suddenly, Marigold announced, "W-Wait! We forgot to blow out all those c-candles! There could be a f-fire!"

Jus said, "No worries, mon. Be happy. The Proprietor always likes to be takin' care of that. He has a special light dissolver, which he is usin' after each of our meetin's. It's bein' different from the fire stick that he lights the candles with. Anyway, it's time to be gettin' home; school is tomorrow and lots to do."

As everyone started following Jus, on what Marigold figured was the return route, she wondered what the "lots to do" was. She knew she needed to do some homework, like the science questions, and she wanted to pack a snack to share with the Misfits in the cafeteria tomorrow. She surprised herself by realizing she hadn't thought about her suitcase and running away for awhile, but instead, was thinking about plans for tomorrow at school and lunch with her new friends.

Back they went through the same alleys (well, at least Marigold figured they were the same alleys), but by now she had lost all sense of direction. She was still trying to wrap her dizzy head around everything that had happened that night, and it wasn't an easy wrap. It was more like trying to tape down wrapping paper in a somewhat sort of neat way, when the object being wrapped was strangely shaped, and there was no way to make it look nice and tidy. It was kind of like that, she thought, and nothing could have made the things happening tonight seem "nice and tidy".

No, tonight was more like one big, strangely shaped, unbelievable present to Marigold, and one that made her have chills from the top of her head to the tips of her toes. In addition to the chills, there was a big smile filling her face, because she had been welcomed into a wonderful, amazing world. Plus, she had not only been welcomed, but also wanted there. Marigold Marsha Stroop, who never was wanted anywhere with kids her age (not even invited to birthday parties), had been expected to be there. They needed her gift? Empathy? Really? She never knew she had a gift, and had not even known what empathy was before tonight. She knew she cared about others but didn't know there was a name for that.

"Well, here we are," Jus announced when he came to a halt, in the alley, behind Marigold's house.

"We are h-here already?" How quickly the trip back home had been! Marigold thought the walk home seemed a whole lot shorter than the journey to the shed had been.

"Weee are here, Marigold. Quickly, go through the baaack door. Flip the back porch liiight on and off, head to your room and turrrn your lamp off, on, and off. Then I will snap my fingers. Your mother will awaken and fiiind you in your bedroom, not understanding whyyy she had fallen asleep or realizing that you'd ever left the houuuse."

Highly doubting that all of this was going to happen as Jade had predicted, she still remarked, "Okay, g-guys. Here I g-go." Marigold scampered through the tall back yard's grass to the house, flipped the porch light on and off, then tip-toed to her bedroom, past her mom zonked out in the recliner, entered her room, and turned her lamp off, on, and off again. Looking at her digital alarm clock beside her bed, she saw that it was eleven fifteen! She could not remember the last time she had been awake at eleven fifteen! Well, maybe last New Year's Eve.

She crawled under her sunset comforter and closed her eyes. Hopefully in the morning, I'll have time to pack six snacks and read the rest of the science chapter, then do the questions, she thought. I'm going to have a good night's sleep and be ready to do all of that at six a.m. But now, her heart was still pounding, while her thoughts twirled in giant circles through her head. Remembering all that had happened didn't exactly make it easy to close her eyes and try to sleep.

It was mere moments, before she heard her bedroom door open, and her mother's knees crackle when she knelt down to plant a kiss on her forehead. Marigold's eyes popped open.

"Hi, M-Mom." She was thankful her mother had awakened from the hypnosis.

"Oh, sorry I woke you! That meal was so big, it must have put me right to sleep. I just woke up myself!"

"It's o-okay." Marigold gave a large yawn. "N-Night."

"Good night, sweet daughter of mine," Marsha Stroop said. She stood up and walked from the room, taking the smell of mums with her.

Chapter 12

For some strange reason, Marigold awakened before the ding, ding, ding sounded--an occurrence that just never, ever happened. After turning the alarm off, she grabbed her science book, reread the material, and wrote the answers to the questions in her very best handwriting (again, something that never, ever happened). She ate a breakfast bar and packed a lunch snack of peanut butter on 12 crackers, then she put a walnut on top of each for good measure.

As usual, her mother had placed folded clothes by her bed: an orange ruffled blouse, a yellow pleated skirt, orange socks, and orange and white striped underwear. Oh, no! But two good things were the Nikes and socks by her bed. She yanked on the stupid clothes and, after finding her dirty white socks on the floor, put those on instead of the orange ones. Finally came her new shoes. She hoped her mom wouldn't notice the socks and make her change. When she slung on the red book bag over her old yellow jacket, she knew "colorful" didn't even come close. Oh boy, would Billy and the Droobs have fun today!

As Marigold started the walk from her house to the bus stop, her mom initiated her stance in the front yard. She wore the usual attire: a yellow robe, fuzzy orange slippers, and curlers poking out of her hair like hungry, bobbing birds in a yellow nest. The slimy, venomous taunts from the bus stop started as soon as Marigold stepped, in her new shoes, from her yard and onto the sidewalk. Luckily, she had escaped her mother's eagle eyes regarding her attire and still was wearing the white socks. She hadn't escaped the slobbery kiss on the forehead and the flower hair clip in her hair, however. Billy started the cruel words before the others joined in with,

"Flower Dweeb!"

"St-St-Stutterer!"

"Freak Face!"

"Freakin clothes!"

"Okay--freakin' everything!"

"Yeah. freakin' everything!"

Well, even if Marigold hadn't thought things could have gotten any worse, she was about to find out that, yeah, they could. They really could get much, much worse. Out of the front yard, barreled Marsha Stroop, rolled up newspaper in hand, screeching at the top of her lungs, "Shut up! Do you hear me? Shut your ugly, potty mouths up! Nobody talks to my baby girl, Marigold Marsha Stroop, that way!"

She dove first at Billy, knocked him down, and began smacking his face with that rolled-up newspaper. She, in her robe and slippers, her hair in curlers, sat straddling Billy and pounding the ever-living daylights out of him with the "Freemont Front" newspaper.

Billy swung his pudgy arms back at her as Marigold unsuccessfully tried, with all her might, to get her mother pulled back up to a standing position. She also kept attempting to grab the mighty weapon--that rolled up newspaper. As the Droobs also fruitlessly attempted to jerk her up (Marsha was one mother bear on a mission), the sound of a police siren could be heard approaching.

"Oh n-no!" Marigold figured some neighbor had heard the ruckus and called the cops. "M-Mother! Stop! The police are c-coming!"

But it made Marsha Stroop no difference. She kept pounding Billy with that now shredded-into-long-pieces of newspaper-weapon. "Let them take me away! Let them! Nobody messes with my beautiful, little Marigold!"

The other kids now piled on top of Marsha, and fists were flying. The police zipped up, and the red light on top of the squad car was beaming like some bright, spinning UFO on steroids. The wailing siren was deafening. It screamed out, "You are in big, bad trouble! Really big, bad trouble!" Two police officers jumped out and threw kids off, one at a time, from this moving mound of relentless protectors, attempting to save their leader. They yelled at the cops about poor Billy. To add more lunacy to the situation, the yellow school bus roared up. It braked with a major screeech, and out jumped Mr. Carini, all red-faced, waving his arms over his head.

"You have to get onto this bus-a! You want to be late for school-a?" He wiped off his sweaty face with the back of his ham hock fist. Then, he started helping the police officers yank kids off Marsha; his arm, a giant, swishinng fly swatter. Finally, Marsha was uncovered, all disheveled and perspiring heavily. She teetered to an upright position in her orange, fuzzy slippers. When Billy emerged, he could barely stand, much less walk. His wet hair was plastered down to his head, his shirt raised up to his sweaty armpits, his shorts were at his knees, but thankfully, his Bart Simpson briefs were in place.

One officer had removed a notepad from his front pocket and was busily scratching away, while the throng of kids pointed fingers at Marsha. She was swaying from side to side, trying to position her dislodged pink rollers back into place.

As the Droobs screamed accusations in her direction, Mr. Carini took turns grabbing them under their arms and thrusting them toward the open bus door. Their shouts continued out of the open bus windows, even while the cops calmly escorted Marsha Stroop toward the squad car, giving her the Miranda Rights all the way. Above the mass chaos, Marigold could make out her mother yelling about the "big, bad bullies" and her "precious baby" being a "victim of their cruelty!"

Marigold was the last student to make it onto the bus. Mr. Carini wiped off his face, with a dirty gray handkerchief, and barked at her, "Now, we are going to be late for school-a!"

"S-Sorry."

"Is that your mother in-a that police car?"

Marigold nodded. "Y-Yes."

Mr. Carini put the bus in gear and started out. "Well, she is nuts-a."

Marigold couldn't have agreed more and fell into a seat behind this very angry bus driver. The Droobs' shouts in her direction now increased in volume. She looked out the window and saw the white puffy clouds dancing a waltz in the blue, blue sky. Maybe running away wasn't such a bad idea, after all. Suddenly, from out of those beautiful, white clouds, flew that huge black bird. Her huge eyes watched as it soared and swooped its way over the bus, all the way to school.

Marigold found a seat in the back of homeroom, just like the day before. Billy, again, was getting everything stirred up, while Mrs. Drebel began taking attendance over the uproar. Nothing changed, Marigold knew. Never ever. Same-o, same-o. Except today, with her mother's performance at the bus stop, it was worse. Much, much worse.

She could see that Billy was beginning a black eye and was spilling his guts, clearly giving the kids around him a blow-by-blow description about what had just happened. Those kids, with dropped jaws, stared from Billy to Marigold, and back again. Some pretty girl even jumped up and gave him a big hug, something Billy obviously enjoyed, because his face began a slow blush all around the bruised eye.

Marigold felt completely alone. All the Misfits, with their friendliness and cool gatherings, their magic, wasn't going to make any difference. She was still going to be a victim of bullying, and there was only one solution: leaving. Leaving and going to live someplace different, someplace where nobody knew her. She had no idea where that place was going to be, and she didn't care. She heard people lived under bridges, in big cardboard boxes, and under benches. Wouldn't any place be better than here?

To make matters worse, her mom was now probably behind bars in jail, and who knew when she'd get out. Till then, who was she going to live with? Marigold was so embarrassed by her mom's attacking Billy at the bus stop with a newspaper! Yep, her mother had basically ruined her life. Again.

"Marigold Stroop?" Mrs. Drebel's hollering voice interrupted her thoughts.

Marigold put her head on her desk and covered it with her arms. Just let Mrs. Drebel count her absent; she wasn't going to be here much longer anyway. When she called her name again, Billy was up, punching his arm above his head, and shouting, "Boo! Boo!" Other Droobs now jumped out of their seats and yelled at her:

"Boo!"

"You creep!"

"Your mom's a criminal!"

"Your mom's in jail!

"Die!"

Marigold knew her small body could easily fit through the open, tall window beside her desk. Like a book bag-towing cannon ball, she became a loaded projectile launching through the window and into the grass. She was out of there, blasting forward toward freedom! She would run home, get her suitcase, and then escape. No more bullies shouting cruel words. No more embarrassing mother.

Through the field, she barreled! Mrs. Drebel's yelling words for her to come back became weaker and weaker, with each running step. Nobody was going to stop her now! Nobody! On and on she ran, as fast as she could (which wasn't real fast), but at least she knew she was persistent. Like a blasting cannon ball, with an agenda, she shot ahead.

Now, she was on the other side of the field. There were only a couple of miles to her house, her packed suitcase, then freedom! Her breath had become hot, and as she huffed and puffed, it burned her throat like volcanic lava. With each forward step, Marigold knew she was erupting with all the energy she possessed. On and on and on!

There were sounds of sirens in the distance. Had the school called the police, and now they were hunting her down? Would she soon be joining her mother in a jail cell? Like mother, like daughter? Were they going to be roomies?

There was a tall shrub beside some old house on her left, and she dove behind it; she watched through the branches and saw two police cars zip by. After the sirens had faded into the distance, she was out again, running as fast as her new Nikes would take her. Down into a muddy puddle she fell—-but up again! Go forward! Forward! Forward! She now realized she had to use speed but couldn't get sloppy and end up in jail. Even worse than jail, would be to end up back at school with the Droobs causing her life to be more miserable than ever. Nope, she only had one chance, and that was to be a fugitive--like that guy on the old television show her mom liked to watch. What was it called? Oh yeah, "The Fugitive": A TV series Marsha watched while she nervously nibbled on buttery popcorn.

No TV or popcorn for her mom now-well, at least Marigold didn't think so, anyway. She almost felt sorry for her mother, even though she had ruined her life. At least her mom loved her. Marsha Stroop was crazy, but she loved her-only one who did. Now, it might be only bread and water in a jail cell with no TV or popcorn-for a very long time.

The sirens began coming from the other direction, and Marigold threw herself behind a car parked in a driveway. She watched the two squad cars zoom by as they headed back in the school's direction. Yep, she bet they were hunting her down. Once they had passed, she leaped out and was running. Not much breath left anymore, her legs had become jelly, and her clothes were filthy with mud and grime. Sweat dripped from her face to the ground like a dripping faucet, and when she looked down, she saw her brand new, white Nikes had turned black. She clutched at the cramp in her side and staggered forward, gasping for breath.

Only a block now, and she'd be at her house. She put one shaky foot after the other, not running anymore. She felt relief when she finally saw her little, white, blue-shuttered home coming into view.

But what was this? Her mother was out in the front yard watering the many orange and yellow mums, zinnias, and marigolds she had recently planted? The cops must have let her out of jail! Now, Marigold wondered, how she was going to slip, undetected, inside her bedroom to get her suitcase?

She pressed her body against the side of the house and inched her feet toward the back door. Once there, she turned the doorknob and found it was unlocked. Yes! Holding her breath, Marigold scooted into the kitchen and down the hall to her bedroom. There, she dropped her book bag onto the floor, grabbed her suitcase, made her way to the back door again, and darted outside. Finally!

With renewed energy, she ran into the alley she had traveled the night before. She tried not to think about the Misfits, who had been so nice to her, and tried not to think about her mother, who loved her. She had to concentrate on one thing-herself-and the knowledge she was the only one who could change her life and get away from the Droobs, who didn't care if she lived or died. No, most of the Droobs really hoped she died. And how could she change her life? Easy Peasy. She had to find a new place to live, and now she knew where that place was going to be: under the bridge in Solly Park.

One steady step after the other. Her stomach growled and reminded her she was hungry. What would she eat, if she lived under Solly Bridge, in the park? She knew there were dumpsters located behind restaurants, where she bet she could find some food. Yeah, didn't homeless people do that all the time? And she bet restaurant people threw out tons of food left on customer's plates. Well, the idea of eating food off of other people's plates made her feel pretty nauseated, but ya had to do what ya had to do.

Then there was water. How was she going to get that? She was thirsty from her long run. Really thirsty. Once she got to where she was going to hide, she'd figure it out. There would probably be other nice, homeless people under the bridge, who could teach her how to live outside on her own. Why did I pack such a heavy suitcase, she wondered, and her steps began to slow down.

It was only two blocks to the park, and once she got there, she trudged toward the bridge. Her suitcase now almost touched the grass. For the first time since she had left school, she looked up into the sky, at the beautiful blue sky and the puffy white clouds and-and-that huge black bird soaring above her head! What was that bird doing? Was it following her? A stalking monster bird? Really?

She walked under the bridge and almost tripped over some old, grimy man, with a bunch of glass bottles at his feet, that she clink-clanked across. At first, she almost didn't see him or the bottles; the bridge blocked out most of the sunlight. It smelled like a ton of old, open, garbage cans times one hundred. And the odor was worse than last night's alleys. Then his stench, added to the smell of garbage, made her almost want to put her feet in reverse and skadoodle-skadoodle right out of there.

Almost, but not totally. She asked herself which would be worse: breathing in this horrid smell or going back to school and facing the many cruel Droobs: cruel Droobs who wanted nothing more than to spit horrid words, in her direction, from slimy, lizard lips? Nope, here was better. A stinky man under a bridge was better than a bunch of mean Droobs.

As Marigold's eyes adjusted to the dimness, she could see that this disgusting man was sitting up, but his head was lying on his shoulder at an awkward angle. She knew he was asleep and not dead, because he was snoring. She crouched down a distance away from him. It was dark under there, and hopefully if he did wake up, he wouldn't see her. Every now and then, he coughed up something and spit; she tried not to look at what disgusting thing he had unloaded. Then, after a few moments, he would snort, snort, snort and start the snoring all over again.

She wondered why he was so tired and asleep in the morning? Did he hunt for food at night, like a wolf? Was he sick and dying? That cough he had sure didn't sound too good, and she almost felt sorry for him. Her mom would say he needed cough syrup and a vaporizer running. There was no place to plug in a vaporizer, but she could go back home for meds. Still, those bottles at his feet? Was he an alcoholic?

She had heard about people drinking and getting drunk until they passed out. She wouldn't know; the only alcohol her mother ever had was a little glass of champagne on New Year's Eve when she toasted in the New Year and munched on cold cabbage, which she made Marigold take bites of. Every New Year's Day at 12:01 a.m., she told Marigold that eating cabbage was going to bring them lots of money the next year. Marigold always wondered how that was going to happen, when it sure hadn't occurred the year before, or the year before that, or the year before that-even after crunching down a bunch of cold cabbage at 12:01 a.m., when people outside were banging pots and pans. Then she wondered why she was thinking about New Year's Eve at a time like this.

She pushed her suitcase to the side, where she could put her head on it. Maybe sleeping wasn't such a bad idea, since she might need to be up all night digging in dumpsters behind restaurants. She thought she had quietly gotten herself comfortable (well, as comfortable as was possible with her head on a hard suitcase), but suddenly the grimy man was up. He stood tall, staggered over to her, and shouted in-between coughs, "Who-(cough) are (gag) you (cough again)?" His filthy clothes were in tatters and hung off his bony frame like gray, shredded curtains in some haunted house's window. The man's dark hair was greasy, and if she thought he had stunk before, it was nothing compared to his smell now.

Marigold tried to hold her breath and press herself into the cold concrete behind her. She also tried to somehow find her voice-a very difficult thing to do. He stepped closer, until there were mere inches between his torn pant's leg and her face.

She tried pushing herself even further back into that concrete, which wasn't moving anywhere, and said, "M-Marigold. Marsha Str-Stroop."

Now he crouched down and stared his blood shot eyes into hers. "I caaan't hearrr yooou! Talk louder!"

She cleared her throat, more scared than she thought she had ever been in her whole life. She felt even more scared than she had descending on a curly, twirly slide into the Misfits' underground cavern or zooming upward in their elevator. At least there, the Misfits had been waiting on her. Here, it was just her puny self against this crazy, filthy, frightening man, who could kill her and throw her into the muddy river that flowed just mere feet away. "Pl-Please don't h-hurt me," she said.

"Oh, deary, I like little girls." He grabbed hold of her elbow with a scratchy hand. "I like them a whole lot." His face was almost touching hers, and his breath smelled like a poop-filled sewer. "I can sell you, you know, for a whole lot of money."

Chapter 13

With a great "Hiii-yeee!", someone else entered this space under Solly Bridge. This "someone" was dressed in black and even wore that familiar mask. Della did a quick kick, a chop, and the smelly derelict flew onto his back. Then she grabbed Marigold, pulled her and that suitcase out from under the bridge, and yanked her over the grass, like she was an Alaskan malamute pulling a sled in the Iditarod. Della didn't stop pulling, until they were on the grass, in front of Marigold's house. Her mom's car was gone.

Della angrily made a kick and chop in the air. "You need to go into your house, dump your suitcase, grab your book bag, and get your booty back to school! Do you know what happens, dude, when you leave school without Mrs. Hernandez's permission? You get expelled! How are you going to help the Misfits if you get kicked out? And you would have gotten killed if Jade hadn't told me where you were!"

Marigold was beyond relieved that Della had found and saved her-again. Jade told Della she was under that bridge? She knew Della's angry words were true, but that situation with her mother at the bus stop, and her leaping out of the classroom window, were going to give Billy and Billy's friends major bullying ammunition. The Misfits just didn't understand what she had to deal with when it came to the Droobs. They thought they did, but they had no idea. Who was Mrs. Hernandez? Was she the principal?

After she dropped her suitcase on her bedroom floor and put her book bag on her back, she met Della in the yard and followed her to school. Della didn't say a word during the very long walk; she only made intermittent chops, angry growls, and kicks in the air.

Marigold could smell it was lunch time when they entered Brentwood, and she followed the still-- angry, kicking and muttering Della through the empty halls to the cafeteria. And there were the Misfits, busily throwing bags of food to each other at the back table. Marigold took out her peanut butter crackers, passed them around, and then sat down between Kate and Mo. Jade was perched in her familiar position atop the table, hands folded, eyes closed, and humming.

"Here ya go, mon. Welcome back." Jus made certain the flying food landed in front of Marigold and Della, so they were able to take cauliflower and broccoli, a piece of whole wheat bread with cheese, popcorn, an orange, an apple, and Marigold, of course, took two of her peanut butter crackers. A bottle of water she'd brought completed the feast.

"Better eeeat fast," Jade said.

"Hmmm?" Marigold asked, when she saw Jade was looking at her.

"Better eeeat fast. Your tiiime with us will be short."

"Why?" Marigold took a big bite out of a Golden Delicious apple. That's when she saw Coach Reynolds stomping his way toward their table. His colorful gym shoes came to an abrupt stop once he reached the Misfits, slamming down food.

"Up! Up!" he commanded with an upward-pointing finger, his eyes landing on Marigold.

"M-Me?" she asked.

"Of course-you. Do you think you can jump out a window, leave school, and escape the police without a consequence, you stupid idiot?"

Marigold reluctantly stood and followed Coach Reynold's marching gym shoes toward the office. Once there, the school secretary nodded acknowledgment at the coach, then gestured with an open palm that she was to follow her straight back to the principal's office. Marigold followed this secretary and entered a small office, sat down on a blue upholstered chair facing a desk, and clutched the armrest with sweaty fingers. She could only imagine how dirty she must look with her filthy clothes and muddy Nikes. Stinky, too. She sure hoped she didn't smell like that awful man under the bridge.

Marigold swallowed hard when a very tall, beautiful woman, in a black suit, entered.

Was this woman the principal? The woman held out her hand in Marigold's direction, and Marigold reluctantly shook it with her grimy, perspiring one.

"Hello, Marigold. My name is Mrs. Hernandez. I have not had the pleasure of meeting you yet; although, I knew you were coming to our school. I've been anxiously anticipating your arrival, as have the other Misfits."

"'Other' M-Misfits?" Marigold wondered what that meant.

"Yes." Mrs. Hernandez smiled sparkling white teeth in her direction. Her glistening black hair was knotted in a tight bun on top of her head, and she wore bright red lipstick, along with dangling, silver earrings. She pulled a large, brown leather chair on wheels over from behind the desk to a spot facing Marigold, sat down, and crossed her long legs. She was wearing shiny patent, black, spike heels and swung her top leg back and forth. With very long, sharp fingernails, she re-stuck a hair pin into her bun.

Marigold cleared her throat and somehow managed to get out a "H-Hi." What was going on? Why was this principal being so nice to her? Nice to her, after she had jumped out a window and run away? Plus, Mrs. Hernandez even said she had anticipated her arrival, along with the other Misfits? Marigold chewed at a fingernail and wondered what the heck was happening.

She figured Mrs. Hernandez must have seen the surprised look in her eyes, since she reached out to pat her on the knee. "No worries, Marigold Marsha Stroop. Jade informed me about the bullying you were forced to endure during homeroom this morning. It saddens me that your teacher, Mrs. Drebel, did not come to your defense. I will have a meeting with her after school today to discuss her lack of sensitivity, absence of support for you-plus her very questionable classroom management skills. I have already assigned Billy to after-school suspension today."

Marigold slowly nodded her head up and down and had to force her mouth closed. Why was this principal, the leader of Brentwood Middle School, being so kind to her?

"I understand, Marigold." Mrs. Hernandez looked caring, black eyes into her green ones. "I would have jumped through that window, too, except I wouldn't have fit!" She let out with a loud "Caw!" and continued, "I guess I would have simply had to fly from the room and out the school's door. Then I would have continued traveling as fast as I could (which would have been very fast, by the way). I can be quite swift, or so I've been told, but I'm not as fast as Mo. No one is as speedy as that boy! Caw!"

Marigold was speechless.

"From now on, know you can come here to me, in this office, anytime you are a victim of such cruelty, or if you just want to chat, tweet, or twitter. Caw! Caw! Caw!"

Well, now Marigold was incapable of even a head nod. She couldn't move a muscle. She watched Mrs. Hernandez swoop her long black sleeves above her head, then slowly lower them.

"I know all of this might come as a shocking experience for you-support in a school by a principal, when you haven't experienced that before." The principal's dark eyes moved quickly back and forth, as if she were deep in thought. "But you shall find it's different here at Brentwood. Very different."

"It-It is?"

"Oh, yes. And let me interject that I understand you more than you even know. Plus, Mrs. Toon and Ms. Henley are on the same page as I."

"Y-You do? Th-They are?"

The phone on Mrs. Hernandez's desk rang. She smoothly glided over to it, her large sleeves billowing in the breeze she created with her movement.

"Hello? This is Mrs. Hernandez." (Pause) "Yes, she is, in fact, sitting in the office with me right now. Yes, she arrived back at school, Officer Jackmon. (Pause) "No problems, no problems at all." (Pause) "No, we do not need to send her to Juvenile Detention. I dare say, I would have escaped this place, had I been in her same position." (Long pause) "I will impart that information to Marigold; I am certain she'll be happy to hear it. Thanks."

Now Marigold was wondering exactly what she was going to be "happy to hear".

The principal clicked off her phone and lowered it down. Then she drummed her very long, sharp nails on the desk's shiny surface. "Marigold, your mother has been released from jail, which Jade already told me you are aware of. Your mom told the policemen that she had some chores to complete at home, before heading to work; her income was essential for the two of you to have clothes, food, etc. She said she broke her back every day to provide for both of you." Mrs. Hernandez raised her dark eyebrows.

"Y-Yeah. Sounds just like my m-mom." Marigold rolled her eyes.

"She works hard every day?"

"She d-does. Works her f-fingers to the bone. Just ask h-her."

Now Mrs. Hernandez closed her eyes, leaned back in her chair. "I see. Well, she is at work, and I'm sure she will be returning to your house at her usual arrival time. Officer Jackmon said they talked to your mother, and after hearing about Billy's antics, well, they informed his father. Billy's dad is a police officer and stated he will deal with his son at home. They did give her a warning, however, and said that the next time, she will have to face jail time. Assault by an adult to a child won't be tolerated."

"W-Well, I hope she listened. She will d-do anything to protect me."

Mrs. Hernandez scrawled a pen across a pass and walked toward Marigold. "Now, to class, dear."

Marigold walked backward toward the door as she watched Mrs. Hernandez throw her arms over her head and cry a loud, "Caw!". Then her jaw dropped open when this principal appeared to levitate a few feet above the floor as she cawed again!

"Nope," Marigold said aloud, when she shakily turned the doorknob and escaped through the door. "Only my imagination. Had to be my imagination."

After leaving that room, Marigold found Jade holding the outside office door open for her. The telepathic wonder said, "Sometimes things are truuue and not imaginaaary, my friend. Ommm."

Oh, boy, oh boy, oh boy, Marigold thought. Things just kept getting crazier and crazier.

Marigold started for gym, not as afraid of the mean girls' rudeness as she might have been before, since Jade and Della had helped with that. The halls were silent when Marigold marched her dirty shoes toward class. Not only did she have the support of the Misfits; now, the principal had her back. Plus, there were two teachers named Mrs. Toon and Ms Henley, who were "on the same page".

She held her head up higher, and it wasn't just because there was nobody in these halls to criticize and taunt her. To gym she went, and straight into the locker room to put on her crazy, colorful outfit. Then she ran into the gymnasium, where the girls were hitting volleyballs over the net.

After handing her pass to the gym teacher, Miss Smith, she prepared herself for the cruel words about to verbally smack her across the face, smack her harder than those Droobs were hitting the balls. But when the Droobs just ignored her and kept on playing, she understood Della had certainly done a number on them yesterday in the locker room. Again, she sent a silent "thank you" to Batgirl, with her kicks and chops and to Jade, the message-sender. Marigold grabbed a ball and began hitting it against the wall. She wasn't ready to join the group of girls. Not yet, anyway. The teacher didn't seem to care and only stared at the big clock on the wall, obviously counting the minutes until this period ended. Marigold bounce, bounce, bounced the ball against the wall for the remainder of the period.

After a very quick change, it was on to last period, social studies. She sure hoped Jus was in class today. She rushed through the door, scanned the room for a tall guy with dreads, and spied him sitting at a back desk. An empty one, beside him, seemed to call her name. She smiled when he waved his long hands, with sparkling rings, in the air. Unfortunately, as she sped in her little dirty Nike shoes right past Billy, he stuck out a foot. She landed with a thud onto the brown tile. Her skirt flew up, obviously showing her striped underwear to anyone looking, and the book bag on her back ka-whumped onto the floor like an earthquake's aftershock. The class was in an uproar.

Like a struggling turtle on its back, she rocked about but finally managed to sit up. Thankfully, there was Jus, standing beside her with his hand outstretched. She grabbed hold, and he raised her to a standing position. Billy, also now standing, sang, "Marigold's wearing stri-ped underwear, Marigold's wearing stri-ped underwear..." Of course, the other kids joined in, repeating the chant, jumping in place, and punching the air.

Waving a referral form over her head, Mrs. Johnson ran, on her black rubber-soled shoes, toward Billy. "You bad boy! Go to the office! You are in big trouble!"

Marigold could barely hear the teacher's words over the shouts, "Stri-ped underwear!, stri-ped underwear!" Marigold wondered, did Billy have an even blacker eye?

Amidst it all, Marigold found her way back to that desk in the back, Jus at her side. Mrs. Johnson screeched for the kids to get quiet and sit down. They didn't. Black-eyed Billy kept swiping his arm in the air, encouraging the others to continue with the steady chant. He ignored the referral fluttering from Mrs. Johnson's hand. The teacher stomped over to her desk and started talking to someone on her phone. It wasn't long before Mrs. Hernandez appeared in the doorway.

Immediately, kids lowered their behinds into their seats, and their voices started quieting, as well. Obviously, they recognized the principal and knew they'd better stifle it, if they didn't want to get into trouble, too. Not the kind of trouble their bullying leader was probably going to get in.

Mrs. Hernandez stood in front of Billy. "Go-to-the-office-now!" She planted her spiked heels firmly on the floor and crossed her arms over her chest.

"Make me!" Billy looked behind him to see if the other kids were impressed. There was only a collective gasp from his supposed allies. They looked from side to side at each other, as if they could not believe even Billy would talk like that to the principal.

But Mrs. Hernandez didn't seem a bit ruffled. She took her phone out of her pocket and began talking to someone. Soon, two school police officers were at the door. Mrs. Hernandez spoke quietly to them, and they both nodded. One officer said, "Billy, you need to go to the office right now, or you're going to wish you had."

That's when Billy said something Marigold didn't think anyone was expecting; in fact, she thought she must be hearing things when he said, "Maake meee."

One of the officers stepped forward. "What did you say?"

You could have heard a dry-erase marker drop.

He hissed, "I said, 'Make me'!"

This officer took out a pair of handcuffs from his pocket and put them on Billy. They closed with a click, a sound which reverberated loudly in this now-silent room. He commanded, "March!"

When it didn't appear that Billy was going to move, much less march, each officer curled a hand under one of his sweaty armpits and carried him out the door. Marigold looked over at Jus, who looked as shocked as she knew she must appear. The second day of middle school and Billy was taken out of the classroom-by the police-in handcuffs?

With a trembling hand, Mrs. Johnson wrote an assignment on the board. Marigold opened her book and started reading. Most of the others did the same, and everyone remained quiet for the rest of the period. Jus, however, had opened his notebook and begun a new drawing of a big, black bird soaring through the clouds

When Marigold looked at his drawing, then at him, he ignored her attention and just kept sketching. Why the black bird? Did this bird have anything to do with the one she had seen? Was Jus sending her a message, or did he simply like birds? Had he also seen the big, black bird, a bird that looked larger than the hugest crow she had ever seen in her life? It was like a prehistoric, gigantic crow! She had heard about ravens, even condors-but this bird? Well, she had never seen anything like it before. Not even in books.

When the bell rang ending this last period and the end of the school day, Marigold gathered up her things and looked down at her legs for the first time. No blood from the fall in the classroom. That was a good thing.

Jus touched her arm when they stepped into the hall. "Tonight, same time, mon. Be watchin' for us, cause that way, Della won't have to be kickin' in your window." Then, he gave her a long fingered wave and was off in his colorful, red pants and sparkling, green shoes.

Chapter 14

Marigold stood in the hall and stared after him. Same time? Be watchin' for them? She figured that meant they were going to be at her bedroom window tonight. Yeah, tonight she would be watching for them for sure; she didn't need a broken window. That would not be good and might make her mom start suspecting something weird was going on. Then what? Marigold knew a broken window would make Marsha Stroop call the police, because she suspected somebody was trying to break into their house.

Marigold hurried to her locker and then onto the bus. There was a cop car parked in front of the school, and Marigold saw Billy in the back seat. She wondered how long the police would keep him. Would they put him in that Juvenile Detention place Mrs. Hernandez had been talking about, to the policeman, when she'd sat in her office today? Would they lock him up for a very long time? Without Billy as the ring leader, would the Droobs settle down, or would somebody else take his place-like Mike Botowski?

She had no answers and sat down in the front behind Mr. Carini, who was fanning his face with his huge hand. The other kids seemed subdued, probably because their leader now sat in a cop car. Thankfully, no rude Droobs.

Her mother was home when Marigold arrived. "Have a good day?" she asked as soon as her daughter placed one dirty shoe into the living room.

Heading to her room, Marigold said, "Y-Yeah." She knew it would do no good to get mad and yell at her mom about how terribly she had embarrassed her at the bus stop. No good at all. Her mother would just act all sad and tell her she had done that because she loved her so much.

So she simply went to her room and shut the door, changed clothes, and plopped down on her stomach across her sunset comforter. Evidently, her mother hadn't heard about her escaping from school. That was good. She sure didn't want to explain about being a pretend fugitive and about the homeless man under the bridge. Boy, would that make her mother freak out, and she didn't need Mother Marsha freaking out either. No way.

A knock, knock came on her bedroom door.

"What?" Marigold asked, her eyes closed.

"Can I come in?"

Because Marigold knew she had no choice, she said, "Sure." But she wondered why she couldn't have just five minutes to herself.

The door cracked open, and Marsha Stroop stepped inside. She sat down on the bed, stroked her daughter's back. "Was your day really good today?"

"Uh h-huh."

"Really?"

Marigold turned over onto her side. "I-I told you it was, didn't I?"

"Well yes, sweetheart, you did, but you don't seem very happy-you know-like you really had a good day."

Marigold felt her breath coming in short spurts. Her mother just didn't get it. Would never get it.

When Marigold didn't respond, Marsha said, "It looks like you were in a war zone, from the look of your clothes and shoes, I mean."

Marigold stayed quiet as Marsha eyed the dirty clothes and shoes on the floor.

"But don't you worry." She patted Marigold on the head. "I can go to Tracies after I get my next check Friday and buy you some new, cute, yellow shoes."

Marigold's silence was now broken when she shot up and said, "No, M-Mother. I do not w-want any more yellow shoes. I like these sh-shoes. I c-can wash these shoes."

Now, Marsha stood. "Well, okay, okay. I was just trying to be helpful. I break my back every day, trying to put food on our table, a roof over our heads, and clothes on our backs." Her eyes shifted to Marigold's filthy shoes. "And I guess that means shoes on our feet. You are the most important person in my life. Do you know that? Have I told you that before?"

Marigold said, "Oh, yes, Mom. I think you have told me that before." She walked out of the room, didn't want to say too much, didn't want to hurt her mother's feelings. After all, she knew her mom loved her, and she loved her mom, as well. But why did her mother have to drive her craaazy?

Marsha Stroop scurried after her daughter. "Are you headed to the kitchen, honey? Hungry?"

Marigold carried her shoes into the laundry room and ran a soapy paper towel over them. "N-no. Not h-hungry."

"You know, if I buy you some cute yellow shoes, you won't have to clean those white ug--I mean, plain, white ones."

Continuing to scrub, Marigold mumbled, "I l-like these shoes, Mother. Have I-I told you that before?"

"Well, yes, I guess you have."

And Marigold knew her mother didn't realize she was just repeating her very own words.

"Well, then, would you like leftovers for supper tonight?" Mrs. Stroop asked.

"Y-Yeah. That would b-be good." As Marigold walked to her bedroom, she said, "B-But I need to do my homework f-first."

"Okay, sweetie. I will have your dinner on the table at five o'clock. I am so proud of you for doing your homework. I bet you will be a straight "A" student this year, my brilliant girl!"

Marigold shut her bedroom door behind her and lay across her bed, pulled her social studies book out of her book bag, and started reading the first chapter. Her mind kept slipping away, however, to her nuts-o mother at the bus stop and her arrest; her own escape from school; the homeless, scary man; Della's arrival and saving her; mean Mr. Reynolds; the kind principal; Billy tripping her and his words; her underwear showing; all the kids chanting; the policemen's arrival; and then Billy being removed in handcuffs and put in a squad car. Man! What a day. Finally, she saw in her mind the picture of the bird Jus had drawn on his paper-that soaring bird in the sky.

After she'd finished reading and writing out the answers to the questions in social studies, she closed the book and put it, along with her notebook, back into her book bag. Marigold sprawled across her bed and closed her eyes. It didn't seem like she had drifted into dreamland for more than a few minutes, before her mother was knocking on the door, announcing dinner.

"Time for your favorite supper, Marigold! Two days in a row!"

Marigold sat up and put her feet on the floor. She knew that the sooner she got supper eaten, the sooner she could be on the look-out for the Misfits outside her bedroom window. She wondered why Jus had said they would be back. Did they have something to tell her? Maybe they were going to kick her out for splitting the joint, otherwise known as Brentwood Middle School?

Stumbling out to the kitchen, Marigold breathed in the familiar odors from last night. And there, on the kitchen table, were the same dishes of food: lasagna, salad, green bean casserole, garlic bread, broccoli in cheese sauce, and on the counter, carrot cake. Then her mom lit the red candle. She sat down in a chair and let her mother serve her without argument. It made her mom happy to treat her like a baby, and when her mom was happy, life was just so much easier. Marigold didn't want to witness another kid-attack by Ninja-Mother tomorrow at the bus stop.

"Yum," Marigold said after the first bite of lasagna.

"Do you like it? Is it as good as it was last night?" Marsha Stroop stood above Marigold and made comments like she was some sports commentator on TV. Words like, "There ya go, that's the way to fill your tummy, chew a hundred times now, don't want to choke"-words like that seriously made Marigold feel that she was going to gag on her food, instead of swallow it.

Why did her mom have to make eating some major event, instead of simply a normal happening? Was watching her daughter eat supper the most exciting thing in her life? Well, probably not today. There were probably more exciting things that happened in her life today, like attacking Billy, being arrested, and then driven down to the police station.

After Marigold had forced down half a piece of carrot cake, and her mother asked her if she was okay, if there was something wrong with dessert because she hadn't finished it, Marigold stood up from the table. She couldn't take it any longer. "No, M-Mom. It w-was great. I'm just f-full."

Only after Marigold had finished supper, did her mom sit down at the table, serve herself, and begin eating the now-cold food. "Where are you going?" she asked between mouthfuls, when Marigold made her way back to her room. "I thought we could play some cards after supper."

"Don't w-want to play. Thanks for dinner. It w-was delicious, but I need to get some rest, you know, so I-I can be that straight A student and someday m-make you rich." She continued through her bedroom door and closed it quietly.

"Well, okay, sweetheart! Get some rest! I will lay your clothes out for you by your bed after I finish eating and do the dishes!" Marsha Stroop hollered.

Oh, no! What if her mom came into her room at the same time Jus and the Misfits arrived outside her window? What then? Marigold retraced her footsteps back to the kitchen.

"Back so soon?" Her mom had begun on the cold lasagna. Ready for cards?"

"N-No, but I was j-just thinking, Mom. You work so hard for me every day--break your b-back, even. H-How about I pick out my own clothes tonight?"

Mrs. Stroop stood and piled dishes into the sink. "Oh, honey, I don't mind. Really, I don't. I love getting my baby girl's clothes all ready for her to wear in the morning."

Marigold ran to the laundry room and found some of her clothes, smelling like flowery fabric softener, piled on top of the dryer. She returned with what she thought were ridiculous clothes, ones her mother would really like. She held them out at arm's length toward her mom.

"H-Here. How about these?" Pulling items out, one by one, she said: "H-How about this orange and yellow plaid dress, green and yellow striped s-socks, yellow ruffled underwear?"

Mrs. Stroop, self-proclaimed fashionista, peered at this presentation like she was an art critic analyzing a famous painting. "Well, I suppose. Just wish you had yellow shoes to complete the beautiful ensemble."

Marigold nodded. "I know. B-But guess these will h-have to do."

Marsha drew in a deep breath. "I hope you lay them very carefully on the chair by your bed. Don't want them to get the tiniest wrinkle, you know."

"I w-will. No wrinkles, I-I promise."

Marigold took her mom's nod as approval and scurried back to her bedroom with the ugly clothes in her arms. Once inside, she threw them on her chair and turned out the lights. Time to wait for the visit from the Misfits and whatever they had planned. She sure hoped her removal wasn't going to happen.

Time goes so slowly when you are waiting, wondering, and waiting some more. She watched the minutes drag by on her digital clock; those red numbers increasing by one number, then the next, then finally the next until an hour went by. She must have been at the window to peek out at least fifty times, before she gave up and sat on the edge of the bed. Had they decided not to come? The wind whooped and walloped against the house and made Marigold hope the already-cracked window could withstand the force. Maybe it wouldn't take Della's fierce kick to break it. Maybe Mother Nature was going to make that occur. She donned a yellow fleece sweatshirt, orange sweatpants, and put on her clean Nike shoes.

Knock, knock, knockety-knock sounded at the window at exactly 10:03. She parted her curtains and saw all the Misfits standing in the yard. There was no golden moon tonight; gray clouds skidded across the sky, like ghosts playing tag, and Marigold slipped from her window and out into the darkness.

Chapter 15

"Glad you were waitin', mon," Jus said, his dreads blowing crazily in the wind. Mo had a hand on his turban, while Kate and Della wore caps. Jade's black hair was not going anywhere; it perched atop her head in a tight knot, like a very carefully created bird's nest.

"Wh-What took you s-so long?" Marigold reattached her flower hair clip, since it had been blown down a strand of hair and was about to slip its way off. She was happy she had put on warm clothes. The wind was fierce-and cold.

"Stuff to get ready and important things to see, mon," Jus said, his long legs loping toward the alley. "You are gonna be havin' some special Misfits to meet tonight, too."

"More M-Misfits?" Marigold pushed herself forward, with all of her might, and wished she weighed more. This wind acted like it was going to lift her up and carry her into the sky.

"Yes. Some morrre Misfits. Ommmm," Marigold wondered how Jade was going to walk wherever they were going tonight, scooting through the darkness with closed eyes. It was hard enough walking into this wind by lifting her own feet and being aware of her surroundings.

"Nothing to beee worrying about," Jade said. "I can make my way quiiite easily. By the waaay, your mother fell asleep quickly, just like last niiight."

"O-Oh. Thank you, J-Jade," Marigold said.

Down the alleys they went as flying leaves, paper, even sticks hit Marigold in the face. There was the familiar crunching glass, awful odor, and Marigold wondered if they were going to go to the same place they had gone before. Fighting the wild wind made this trip more difficult than last night;

Marigold held her arm in front of her face and attempted to walk in a forward direction without falling down. This journey was taking forever!

A loud cawing sounded above, and Marigold managed to twist her neck and squint up into the black sky, mottled with whipping clouds. With these surroundings so dark, and leaves flying about, it was hard to discern the source of the sound. But when the blur, in the blackness, became a moving shape, she cowered and wrapped her arms around her head. No, it couldn't be happening. She forced her eyes upward once more. Was that same large, black bird careening through the sky, flying through this wild night?

Should she alert the other Misfits about the monster-fowl sweeping over their heads?

Didn't only owls fly at night? Owls and bats? And Marigold bet neither of those were out tonight; they were probably safely hunkered down in their hidey-holes. But this huge bird? Why was it swooping above? Could that bird be hunting for prey, and could the Misfits provide an early midnight snack? That thought made her wrap her arms more tightly around her head and surge ahead.

Marigold yelled as loudly as she could, to be heard over the wind, "H-Hey! Do you see that big b-bird?"

No one replied, and Marigold didn't think that was because they didn't hear her. Obviously, they either knew about that crow on steroids or they just-didn't-care.

"Only a little bit more, mon," Jus yelled from the front of the line. He was some general leading his soldiers into a safe haven. She didn't look up anymore, only concentrated on one foot and then the other, following those trudging before her. Just as she doubted Jus's encouraging words were true, the line in front of her came to an abrupt halt. Amazingly, they had stopped right before the same rusty, old shed.

With the powerful wind, it required all of Jus's strength and the help of Della's muscles to open the metal door. One by one, they took turns going into the shed and disappearing. Like the previous night, Marigold was the second to the last to sit down onto that slippery slide and twist and turn her way through the darkness, before landing with a ka-wump onto the soft blanket in the candle-lit space. She swiftly moved her position to the left, mere seconds before a giggling Jus landed beside her.

"I am just lovin' that trip down," he said.

Mo grinned. "And you say that all the time!"

"Cause I am meanin' it all the time, mon."

Everyone stood when Jade went to the large chest and removed capes. This time, however, she started with Jus, who then immediately tied one around her. After that, she went to every Misfit, wrapped them in the regal goldness, and tied the black ribbon under each chin. When she placed the cape around Marigold, the same feeling of warmth, along with importance and belonging, helped her understand she didn't want to run away anymore. Now, she realized she was right where she belonged.

"Youuu must remember this feeling of contentment and of happiness when you starrrt thinking about becoming a fugitive again, duuue to the Droobs' words and actions. This is the saaafe place where you belong. We neeed and care about you." Then Jade closed her eyes, made the "ommm" sound, and folded her hands in front of her chest.

Kate nodded. "In actuality, what Jade has professed is entirely correct."

Della yelled, "And no more running away, dude! No more Plan!"

Everyone joined hands, and Jus said,. "The Organization of the Misfits will now come to order." This time, after saying the "ommm", they simply stated the oath once (instead of echoing the words after Jus had said them):

"For Right,
Not Might
For the greater good
To all upon this planet earth,
And for all who have met on these hallowed grounds
From Time Unknown
Until Time We Know."

Marigold stumbled through the words but knew, in time, she would learn them. To her, this sacred oath meant they were following the beliefs of those from the very beginning of the Misfits' organization until now--the promise to help other people "for the greater good". It sent chills up and down her spine in the cool place, and she was happy she was able to be part of this group. These bullied kids, who might need someone to stand up for them, were using their gifts to help others. How wonderful was that?

Jus said, “Well, I am thinkin’ that it’s time for a visit from The Proprietor, mon. He needs to join us.”

As if on cue, the wee little man emerged from the same door in the side of the cavern. He hobbled on crooked legs, over to Marigold, and lifted his gnarled finger at her. In the candlelight, Marigold could see his ancient blue eyes were very light in color, almost transparent. He rubbed a finger across a wrinkled cheek and stopped a bead of liquid escaping from the corner of his eye. Marigold wondered if he was crying, and if so, what he was so unhappy about.

“Heee carries the sadness of the world upon his shoulders, with hisss gift of sensitivity,” Jade said, as if in reply to Marigold’s thoughts. The Proprietor nodded and stopped another tear slipping down his face.

His very old voice creaked, “So many, in need of so much.” Then he motioned with his hands that Marigold was to walk closer, and when she did, he stuck out his left bony elbow for her to grasp. She hesitantly placed shaking fingers there, and he began scooting his bare feet back to the door from where he had just emerged.

“Y-You want me to c-come with you?”

“I do,” he said, in his very squeaky voice.

Marigold looked at Jus for some kind of a signal that it was safe to accompany this little, old man. When Jus gave her a nod, she stooped way down to fit through the tiny door the Proprietor held open for her. Once inside, she had to crawl on her hands and knees through a narrow tunnel. She didn't realize what she wiggled through like an earthworm, was an entrance to a huge room!

"Up with ye!" the wee man directed from behind her.

Marigold placed one gym shoe, then the other, beneath herself and pushed upward. Soon, she was in a standing position. No need to worry about bumping her head on any ceiling, since when she looked up, she realized there was no ceiling--just a vast blackness of empty space above, like in The Meeting Room.

This candle-filled area was very large, and a huge table took up most of the space. Made of heavy, dark wood, the table must have stretched a distance of at least twenty feet, and its legs were probably as tall as she was. Ten intricately carved, tall chairs stood five on each side. There were what appeared to be two, tall thrones, each draped in a bejeweled, red velvet covering, at either end of the table. The many tiny red, green, blue, and yellow gems, sewn to the cloth, sparkled in the candlelight.

After climbing up onto a stool beside the closest throne, she saw white plates and blue goblets had been placed on the table before five of the chairs (three on the right side and two on the left) and also in front of each throne. A very tall, silver candle stood burning in the center, and gold cutlery had been arranged at the side of every plate. A big bronze bell sat before each throne, and wood, burning in a corner stone fireplace, filled the room with the sweet smell of smoldering timbers. Marigold also detected a delicious aroma of cooking food, but she didn't see any pots or pans above the fire.

With tight lips and a grunt, The Proprietor used all of his strength to scoot out a chair located at the right side of the table and motioned for Marigold to sit on it. She stepped down from the stool, walked over to the designated chair, and placed her foot on the lowest of several rungs attached to its side. Finally, she climbed up.

Sitting like this, she had an even better view. How was there enough room in the cavern for The Meeting Room, where they had met, and now a room that had a giant table with chairs? All of this space under the ground amazed her! But the Proprietor broke into her thoughts, when he walked back to the emerging tunnel and yelled (well, in as loud of a creaking and crackling yell that he could muster).

"Come into the Dining Room!" He scurried on his bony legs to the throne at the table's far end.

Into the room, the Misfits entered on hands and knees before standing upright. Jus took a seat on the first throne; then Mo, Jade, Kate, and Della climbed up, like Marigold had, into the tall chairs. Mo and Della sat across the table, while Jade and Kate sat on either side of her. The Proprietor sat on the far throne, opposite Jus. Finally, the very ancient man nodded, smiled, and rang the bell, which was on the table beside his plate. The clang, clang, clang echoed in the large space.

Out of a door behind The Proprietor's throne, came three purple, bald creatures-even smaller than The Proprietor! Marigold rubbed her eyes. Two wore black suits, one a black dress, and they carried wooden trays filled to the brim with so much food, Marigold wondered how it remained there. Why didn't the weight cause these wee creatures to drop the trays, fall over, or both?

"They are Timmmers," Jade said to Marigold.

"T-Timmers?"

"Timmmers. They are verrry agile."

"A-Agile?" Marigold asked.

The coordinated Timmers took turns climbing up the many rungs of The Proprietor's throne, and he reached down to stab various, colorful vegetables with a fork and put them onto his plate. He followed the same process with a tray of oranges, grapes, melon slices, peeled bananas, and then slices of whole grain breads. After that, came a crystal plate of beautiful cakes and pies, and a clear blue bowl holding a layered, creamy, cherry dessert. He continued, by placing each selected food on top of his food-mountain, and chuckled. He thanked the servers, and the three Timmers giggled.

Marigold didn't blink. Three little purple creatures were serving food to The Proprietor?

They next went to Jus, and he filled his plate. After that, Kate, Jade, Marigold, Della, then Mo were served. They took turns saying, "thank you" to the Timmers. When it was Marigold's turn, she only took a small amount of food, since she was still full from the feast her mom had made her a few hours earlier.

She noticed the goblet in front of her was filled with water, and she was very, very thirsty. After reaching for the glass to take a drink, Jade, sitting beside her, gently placed a hand on hers.

"Weee must wait," she said.

The Misfits and Timmers all bowed their heads, but no words were spoken. When Marigold raised her eyes, she saw that The Proprietor was eating. Then Jus began. Finally, Jade raised her hand from Marigold's and said, "Weee may begin now. The Misssfits show respect."

Marigold quickly brought the cobalt goblet to her lips, and she let the cold water fill her dry mouth and slide down into her throat. It was possibly the best water she had ever tasted.

"Yes. Thaaat's because it's spring water, fresh from a bubbling spriiing in The Kitchen. Our wonnnderful Timmers capture and bottle it for us each daaay."

Shifting her eyes toward the opening, the place where the small people had emerged, Marigold asked, "There is a k-kitchen back there?"

"Yes, The Kiiitchen is in there. It's where all the vegetables and fruuuits are grown and prepared by the Timmers."

Well, now Marigold knew her eyes were probably rounder than the plate in front of her. A Kitchen? How could there be room for a Kitchen down here? First The Meeting Room, then The Dining Room where they sat; now Jade said there was a Kitchen?

Even though she was still full from her previous meal, the taste of warm bread, apples, carrots, cauliflower, chocolate cake with creamy vanilla frosting, and the cherry dessert were delicious.

"It's callled a parfait. The cherry dessert? A cherry parfaaait."

These were the best veggies, bread, and cake she had ever, ever tasted. And the parfait? She had never had a parfait before, but as good as it was, she sure hoped she would have it again. What magic did these Timmers perform to make the food taste this good? Did it all happen in The Kitchen? These Timmers must be better chefs than she'd ever watched on the Food Channel.

Without speaking, all around the table hungrily delved into the food, and it didn't take long before the plates (except for Marigold's), were empty. One of the Timmers climbed up the rungs of Marigold's chair and peered, with one red and one silver eye, at her plate and then at her.

"I-I'm sorry. I just h-had supper at home."

The Timmer now appeared sad, but The Proprietor quickly interjected, "It's okay, Certil. Marigold loved your food; she just was full from a prior meal."

Marigold quickly nodded her head up and down. "Y-Yes. Your food was wonderful, so w-wonderful. I'm sorry my tummy d-didn't have any room."

Certil pulled a napkin from his apron's pocket and blotted Marigold's lips, then winked his silver eye at her. After that, he was down the rungs and on to the next person. The other two Timmers followed Certil, with buckets of warm water and cloths, which they used to wash everyone's hands and faces.

"I-I hope I didn't hurt his feelings. The f-food was delicious."

The Proprietor climbed down from his throne and slowly walked over to Marigold's chair. Up his bare feet mounted, one rung after another, until he could peer his transparent, blue eyes into her green ones. "Because of your gift of empathy, this feeling that you might have hurt Certil breaks your heart, right?"

Marigold nodded. How did he understand this?

"Heee has the wisdom of the aaages. Plus, heee's sensitive."

"Do not worry, Marigold," The Proprietor continued in his crackly voice. "The Timmers are strong, as well as very kind. You did not hurt Certil's feelings; in fact, right now he is probably planning on simply giving you a smaller portion at our next meal."

Certil, at Jade's place where he was busily blotting off her face, looked over and gave Marigold another wink, but now with his red eye.

"Oh, g-good," Marigold said.

The Proprietor said, "The other two Timmers are Camtrel, a male, and the female, Convel. I did not ask the three of them to serve us this food and water, to wipe off our faces or wash our hands. That is something they want to do. They came to us from the planet, Tinderf, and were royalty there thousands of years ago. When they arrived here to help the first group meeting in this place, well, they asked if they could remain and help our cause."

"They d-did? How did they g-get here?"

"How did they get here, Jus?" The Proprietor asked, pointing a crooked finger into the air.

"Well, mon, in a flyin' saucer, of course."

"A flying s-saucer?" And those around the table nodded their heads, except for Jade who was still having her face wiped by Certil.

"The Timmers do not speak-except to themselves," The Proprietor continued.

Marigold tuned her ears to listen carefully and was able to detect very soft grunts and squeaks. "I h-hear them. And they understand e-each other?"

"They do. Like dolphins in the deep blue sea, like chimpanzees in jungle forests, like all living creatures, they hear and understand each other." The Proprietor climbed down to walk toward his throne.

"W-Wow. That's a-amazing."

"Yesss," Jade now said, since Certil had moved on to Kate. "Very amaaazing."

"And do you know what the Timmers' gift is?" The Proprietor asked, after he climbed up and sat back down on his throne. "They are also Misfits and must possess helpful gifts to be part of this group."

Marigold thought about how they had come from the planet, Tinderf, probably leaving their families to come here to this new home. "I-I know!"

"No, youuu don't," Jade said.

"Y-Yes, I do!"

"No, you dooo not."

"Y-Yes, I do. It's bravery. They are br-brave!"

The Proprietor smiled. "I understand why you would say that. They are brave, but that's not it."

"It's n-not?"

"Told youuu," Jade replied. "Think about whaaat they do here."

"Well, they grow a-and serve us food. They m-make bread, desserts, and get w-water from the spring in The Kitchen. They wipe off our faces and w-wash our hands. Now, I-I know!"

"You do?" Kate asked, now that Certil had traveled over to Mo. "Please enlighten us with your well thought-out deduction."

"No. You are not corrrrect," Jade said.

Marigold ignored Jade and shouted: "Hard w-work! Their gift is that they work h-hard!"

Now, The Proprietor chuckled and Marigold could feel her cheeks getting warm. "Please do not feel embarrassment," he said. "I understand your reasoning, because yes, they were brave to move here from a planet in another solar system. And yes, they certainly are hardworking. But what is the reason they would want to move here and help us with their hard work?"

"B-Because-because-"

"Now, you are riiight. Just saaay it."

"B-Because they are kind. They c-care about all of us sitting here and everyone who used to s-sit here."

Now, The Proprietor stood atop his throne and punched his bony arms above his head. "Yes! Yes! You are right! Kindness is their gift!"

The Timmers quickly joined tiny hands and danced in a circle, making high-pitched squeaks and grunts.

"They s-seem very happy."

"Yes, they are verrry happy."

"Such an excellent deduction you have succinctly stated, my friend," Kate said.

"You knew, mon, that they were bein' happy, because of your gift, Marigold."

"M-My gift of empathy? Is empathy l-like kindness?"

"Empathy is being able to understand how someone feels on the inside. It differs a bit from kindness; however, you are definitely kind," Kate explained.

"O-Oh," Marigold replied.

Pointing at her forehead, Kate continued, "Kindness and empathy both begin in the limbic system of the brain. It may seem a bit daunting, I realize."

"Ooooh, my. Why can't you just talk with normal worrrds? 'Limbic system? Dauuunting'?" Jade shook her head and groaned.

"Oh, just google it!" Mo said, as he leaped down and ran in circles around the table, while everyone giggled-even Kate.

Della jumped down from her chair and began kicking at some imaginary adversary. "Google it, dudes!"

When the laughter died down, The Proprietor said, "Now, I think it is time for Marigold to visit The Kitchen."

"The beautiful Kitchen." Della said, "Chop! Chop!," while the Timmers raced ahead of them through the next door.

Chapter 16

The Proprietor marched on his toothpick legs to the door at the end of this room. As the Misfits followed him, Marigold took the rear. Once inside the next room, The Kitchen, Marigold sucked in a breath. Was this real? Would the unbelievable ever become believable? How could a place like this room even exist? They were in a cavern, under ground, and she'd already seen three large rooms!

"It is very reeeal," Jade said, once the group stopped in place. Marigold stared in wonderment.

In front of her was a garden-not like a normal garden, in someone's back yard, but one that stretched so far, she couldn't even see the end of it. Green cucumbers, bright orange pumpkins, and watermelons, on curling vines, carpeted the area on each side of the dirt path where they walked. There were also many tomatoes, strawberries, and blueberries. Tall, brown stalks of wheat and various vegetables grew profusely, while trees bearing apples, cherries, and peaches abounded. Marigold noticed and pointed toward an unusual green and orange fruit bunch, hanging from the top of a tree by the path.

"Those are paaapayas," Jade said.

"Normally only prolific in tropical areas; however, due to this climate-controlled environment, the Timmers are able to grow them here. The papaya is of the class Magnoliosida, genus Carica. In the center, are many, many small seeds that are very good for you, although they taste like mustard and black pepper. The seeds contain the enzyme papain which can rid your body of parasites, such as intestinal worms. Now, I doubt that you have intestinal worms, however..." Kate pursed her lips when she realized all eyes were on her.

Jade had stopped humming and took a step in Kate's direction. "Willl you just quit with your smartness? Nobody cares about papaaayas!" She closed her eyes, paused a few seconds, then said, "Well, maaaybe somebody does."

Marigold put her hand on Kate's arm. "Actually, I do c-care. I think finding out about p-papayas is very interesting!"

"Well, thank you, Marigold Marsha Stroop." Kate patted Marigold's arm.

"Plus, I know y-you are only trying to keep us informed about things, e-even getting rid of parasites."

Kate quickly nodded and smiled. "Yes, I am."

"Well, I don't want to know about yecky parasites!" Della shouted, just before kicking her foot.

Jus said, "Then, mon, you don't have to be listenin'."

"You would care, Jade, if you had parasites." The Proprietor patted his belly and said: "Even if I've never had any-not that I know of, anyway."

"Let's have the Timmers start explainin' to us about this space they were so artfully designin'," Jus said, clearly attempting to change the subject.

"B-But can they talk to us? I don't want them f-feeling frustrated."

"Ooooh, but they have another way of communicaaating-"

With many grunts and squeaks, the Timmers danced about and pointed at a huge waterfall streaming down a rocky wall. This crystal, clear water turned a wheel which, Kate explained, supplied an irrigation system that watered all the plants and trees.

"W-Wow," was all Marigold managed to get out.

The Proprietor gestured a wrinkled hand toward the waterfall. "Yes-wow."

Next, these wee Timmers pointed up, up, and up to the many shining lamps hanging down from who-knew-where. They shed bright light onto the green plants and trees. Such happiness for these lights was evident as they leaped about, twirled in circles, and filled the air with merry squeals.

"Where do they plug th-the lights in?" Marigold turned her eyes to Kate.

"No plugs. Solar panels, I understand. Solar panels that are located in areas not discernible to our eyes." Kate opened her mouth, probably to expound on how solar panels worked, but must have changed her mind, because she looked about and then closed it. Mo smiled and gave Kate a thumbs-up.

Birds chirped and flew through the air; squirrels scampered across the ground. Marigold even spied a deer peering from around one of the papaya trees, as a bunny hopped by. The Proprietor knelt down and held out an open palm holding small yellow seeds. The deer, several bunnies, birds, and a squirrel flew, hopped, scurried, or walked over to eat from his hand. When his palm was empty, he produced more seeds from his pocket, and they resumed munching away. After three overflowing handfuls, he stood up.

Next, the Timmers skipped toward a large black kettle cooking something delicious (it looked like a vegetable stew) above a fire pit, filled with glowing orange embers. They pointed with happy shrieks at a long wooden table topped with cutting boards, trays, many white plates, large blue bowls, gold cutlery, several cobalt-hued goblets, pitchers, and clear glasses. Beside this table were stools and ladders, obviously, so these small Timmers could climb up and down to do their work. The three wee folk ran to a large crystal pool, fed from a gurgling spring in the ground. Within this transparent-like-glass pool, several huge fish swam in swirling circles.

Marigold squatted down, put her hands in the cool water, and felt the orange and white marbled fish swim through her fingers. "They are b-beautiful," she said.

Kate cleared her throat before expounding, "The fish are called koi; however, they are really jinli, a type of carp."

"R-Really?" Marigold said.

The water from the pool sent its clear liquid through a large filter into a marble basin. Certil showed them, with a plate he had quickly grabbed from the table, how they washed the dishes in this sink. He also filled his hands with the water, as it spurted through small spaces in the filter, and raised them to his mouth. As water dripped down his chin, he motioned for Marigold to do the same.

Camtrel and Convel ran over, and each stretched a hand up to grab one of Marigold's, then guided her over to the filter. They dropped their hands, and she let the cool water fill her cupped palms, raised them to her mouth, and drank the liquid. Like what she had sipped from the blue goblet earlier, it was unlike any water she had ever drunk from a faucet. It tasted sweet, pure, and cool. She thought she could have allowed that water to fill her mouth and slip down her throat for a very long time.

"Time to be movin' on," Jus announced. "More to be seein', mon."

"M-More to see?" Marigold could hardly wrap her mind around the possibility that she was going to see more.

"Yessss. Be prepared for another rooom."

"A-Another room? How is there space for another r-room?" An amazed Marigold wiped her wet hands on her pants, then followed as Comtrel, Convel, The Proprietor, Jus, Kate, Jade, Della, and Mo went through another door that Certil held open in a far wall. Once inside the next room, The Proprietor stretched out his arms, seemingly to invite Marigold to marvel at the beautiful paradise before her.

Now, the overhead lights weren't as bright. The area felt warm and a bit muggy, even though a multitude of twirling floor fans moved the humid air about a thick, green forest. Marigold rubbed her eyes. Where was she? A forest? A forest of trees filling a room in a cave?

So amazed, Marigold could barely move her feet forward in the black dirt beneath her, and it took Della's strong grip to pull her along. Colorful, tropical birds flew through the air, making raucous cries, and flitting from branch to branch, within this canopy of greenness.

Have we journeyed to another land across the ocean? Marigold wondered. Where am I? She spied a monkey hanging upside down from a swaying limb, as giant-leafed plants and tropical flowers covered the ground in tangled foliage. From visiting Greta's Garden, she recognized some of them: birds-of-paradise, lobster claws, lilies, and very large philodendrons. They seemed to shout, "Stop and admire me," with their bright yellow, red, green, and blue hues. A feathery, wet mist covered Marigold, the Misfits, and everything surrounding them.

Bubbling gurgles could be heard, and the troop carefully scooted their feet around the vegetation to arrive at its source: a turquoise, dancing stream. Marigold made out jagged gray rocks and schools of bright blue fish with yellow fins, beneath the surface.

"This place is a tropical r-rain forest! It looks like pictures I have seen in my geography b-book at school!" Marigold excitedly pointed. "There are b-bamboo trees! They can grow a y-yard a day!"

Kate said, "The Timmers have replicated those geographical areas in this Tropical Rain Forest Room, where we now stand. They are hoping, by creating this type of environment, within this secure space, birds, plants, trees, and various animals (many of whom are currently well-hidden), will live and not be forced to succumb to a cruel death and ultimate extinction."

The Proprietor wiped away another tear slipping from his eye.

Marigold took in her surroundings and only managed to squeak out, "W-Wow," again.

Della gave a chop and kick. "Yeah, 'wow', dude. Major wow-za. Do you know that there might be a cure for cancer and major diseases hanging out in rain forests? Especially in the Amazon Rain Forest."

"N-no, I d-didn't know that."

"It is truuue, Marigold Marsha Stroop. Possible cures for many diseases, within yet unknown plants, are beeeing destroyed. Treees, plants, grasses, and-ultimately- animals' hooomes are chopped and mowed dowwwn. As a result, many animals die; some become extiiinct."

"That is t-terrible! So why are people ruining the r-rain forest?"

Mo ran in place. "Because they are full of greed! They are selfish and don't care about the environment! They want to grow their own crops, and the soil in the rain forest is the best! They want to mine gold, copper, diamonds, and other precious metals, found in those areas, so they build roads through the many tropical trees and plants to travel on!"

Jus swept his arm across the space. "Be lookin' at this beauty, mon. Gorgeous, right? But greed is rulin' some people's lives, and they only are thinkin' about this." He rubbed his fingers together.

Marigold repeated his motion. "What's that m-mean?"

"Money. Some people are putting their love for money above their love for the environment," The Proprietor said, while he stared sadly into the clear water.

Kate continued, "Do you realize islanders in Dominica, a Caribbean island, often live in tiny shacks and possess little or no material possessions? Still, they put their love for the environment above their need to own grandiose mansions, with opulent furnishings, or eat expensive cuisine? Instead, on that island where tropical rain forests abound, there are very strict laws regarding their environment. A jail sentence is a consequence for disturbing plants, animals, all life on their island."

Marigold watched as Certil knelt down and ran his hand over the back of a gargantuan white crab, something she had first believed to be a rock. It twitched at the feeling of the Timmer's touch and opened, then closed, its claws. "The p-people on Dominica must r-really care about their island."

"You are bein' right about that, mon, and so do these Timmers." Jus laughed when the three purple folk squealed and jumped up and down, causing the white crab to scuttle into the water.

The Proprietor smiled a wide, toothless grin. "Certil, Comtrel, and Convel care about their environment, like those on the island of Dominica."

"Yesss, the Timmers believe in protecting this world down here, wheeen our world above, is beeeing destroyed." Jade folded her hands and said, "Ommm".

Jus pointed into the deep forest. "But now, Marigold, are you seein' the hammocks tied between the trunks of those trees?"

After much peering into the darkness, Marigold saw four canvas hammocks, tied to trees, and swinging in the breeze the fans created. "Three t-tiny ones, low to the ground, and one l-larger one that is a little bit h-higher up?"

The Proprietor laughed, before scurrying over to the larger one and sitting on it like a swing. Then he swung his bony legs back and forth, before throwing himself deep down into the rocking canvas and was no longer visible.

A brown animal scampered down the trunk of a nearby palm tree, and over to The Proprietor's hammock. It barked, as it raised itself up onto its haunches, then made an insistent screech, until The Proprietor stuck out an arm and raised the brown furry creature, with a pink nose and long tail, up to join him. Soon, they both were swallowed up in the canvas, and the animal's barking sounds were silenced. This made the Timmers spin in circles, and the other Misfits laugh.

"The Proprietor always is raisin' Homerel, his honey bear, into the hammock to be sleepin' with him, mon." Jus giggled.

The sound of snoring resonated from that hammock. "Is that where The Proprietor sl-sleeps, with the honey b-bear?" Marigold asked.

"Yes, The Propriiietor, with Homerel and the three Timmers, sleeep in the hammocks."

As if on cue, the Timmers raised their tiny purple hands to their mouths in giant yawns and ran over to the other three, low-slung hammocks. They jumped into them and, like The Proprietor, soon were no longer visible. Within seconds, their high-pitched snores joined The Proprietor's. The lights began to dim even more, and the sound of night creatures filled the air.

"And now, Miss Marigold, you are needin' to be goin' home and gettin' some sleep, too," Jus said, with a yawn. "Guess we all are needin' some rest."

Jade said, Jus is riiight." She also yawned.

"I am still so full of energy, though, I don't know how I will ever be snoring like them!" Mo ran toward the door leading back into The Kitchen.

Kate started in Mo's direction. "But sleep is quite essential for good health. Especially REM sleep which is the time of your deepest slumber, when you dream, and necessary for the subconscious to release your deepest feelings. Your hopes and dreams become apparent then. Did you ever make a decision to keep a dream journal? It is important to record your dreams when you first awaken, however, before they slip away into oblivion. I have often written-" She stopped, when Della made a flying kick in her direction.

"Stop! Just stop, dude! Even I, who probably has more patience than anybody else here, is so tired of hearing you go on and on with your brainiac stuff!"

"Youuu have patience, Della? Riiight."

"Is that sarcasm, Jade?" Mo laughed and ran back in her direction.

"We just need to be gettin' home. We are all bein' tired," Jus said.

"I'm not tired!" Mo hop, hop, hopped in place.

Jus pointed a finger at Mo. "Except for you, mon."

Kate hung her head. "Sorry. So sorry. I just can't seem to help myself..."

Marigold walked over to Kate. "It's o-okay, friend. I didn't know all of-of that about dreams and j-journals. Thanks for t-telling us."

Kate gave a slight smile. "You are extremely welcome. Anytime."

"Oh, my gosh." Della kicked her way toward the door. "Please don't encourage her, Marigold."

Mo held the door open, and everyone passed through, from The Tropical Rain Forest Room, into The Kitchen, The Dining Room, and finally, they walked into The Meeting Room. Marigold was surprised to see The Proprietor had joined them, accompanied by Homerel, scampering alongside.

The Proprietor said, "You get home and go to bed. Get lots of rest! Big night tomorrow for all of you! But now? Homerel and I need to put out the candles." He pulled the very tall ladder away from the wall. "Go! Off with ye!" He pointed a crooked finger above his head.

Jade removed all the capes and put them back into the chest, before Jus walked quickly to the elevator's entrance, and everyone followed.

It was evident to Marigold that when The Proprietor directed the Misfits to do something, there was no delay in their response. This time, she felt only a little fear about the ride to the shed, as up, up, up she traveled. At last, she joined the others in the cool night air, feeling glad she wasn't as dizzy as last night. Mo ran loops around them, Kate studied the gray sky, and Della flew through the air, with some mighty kicks. Jade made the "ommm" sound, holding her hands in prayer position, and Marigold watched them all. Finally, a giggling Jus arrived.

"I am lovin' that elevator ride. Not as much as the slide, mon, but it's still tons of fun. I was thinkin', on my way up, maybe I should be wall paperin' its interior."

"Oooh, brother," Jade moaned.

Jus giggled and did his little, green-shoed dance. "Maybe the walls of the shed, too, mon!"

"Th-That's a good idea," Marigold added with a smile. "A bright, fl-floral pattern."

Onward!" Mo hollered. He had already galloped ahead of them down the road.

Chapter 17

As they walked down an alley, Marigold wondered what The Proprietor meant, when he said the next night was going to be "a big night". She didn't ask the Misfits, though. She knew nobody would tell her anyway, so why ask? She figured they wanted it to be a surprise again, but she doubted anything could amaze her more than what she'd seen in the Misfits' cavern these last two nights.

All of her experiences, clumped together, rocked her mind. Am I going to wake up and discover I have been dreaming? None of this has been real? But after she slid over the top of a liquor bottle, tripped, and only regained her balance by grabbing onto Kate's jacket sleeve, Marigold knew she wasn't dreaming. She was very much awake.

Last night, she had begun her adventure by sliding into a cavern where the Misfits met and The Proprietor made his entrance. Tonight, she met little purple Timmers, who served them food in The Dining Room; saw the large Kitchen, with growing crops; and took a walk through The Tropical Rain Forest Room, where animals, trees, and plants abounded. There were hammocks in the trees: beds for The Proprietor, Homerel, and the Timmers. Oh, and so much more!

She could write the best book ever, about what she had seen, and it would be nonfiction, not fiction, since it would be true. She never would, though, because it was all a secret. She had promised the Misfits she would never share her experiences-not even with her mom. Nope, she would never tell, but Marigold also understood nothing during her next visit could surprise her more than what she had already seen. And there couldn't be space for any more rooms!

"I wouldn't beee so sure about that, Marigold," Jade said before resuming the "ommm" sound and scooting her way down the alley. Mo stopped suddenly when they reached Marigold's back yard.

"Be seein' ya in first period, mon. It's late tonight so you are havin' to be shuttin' your eyes and gettin' in as much sleep as ya can."

Mo ran further down the alley, but yelled over his shoulder, "You are needing rest to prepare your mind and body for what you will experience tomorrow night, Marigold Marsha Stroop!"

"What will I-I experience?"

There was no reply, of course.

"Remember tooo blink the porch light and the lamp in yourrr bedroom on and off. Then I will awaaaken your mother," Jade said.

"O-Ok." Marigold ran through the back door, blinked the porch light on and off, and then zipped past her snoring mother in the recliner. She smiled, since her mom was snoring much louder than The Proprietor, Homerel, and the three Timmers put together.

In her room, she flicked the lamp on and off three times, put on her pajamas, and crawled into bed. The alarm clock on her nightstand said 12:02, and she rubbed her eyes. A little after midnight? Not going to be much sleep for her tonight! She set her alarm for 6:00, pressed her eyelids tightly together, and wondered how sleep was ever going to happen, after all the excitement she had just experienced.

Within minutes, her mother opened her door and Marigold could hear the shuffle, as she knelt down, with crackling knees, and planted a kiss on her forehead. "Good night, my darling. I hope you are having sweet dreams."

Marigold softly whispered, "Sweet dreams, Mother? I'm living the dream." She rolled over and closed her eyes. Little purple creatures danced behind her eyelids.

"And now you are talking in your sleep, my darling? I wish you would wake up and talk to me. You know, I would do anything for you-even go to jail."

Marigold made a low moan at her mother's words.

Marsha pulled the sunset comforter up, bunched it across Marigold's shoulders, then walked from the room, taking the smell of orchids with her.

***

Marsha Stroop, in her yellow robe with an orange scarf tied around her curlers and wearing her orange, fuzzy slippers, stood in the front yard and screeched to her daughter to "have a good day." Then she added in an even louder voice, that she would "attack anyone, if they said mean things to her precious baby;" words that mortified Marigold, who was making her usual trek to the corner. Marsha emphasized the words "at-tack an-y-one," punching her newspaper-dagger into the air with each syllable.

The strange thing was that none of the kids yelled the usual rude words in Marigold's direction, even though she was wearing weird clothes (except for her cool shoes that she had cleaned that morning). Cool shoes, with stupid orange socks, since she refused to wear dirty, white socks two days in a row. The Droobs just talked quietly among themselves instead, and actually seemed to ignore her. Huh? What was happening? Had her mother's actions yesterday morning really made an effect? Were they afraid of her mom, Ninja-Mom Marsha?

They stood whispering and intermittently casting looks at her. She didn't care. Whispering, even if they were saying unkind words about her, was bearable. Again, wearing a Band Aid was better than having to put on a cast. What would have been bad is if their words had caused her mom to run, like some ancient Spartan warrior, and launch herself on top of the mouthy kids, her newspaper-weapon stabbing every Droob in her path. Yep, that would have been real bad. That action could have meant more than just a few hours in jail for Marsha Stroop. Her mom might be locked up, having only bread, water, and no TV, for a very long time. And she? She could be placed in some foster home and missing her mom.

Instead of letting her mind go there, Marigold focused on the blue sky and puffy white clouds. It was so beautiful up there! Then, from behind a large clump of clouds, soared that big black bird! It made a great swirling circle, a loud caw, then flew away. As before, the other kids didn't notice, and she wondered why they still didn't seem to see such a huge, flying, black bird !

Well, she didn't have much time to ponder this, because the yellow school bus pulled up, and the kid-cluster broke apart to clamber up the steps. That's when Marigold knew why they had been quiet and not shouting the usual cruel words. Even though Mike was there, Billy wasn't. Maybe the police, who had taken him away, had locked him up. Their not bullying her wasn't due to her mom's actions yesterday morning. Their ring leader wasn't there, and they were obviously nothing (at least not daring Droobs), without Billy to initiate the terrible taunts.

And Mike? Was Mike not enough of a leader, without his best bud by his side? After all, it had been Mike, who had tripped her in the hall and caused her bloodied knee. But had Billy already ordered Mike to do that? In the back of her mind, she could almost remember seeing Billy's face in the crowd of kids encouraging Mike, who was throwing her papers all over creation and mutilating her book bag.

Yes, as she concentrated on that incident, Billy had definitely been there, watching it all happen. Mike was Billy's puppet. Maybe there was hope for him yet, if Billy was gone. So deeply involved in her thoughts, she didn't realize all the other kids had entered the bus, and only she stood at the bottom of the steps.

"Whats-a matter with you? You-a wanna make-a me late? Get onto this-a bus!" Mr. Carini shouted. His face was crinkled up in anger, and he wiped it with a brown napkin, while he waved his other hand over his head.

As she hopped up the steps and looked for a place to sit, he said: "Well-a, the boy your mother beat up yesterday? He got kicked off-a this bus for today." He took off with a roar, again knocking Marigold into a "seat-a"..

A small, African-American girl entered the bus at the next stop and sat behind Marigold. She tapped her on the shoulder, and said, "Do you want to sit beside me?".

Marigold wasn't sure she'd heard her words correctly, but when the bus paused at a yield sign, Marigold moved to the vacant seat next to the girl anyway.

The bus driver cranked his head, on his huge neck, to the side and hollered, "Whats-a matter with you? You don't move-a from your seat once you have sat down-a!"

Marigold gave him a thumbs-up, but stayed where she was. The loud kids, jumping around, now occupied his attention. He wildly waved his hands in the air, while he shouted profanity, and Marigold wondered if he should put his hands back on the steering wheel and take anti-anxiety meds, like her mom did. Of course, her mother's actions yesterday morning, when she beat up Billy, made Marigold seriously question the medicine's effectiveness. Maybe her mom needed to visit the doctor, get a dosage adjustment, and she should take Mr. Carini “along-a”.

“Do y-you really want me to sit here b-beside you?” Marigold asked her.

This pretty girl nodded and said, “Yes. My name’s Latasha Trine. I go by Tasha”

“My n-name’s Marigold Stroop. I go by M-Marigold.” She was surprised this nice girl had invited her to sit beside her. “Thanks for l-letting me sit with y-you.”

“You are welcome. I already knew your name. Pretty much everybody knows your name.” The pretty black girl brushed a crumb off Marigold’s collar.

“They d-do?”

“Uh huh. We know, cause Billy and his friends yell it sometimes when they bully you.”

“Oh, yeah. But they m-mostly call me other names like Sunshine Girl or D-Dweeb--.”

“Right. But sometimes Billy or one of his friends, calls you Marigold. That’s how kids know you.”

“Great. S-So nice to be famous for being a w-weirdo.”

Tasha looked her big brown eyes into Marigold’s green ones. “Not everybody is a bully, you know. Lots of kids just stay quiet cause they’re scared of Billy, or his friends, and don’t want to get beat up. Some kids look up to Billy, cause he acts like he’s ‘all that’ and nobody’d better mess with him.”

"Well, I understand s-self-preservation and the n-need to feel important, I g-guess,"

"Kids have said mean things to me for forever, since I'm black. Some kids are still racist, even though we live in the twenty-first century."

"Sorry. I-I think you're beautiful." Marigold remembered Jus's words regarding racism and thought Tasha would certainly relate to what he'd said.

"Well, I think you're beautiful, too."

Marigold smiled. "Thanks, but I-I don't think I'm beautiful. I d-do have a gift though. I know you have a g-gift, too." And she knew she would have never said that, without the Misfits telling her she had empathy.

"A gift?" Tasha asked. "What kind of gift? I'm from a big family, and we don't get many presents."

"No. Something that m-makes you special," Marigold said, when the bus stopped, and the kids ran down the steps and through the school's red doors. In the moving throng, Marigold lost sight of Tasha.

When she stopped at her locker, she glanced from side to side to ready herself for Billy's yelling at her in the hallway, but he was nowhere in sight. Well, without being able to ride the bus, maybe he was going to be late-or he was locked up.

Marigold spun her combination lock, and when it clicked open, she raised the metal lever, and whispered, "Wh-What?" There, on the top shelf, was a package of six pairs of new, white, crew socks, along with a black T-shirt, folded under them! And if that wasn't enough, a pair of brand new jeans (with tags still on them), hung on the hook and completed, what her mom would call, the "ensemble"! Taped to the inside of the locker's door was a note that said, Change into these in the restroom, if you want. Here's a pass to get into homeroom. Enjoy, Ms Henley.

Why was Ms. Henley being so nice to her, Marigold wondered, grabbing the clothes and tearing to the bathroom. Two pretty girls stood in front of the mirror, combing their hair and analyzing her, when she zipped in and quickly opened, then closed, a stall door. After throwing off the orange and yellow dress, orange socks, hair clip, and white shoes, she put on the perfectly fitting new shirt, jeans, white socks, and gym shoes again. She was done so fast, Marigold thought she would have made a good quick-change artist in some magician's act in Las Vegas her Aunt Mary had told her about. Then she dashed through the open stall door and found the pretty primpers were gone.

She stuffed her old clothes inside her book bag (throwing them out in the big trash can was tempting, but her mom would be upset), and tore back to her locker in the silent hall. There, she jammed the old clothes and hair clip onto the shelf, and grabbed books for her morning classes. As she jogged to homeroom,

Ms Henley strolled by and gave her a wink, along with a "twitter"..

"Th-Thank you," Marigold said to the smiling teacher, and she wondered how Ms Henley had known what size she wore. Then she made a quick turn into homeroom and dropped the pass onto Mrs. Drebel's desk. The yacky kids became suddenly silent, when she, in these cool clothes, walked to her seat in the back. Even the teacher stopped taking roll while Marigold strolled to her desk. There was no Billy sitting in the front row; his desk was empty.

Well, it was much easier to hear Mrs. Drebel take roll with the class more subdued that morning, and when she said, "Marigold Stroop", Marigold stood and waved her hand in the air. "I'm h-here!" she shouted. The rest of the class turned and looked at her, clearly surprised at this "new" girl--new clothes, new confidence. Marigold sat down with a large smile on her face.

The rest of the day was uneventful, and no kids were cruel. Some stared at her, many whispered, but nobody shouted ugly names in her direction. After school, Marigold ran to the restroom to make another quick change, and she put on her old clothes. Then she jetted to her locker, where she carefully hung the new clothes on the hooks (didn't want them to get the tiniest wrinkle), and placed the white socks on the top shelf. Next, books with homework to do, went inside her book bag, and she was off! Amazingly, she made it to her bus on time, and she plopped down in the seat beside her new friend, Tasha.

"How was your day?" Tasha asked.

"I had the best school d-day I think I ever h-had."

"Well, that's good. Mine kind of sucked."

"H-How come?"

Tasha wiped her eyes with balled up fists. "There is a bully in eighth grade-his name's Tyler. Tyler calls me names, cause I'm black."

"I-I'm sorry. What d-does he call you?"

"Every day, it's something different. Today it was Black Licorice and Fuzz-Ball Hair. Then a bunch of kids around him started laughing."

"Why are they so mean t-to you? Your skin is the prettiest c-color ever, and your h-hair is so shiny and black. You are r-really, really pretty. I w-wish I looked like you."

"No, you don't, cause if you did? You would get bullied even more. Bullied for being black, on top of everything else they call you."

"Y-Yeah. Some kids will make up anything to be m-mean. B-But you know what?"

"What?"

"You have a g-gift that makes you special: something you c-can do really well. Something probably n-nobody else can do-not like y-you, anyway."

Tasha shook her head. "No, I don't."

"Y-Yes, you do."

"Huh uh. There isn't anything I can do really well-except-except, but it would make me feel real embarrassed to tell you."

"Y-Yeah? What is it? Don't b-be embarrassed!"

"It doesn't matter. It sounds stupid to say it out loud."

Marigold touched Tasha's arm. "L-Listen, I promise you it won't sound stupid--not t-to me, anyway."

"Well," Tasha began, just as the bus came to a fast stop, almost throwing kids out of their seats.

"This is my stop. See you tomorrow, Marigold." Then Marigold watched as her new friend was shoved by other kids out the door.

Marigold heard some girl bringing up the rear saying, "Hurry up, Tasha! You are such an ugly monkey!" Then she pushed her down onto the sidewalk.

In disbelief, Marigold saw Tasha, on her hands and knees, trying to gather her stuff together, after that horrible Droob had knocked her down! Well, that all seemed way too familiar to Marigold, and she stumbled to the front, where Mr. Carini had turned a metal device to close the doors. He glared at her, standing beside him.

"Whats-a matter with you? Get back-a to your seat! You want to make-a me late?"

But Marigold held onto the back of the bus driver's seat and yelled, "D-Didn't you see what just happened? That m-mean girl pushed Tasha down onto the sidewalk, after she called h-her an ugly name!"

"Yeah, I saw it. You need to be minding your own-a business! Now, sit down-a!"

But Marigold stood firm, even after the bus pulled away from the stop. "N-No! I'm not sitting d-down! You are an a-adult and in charge! You should have gotten off the b-bus and helped Tasha! You should of g-gotten the bully's name and m-made sure she never rode on this bus again!"

The driver came to a sudden stop and sent Marigold flying to a spot on the dirty bus floor. "You see-a what happens when you don't follow my-a directions?" He waggled a fat index finger at Marigold, still on the floor. "If you ever cause-a me more trouble, you won't ever ride on this bus-a again!"

Marigold crawled over to a nearby, vacant seat and pulled herself up, as the bus began its rock-n-roll to the next stop, a stop which happened to be hers. As she walked shakily to the steps, Mr. Carini glared at her and spit on the floor.

Spit on the floor? She stumbled out the door, but when she turned and looked back at Mr. Carini's snarly face, it appeared like he would have spit on her, if she were closer. That bus driver was a bully, too? Yep, Marigold knew he was a very mean man, and she wondered just what he was capable of doing.

As she stepped from the bus and onto the sidewalk, Mike hissed through the space in his front teeth, "When Billy comes back to school, you had better watch it, Sunshine Girl. Your mom messed with the wrong guy."

Marigold brushed the bus floor's dirt off the front of her dress and, with shaking steps, walked home.

Chapter 18

"So how was your day, sweetheart?" Marsha Stroop held the screen door wide open.

"G-Good."

"Good? Really?"

"R-Really." Marigold stepped into the living room. "Yes, Mother. It's all c-cool. No need t-to attack anybody."

Her mom jumped up and down in place and clapped her hands. "Oh! I am so happy! But you know I would knock anybody down, anybody who causes you problems."

"O-Oh, I know that, Mom. I think everybody at the b-bus stop knows that. Everybody at th-the school, even the police department, t-too."

"Well, that's good. Now, everybody knows not to mess with you."

"O-Oh, yeah. Everybody knows that and-and a whole lot m-more."

"They do? What else do they know?"

Marigold wanted to add that they knew her mother was nuts, but she didn't. Instead, she said, as she walked to her room, "N-Nothing, Mother."

"Nothing?"

"N-Nope." She peered back with a forced smile.

"Did anyone tell you how beautiful you looked in your lovely clothes today?" Marsha opened her arms toward her daughter with a broad smile. Evidently, self-proclaimed Miss Fashionista, took full credit for the artistic creation adorning her daughter, otherwise known as Marigold Stroop.

"No, d-didn't say a word." She opened her bedroom door and closed it behind her.

Marsha was soon tapping on the door, however. "Marigold?"

Marigold had burrowed under her comforter and closed her eyes. She knew she needed a nap; who knew how late she was going to be up tonight?

"Marigold? We are out of leftovers. Would hot dogs be okay tonight?"

"Y-yes, Mother. Thanks so very m-much." She forced out the words through gritted teeth.

"Okay, sweetie."

Marigold closed her eyes and slept deeply. She dreamed she was rolling around and around and around through the clouds-soft, puffy, white clouds-that wrapped about her, while she wore cool blue jeans, a black T-shirt, and nice white shoes, with white socks. The flower clip in her hair came loose and went spinning in tiny circles through the wind, until Marigold couldn't see it any longer. She smiled, knowing she was in her happy-nest, a safe, warm place she never wanted to leave.

Then came the tap, tap.

It seemed she had closed her eyes only moments earlier when the tap, tap sounded again on her door. She pulled her comforter up over her head and tried to go back into puffy, soft Cloud Land.

"Marigold, sweetheart?"

Cloud Land wasn't going to happen anymore, Marigold was certain.

The door opened. "Honey? It's me, your mother."

She lowered the covers. "I-I need to get some more sleep. S-So tired."

Marsha Stroop was inside, sat down on the bed, and put her hand on her daughter's forehead. "I wonder why you are so tired. You aren't sick, are you?"

"N-No, I'm not sick. I'm t-tired."

"I am thinking I need to call Dr. Morehead. Maybe you need a check-up. After all, you are almost a teenager, your hormones are changing, or your immune system could be compromised....."

Marigold bolted upright. "I do n-not need to see Dr. M-Morehead! I am not sick! I-I am tired!"

"Didn't you get enough sleep last night? When I checked on you around midnight, you were sleeping. It looked like you had been sleeping a long time and even talking in your dreams."

Knowing there was no longer any choice in the matter, she put her orange-socked feet on the floor. "I-I'm up. I'm up. Are you h-happy, Mother?"

"I only hope you aren't sick; you are sleeping so much and being grumpier than you have ever been before. I'm calling the doctor tomorrow and making an appointment for a check-up. Maybe you need a shot of vitamin B-12."

Marigold forced a smile and stood up. The last thing she wanted was a B-12 shot. "S-Sorry, Mother. I'm fine. Really f-fine. Can't wait to eat yummy hot d-dogs."

"Oh, I'm so glad," Marsha said with a clap of her hands and a jump in place. She ran her fingers through Marigold's messy hair. "Where's your hair clip?"

Uh oh. She had forgotten her hair clip-left it at school in her locker, not Cloud-Land. "Um, I-I bet it's at school. T-Tomorrow, I'll check the Lost and Found."

Marsha nodded and patted Marigold on top of the head. "Okay, sweetie, check the Lost and Found. But until then? I have several others in my secret box under the bed, the place where I keep my treasures, my most precious belongings."

And I bet you do, Marigold thought.

Supper went okay: veggie hot dogs with beans, chips, and lots of ketchup; a tossed salad; more carrot cake (left over from the last two nights); plus, almond milk to drink. This was a much better supper than the last ones, Marigold thought. Veggie hot dogs were always good, and she didn't feel so stuffed. If the Timmers had dinner for all the Misfits tonight, she wanted some room left. She really hoped that if they served them dessert, it would be more of that cherry parfait. It had been yummy.

Marigold figured she must have been staring dreamily into space, imagining that creamy pudding, with juicy cherries and whipped cream, because her mother said, "What are you thinking about, honey? Do you have a boyfriend?"

Marigold stopped chewing a piece of hot dog, mid chomp. "A-A boyfriend? No, I-I don't have a boyfriend! Why would you b-be asking me that?"

"Just because you were smiling, like you were thinking about something real special-like a boyfriend." Marsha giggled and sing-songed, "Marigold's got-a-boyyy-friend."

Marigold stopped up her ears with her fingers. "N-No! I don't!"

"Nothing to be embarrassed about, sweetie. I wouldn't be surprised if a whole lot of boys think you are pretty, with your beautiful clothes and hair! Your lovely smile! The pretty, flower hair clip, when-you-wear-it."

Staring down at her plate she said, "I-I-do-not-have-a-b-boyfriend."

"Well, I hope when you do, you will tell me?"

"You will be the f-first to know, Mother. The v-very first to know. But I d-don't."

"O-ka-aay," her mother said with a grin, like she still thought she had a boyfriend.

Marigold stabbed the last bite of cake with her fork.

"Tell me about your school day," Marsha said.

"N-Nothing to tell."

"Nothing? How were your classes?"

"O-Okay."

"Just okay?"

"Yeah, n-nothing special."

"Hmmm. Why do I think you are hiding something from me?"

"I-I don't know. Why d-do you think I am h-hiding something from you?"

"Just because I know you so well. I gave birth to you, after all."

Marigold rolled her eyes. " You d-did?"

"I did. Eleven years ago. It took me almost two days to birth you, and it was a very long and a very painful birth. You are the most important thing in my life. Did I ever tell you that before?"

Marigold walked over to the sink and began washing off her plate, glass, and fork. "Y-Yes, I think you did."

"Well, then don't forget it, not ever."

"Oh, I w-won't forget." Then she mumbled as she walked to her room, "C-Cause I'm sure you will keep r-reminding me, about a-a billion more times."

"Did you say something, sweetheart?"

"No, M-Mom. Now, I'm going to do some h-homework."

"I'm so proud of you, my brilliant daughter!" Marsha hollered, when Marigold closed her door.

After she had finished her science and language arts homework, Marigold closed her eyes but couldn't sleep now. Awaiting the knock on her window caused too much tension. What in the world could be more exciting than what she had already seen the last two nights?

Also, in the back of her brain, was what had happened to Tasha at the bus stop, and the bus driver's reaction. Plus, what was the gift Tasha had mentioned? Maybe she would tell her on the bus tomorrow.

The next tap, tap, tap that occurred was on her bedroom door again.

"Y-Yes?" Marigold asked.

"Honey, it's your mother. Can I come in?"

Really? It wasn't the Solly Bridge homeless guy, with a big knife? "Yeah, M-Mom."

Marsha Stroop entered and sat down on Marigold's bed. She patted her leg.

"Honey, why aren't you asleep? It's almost ten o'clock, and you're still wearing your pretty school clothes. Normally, you'd be in your jammies and fast asleep, under that warm sunset comforter."

"Just not t-tired yet, I guess." She hated lying to anyone, especially her mom, but it was true, right? She was too excited to go to sleep.

"But you are always asleep by ten. I think something, maybe something really big, is bothering you. Am I right? Are you going to run away?"

"N-No, Mom. Nothing is bothering m-me, and I'm not g-going to run away."

"You are the most important thing in the whole world to me. That's why I break my back at the florist shop, every-single-day, to put food on the table and clothes on our backs."

Marigold bit her lower lip.. "R-Roof over our head. Think I-I know that, Mom."

"Do you need me to come to school and beat up the bullies? I would do that for you, you know. I would do anything for you! You saw me in action!"

"No, Mother! D-Don't come to school! Promise me y-you won't come to school!"

"Well, okay, for now. But you need to promise me something..."

Swallowing down a big lump in her throat and taking a deep breath, Marigold said, "What's that, M-Mom?"

"You need to promise me that if anyone, and I mean anyone ever--"

There was the sound of pebbles hitting the glass.

Marsha sat up straight. "Did you hear that? I think I just heard--" Then her eyes closed, and before Marigold knew what was happening, her mom had instantly fallen asleep-right across her legs.

Oh, great, Marigold thought, as she attempted to pull her legs out from under her mom's 120 pound, sleeping-like-a-rock, body. One leg, then the other, all as pebbles had begun to hit the window with even more fervor. Finally, she wriggled out from under her mom, jerked open the window, and climbed out-- just as a pebble hit her in the face.

"Ouch! Will y-you stop? I-I'm out!" She pushed the window closed and glared at Della.

"Weee are in a hurry, Marigold."

"And you should've known my m-mom was in my room, before y-you started throwing stones! J-Jade, you should h-have told everyone!"

"Everythiiing was timed perfectly. I couldn't exactly teleport your mother to the liiiving room. Don't dooo teleportation of big objects. Starting to do that, though. I put her to sleep, right in your rooom."

"I know y-you did, but she h-heard the stones on the window."

"Sorry about that. My timing was a little off, dude." Della kicked and chopped the air.

"It doesn't matter, mon," Jus said. "We are all bein' together now."

"That's right!" Mo ran back and forth in front of them. "Let's get going!"

"The meteorological reading I did, before I exited my house, was indicative of a clear night with no precipitation or high winds. The moon, as you will see, if you turn your eyes upright into the sky, is at three-quarters and will lend enough light for us to see clearly, while we traverse the terrain before us. It should be an easy trek, and I, for one, am extremely grateful for that fact." Kate pointed at the sky.

"Oh, my gosh! Let's get moving, dudes!" Della did more kick, kick, chop, chops.

"Della, maybe you need t-to be kind!" Marigold pointed a finger at her. "Your words probably h-hurt Kate's feelings. By the w-way, Kate, I appreciate your t-telling us about the weather c-conditions."

Kate smiled in Marigold's direction and adjusted her thick glasses on her nose. "Thank you, friend. I am glad you possess the gift of empathy. Obviously, that is not a trait shared by all." She stared directly at Della.

Mo now began a looping lope around Kate and Marigold. "Come on! The others have started out! Quite an experience tonight!"

Kate and Marigold quickened their steps to catch up with the rest of the group. Kate's meteorological study had been right, much to Marigold's delight. It was a very easy walk through alleys, and before she knew it, they had arrived at the shed and the opening to whatever excitement awaited them.

"Weee are here," Jade announced, like nobody could figure that out by themselves.

"Okay, Misfits, you are knowin' the drill, mon." Jus yanked the door open and, one by one, they sat on the slide and spun their ways down to their soft spots, in the candle-lit Meeting Room.

When Jus landed, with a thump, next to Marigold, he immediately stood and inspected the group; he was a ship's captain, giving the sailors under his command the once-over. "You are all bein' here and accounted for. Tonight is a night unlike any we have been experiencin' before, mon. Not just bein' new to Marigold, but to all of us, too. Except, for our telepathic Jade. Jade is always knowin' everything."

The other Misfits looked at each other. Marigold wondered what this new experience was going to be. Jade nodded, verifying Jus's words, and he motioned for all of them to stand.

"Jade?" Jus asked.

Jade opened the chest, then she placed a gold cape around Jus and the others. Jus wrapped one around her, before they all joined hands in a circle and said the oath:

"For Right,
Not Might,
For the greater good
To all upon this planet earth,
And for all who have met on these hallowed grounds
From Time Unknown
Until Time We Know."

Marigold smiled, since the words were becoming much more familiar, and she ended this oath by squeezing both Kate's and Mo's hands, standing on either side of her. They squeezed her hands back, and Mo squeezed with so much strength, she almost yelled out. Then, as five Misfits sat down on their soft blankets, Jus sat on his stool.

For what seemed like an eternity, Jus looked about the candlelit room and didn't say a word.

Everyone stared intently at their leader. Even Jade had her eyes open, her gaze on Jus, unbroken.

The only sound was the trickling water slipping down the walls and onto the ground.

Finally, Jus said, "It is bein' time for dinner and the business at hand, mon." He stood from his stool, walked over, opened the door that revealed the secret passage, and then, he motioned them inside. They crawled on hands and knees through the tunnel, like ants in an ant farm. Finally, each stood up and climbed into the same chairs, where they had sat the night before. Jus sat at the end, on his regal throne.

The Timmers quickly entered, with trays of many roasted vegetables, breads, and clear glass water pitchers. The food and water were passed around, family style. Marigold certainly viewed this group as her new family; however, she looked at the empty throne and wondered where The Proprietor was. One family member was missing.

After everyone observed the moment of silence, Jade said, "Heee will be joining us shortly. Currently, heee is involved with preparing the others for what is about tooo happen."

Marigold nodded, again knowing not to ask any questions. Questions were fruitless. Instead, she delved into the delicious food, but saved room, for what she hoped, might be dessert. She watched, as the little purple Timmers bounced about with glee. They appeared happy, seeing the Misfits chowing down .

"Thank you s-so much for all of this good f-food," Marigold said. "I-I am sure you have worked hard t-to grow, prepare, and s-serve it."

With a happy squeal, Certil climbed up the rungs of her chair, and Marigold grinned when she saw the cherry parfait, nestled within a glass dish, being handed to her.

"Y-Yummy! I was h-hoping you were going to make this for us t-tonight."

With much laughter, spins and dances, all three Timmers climbed up to the various Misfits and gave each of them this luscious dessert. Like Marigold; Mo, Kate, Della, and Jade began spooning down the creamy goodness and thanking the Timmers between mouthfuls.

Marigold noticed that Jus, however, was not smiling like usual, and he did not eat with the same vim and vigor as before. He rested his cheek in his hand, and Jade nodded understandingly in his direction. Marigold wondered what was going on. Slowly, the room became silent, as the others apparently also realized there was a very serious concern affecting their leader.

"Marigold, I was tellin' ya tonight would be different from the others, mon. The other Misfits, except for Jade, who knows all, are also wonderin' what's goin' on. They are understandin' it's important, but that's all. Now, I'm thinkin' The Proprietor will be leadin' us to the Contributin' Room real soon."

"The C-Contributing Room? Another r-room?" Marigold knew her surprise was evident to all around the table. She also knew she was safe traveling to another space, surrounded by these Misfits, her new best friends. She trusted these five other kids who fought for the rights of others, bullied like them.

"Anotherrr room." Jade opened her eyes long enough to wink at Marigold, then closed them again.

"It is a room that you won't believe, dude!" Della chop-chopped the air.

Kate nodded. "What Della has just stated is accurate, and I think you will have difficulty believing the beauty, soon to be displayed before your eyes."

"I-I will?"

Mo shifted the white turban on his head. "Oh, yes, you will! Prepare yourself for the unbelievable, Marigold Marsha Stroop!"

Chapter 19

Marigold followed the other Misfits, as they clambered down the rungs from their chairs in The Dining Room. Everyone stood quietly, and she figured they were awaiting what would occur next. Even Della had stopped the chops and kicks, while Mo didn't bounce in place on his huge feet. The telepathic wonder, Jade, folded her hands in front of her chest and hummed, and Jus, their leader, stared straight ahead. Kate had folded her arms across her chest and contemplated the ceiling; Marigold wondered what Kate, with all of her great intelligence, was thinking about.

From the door leading into The Dining Room from The Kitchen, came a very serious Proprietor. This ancient leader was dressed as he had been the past two nights, in burlap and still barefoot.

"Can you be leadin' us, mon, to The Contributin' Room?" Jus asked.

The Proprietor stopped a tear traveling down a ravine on his ancient face and began walking into The Kitchen. Marigold wondered why The Proprietor was sad about going to this Contributing Room, wherever that was.

Jade said, "He isss not sad about going into that room; he is sad, duuue to the reason we must visit it. The plan was for you to meet two otherrrs; now, we have an additional reeeason to come together."

Marigold took the rear and followed this single line of Misfits through the area where the Timmers busily washed dishes in the basin. They smiled and waved happily, while the Misfits passed by. Marigold smiled and waved back.

Next came the beautiful Tropical Rain Forest, and Marigold watched creatures scamper; she heard birds sing out noisy cries. The four hammocks were swinging and twisting in the blowing air, entangling themselves within branches bearing bright green leaves. They strolled past the stream, and Marigold almost tripped over her feet when yes, The Proprietor opened another door at the end of this room.

If Marigold had been surprised at the sight of The Meeting Room, The Dining Room, The Kitchen, and The Tropical Rain Forest Room, well, those places had been only entry-level experiences, compared to what she saw in this room. She was so overcome when she stepped inside, her feet went out from under her! She simply slid down onto the black and white slippery, marble floor, and she couldn't do anything but sit and stare.

"Are you all right, Marigold?" Kate was at her side. "At times of great stress or shock, blood leaves our limbs and transports itself to the heart so that we stay alive. Oftentimes, this results in a ringing of the ears and falling down, or sometimes even collapsing into a fainting unconsciousness. I have actually--" Again, she pressed her lips tightly together when she realized Della was glaring at her, and said, "Sorry."

"Interesting info, K-Kate," Marigold said from the floor.

Della raised Marigold up in one fell swoop. "There ya go, dude."

"Thanks. Th-This room is beautiful," and Marigold decided she must be in a lovely palace. There were crackling fireplaces in all four corners, and a swirling, blue design covered the white marble walls. Crystal chandeliers, with many tiers of glass pendants, hung from above and filled the room with soft light. A very long brocade couch faced three intricately carved, silver thrones located at the top of marble steps in the front. Open wooden chests, lining the walls, were filled to overflowing with rubies, emeralds, and sapphires, along with gold and silver coins.

"Loook up," Jade said.

Marigold looked up and saw a black sky filled with shining stars-hundreds and hundreds of shining stars.

"The stars are diiiamonds," Jade said, as Marigold's eyes became lost in the spectacular view. "But not hundreds; there arrre thousands and thousands of diiiamonds."

"W-W-Wow."

Jus motioned with his arms that everyone was to be seated. As the Misfits sat down on the couch, Jus and the Proprietor each sat on a throne. Jus took the far right one, and The Proprietor sat on the left throne. The one in the center stood vacant.

Who is going to sit in that middle throne? Marigold wondered.

"Juuust wait, and you shall see," Jade whispered, pointing upward.

Marigold didn't have to wait long, for out of an opening in the diamond-laden sky, glided a creature dressed all in black. Wearing a long black gown, cape, and a scarf wrapped around its head, it slowly descended. Then, as if riding a softly blowing breeze, on a downward draft, this creature fluttered its arms and slipped easily into the middle throne.

Well, if Marigold was surprised to see this creature float down from the sparkling sky to sit in the middle throne, she was beyond amazed to hear a familiar "Caw!" and see a flash of those white teeth inside beautiful red lips.. Could her eyes be deceiving her? Was this really happening?

As the creature unwrapped the scarf and revealed her face, she said, "Good evening, Miss Marigold Marsha Stroop. I am certain you are in disbelief, seeing my arrival and my sitting on this throne."

Marigold slowly nodded her head up and down. "Y-Yes."

"It is I, your school principal, Mrs. Hernandez. Caw!"

"Y-You are Mrs. H-Hernandez?"

Mrs. Hernandez nodded. "I am. Like the Proprietor, I have been a Misfit for over a hundred years."

"B-But you are the principal. The pr-principal of our school--"

"Being the principal of Brentwood gives me an advantageous proximity to you, as well as the other Misfits sitting here. I can be your advocate at school and relay important information, when needed."

"And y-you are a bird?"

Not entirely, but because of my close affinity, my love for birds, I am inclined to display bird traits.

You saw how I glided down from the sky, and you heard me caw. The problem is, I cannot fly long distances, and there are many times I wish I could." She flipped off her shoes and stretched her toes.

"Y-You wish you could fly?"

Mrs. Hernandez nodded and smiled at Marigold. "There are times when the Misfits need someone who can keep an eye out on what is happening from, may I say, 'a bird's eye view'. I can float but cannot fly. Caw!"

"She can't do that, mon, but there is someone who can," Jus said with an upward gesture. Marigold wondered who that would be, but the answer to that question soon presented itself.

The huge black bird Marigold had seen in the sky at various times, the bird Jus had sketched in his notebook, the bird she had met in her dreams-that bird dove down, with a wild fury, from the black, diamond-studded sky above, out of the same place where Mrs. Hernandez had emerged. But instead of gliding, this gigantic crow whipped its wings about and caused Marigold's hair to swoosh crazily in the wild wind they created. Feathers flew everywhere.

"Caw! Caw!" it screeched, before zipping in several directions and finally resting on the marble floor, before Mrs. Hernandez's throne.

"There, there, baby," Mrs. Hernandez said and ran her toes over the bird's glistening head. The bird rolled over onto his back like a pet dog, and Mrs. Hernandez continued the toe massage on his belly. To Marigold's surprise, this gigantic bird, who was at least ten feet long, with a huge wing span, made happy little chirping noises.

"Sinbad is one happy bird!" Mo said, jogging in place before sitting back down.

"Sinbad?" Marigold asked.

Kate stood and faced Marigold. "Sinbad is named after a fictional sailor, who was of Middle-Eastern origin. He was supposed to have done heroic acts, along with having fantastic adventures, while encountering monsters and supernatural events during the eighth and ninth centuries." She sat down.

"Sinbad's been watching over you on your journey to the bus stop and other places. Then he has reported back to us about the bullying and your location," Mrs. Hernandez said.

"H-He talked t-to you?"

"No. Jade can read Sinbad's thoughts," Mrs. Hernandez said.

"R-Really? Read a b-bird's thoughts? Birds c-can think?"

Mrs. Hernandez frowned. "Of course, birds can think. They are very smart-can solve problems, use tools--"

"Birds are quite intelligent. In proportion to their head size, their brains are very large; in fact, the proportion is similar to that in monkeys, apes, even humans." Kate nodded at Mrs. Hernandez.

"Caw!" the principal said, throwing an arm above her head.

"B-But why, when I saw Sinbad flying above me, the other kids didn't s-seem to notice?"

Mrs. Hernandez switched feet, while she rubbed Sinbad's belly. "Sinbad is invisible to all, except for us."

"H-Huh? I don't understand--"

"Sinbad is visible only to Misfits, or to those about to become Misfits," Mrs. Hernandez explained. "You were hopefully about to become a Misfit, so you were granted the ability to see him."

"Mrs. Hernandez, could you please be sharin' information Sinbad was tellin ya?" Jus proceeded forward with the agenda.

At this, The Proprietor began with, "Oh, no,no, no."

Mrs. Hernandez rested a hand on The Proprietor's arm, before stating, "I know you already have been apprised of what Sinbad saw."

The only sound was Sinbad's chirps. There was a quiet expectation, a waiting for important information, which Marigold decided must be bad since it made The Proprietor cry. Everyone watched Mrs. Hernandez.

"As you know, Billy Smith is a bully," Mrs. Hernandez said.

There was a chorus of agreement from the Misfits and Jus commented, "Well, that goes without sayin', mon."

Mrs. Hernandez nodded, reached deeply into her cloak's pocket, and withdrew a black, video camera. It looked to Marigold like the video camera her mom had used at birthday parties and holidays, years before she began using her phone to record celebrations. The principal pushed a button on the wall, which lowered a large, white screen behind the thrones. The room was darkened, and those on their thrones walked over and sat on the couch, with the other Misfits, evidently to watch what Mrs. Hernandez was going to display on that screen. Sinbad remained sleeping on his back in the same spot.

"Sinbad has been doing a lot of investigation and video recording at the Smith residence, especially after Billy was removed from school yesterday. This is a scene that occurred tonight at the Smith's supper table." Their principal turned on the camera.

What filled the screen could have been Marigold's own kitchen, she thought. There was a brown worn table, with four matching wooden chairs, and green, plastic place mats. A white refrigerator, dishwasher, and stove, along with a black plastic clock on the wall, completed the room.

Into the room trudged Billy, and he slumped down on a chair at the end of the table. Resting his chin in his hand, he stared sadly into space, and Marigold couldn't help but think how different he looked here at home, compared to his bad-boy self at school.

Next, came his younger sister, Lila. Marigold had seen her only a couple of times at school, since she was in kindergarten last year, and her classroom was on the other side of the school. She wore her long dark hair in a ponytail. She squeezed down into the chair, with its back against the red and yellow flower-patterned wallpaper. Billy's mom, with long black hair, a purple T-shirt, and skinny jeans stirred something in a large, black pot on the stove.

"It smells good, Mommy," Lila said.

"Well, thank you, Lila. It's chili." She turned her pretty face and smiled at her daughter. Then she shifted her gaze to her son. "You okay, Billy?"

Billy blinked quickly, like she had interrupted his thoughts. "Yeah, why wouldn't I be? Just spent time in kid lock-up, but what the heck?"

"You're lucky your dad signed you out tonight."

When he ignored her, she turned back to her task of stirring the chili.

With a heavy tromp, trudge, tromp came a black haired, burly man, wearing a blue police uniform. He threw himself down into the chair at the end of the table opposite his son. "It's 5:02. You know supper is supposed to be on the table at 5:00, Meghan," he grumbled.

Meghan filled a large, blue bowl with chili and gently placed it in front of the man. "Here ya go, Jake," she said with a forced smile.

"About time." He quickly guzzled down a can of beer she handed him, then crumpled it up and threw it into the sink across the room. "Billy? Get your fat butt to the fridge and get me another one." He belched-long and loud.

Billy popped up, like the clown in a Jack-in-the-Box, and tripped over his shoes getting to the refrigerator.

"Walk much?" Jake snorted.

Billy busily moved things around in the fridge, until he located a can and tossed it to his father's open palm. Jake caught it, popped it open, and sucked it down. Meanwhile, Meghan filled two more bowls and placed one in front of Lila and Billy, poured them each a glass of milk, and set those on their green place mats. Finally came her own bowl of chili and a glass of water, before she lowered herself down into the chair across from Lila.

"After taking a huge bite of chili, Jake swallowed and said, "What's this crap supposed to be?"

Meghan stared down into her bowl and said, "Chili."

With a great heave, Jake threw his bowl across the room, and it shattered into many shards of glass against the wall. Marigold thought the red chili, splattering on the flowery wallpaper, looked like a vicious, bloody murder had just happened right there in that kitchen. Billy, Lila, and Meghan paid this action no mind and just kept eating, one bite after the other. Marigold made an audible gasp and raised her hands to her cheeks.

"Billy, you ton-a-lard, make yourself useful." Jake pointed at the refrigerator.

Billy was up, pronto. After searching the fridge and apparently finding no more cans of beer, he looked at his mom with raised eyebrows.

She shook her head. "I guess we're out of beer."

"Out of beer. What do you mean we are out of beer? Why didn't you go to the store and get me my six pack today?" A red color raised itself from Jake's neck to his cheeks, then up his forehead to his receding hairline, and Marigold watched for an explosion to occur.

Meghan looked into her chili again. "Car wouldn't start."

"The car didn't start? So what? Something wrong with your legs?"

"It's almost two miles to the store--" Meghan bit her lower lip.

"And you can't walk two miles? Really? Your fat belly could sure stand a two mile walk."

Meghan said, "Billy, Lila, would you like more chili?"

"Let them get their own chili, Meg. You aren't their slave-you are only my slave." And he glared at her with blood-shot eyes.

Marigold forced herself to breathe (since she must have stopped), and she watched the horrid scene unfold on the screen before them. What a wicked, cruel man Billy's dad was! She attempted to find The Proprietor in the darkness. How was he managing to watch this?

Jade said from beside her, "Heee left; he couldn't take it. He will be baaack when it's over."

Marigold reluctantly forced her attention back at the video Sinbad had recorded.

Jake stood up and yelled: "Billy, get your ugly face over here!"

Billy tried to cover his left eye with his hand, as he made his way closer to his dad, now leaning against the kitchen door frame. "Yes?"

"Yes-what?" his dad demanded.

"Yes, sir--"

"Yeah, and don't you forget it. I'm your boss; you got that?"

"Yes."

"Yes what? Are you a slow learner, boy?"

"No-um, sir."

Jake muttered, "Put your hand down."

Billy lowered his hand and revealed his black eye.

"Why is your eye that color? How'd you get a black eye?"

Billy shuffled his feet and looked down at the floor. "Um, somebody beat me up at the bus stop yesterday morning. Black eye's just getting darker, I guess."

"Some kid beat you up at the bus stop? How'd you let some kid beat you up? You a weinie butt? You a girl?"

"No, sir." Billy covered his eye again with his hand.

"Well, if you let some kid give you a black eye, then you are a piece of chicken crap. That's all you are, and I'm embarrassed to call you my son."

"It wasn't a kid, sir. It was an adult."

Now Marigold cringed. "Oh, no!"

"What do you mean it was an adult?" Marigold swore she could see sparks of fire shoot out of Jake's eyes. "Who was it?"

"It was Mrs. Stroop, Marigold Stroop's mom."

"That Stroop lady who lives a street over? The crazy one who wears her robe in the front yard?"

Billy nodded enthusiastically, seemingly proud to have his dad on his side. Marigold, on the other hand, thought she was going to pass out.

"Why would that crazy lady hit you in the eye?" Billy's dad formed his huge hands into fists at his sides, over and over again.

Billy stepped closer to his dad and said, "Cause she's nuts, Dad. She's bonkers."

"Well, I already know she hit ya, Billy, so it's good you told me the truth. She told everybody you were a bully at the station, and she's going to have to answer to me soon, real soon. But till then, you know what I'm going to do, Billy?"

Billy looked admiring eyes up at his dad. "What, sir?"

"This." And Jake, thrusting a fist out like an oncoming train, hit Billy in the other eye. Punched him with so much power, Billy sailed backwards and landed flat on his back on the kitchen floor.

Billy wailed at the top of his lungs and clutched at his other eye. Marigold found herself covering her own eye, feeling his pain.

"Why'd you do that, Dad? Why'd you punch me so hard?" Billy yelled.

"Why? Oh, because you let a wimpy woman hit you in the eye. A real man never lets that happen. Now, your eyes match!" Then he let out a wild guffaw, as he stepped into the living room.

But Meghan was up now, since Lila had covered her eyes. "How dare you? You mean, awful man! How dare you hurt our son like that?" She took a step toward him.

"You questioning me, Meg? Really? You want to go there?"

"I am not afraid of you, you monster! You have broken so many of my bones, tried to crush my spirit, but you know what? I keep bouncing back, and someday-someday-I will--"

With the back of his hand, Jake slapped Meghan so hard, she flew onto the living room floor. When she sat up, blood trickled down her face from a cut above her eyebrow. Marigold cried out.

"Now, I'm off to Lenny's," Jake said, "my real home where they never run out of beer, and I can get me some delicious food. Not your for-crap-chili. Plus, there's a pretty waitress there with a good body, not ugly like you, Meghan. Don't wait up," he said, right before he slammed the front door behind him.

Just as Meghan stood up and made her way to Billy, crouched down, and stroked his head, the screen went blank.

Chapter 20

The light in the crystal chandeliers came back on when Jade snapped her fingers, but silence filled the room like a gray cloud covering the sky on a very gloomy day. Mrs. Hernandez and Jus returned to their thrones, as slowly but surely, The Proprietor entered and stepped back up into his seat. He was sniffling and dabbing his eyes with a white handkerchief.

Mrs. Hernandez cleared her throat and said, "To say that was difficult for all of us to watch is quite an understatement, I am certain."

The Proprietor now had started sobbing, and Mrs. Hernandez patted his arm. "There, there. You care so very much, with your gift of sensitivity, and it saddens you when such evil happenings occur."

The Proprietor nodded, and wiped his nose with the handkerchief. "Yes."

"I regret having to put all of you through this traumatic experience, but it was necessary," she continued. "Jade, you knew what was happening but had not seen it like you just did on the screen."

"Riiight. Much worse in the visuaaal format."

"That was j-just awful." Marigold covered her eyes." I-I wish you hadn't shown us that video."

"But it was extremely urgent that we viewed it, in detail. It was the best method for our conscious psyche' to see and absorb the cruelty pervading the residence that Billy Smith inhabits; watch what he, his mother and sister, are forced to endure." Kate nodded her head at Marigold, as if willing her to hear and understand this explanation.

"I-I just feel so sorry for Billy. For his mom and h-his sister."

Mo ran in circles around the space from the place where the Misfits sat, up to the thrones, around and around and around, like he was a galloping race horse at the Kentucky Derby.

"Mo!" Jus hollered. "What's up, mon? You need to be sittin' down!"

"Heee has no choice and needs to burn off the great deal of anxiiiety he is currently feeling."

"He still is needin' to be sittin' down. That runnin' around is causin' all of us anxiety, mon."

As if motivated by Mo's swiftness, Sinbad batted his huge black wings and created such a great gust of wind blowing about the room, Mrs. Hernandez had to hold onto her hair to keep it in place. Then he was off, with a great surge upward toward the black, diamond-studded sky; next, he dove down, down, down, till his beak almost touched the ground; and finally, he looped in slow circles above their heads. At last, he landed with a great boom-a-boom-boom at the principal's feet, once more.

Sinbad rolled himself onto his back, and Mrs. Hernandez began the belly massage again, then said, "I suppose he gets rid of his anxiety in the same manner Mo does."

A huffing and puffing, now-seated Mo, gave her a thumbs-up.

"Thank you, Mo. I am needin' ya to be sittin' now and participatin' in some important decisions we are havin' to make, mon."

Mo now gave Jus an affirming nod. Marigold thought if that was the best way for him to get rid of anxiety, well, she understood why he needed to run around.

Jus stared up into the black sky; the wood logs in the fireplaces were still crackling and filling the space with a wonderful aroma. But even that smell, bringing back memories of campfires and roasting marshmallows, could not erase the awfulness Marigold had just seen on the screen.

Finally, Jus said, looking at all of the Misfits seated on the couch, "I have been attemptin' to design a plan to save Billy. It is takin' lots of creativity to be comin' up with a way to get Billy out of such a negative situation, along with rescuin' Mrs. Smith and Lila. We have to be makin' sure Marigold's mom isn't gonna be gettin' hurt either, mon."

Marigold swallowed hard. "My m-mom might be getting h-hurt?"

"Mr. Smiiith is capable of doing anything. He is embarrrassed that his son got injured at the bus stop by a woman, a woman whooo happens to be your mom. Remember, heee said she was going to have to answer to hiiim."

"Oh, n-no! So Mr. Smith might h-hurt my mom..."

"This is what I want to do to Billy's dad, dudes!" Della shredded the air with mega-punches and mighty kicks.

"I am not so sure Billy is innocent! After all, think about how he has been bullying Marigold and other kids since kindergarten!" Mo stood up and ran in place.

"Studies have shown that by the age of five, a child's personality has been basically formed. Genetically, Billy may be predisposed to displaying this aggressive, negative behavior, due to his father's temperament. The 'New York Times' reported that one third of adults, who were abused as children, go on to abuse their own children," Kate said.

"Whaaat do you do in your spare time? Sit at home and read 'The New York Tiiimes'?" Jade asked.

"Sometimes. Sometimes I do. I find that publication to be unbiased and quite informative," Kate said.

Marigold raised her voice. "B-But only one third? To me, that s-sounds like there is a chance to save B-Billy. There is a two-thirds p-possibility he will be okay!"

"You, who have been bullied by Billy so many times, possess it within yourself to actually want to try and save him, Marigold? I am not certain that is such a good idea." Mrs. Hernandez quickly flapped an arm in the air and gave a loud, "Caw!".

The Proprietor said with a kind smile, "But Marigold has the gift of empathy. That is why she feels the way she does. Thank you, Marigold."

"It is probable that Billy's father was also physically and verbally abused as a child. As a result, he abuses Billy, Meghan, and probably Lila. In my educated opinion, since a child often inherits his parent's temperament, there is a great possibility that this abuse Billy demonstrates is irreparable, and that he will repeat those actions." Kate looked sadly at Marigold.

Della was back up. chopping and kicking. "This is what I want to do to Billy and his dad. They aren't going to have a chance. Remember, 'Might for Right'? Well, I have the 'might' and it is only 'right', dudes, to punish them for hurting others!"

"'Right, NOT Might'!" Mo jumped toward Della.

"I dooo think Jake Smith waaas abused by his daaad."

"B-But there is only a one-third chance Billy will turn out like h-his father. He's o-only eleven. Maybe w-we can help him, if we start now."

Jus closed his eyes and said, "Designin' this plan is more difficult than I was plannin' on. I'm thinkin' we need to be takin' it to a vote."

"So exactly what are we voting to do?" Mrs. Hernandez asked.

Jus twirled the rings on his fingers. "We will be votin' for the followin', mon: One, savin' Billy and stoppin' his dad from harmin' anybody else-ever. Two, not savin' Billy and still stoppin' his dad from hurtin' anybody else-ever. In number one, we are savin' Billy but removin' his dad from the situation. In number two, we are removin' both Billy and his dad from the situation."

"I guess I-I need to be knowing two things: How are you going to r-remove Billy's dad and maybe Billy, too, and h-how are you going to save my mom?"

"It is probably easily understandable that if we remove Billy's dad from being around anyone he could possibly hurt, your mother will be safe." Mrs.

Hernandez switched feet on Sinbad's feathered underbelly. Sinbad stuck his legs above him and curled his claws.

"Billly would not injure yourrr mom," Jade said.

Marigold nodded. "Where w-would you take B-Billy's dad ?"

"That will be decided after much discussion between The Proprietor, Mrs. Hernandez, and Jus. They will deliberate and make the final decision. We, the rest of the Misfits, will utilize our many gifts in order to help assist, in the process, which they will design," Kate said.

"In other words," Della said with a big kick, "the three up there will decide, dude. Then we'll help them out."

"O-Okay. I-I hope you aren't going to use a gun or a weapon. You aren't g-going to kill either one of them?"

The Proprietor climbed down from his throne and slowly walked in Marigold's direction. Once there, he grabbed her hands and pulled till she stood up. He looked his moist, blue eyes up into hers. "We, the Misfits, are not killers. The only weapons we use are our gifts, which does, of course, include Della's martial arts. But she knows she can only use her gift if she, one of us, or one of our loved ones are being physically threatened. I am glad she is constantly practicing her skills. Della's body is, indeed, our weapon. Now, if someone is in danger of being killed, well, we must resort to stronger measures."

At that, Della was up kicking and girating in the air.

"Y-Yes, I am glad about Della's strength, t-too."

"Good," the little man said, blowing a kiss at Marigold, before turning on his twiggy legs and walking back to his throne. Everyone waited until he arrived, and then Jus stood up.

"It is now bein' time for the vote, mon. Say 'Yay' for 'Yes'; 'Nay', for 'No', and the majority will be rulin'."

Marigold looked at the group of friends surrounding her. It was apparent they were all concentrating deeply on what they were about to do: save Billy or not save Billy.

Kate explained, "Marigold, either we will develop a method to try and assist Billy come to terms with the years of abuse he has endured and become a new eleven year-old who doesn't bully others, or we will remove him."

Jade added, "It haaas already been decided that Mr. Smith will beee removed since he is a danger to Billy, Lila, Meghaaan, and now your mother. You may beee assured that this removal is not going to include weapons (except for possibly Della's body), and nobody will get killled."

Jus stood and was silent for a very long time. Finally, he said, "Let me be remindin' ya, if you say 'Yay', you are votin' to save Billy and tryin' to help him, mon. I think it is goin' without sayin' that if we try savin' him but savin' him isn't workin', we will take another vote for a possible removal. If ya vote 'Nay', you are sayin' Billy is beyond bein' helped, and he needs to be removed, like his dad. He, along with Mr. Smith, will be gone forever."

Marigold closed her eyes and chewed on a fingernail. It blew her away that this group had the power to determine the fate of Billy and Billy's dad. She already thought Billy could be saved, but what about Billy's dad?

"I can guaranteee you that there is no help for Jaaake Smith. He became cruel and hateful a verrry long time ago. He will only continue tooo abuse his family members, and who knows what heee will do to your mother. Right now, he is most likely forrrming a plan to hurt her. We can beee thankful for our police officers-they protect us, but not Officerrr Smith. He isss the exception."

The others agreed with words of:

"Yes!"

"That's right, mon."

"We have to remove him!"

"Are you in a place where you can be votin', Marigold? You need to be understandin' we have to be takin' care of the majority: Billy, your mom, Meghan, Lila, and other victims, who will be crossin' Officer Smith's path in the future," Jus said.

Marigold nodded. "B-But if both Billy and his dad are removed to the same place, won't that mean h-he will still hurt Billy?"

"Weee must trust Mrs. Hernandez, The Proprietor, and Jusss will make the correct placement, so that doesn't occurrr." Jade closed her eyes and hummed, "Ommm".

Mrs. Hernandez's black eyes flitted around the room. "It is certainly apparent that your gift of empathy is at work, but you must place your trust in the three of us, seated up here. We will not allow Billy to be abused any longer by his father. If Billy is removed, he will be placed in a location where his dad cannot locate him."

Marigold nodded. "O-Okay."

"Are we bein' ready for a vote now? Jus asked. "Anybody else havin' a concern that should be addressed before we do, mon?"

Silence pervaded The Contributing Room.

"All right, please be givin' the group a 'Yay' or a 'Nay'."

All of those on the couch sat stiffly upright, clearly ready to state their votes to the other Misfits.

"Kate?" Jus said clearly and loudly.

"Nay."

"Mo?"

"Nay!"

"Marigold?"

"Yay."

"Della?"

"Yay. But I'm gonna kick Billy if he screws up!"

Jus said, "Only a 'Yay' or a 'Nay' will suffice, mon."

"Jade?"

"Yaaay."

"Mrs. Hernandez and The Proprietor, please be notin' we are havin' two nays and three yays. Now, we are needin' your votes, mon."

Mrs. Hernandez looked over at The Proprietor, and when he drew a big breath and nodded, she said, "We are ready, Jus. Caw!"

"The Proprietor?" Jus asked.

"Yay," he said.

"Mrs. Hernandez?"

"Nay", she said.

"That's bein three 'nays' and four 'yays', mon."

Mrs. Hernandez said, "Your final vote, Jus, will determine if it is a tie or not."

Jus turned his face upward. When he looked back at the group, he wore a huge smile. "Yay", he said.

Mrs. Hernandez announced, "Misfits, the group has spoken with three 'nays' and five 'yays'. We will attempt to save Billy, and we will remove Officer Jake Smith."

"What w-would have happened if it had been a t-tie?" Marigold asked.

"If it had been bein' a tie, mon? Then we would have revoted, and if it was still bein' a tie, we would have had to drop our plan. Everything woulda stayed the same--just like it is bein' now," Jus explained.

"I am so glad it t-turned out the w-way it did."

"Meee, too." Jade closed her eyes and hummed.

"I am certainly happy we did not have a tie, and instead, we can proceed forward with, hopefully, a positive result," Kate said.

"But you voted 'n-nay'. How can you be h-happy the vote went with 'yay'?"

"You must have noticed that we don't always agree with each other on all matters? I have perturbed some, due to my intelligence and my excessive elaboration regarding certain topics I have researched.

Some correct Mo for his activity level at, perhaps, inappropriate times. And then there is Della with all her kicks and chops? There are Misfits who may believe she should practice someplace else-"

"Hey! My body is my weapon-and yours, dude." Della leaped up and did a kick, slice. "You ought to be happy--"

"Dellla, cool it. Let Kaaate finish!"

"Thank you Jade, even though I am a thorn in your side, at times," Kate said.

"H-Huh?" Marigold asked.

"Just that at times, Jade is one of my most assertive critics. But all of that doesn't matter. Do you recall the time Della rescued you from a life-threatening experience that certainly was not in your best interest? I imagine she exuded great displeasure at your choice?"

"Yeah. The t-time she saved me from that h-homeless man under the bridge?"

"Exactly," Kate said.

"S-Sorry, Della--"

"No apology necessary, dude. Just glad I got there in time, thanks to Jade."

"M-Me, too. Or I might not be s-sitting here."

"No, you would not beee here," Jade said, and Marigold bit off a fingernail.

Kate continued, "All of us are a family seated here in this beautiful space. We are able to relate to the emotional turmoil each of us has experienced. Some may not have expressed to you the exact cruelty he or she has known, but you may be able to guess-"

At this, Mrs. Hernandez stood and waved her arms furiously in the air. "Caw! Caw!" Sinbad aimed an annoyed look at her sudden motion and noise. "Sorry, baby," she said, and quickly seated herself to resume the toe activity. Sinbad stuck his legs back up into the air and made several chirps.

"You have just objectively observed an example of Sinbad's irritation at Mrs. Hernandez. He didn't agree with the abrupt altering of her activity. Did that mean he still didn't care about her?" Kate asked.

"N-No."

"That's how it is with us, Marigold!" Mo exclaimed while running about. "We may not agree with the way everyone acts or thinks, but we still care about each other!"

"Your mother drives you nuuuts sometimes. That doesn't mean youuu hate her."

"R-Right."

"That's just how we are feelin' about our votin', mon. We may not all be agreein' about what should be happenin' to Billy, but we are still willin' to go with the majority. It's bein' how a democracy works."

Marigold nodded at Jus. "I-I get it. I really get it. And I thank you for not g-giving up on me. Thanks for letting me b-be part of this family."

"Thank you for being an essential element of the Misfits. Thank you for sharing your beautiful gift of empathy, Marigold." Kate gave her a hug.

"Even if I don't think we are going to save Billy!" Mo said with a bounce, bounce, bounce in place. "He's way too gone, man! You will see!"

"That is to be seen, to be seen," Kate stated.

"But now, the time has arrived for those on the couch to journey home. I am certain it is very late, and I must be in my office at school by 6:00 a.m. in the morning." Mrs. Hernandez yawned.

"Yeah, you all need to be travelin' back now," Jus said. "The four of us will be stayin' and creatin' the plan to start tomorrow, mon."

"Four?" Marigold asked.

"Sinbad is an integral piece in implementing their plan," Kate said, standing up.

Marigold raised herself up to follow the line led, this time, by a bouncing Mo. "Oh, I-I see. Sinbad is a M-Misfit, too."

"Yesss he is," Jade whispered. "Oh, yess, he certainly is. Tiiime to head home. Ommm."

Chapter 21

After Marigold flipped the back porch light on and off, then went to her bedroom to do the same with her lamp, she found her sleeping mother still sprawled across her bed. She breathed a sigh of relief, since the back door had been left unlocked. What if Billy's dad had decided to hurt her tonight? The thought of her mom getting injured, or worse, scared her. Two things for sure: She would need to make certain all doors were locked, before she left with the Misfits, and she had to take a key in her pocket from now on.

As Marigold was forming that future plan, she quickly changed into her pajamas, slid very carefully on top of the sunset comforter, and tried to work around her mother's sprawling limbs. She noticed the clock on the nightstand read 2:08. Oh, my goodness, she thought. She was only going to get a few hours of sleep! Still, tonight had been the most important meeting so far. Getting only a few hours of sleep was minor, in comparison to what the Misfits had decided: Try to save Billy and remove Mr. Smith to who-knew-where.

With a great start and a jump out of bed, Marsha Stroop cried, “What? I have been sleeping here, in your bed, till two in the morning?”

Marigold had her eyes pressed closed and smiled, giving Jade a silent thank you. Obviously, Jade understood the dilemma she faced-get into pajamas and bed, before her mom woke up.

Marsha bent over and kissed her daughter’s forehead. “Good night, sweet girl. Let’s pick out your clothes in the morning.” She gave a huge yawn. “I’m too tired to arrange your beautiful outfit tonight. I hope you don’t mind.”

After her mom closed the door with a quiet click, Marigold wiggled her way under the covers and fell asleep. It seemed like only a few minutes later, her alarm clock rang, and she was surprised at how wide awake she felt. It must be due to the excitement of last night, she thought. She also understood she was anticipating the day and hearing what the Misfit leaders had decided to do regarding saving Billy, removing Billy’s dad, and preventing her mom from injury, as a result.

Her mom had a breakfast of eggs and toast, hash browns, and orange juice on the table. “I don’t know when I have slept so well, sweetie! Did you know I fell asleep early on your bed and didn’t awaken till two in the morning? You should have woke me up, so you could have gotten under the covers. You had to have been so cold and...squished!"

"It's o-okay, Mom," Marigold said with a smile. "I'm glad you slept w-well." But she thought how her mother could have been hurt-or worse.

"I thought today I would let you pick out your pretty outfit. You are getting to be a little older, you know."

Marigold nodded and knew that was okay, since she was going to change clothes as soon as she got to school, anyway. But she would need to change fast, since she wouldn't have a pass today to get into homeroom on time. Then she started chowing down.

"You must be real hungry," Marsha Stroop said.

"Mmm mmm," she said. "It t-tastes real good. Thanks for breakfast, M-Mom."

And she meant it. Yeah, her mom might be way too overprotective (a smother-mother), but she was her mom, whom she loved so much. The thought that Billy Smith's dad could hurt her, as a result of her only trying to protect her daughter, scared her-and scared her badly.

"Well, you are so welcome, darling. Now, you can go decide on your beautiful clothes to wear today. They are folded on top of the washing machine."

Marigold took the last bite of the food on her plate. "O-Okay, Mom. I w-will." Then she carried her dishes to the sink, rinsed them off, and put them in the dishwasher. She packed six celery stalks with hummus. Mo would be happy they weren't stuffed with peanut butter, pickles, and radishes, she knew.

As Marsha began clanking pots and pans, Marigold scrambled to the laundry room and picked out the ugly clothes she was going to wear to school that day: a green and orange striped dress, yellow underwear, orange socks. Then she was off to the bathroom for a shower, brushing and flossing her teeth, and dressing. After that, she started through the front door while her robed mother stood at her post in the yard. Marigold figured some things weren't ever going change.

"M-Mom, promise me something, o-okay?"

"Yes," her mother said, after placing a flower clip in her daughter's hair and planting the familiar kiss on her forehead.. "Anything for you, darling."

"When y-you are in the house or when you l-leave, promise me you w-will keep the doors locked."

"But we never lock the doors. We live in such a safe neighborhood, there is not a reason to ever, ever worry, sweetheart."

Marigold, who had just reached the sidewalk leading to the bus stop, turned on her heels. She knew she couldn't share with anyone, not even her mom, what she had discovered at the Misfits' meeting last night. But she had to protect her. Marigold ran back to her mom's side and said, "M-Mom, you promised you would do whatever I asked y-you to do."

"Okay, Marigold Marsha Stroop. I promise I will always keep the doors locked, when I'm here and when I'm not."

Then Marigold did something, something she never ever did. She placed a kiss on her mom's cheek and said, "Th-Thanks, Mom. I love y-you." And she didn't even care that the Droobs were laughing uproariously, while she made sure not to step on the cracks in the sidewalk, on her way to the bus stop.

Just as she figured, Billy was there. Yes, the gang leader stood there, but when Marigold looked at his face, she didn't see any black eyes. What was going on?

"Wow, creepy Sunshine Girl! You sure are bright this morning!" Billy yelled.

"Yeah, bright for sure! Look at those orange socks, even though she thinks she's wearing cool shoes!" It was Mike Botowski, no body space between him and his idol, Billy Smith.

"Don't you know you are supposed to be wearing white socks with your Nikes?" Billy gave a laugh, and, of course, everybody else joined in.

A boy, Jon, said, "Wonder where she got her cool shoes?"

"Probably out of some trash can," Billy chuckled. And for a moment, Marigold wondered if Mo had been right-there was no hope for Billy. Maybe he ought to be removed to someplace, just like his dad.

"Caw! Caw!" Marigold looked up and saw Sinbad burst through a cloud and dive down in her direction. He made a great, low swoop above her, like he was going to hit her in the head, but he didn't. With a great, "Caw!", he zoomed back up again into a cloud. Sinbad was watching over her. She smiled, knowing nobody else at that bus stop but she had seen the giant, protective, black bird.

Well, that special feeling was only short-lived because Billy said, "Hey, why are you smiling, Freak Face? You shouldn't be, since your mom is dead meat. My dad is going to take care of her, big time!"

That started the kids screaming in glee. The bus stopped in front of them, and Marigold felt her heart pound like a bass drum in her chest. Yep, her mom was in big, bad trouble. She sat down in her usual seat and bit at a fingernail.

As the bus drove by Marsha Stroop, waving like a nutcase at her daughter's face in the window, Marigold knew her mom had better keep the doors locked. Sinbad soared, above the bus, in great soaring circles, but even that didn't remove the fear she felt knowing her mom could be hurt, really hurt, by the time she got home. Hopefully, the Misfits had a good plan, because even a call to the police station wouldn't help. After all,

Jake Smith was a policeman, and he probably had lots of good friends there. When the bus stopped at Tasha's bus stop and she didn't board, Marigold wondered where she was.

She dashed to her locker to find the clothes she had worn yesterday, only to discover they were gone, but had been replaced with a new pair of jeans and a blue T-shirt. There was also a note and a pass into homeroom. The note said, Your friendly laundry service at work! Both the note and pass were signed "Ms. Henley and Mrs. Toon." Mrs. Hernandez had said Mrs. Toon and Ms Henley were on the same page. Plus, Marigold had heard them both make bird noises, "tweet" and "twitter.". Was there a connection between the two teachers and Mrs. Hernandez, who said, "Caw"?

Jade surprised Marigold when she approached, seeming to glide on air. "They are sissssters."

"H-Huh?" Marigold asked.

"Sisters. Tripletsss; although, Ms. Henley and Mrs. Tooon are not as closely affiliated with the bird kingdom as Mrs. Hernandez. Not yet, anywaaay." Then Jade shuffled away.

Mrs. Hernandez, Mrs. Toon, and Ms Henley were sisters? Well, Marigold decided that explained a lot-a whole lot. That meant they must be really old, too, since they were triplets! To the restroom she traveled, with the new clothes and a pair of white socks fresh out of the package in her arms. She ran past the same girls at the mirror, eyeing her suspiciously; went into quick change mode; and then jogged to homeroom.

She tossed the pass onto Mrs. Drebel's desk and slid into her place in the back. Of course, because Billy was there, the class was rocking and rolling again. The teacher stood stomping her feet, then screaming with an order for silence, then stomping her feet again. Kids shouted unkind words in Marigold's direction, but she let them roll off her like "water off a duck's back", her mom's expression.

On she scrambled to first period and to her regular seat, only to discover Jus wasn't there. She sure wondered where he was, but thought with his early morning meeting, perhaps he was going to be too tired to make it to school today. Marigold mega-missed him and had tons of questions regarding what they had decided; she didn't want to have to wait until tonight to find out.

She doubted Jus could tell the Misfits anything at lunch, anyway. There was probably no way he could share the leaders' decision, with the other kids around them in the cafeteria. And mean Mr. Reynolds, who seemed like he had traveled over to the dark side (or had always lived there), might hear Jus. Marigold didn't know just what Coach Reynolds was capable of doing.

After being given a math assignment on the board, and working the rest of the period on it, Marigold ran on to second period after the bell rang. Because she arrived early to the classroom, just after Billy had, she saw him pull out some kind of makeup stick from his pocket and slick it around his eyes. Well, that's why the bruises weren't apparent.

Although she attempted to creep quietly to her seat, Billy still noticed and said, "Hey, Creep Girl! If you tell anybody about what you just saw, I will take care of you, just like my dad is going to take care of your mom. I will make sure you die-like her!"

He was interrupted by a throng of kids, pushing each other through the door, and quickly shoved the makeup stick back into his pocket. As the many kids began shouting cruel words toward Marigold, Mrs. Toon aimed her footsteps back in her direction.

Mrs. Toon whispered, "Marigold, I just received a message from Della in the hall. An emergency meeting has been called, and you are to hurry to Mrs. Hernandez's office, ASAP!"

Marigold didn't have to spend any time thinking about that directive. She grabbed her book bag and leaped from her chair. What was happening? A fear of what it could be, scared her.

As she ran through the classroom door, Billy yelled, "Hey! Where is that ugly girl going? You know she has to get all her clothes from the dumpster? Maybe she's hurrying to a garbage can right now! Maybe there's a dumpster sale close by!"

"She probably gets her food out of there, too!" somebody else shouted. Then some other kids joined in with titters and giggles.

"Billy!" Mrs. Toon raised her voice above the tumult. "You get quiet, or you will be back in the office! Do you want to be absent from school another day?"

The voices faded away, and Marigold thought about the video they had watched last night. Having seen the beast Billy's dad was, she bet home was the last place he wanted to be right now.

As she ran into the school's office, she was directed by the secretary, Miss Pinlay, back to Mrs. Hernandez's office. Their principal was pacing and waving her flowing-armed blouse over her head. "Caw! Caw!" she cried. In chairs around her desk, sat Jus, Jade, and Kate. Della was chopping and kicking, while Mo bopped up and down in place. Marigold feared something very bad had happened.

Chapter 22

"We are all here," Mrs Hernandez said. "All here and ready to implement the plan, much sooner than we had decided on, however."

"Wh-What's the plan?" Marigold asked.

Jus cracked the knuckles of his jeweled fingers. He frowned and cleared his throat. Seeing him like this, Marigold knew whatever had happened wasn't good. Jus, who was usually displaying his "be happy," Jamaican self, was clearly upset.

"Welll, tell the group, Jus," Jade said.

Jus looked at Marigold. "Your mother was not appearin' at work this mornin'. The owner of Greta's Garden called here at school to be askin' if you knew why, mon. She wondered if she was bein' sick?"

"No, she w-wasn't sick. Why wasn't she at w-work? Where c-could she be? She's n-never late!"

"We didn't figure she was ill, and Jade called on Sinbad to try and find her." Mrs. Hernandez ran on her very long legs to the window and peered out.

"But h-how is Sinbad going to tell you where m-my mom is?"

"Remember, Jade can read Sinbad's thoughts," Mrs. Hernandez said.

"Why c-can't you tell us right now, J-Jade?"

"Caw! Jade is waiting for Sinbad to find your mother and transmit his thoughts to her."

"Oh, r-right. My mom's not a M-Misfit."

Tapping the window sharply with her fingernail, Mrs. Hernandez said, "Hurry up, Sinbad!"

Jade stood motionless, with her eyes closed. Finally, she said, "Oh no, oh nooo, oh no--" She shuffled over to whisper in Mrs. Hernandez's ear.

"This is not good. Caw!" Mrs. Hernandez flapped both arms.

Marigold felt like she was going to crawl out of her skin. "Wh-What is not g-good?"

"It is essential that weee leave now," Jade stated.

"Tell us what is going on!" Mo exclaimed, hopping on one foot.

"Marigold's mother is in great peril at this very moment, and Sinbad has begun the first plan of action. Caw!" Mrs. Hernandez's arm flaps began again, and she whispered in Jus's ear.

Marigold darted to Mrs. Hernandez's side. "What is h-happening to my m-mom?"

Jus said, "The plan to be removin' Officer Jake Smith is soon to begin, mon. Sinbad will fly Mr. Smith to a location in the Pacific Ocean. He will be placed, on an uninhabited island, that Sinbad was checkin' out this morning, an island where he will be existin' without human contact, a place where he will be foragin' for food, buildin' his own shelter, livin' a life totally on his own."

"Caw! Caw! This is the design Jus, with all his creativity, formulated for us in the very early morning hours today. It was approved by The Proprietor, Sinbad, and me. But first, does this plan meet with your empathetic gift, Marigold?"

Now Marigold was jumping in place like Mo. "Yes! He w-won't be killed, and you already said h-he was beyond h-help! We need to g-go now to save my m-mom!"

Mrs. Hernandez continued quickly, "Jade, do you think the best route, to the Solly River, is to run through the woods across from Jone's Grocery Store? Will that be the least obvious way, so as to not be seen by others?"

Jade closed her eyes. "I beeelieve that would be the best, secretive route."

Still, Mrs. Hernandez was not finished. "Jade, as you gaze into the future, are you able to ascertain that we will have a safe arrival and Mrs. Stroop will be unharmed?"

With hands folded before her chest and eyes closed, Jade said, "Yes to both, if we leave in tiiime. Sinbad needs our help, before heee can proceed."

"Yes! We have to g-go!" Marigold shouted. "My mom's at the r-river?"

Much to Marigold's astonishment, Mrs. Hernandez placed her black shoe onto the wall beside her office window, and pushed. A door to the outside opened, and everyone ran through it.

In the cool air, Mrs. Hernandez pointed a long, sharp fingernail at Mo. "Lead the way with your swiftness." Then the fingernail was aimed at Della. "You must accompany him, at a quick pace, since your strength will help take Jake Smith down. The rest of us will run behind you. Go! Caw!"

"Why don't w-we just go in your c-car?" Marigold asked.

"Questions, questions! Caw! We cannot go in my car! We must travel through the woods, so we aren't discovered by other human beings. Now, move, please!"

Marigold dashed ahead of Jus, Jade, Kate, and Mrs. Hernandez. Mo and Della had already vanished from sight. Through the woods she ran! Long tree limbs scratched her face, and brambles grabbed at her ankles. The others caught up, as on and on they jogged, without a word. She knew everybody had two agendas: save her mother, and witness Officer Jake Smith taken to some uninhabited Pacific island, where he would never be discovered, or hurt anyone again.

At long last, after Jade, Mrs. Hernandez, Marigold, Kate, and Jus barreled from the woods in Solly Park, Mo and Della met them. Marigold was surprised that Mo was only a bit out of breath after running the distance. Della, on the other hand, bent her upper body over her legs and desperately sucked in air.

"Mo is really—really fast, dudes," Della said between gasps.

"I see Mr. Smith on his hands and knees over there," Mrs. Hernandez said. "There is someone lying beside him."

Marigold squinted and made out a colorful blur by the river; she knew who that "someone" was.

"It is time!" Mrs. Hernandez shouted, with a wild flap of both arms. "Caw!" They all sped ahead in one attacking group, on a mission, determined to save Mrs. Stroop.

The sound of the "Caw!" and the great swooshing movement alerted Billy's dad he was the victim of a coup. He jumped to his feet and whipped out a gun from his holster. Aiming the revolver at this group, he barked, "Take one more step, and all of you are dead!"

"Help me, help me," Marsha Stroop weakly cried.

Fear clutched Marigold's heart. She feared her mom had been majorly injured, and if they hadn't arrived when they did, she could have been killed. Was she going to be totally out of danger, though?

"Hi-yee!" In one wild flurry, Della flew through the air with a giant kick and then another. Like some kind of military machine, she charged at him. Well, Marigold didn't know if it was Della's black Batgirl outfit, her cry, or her unstoppable actions, but Officer Smith stumbled backward, fell over, and landed in the river.

He lost his gun somewhere in the process, and Mo rushed up to locate it. He had just raised it from the water, when Jake grappled for it with his huge hand and tore it away from Mo. Mrs. Hernandez gasped when a shot was fired into the air! Marigold wondered if they all were going to be dead meat!

Like a mad flash, Mo jumped on top of the policeman's back and grabbed the gun. Then, he threw that weapon far out into the river. But the mad man was back up, sending Mo flying through the air, and he went charging toward the group of Misfits.

Still Della, being a true powerhouse, was on it. Kicking him in the face with the hardest kick Marigold thought any martial art's athlete had ever planted on an individual, she let out with a "Hi-yee-ayyy!" Jake succumbed to Della's strength and fell onto the ground beside the river. His eyes rolled back into his head. Marsha cried and covered her face.

Della gave his body a few chops for good measure, then Kate ran up. She took the pulse in his neck and nodded. "Still alive," she said in Marigold's direction. Marigold knew that was to reassure her that her request he not be killed, had been honored.

Then, from out of the top of a very tall tree behind them, flew Sinbad. He made great circles in the sky, then dove down and picked up Officer Jake Smith by the back of his blue policeman's uniform. Up, up, up they traveled, until they were in the clouds, and Marigold couldn't see them anymore.

"Safe travels, my bird," Mrs. Hernandez said, then chirped. "Sinbad will be back by tonight for our meeting, I am sure."

"Mom!" Marigold tore over to her mother's side. Soon she was joined by the others.

Marsha Stroop uncovered her eyes and managed to sit up. She tentatively touched her bleeding face and looked at her bruised wrists, tied together. Mrs. Hernandez shredded the binding rope apart with her sharp fingernails and removed it.

Marigold wrapped her arms around her mother. "I'm s-so sorry you got hurt, Mom."

"How did you know where I was? How did you find me?" she asked.

"We are just very sorry it took us so long," Mrs. Hernandez said, taking Mrs. Stroop's hand in her own.

"By the way, I'm Mrs. Hernandez, school principal. Someone reported to us that they had seen something suspicious down by this river, so we came over."

"Someone told you? Why did they tell you and not the police?" Marsha asked.

"Oh, I suppose because they thought we could take care of it," Mrs. Hernandez explained. "Caw!".

"What was the sound you just made?" Marsha asked.

Mrs. Hernandez smirked. "Oh nothing. I guess I just have a cawph."

Weakly, Marsha Stroop pushed herself up. "That man who hurt me, who was going to kill me? He knocked on our door (which I locked, sweetie) and said he needed to come in to talk with me about break-ins in the neighborhood. Well, since he was a policeman, I let him in. Policemen are our friends."

Marigold said, "Well, m-most policemen are. Then what h-happened?"

"Before I knew what was occurring, he'd put a gun to my back, forced me into his car, and drove me here. He told me I would never touch his son, Billy, again, and that he was going to make sure I didn't. He told me I would never make Billy look like a wienie butt. He tied my wrists together and said he was going to kill me and throw me into the river." She put her head in her hands and sobbed.

"Don't worry about him. He will never hurt you or anyone else again," Mrs. Hernandez said, staring into the sky.

Marsha cranked her head in all directions. "Where did he go?"

"D-Don't worry, Mom. He went f-far away—"

"He did? Where is he? I never even saw him leave! I was so scared, I had my eyes covered!"

"M-Mother, I'm just s-so glad you are alive!"

Marigold's mom smiled. "Me, too. Thank you all for saving me!"

"You are very welcome," Mrs. Hernandez said.

"And where that evil man went? I guess I don't even care, since you said he won't hurt me or other people, ever again. Don't know how you know that, though. He might have run back into those woods." Marsha pointed toward the tall trees.

"We can be promisin' ya that he didn't, mon." Jus raised his eyes up into the sky, too.

"Well, good. Now, can I be taking my daughter home, Mrs. Hernandez?"

Mrs. Hernandez glanced at her watch. "Marigold still has lunch and classes left. I will leave that decision up to your daughter."

Marigold thought escaping the Droobs sounded mighty inviting but looked at her circle of friends and said, "N-No, I had better go back to school, M-Mom." The other Misfits gave her smiles, nods, and "thumbs-ups".

"May I call school and get Mrs. Toon to drive here and take you home, Mrs. Stroop?" The principal pulled a phone from her pocket. "I know the secretary, Miss Pinlay, will be happy to watch her class."

"Oh, that would be super. Thanks." Then Mrs. Stroop added, "I am just so happy my daughter has found some new friends. She never had any little friends before, and the way she likes you, I think you all must be very special."

"Your daughter, mon? She is bein' very, very special." Jus smiled at Marigold.

Marsha grinned at Jus. "Are you her boyfriend? I bet you are her little-um, tall-boyfriend."

Jus did a happy dance in his green shoes. "No, I can be guaranteein' ya I'm not her boyfriend! Not the kinda boyfriend you are meanin', anyway."

"Well, you must be returning," Mrs. Hernandez said, while her small black eyes focused on each individual Misfit. "I will remain here, until the transportation for Mrs. Stroop and me, arrives."

As the Misfits began their return trek through the woods, Marigold heard, but didn't respond to her mom, when she shouted, "But where are your pretty clothes, Marigold?"

Although she knew the Droobs awaited, Marigold followed her friends, the Misfits, through the woods. Onward to Brentwood Middle School and who knew what else awaited. Whatever it was, she knew she would survive, because even though Della, Mo, Jade, Kate, and Jus tromped ahead of her-well, they also had her back.

Chapter 23

The clamor of lunch trays banging against cafeteria tables, the kids' loud voices, a flying apple, as well as the smell of hamburgers and french fries, announced it was lunch time. Marigold ran into the cafeteria and made her way to the back table, where Mo, Della, and Jus sat.

"What a morning, huh? Wow!" Mo said, when Marigold lowered herself down onto the bench.

"O-Oh, yeah. I never, and I mean never, had a morning like w-we just had." She unzipped her book bag and removed the bag of celery with hummus to share.

"Hey, Jade. Welcome, mon." Jus gestured with open arms, as Jade scooted their way and sat on top of the table. Once there, she arranged her legs in a crisscross position, closed her eyes, and put her folded hands in front of her chest. "Kaaate is approaching. Ommmm."

And just as she predicted, Kate arrived. "Hello! Today has certainly begun in a monumental manner. The remainder of this afternoon and evening will hopefully be much less stressful." She sat down gently at the table.

"Well, now that we are all bein' here and present, mon, I think it's time to be slammin' down some food." Jus removed a clear bag of mixed nuts and cheese.

"I agree!" Mo bopped up and down in place. "I have worked up quite an appetite!"

"Annnd you surely have. Your energy level is very hiiigh." Jade opened her eyes and winked at him.

"Okay, dudes. Start the food toss, cause I also have used up tons of energy today." Della did a chop, chop in the air.

Marigold smiled. "I think we all h-have used up 'tons of energy today'."

"But I used up the most, man!" Mo was up and made a loop around the table.

Della jumped from her seat and performed a kick into the air. "Nope. Nothing compared with the way I took him down, dude."

The table became instantly silent when Jus raised a finger to his lips. "Shh! Are ya nuts, mon? Do ya wanna get all of us in trouble?"

"Sorry, dude. I guess I wasn't thinking." Both Della and Mo sat back down, and just in time.

"Are we acting crazy again, you weirdos?" Mr. Reynolds slinked up to the table, like some weasel approaching. "Do something else wrong, and you are mine. I know you skipped school this morning, but when I reported you rejects to Mrs. Hernandez, she said she had it all under control. Read my lips: 'All under control'. I bet you jerks are going to get called into the office and expelled real soon. You are in big trouble. But if you aren't--"

In his wake, charged Billy. "And Marigold's mom? She's going to be dead meat. You see, my dad's a cop." He smiled widely at his hero, Coach Reynolds.

"What's wrong with your eyes, Billy? Are they black?" the coach asked.

Billy raised his fingers to where the makeup had begun dissolving. "Uh, no, Coach. I mean--"

"Hey, Billy, no problem. I'm thinking you were in a fight, right?"

"Right. That's right, Coach Reynolds. A big fight."

"Does the other guy look worse?" The coach's smile revealed his chipped, yellow teeth.

"Oh yeah. Lots worse than me."

Mr. Reynolds patted Billy on the back. "Good. That's real good. I like a tough guy. That's why you're on my football team, right? You're going to get lots more bruises playing football."

"Right." Billy's eyes shifted from side to side, as if he wasn't so sure about the "lots more bruises".

"Well, great. Hey, let's get in line and get us some food--lots of protein to build big muscles."

Billy charged away, but not before giving Marigold an evil eye and mouthing the words, dead meat.

Mr. Reynolds followed him, and the Misfits began throwing food around. Bags of celery with hummus, popcorn, nuts and cheese, slices of bananas, apples, oranges, and broccoli (dipped in ranch dressing) bounced about the table, and everyone devoured the food. Marigold's thoughts went to what had just happened to Billy's dad that morning. As awful as that man was, she still hoped he would be able to find food on that island, somewhere deep in the Pacific Ocean. She also remembered how her mom had almost gotten killed, as well as Jake's vicious cruelty to Meghan and Billy the night before. As she chomped on a piece of celery with hummus, she knew the Misfits had done the right thing.

"Yes, we did the onnnly right thing," Jade said, crunching down on an apple.

Marigold didn't make a response for two reasons: She didn't want anyone around them to hear her words, and she knew Jade was correct.

The bell rang ending lunch, and Marigold threw the apple and orange into her book bag; they'd be snacks for later. After hearing Jus say, "See ya all tonight, mon", she ran to her locker to exchange books and get to gym. On her swift walk, Mrs. Toon swished up and handed her a piece of paper.

Marigold opened the note and read her homework assignments from the classes she had missed that morning: science, language arts, and art. She said, “Th-Thank you” to Mrs. Hernandez’s sister.

Gym and social studies were both benign; they didn’t cause her any grief. On the bus, still no Tasha, and Marigold hoped she was all right-both physically and emotionally-after her bully encounter the day before. Were the bruises she had probably gotten yesterday at the bus stop embarrassing to her, or was she afraid she would get bullied again? Maybe both? Marigold also hoped she would be back soon and tell her about the gift she had mentioned. Was Tasha’s gift one that would help the Misfits? So lost in her thoughts, she only sorta-kinda heard the mean words yelled at her from the Droobs.

As she was climbing down the bus’s steps, Billy came up behind her and shoved her down onto the grass. Of course, Mr. Carini, who she was very certain had witnessed the act, didn’t make sure she was okay-didn’t even correct Billy. After she managed to stand back up, Billy wasn’t done with her yet. He looked his very scary, makeup-smeared eyes into hers and said, “Don’t be surprised, when you open your door, if you see your mom is dead in the living room. I bet my dad killed her today.”

Marigold felt a chill, even though she knew Billy was wrong. Then, as she watched him trudge away, she thought how he was the one who was about to have a very big surprise today.

"Caw! Caw!" Sinbad cried, doing his loop-de-loops above her head. When she looked up, did he actually wink at her? Mission accomplished, she figured. He was back in time for tonight's meeting, just as Mrs. Hernandez had said he would be.

The door was locked, and Marigold used her key to get in. Instead of finding her mother dead on the living room floor, she found her sitting inches away from the television set.

"Hi, honey!" she said. She had plastered several cartoon Band Aids on her face. "Look at the special news report! There's his car by the river!"

"Officer Smith's police car has been located," the local news reporter said. "If you know his whereabouts, report this to the police immediately."

Marsha Stroop slipped on a sweater from the closet by the front door.

"Where are you going, M-Mom?" Marigold feared the words that were about to come out of her mouth.

"To the police department, of course. The reporter said anyone having any information should come down and tell the police right now. They are searching the river, as we speak! I need to tell the officers when I saw him. How he almost killed me, but then disappeared!"

Marigold was at the front door, her small arms stretched across it. "No! No, M-Mom! Do you want the police to arrest y-you for killing him? D-Do you?"

"Well, no..." Mrs. Stroop said, taking a few steps backward. "But--"

No buts, M-Mother! You were the l-last one to see him. They will probably arrest y-you, especially with your history of v-violence!"

"My 'history of violence'? I don't have a --"

"Are you k-kidding me? You beat up B-Billy, Officer Smith's son!"

"But I only did that to try and protect you from that bully!"

"M-Mom! The police aren't going to care why you beat up B-Billy at the bus stop! They already put you in j-jail for doing that! Can you imagine what they will d-do to you if you say you were the last p-person to see Billy's dad alive?"

Marsha Stroop slowly closed the closet door and looked at the TV. "I guess you are right..."

"Y-Yes, I am positively right, Mom. There is no 'g-guess' about it. You m-must never, ever talk about it to the police or anyone. If you d-do and they put you in jail, well, where w-would I live without you? The court would take m-me out of this house, and I-I would be put in a foster home."

"Oh, no! That would be awful if I had to go to jail, and you couldn't live here anymore."

"Ya think? D-Did you kill him, M-Mother? Did you k-kill Mr. Smith?"

"Of course not! You know I didn't kill that wicked man!"

A video shot of the river being searched by two scuba divers filled the screen.

"Then, you must n-never tell anyone what happened, M-Mom."

"Well, will the principal or any of your little friends tell the police?"

"N-No! He was a k-killer, Mom. Mrs. Hernandez told you he was g-gone for good, and you ought to be glad that's the case. You h-have to promise me you will never tell anyone about how he attacked you, or h-how you were saved."

"And how he disappeared. Isn't it strange how he just disappeared into thin air? He was right there, and then, when I uncovered my eyes, poof, he was gone!"

"Y-Yeah. S-So strange."

"Well, okay, Marigold Marsha Stroop. I promise you I won't ever tell anyone, just like I promised you I would always lock the doors. By the way, is the front door locked?"

Marigold twisted the dead bolt closed. "There. N-Now it is."

"Well, good. Never can be too careful in this town, especially after what happened this morning."

"Right, M-Mom. And we can't ever o-open the door, not for anyone."

"Yes, but I have another question."

"What, M-Mother?"

Marsha scanned her daughter from the top of her head to her toes. "Where are the pretty clothes you wore to school this morning?"

Marigold realized, with a jolt, that she'd forgotten to change back into her other outfit, the outfit her mother "broke her back" at the flower shop to be able to buy her. Uh-oh. She sure didn't want to hurt her mom's feelings.

Mrs. Stroop quickly said, "You look so cute in the ensemble you're wearing. Just like your little friends. Why do you wear those bright, crazy outfits, when you look so cute in nice jeans and a T-shirt?"

Now a bigger jolt. "W-Well, maybe because you w-wash and put the bright clothes out f-for me?"

"And it's high time you start learning to use the washer and dryer. I won't be around the rest of your life to take care of you. I can't keep washing, drying, and folding clothes to put on the chair by your bed. Do you have any idea how tired that makes me?"

"W-Well--"

"That settles it. Tonight, I show you how to do the laundry, and it's not an easy task, I warn you." Marsha Stroop turned to walk into the kitchen. "Now, time for supper, another job that makes me so tired. Something else you need to learn to do, and then you can make supper for me." But Marigold saw the spring in her mom's step, as she skipped ahead and began the job that made her so tired.

Instead of retreating to her room, Marigold helped her mom prepare grilled cheese sandwiches, tomato soup, and a big salad-—her mom guided and gave detailed instructions all the while. Marigold stifled the sarcasm, when her mother told her how to butter the bread, cook the sandwiches, pour a can of tomato soup into a pot, assemble the big tossed salad, and even cut up some fruit. Marigold pressed her lips together, as her mom told her exactly how to perform minute methods of getting dinner together; she kept her mouth shut, even though she certainly knew had to do such simple tasks. But she understood how important these ways of making such a simple supper were to her mother.

Yes, she just did as she was told, knowing the whole time that her mom could have been dead tonight. The realization that her mom had been within minutes of being killed, made her tremble. She needed to thank the Misfits for saving her mother, the most important person in her life. She also wanted to tell them how grateful she was that Officer Smith had been removed to a remote, uninhabited island, somewhere in the Pacific Ocean. The knowledge that Billy's dad would never hurt her mom, Billy, Meghan, Lila-and probably so many others-caused her to breathe a sigh of relief.

"Why do you look so happy?" Marsha asked her daughter, cutting tomatoes into thin slices. "Are you having fun making supper, sweetie?"

"Yes, M-Mom. That's why I-I'm smiling." She was glad her mother hadn't asked about a boyfriend. She couldn't handle that tonight.

"Well, good. It is fun, but it's also hard work, after you have been so busy today, right?" She turned and gave Marigold a wink.

"R-Right," Marigold said, even though she really didn't see what was difficult about making such a simple supper.

"Yes! After I have almost broken my back at work, sometimes it's all I can do to make supper. But you know why I do it?"

"Um- b-because you love me?"

Marsha Stroop gave her a high five. "You got it, baby."

After what Marigold would term a yummy supper, she helped rid up dishes and fill the dishwasher.

After that, she made a snack of green pepper, red pepper, and chunks of cheese on toothpicks; put them into snack bags; and placed them into the fridge for tomorrow's lunch at school.

"Thanks for all your help," Marigold's mom said, squeezing her around the waist. "Time for homework, and then bed?"

"Y-Yep, Mom. So maybe I-I will say good-night now, so you don't have to come into my room tonight? I-I mean, after everything that happened today, you must be so t-tired."

Marsha Stroop nodded. "Yes, but we have another task to perform, before I collapse into a tired heap-"

"W-We do?"

"Yes. I need to teach you how to do laundry, and you must wash your jeans and T-shirt, plus any other clothes, that are building Mount Everest, in the middle of your bedroom floor."

"O-Okay, Mom," Marigold said, as she dashed to her room and returned with a big pile of laundry. Even though there were crazy clothes in that mountain, she figured they needed to be washed, too.

As her mother taught her how to perform laundry duties, Marigold patiently followed the directions. After she had loaded the washer, her mom said when the cycle was over, she would help her out by putting the clothes into the dryer. That way, Marigold could do her homework, get straight A's, become a doctor, and support them for the rest of their lives.

Marigold said, "Thanks, M-Mom."

"But I won't be coming to your bedroom tonight, since I will be too tired to tuck you in, sweetheart. My hip had a 'hitch in the giddy-up', after falling asleep on your bed last night. Don't want that to happen again."

Marigold asked, "A what?"

"'Hitch in the giddy-up'--pain in my hip. Grandma used to say it."

"O-Oh, I get it, since she had horses. Well, night, M-Mom." Marigold gave her a quick smooch on the cheek. "Sweet dreams."

"Sweet dreams, darling."

Marigold was relieved that her mom wasn't going to fall asleep on her bed tonight. Otherwise, Marsha might hear the pepples hit her window, peek outside, and see the Misfits waiting in the yard. That would not be good. Nope. Not good at all.

Chapter 24

As Marigold, Mo, Della, Jade, and Kate sat in their gold capes on the couch in The Contributing Room, Mrs. Hernandez massaged Sinbad's belly with her toes. Jus and The Proprietor flanked her on either side, and Sinbad's snores were rockin' the house. That flight with Officer Jake Smith held tightly in his beak, over to some remote island in the Pacific Ocean, must have really exhausted him, Marigold thought.

Mrs. Hernandez looked over the group and gave them a smile. "Mission accomplished. Officer Jake Smith was lowered and placed, quite gently, on an uninhabited island in the Pacific Ocean. He will never be found, but is unharmed. We owe his arrival to this beautiful bird lying here. Caw!"

Everyone clapped enthusiastically, but even that didn't awaken Sinbad. Thinking of Sinbad got Marigold wondering about Mrs. Hernandez, his "family member" and his belly masseuse. Yes, Sinbad's gift was obvious--he could fly. But what was Mrs. Hernandez's? Her mind ticked off:

Jade-telepathy and hypnosis
Jus-creativity and design
Kate-intelligence
Della-strength
Mo-speed
Herself-empathy
The Proprietor-sensitivity
Sinbad-flight
The Timmers-kindness

Then Kate, on Marigold's other side, said, "Mrs. Hernandez has the gift of sight. Humans can see light in a combination of the colors red, yellow, and green, but it may be quite interesting for you to know crows see a combination of four colors. Crows are able to see better than human beings, so we are fortunate Mrs. Hernandez, who possesses many of the crow's characteristics, has unselfishly offered this gift to the Misfits. Did you happen to notice how she immediately saw Mr. Smith bending over your mother at the river this morning? She was the first."

"Y-Yes! I d-did!"

Mrs. Hernandez stood. Her movement did not cause Sinbad any distress, and he just kept sleeping. She pulled the video camera from her large pocket, and the screen came down. She, The Proprietor, and Jus moved to the couch, as the chandeliers dimmed. The fireplaces' burning wood provided the only light.

"Even though Sinbad was very tired after his long journey today, he still managed to make a discreet visit to the Smith's open window at supper tonight. Now, he has earned a much deserved rest." Mrs. Hernandez looked lovingly over at her "baby", the one in her charge.

Then their principal aimed the camera at the screen, and the group was able to observe Meghan, Lila, and Billy sitting at the table. A small TV was on the counter, and the newscaster related that the search and rescue team had not found Officer Smith.

"Where could he be? Where is my daddy?" Lila asked.

"I don't know, sweetheart," Meghan Smith said. Tears streamed down her face. "I just don't know." Marigold could see a dark, blue bruise on Billy and Lila's mother's face, proof of Jake's behavior the night before.

Billy stared straight ahead with no emotion; the black circles ringing his blue eyes were also visible. "It doesn't make sense. It's like he disappeared into thin air."

"And heee did," Jade said.

Meghan raised her face from her hands and sniffed. "Yes, thin air."

Lila started crying. "Where's my daddy?"

Meghan walked over and raised her daughter into her arms. She rocked her back and forth, as if she were a tiny baby, and sang, "Hush, hush sweet Lila. Lila, don't you cryyy--" But Lila continued to cry.

"Be quiet, Lila. Your crying isn't going to bring him back." Billy picked at the noodles on his plate.

Meghan sat down and held her daughter on her lap. "It's okay to cry, Billy. Nothing wrong with showing your emotions."

"Well, I'm not crying. Dad wouldn't like that-he wants me to be tough." Billy walked over and stood in front of the television set. "His car is at the river, but nobody found his body. That means he's still alive someplace."

"But where." Meghan touched the bruise on her face and winced. "Where would he be?"

"I don't know, but I'm going to find him." Billy got up and slipped on his jacket.

"Billy! You can't go out in the dark! You won't find him in the night, and you could end up getting hurt. Whoever took him might take you," Meghan said.

"I'm going down to the river. I bet he's someplace close to there, and I might find footprints or something." Billy was out the door, leaving Meghan and Lila sitting alone in the kitchen.

"I d-don't get it. Mr. Smith was so m-mean to them. Why do they m-miss him?" Now, Marigold was wondering if the Misfits had done the right thing; maybe Sinbad's taking him far, far away hadn't been the right choice.

"Would youuu have wanted Meghan, Liiila, Billy, and your mom to beee killed?" Jade asked.

"Of course n-not. But Billy, his s-sister, and his mom l-love him."

"A lionnn keeper might love the lion. That doesn't mean heee should be close to him. The lion's genetic maaake-up tells him to kill, and there is nothing that will chaaange that. A lion might kill his keeeper. "

"But why do they still c-care about that man, who could have k-killed them?"

"Because they arrre kind, but that doesn't mean he was worthy of their kiiindness. And let meee assure you, there is more than a verrry good chance that he would have killed one, or alll, of them."

Mrs. Hernandez pointed a sharp fingernail at Marigold. "Please continue to watch the screen."

Mrs. Smith had placed Lila back into her chair and walked to the refrigerator. She took out a piece of ice from the freezer and placed it on her bruised cheek.

"Mama, does your face hurt?"

"Oh yes, sweet girl, it hurts bad--real bad. But your daddy has dislocated my shoulder, broken my jaw, even thrown me against the wall and cracked my spine. I guess a bruised face is nothing in comparison to that."

"Mommy, he shouldn't have hurt you or Billy. That was real mean. Will he ever hurt me?"

"Will he ever hurt you? Well, he hurts Billy and me, but I sure hope he never...."

Lila lowered her head to the table. "But I don't want him to hurt me, Mama."

Meghan raised her tear streaked face to the ceiling and drew a deep breath. Then she looked at her daughter and suddenly, like some wild whirlwind on a mission, she ripped open the refrigerator door. Evidently, she had been to the store that day, because she started jerking out beer cans and pitching them into the trash, before throwing herself back down into her chair.

"Mama, what are you doing? Daddy's going to be real mad, if he can't find his beer in the refrigerator! He might hurt you again!"

"Well, let your daddy get real mad. It could be you next time, Lila. He might hurt you 'real bad', just like he has hurt Billy and me. It's high time I start thinking about you kids and quit being scared of him. We don't need beer-or a monster-here at our house, anymore."

"What are you going to do?"

"I, sweet girl, am going to have the locks changed on the door, so he can't get in. If he tries, I'll call the cops and have him arrested. All the good police officers will listen to me. When I tell the judge how he's been acting, well, he will put him in jail and throw away the key. He won't ever, ever hurt us again."

Meghan crawled up onto her mother's lap. "I'm kinda glad, Mama."

"What are you glad about?" She kissed Lila on top of the head.

"Glad Daddy won't hurt you or Billy again. Won't hurt me."

"That is a real smart way to think." Meghan then reached for her phone, scanned the screen, and punched in some numbers.

"Who are you calling?"

"A locksmith. I just found the number for Stinson Locksmiths, and they have 24 hour service. Going to have our locks changed, before your daddy can get in and hurt us--"

"Ever again." Lila wrapped her small arms around her mom's neck. "Guess it will just be you, Billy, and me living here?"

"Yes, and we are going to be fine, just fine. Even better than fine, Lila."

That's when Billy came through the door. He threw his jacket onto the couch and stomped into the kitchen. "Too dark to see him, Mom, but I am skipping school tomorrow to try and find him in the daytime. I won't let you down."

Meghan lowered Lila to her chair, walked over to Billy, and rested her hands on his shoulders. "Billy, I am having the locks changed tonight."

Alarmed, Billy threw her hands off his shoulders. "What do you mean? Dad won't be able to get into the house if-" Then a look of understanding covered his face. "No! You are not kicking Dad out of this house!"

"Billy, I need to start thinking of you and Lila. It's high time I start protecting both of you."

Billy yanked his jacket back on. "Then I am out of here to find Dad! I love him, even if you don't. I will find him and go with him-wherever he goes!" He was gone, after slamming the door with a loud bam behind him.

The screen went blank, the chandeliers started to illuminate The Contributing Room, and Mrs. Hernandez pressed the button to raise the screen. The leaders resumed sitting on their thrones.

It was so silent in that room, Marigold thought you could have heard a feather drop. Finally, she said: "I-I still don't get it."

"What don't you understand, Marigold?" Mrs. Hernandez asked.

"I-I still don't get why Billy wants to f-find his dad, when his d-dad hurt him and his mom."

"Kate? I believe a psychological analysis is due." Mrs. Hernandez flapped her arms at her sides. "Caw!"

Sinbad continued his snoring, and he didn't adjust his position under his keeper's toes.

Kate cleared her throat and said, "Many psychologists have studied this phenomenon. Although most children love both of their parents, look to them for nurturing and security, the strongest role model is often the same-sex parent. In his life, Billy's father probably was that person. His dad most likely had more influence on him than anyone else--more than his mother, his sister, his friends. That doesn't mean he doesn't love those people, but he probably patterned himself after his father. He feels that he is part of his father and his father is part of him. It is very essential to understand, however, that child abuse can inflict horrid consequences upon the abused: The child's behavior, mood, and mental health are all affected. Billy is fortunate he has a kind, loving mother, whom he can draw upon for support."

"Thank you, Kate. Does anyone else have something to add?" Mrs. Hernandez's black eyes surveyed the group before her.

"It isss very good, Marigold, that Jaaake is far, far away. If he were still innn Billy's life, there would be an excelllent chance that Billy would end up having maaajor mental health issues, not to downplay the fact thaaat he would probably treat his children in the same manner, if heee wasn't killed by his dad first."

Marigold wiped a tear away. "But he l-loves his dad. His dad is so important in h-his life. We t-took that person to a place where he will never f-find him!"

Mo was up and running in circles. "People are loving things that aren't good for them all the time!"

"Mo isss right. Remember what I said about the lion and its taaamer? And take the example of somebody loving tooo drink beer to the point where he or she can't see or think, then gets behind the wheeel, and kills an innocent person in a car crash. Thaaat isn't good. A perrrson who loves heroine, and his kids go without foood, is not good. Babies born with a cocaaaine addiction, because their mother loved that drug, is not goood."

"And k-kids, who love parents-e-even though they beat them up-is not g-good," Marigold said.

Jus ran from his throne and high-fived Marigold. "Yeah, mon. You are bein' exactly right." Then he jogged back to his throne.

"Now, the big question probably looming in all of our minds, is how do we get Billy to a place where we can help him?" Mrs. Hernandez asked.

"And how do we help him?" The Proprietor asked.

Della began her kicks and chops, a round-off across the floor. "Count on me, dudes! I'm on it! I will knock him onto the ground; after that, Mo and I will grab him and take him wherever we can start working on his behavior!"

"No! Y-You can't hurt him!" Marigold started marching toward Della. "H-He's been hurt enough!"

Jade shuffled her feet to where Marigold stood. "Ommm. Marigooold, Della will not do her martial arrrts on Billy. We, the Misfits, willl not allow that. She only attacks if weee, or someone we are proootecting, is in danger." Then her hands were in front of her chest, and she gracefully lowered herself back onto the couch. Marigold sat, as well.

"No, to the Della force-machine, but I have been designin' a plan which I believe will be workin'", Jus said. "I will be wantin' your input this time." Della plunked down onto the couch.

The room was so hushed, only Sinbad's snoring sounded. That, and the intermittant whipping of Mrs. Hernandez's raising and lowering her arms. Marigold wondered if she was about to levitate.

The Proprietor wavered up and stuck one crooked arm into the air. "I believe we are ready to hear your plan, Jus, if you would care to share it."

Jus stood and said, "Marigold, you may have been noticin' that the last time we leaders were makin' a design, we stayed up all night and informed you the next day."

Mrs. Hernandez said, "You made the design, Jus. You are our creative guru."

"Whatever, mon. This time, though, it is really important that all of us are a decision-makin' force. I am havin' some issues comin' up with the best way to be implementin' what needs to happen."

The Proprietor raised his other arm. "Why don't you tell us what you have developed thus-far?"

Jade was humming, but then she said, "I thiiink Jus already has a great starrrt."

Jus looked down, and Marigold thought he almost looked embarrassed. "Okay, mon. I think it goes without sayin' that our agenda must be implemented, as soon as we can be gettin' started."

"I am ready, dudes!" Della flipped her body through the air.

Mo said with a hop on one foot. "I understand the reason for being speedy!"

"How can we be an integral part of this decision-making process, Jus?" Kate asked.

"First we need to be locatin' Billy, in whatever spot he traveled to tonight, mon."

"I believe that Sinbad will be the 'moving force' in this endeavor? Caw!" Sinbad opened one eye, then closed it again.

Jus nodded. "Yeah. Sinbad will be helpin' us by locatin' Billy."

At that, Sinbad batted his wings, darted up, and made large loops through the air.

"After Sinbad is findin' Billy, let's have him bring him someplace, where we can all be meetin' with him." Jus tapped a finger on his chin. "But where, mon?"

"S-So Sinbad will pick Billy up in his beak and t-take him someplace? P-Pick him up in his beak, like he did t-to his dad?" Marigold asked.

"Yesss, and remember Billy will not see Sinbad. He will just know heee is traveling through the air and then put dowwwn somewhere."

Marigold put her hands on her cheeks. "That w-will be so scary!"

"Yeah, but probably not as scary as getting hit by his dad, dude." Della was up with a kick. "Remember how I took Jake down? He didn't have a chance!"

"Yesss, Della, we all remember. Now, siiit down, please," Jade said.

She did, but Mo started running circles around the group. "Yeah, but who found his gun and threw it out into the river?!!"

"You did, mon. But can ya be sittin' down, so we can be makin' some decisions?"

Mo did.

"Now, the question is bein', where should Sinbad put him down?" Jus closed his eyes and rubbed his eyelids.

"H-How about here? R-Right in this room?"

Kate said, "No, Marigold. The ramifications of Billy knowing about this place could be quite disadvantageous to all of us. This is a secretive location, and it has been for thousands of years. Can you imagine what would occur if Billy imparted information about this place to the Droobs?"

"That c-could be terrible."

"Can ya be imaginin' Billy and the Droobs findin' the shed and slidin' down, while we are meetin', mon?" Jus asked.

Marigold shook her head. "N-No. I get it. Billy can't ever know where w-we meet, and he can't know about what we are d-doing here."

"Youuu are right, Marigold--"

"S-So where can we m-meet with him?"

Kate stood. "I propose the location be someplace unfamiliar to Billy, so he will not escape and run home, or relate to the Droobs where he was. Should he convey that information to them, they might invade, while we are gathered there another time. Also, I believe it needs to be a place within a reasonable proximity to our residences. We need to arrive there, do the decided procedure, and depart for home."

"Yeah, Kate, good suggestions. I am right now arrangin' a method to be helpin Billy', in my mind." Jus closed his eyes, and everyone else in the room remained quiet. Even Sinbad ceased soaring, and he settled his feathered-self back down at Mrs. Hernandez's feet.

"I've got it, mon!" Jus exclaimed.

Chapter 25

The Misfits on the couch were silent. Both Mrs. Hernandez and the Proprietor had turned their heads in Jus's direction. Finally, Jus stood and said, "I see it happenin' this way. Sinbad will be flyin' tonight and findin' Billy."

Now Sinbad tilted his head in Jus's direction.

"Yes, first be findin' Billy tonight, and then fly' him to the barn, behind Farmer Maxwell's vacant home. It is located far enough away to be unfamiliar to Billy, but close enough for us to be gettin' there by bikes, mon. Is everyone here havin' a bike?"

Marigold knew her bike hadn't been ridden in awhile, but yes, she had one. She joined those on the couch shouting, "Yes!"

"I will be driving my car," Mrs. Hernandez stated.

"That is bein' fine, but park behind the outbuilding, just to the north of the barn. Misfits, you need to be parkin' your bikes there, too. Can't be havin' Billy or anyone else recognizin' your car, Mrs. Hernandez, or any of our bikes."

"B-But won't he know who we are, when w-we meet with him in the b-barn?" Marigold couldn't figure out how Billy wouldn't recognize them, if he was going to see them face-to-face, in the barn.

"Thaaat will be determined in Jusss's design. How will youuu get there, Mr. Proprietor?"

"I will not be attending this gathering," The Proprietor announced in his creaking voice.

"We are understandin' your wish to be stayin' here, mon. Mo, can you be runnin' and tellin' The Proprietor, as sooon as Sinbad delivers Billy to the barrrn, and Jade notifies youuu?"

"Yeah, man! I can run and do that!" Mo pointed at one of his large shoes and nodded.

"Thank you, Mo," The Proprietor said.

"I can also pedal on my bike really fast to the barn, right after school!" Mo jumped up.

"Great, Mo. Tonight, I will be stayin' in the barn with Billy," Jus said.

Marigold thought Jus's parents would be worried if he didn't come home.

"Jusss doesn't live with his parents. Ommm." Jade recrossed her legs.

"Wh-Where does he live?"

Marigold was interrupted when Della did a round-off, back hand spring and shouted, "Mo, you had better let me ride on your bike's handlebars! You and Jus will need my help, if Billy tries to leave!"

Mo said, "Okay, Dell!"

"W-Won't Billy be upset to b-be kept all night in a b-barn?"

"Nooo, because if it is all right with you, Jus, I will hypnotiiize him, before Sinbad picks him up, and he will sleep until weee all arrive. I can dooo that, since he will be in close proximity to a Misfit."

"Hypnosis? Yeah, mon. That is a good idea. You can be wakin' him up during the time we are tryin' to be helpin' him. We will try to be givin' him ideas on how to change his behavior."

"I understaaand. Sinbad, when you fiiind him, let me know. I will join youuu to hypnotize him before yourrr flight. After our meeeting in the barn, I will hypnotize him again. He won't remember the triiip over, trip home, or any of us. I hope heee remembers what we tell him, though. Ommm."

"Why c-can't we skip school t-tomorrow?" Marigold thought they needed to get started right away.

"Because school is bein' important, mon." Jus looked over at Mrs. Hernandez, who nodded.

"I hope he implements the teachings we attempt to convey," Kate said.

"Yeah, me too." Jus stared up, into the black sky, above their heads.

"It maaay take more than one hypnotic session to chaaange his behavior."

"Yes, Jade," Mrs. Hernandez said. "We understand."

"What happens if B-Billy doesn't change? What if h-he keeps being a bully?"

"Then we vote again, regarding his future," Mrs. Hernandez stated.

As he sniffled, The Proprietor said, "He might have to be removed like his father, but of course, to a different location. I just hate to think that. No hypnosis would have worked on Officer Jake Smith; he was too far gone, into a dark world, of evilness and cruelty."

Marigold said, "I-I sure hope Billy changes and stops acting the w-way he has been."

"Weee all hope that happens, but we can't forrrce Billy to change the way he has been behaaaving for so many years. Heee needs to decide he wants to."

"All we can do, mon, is try. We can be tryin' with all our might."

"C-Can you locate Billy and tell S-Sinbad, Jade?" Marigold asked.

"Nooo. Billy is not a Misfit. But afterrr Sinbad is with him and he alerts meee, I will know his location, get in cloooose proximity, and be able to hypnotize him-liiike I have done with your mother."

"O-Oh. I get it."

"So, have all questions been answered, mon?" Jus scanned their faces.

"Jus, in my estimation, since no one is posing another inquiry, your design--so well developed--is ready to be executed," Kate said.

Sinbad was now up onto his tall legs and beating his wings so hard, Marigold clutched the couch's cushion. Were they all going to be blown away? The Proprietor jumped from his throne and scurried through the door, leading into The Tropical Rain Forest Room.

Jus joined the Misfits, who had backed away to a space by that same door, and stood huddled together. Through a space between her fingers, Marigold made out Mrs. Hernandez, batting her arms energetically up and down, and crying, "Caw! Caw! Caw!"

In great swirls of blackness, Sinbad disappeared through the opening in the sky, and the room became calm once more. Mrs. Hernandez lowered her arms and stopped cawing. She strolled across the space to join the Misfits.

Jus stated, "You all are on your own tonight, mon. I will be headin' out to get my bike, then ridin' to the barn."

"W-Won't your mom worry about where you are, J-Jus?", Marigold asked.

Jus didn't reply. Marigold thought, just another question unanswered.

Jade announced, "As sooon as Sinbad arrives, and I know the locaaation, I will travel to hypnotize Billy."

"Thank you, Jade," Jus said.

"But Jusss, please remember, not everyone can be hypnotiiized."

Jus turned toward Jade. "I am understandin', mon."

"What h-happens if you can't hypnotize h-him, Jade?" Marigold asked.

Kate interjected, "Jade is only capable of placing Billy, into a hypnotic state. if he is receptive to that process. If he is not, we will need to proceed with a new agenda ,which, I assure you, Jus will formulate and present for our understanding and implementation."

Della kicked the air. "Jeeze, Kate. What she is saying, dude, is that Jade can only do what she can do (chop, chop); we need to roll with it (somersault); and if it doesn't work, Jus will come up with something new."

"O-Okay." Marigold smiled in Kate's direction.

"Thanks, Kate. Jade, will you please be informin' the Misfits at school tomorrow what is happenin'? Kate and Jade, can you be ridin' your bikes to Marigold's house right after school, so she can be followin' ya? Mo and Della will have already left. You all need to be travelin' on your bikes in daylight, because of safety reasons, mon. Mrs. Hernandez will be drivin' to the barn right after school."

Everyone affirmed Jus's words with nods and shouts, as Mrs. Hernandez raised her arms and floated up into that black, diamond-sprinkled sky. Marigold watched her exit, marveling all the while.

Just before Jus loped ahead, he pointed a finger at Mo. "Don't forget, mon, that as soon as Jade is transferrin' her knowledge to you, regardin' Billy's location and his successful drop at the barn (not a painful drop, Marigold-he will be carefully lowered), run and tell The Proprietor."

"You got it, Jus!" Mo ran a zig-zag pattern through the space.

"As sooon as I know everything, Mo, I will tell youuu. Ommm." Jade scooted ahead, and everyone started for home.

***

In the morning, Marigold was off to school on the bus, without any major bullying, since Billy wasn't there. She was elated when Tasha boarded the bus and sat beside her.

"I-I am so glad you are here today. I saw how y-you were knocked d-down at the bus stop and worried y-you had been h-hurt. Are you o-okay?"

"Not really."

"Did y-you get cuts and br-bruises?"

"Yeah, but it was worse than that. I faked being sick, so I could stay home."

"What w-was worse than b-being hurt by that Droob?"

"Tyler, Billy's friend? Well, he whispered something, and I heard him cause of my gift."

Now Marigold was majorly tuned in. "Wh-What is your 'gift'?"

"I have really big ears, see?" Tasha flipped back her hair.

Marigold observed the biggest ears on a human being that she had ever seen before, but said, "I-I think you're b-beautiful." And she did.

Latasha recovered her ears. "Well, I have to make sure I keep them covered up, cause kids bully me about them—and cause I'm African-American. They call me black Dumbo, among other things."

"I'm s-sorry. What did that b-bully, Tyler, say?"

"Well, cause of my gift of great hearing, I could hear him whisper, 'Billy and I hate black people. Your kind needs to go back to Africa. We are going to hurt you bad.' Other people wouldn't have heard him, but I can hear anything. Right now, I can hear what kids are saying, clear in the back of this bus."

"You c-can?" Marigold felt a surge of excitement, thinking maybe Tasha could be a Misfit, for sure.

"Uh huh. I can."

Marigold smiled. "I think m-maybe things will start getting better f-for you." Then she added, "You need to t-tell Mrs. Hernandez about the b-bullying, though."

"The principal? She wouldn't understand--"

As the bus stopped in front of the school, and the kids started pushing each other to disembark, Tasha said, "Nope. Nothing will ever get better." Then she was gone, in the throng of kids, entering the building.

Marigold shouted, "Oh, I wouldn't b-be so sure about that!" then wondered if Tasha had heard her.

It was during homeroom, while attendance was being taken, that Della (masked and in black) leaped through the door and ran back to Marigold's desk. She whispered, "Emergency meeting in the office."

Marigold picked up her book bag and started toward the front.

"And just where do you think you are going?" Mrs. Drebel asked.

"T-To the office."

"And you have a pass to go to the office?"

"N-No, mam."

With no Billy to stir everyone up, the class was actually quiet. Marigold smoothed down her blue T-shirt and headed back to her desk. Great. She was needed in the office, but obviously Della hadn't told Mrs. Drebel that.

After Marigold restlessly shifted her body back and forth in her seat for a few minutes, Mrs. Hernandez's voice crackled over the room's speaker. "Mrs. Drebel?"

"Yes."

"Mrs. Drebel, would you please send Marigold Stroop to the office?"

At that, the kids started chanting: "In trouble, in trouble, in trouble--"

"Fine," Mrs. Drebel grumbled.

Marigold was off, jogging down the slippery hall. Once she skidded into the main office, and Miss Pinlay pointed toward Mrs. Hernandez's office, she ran there. Then she collapsed into a chair beside Jade. Della and Kate stood by the desk.

"Mrs. D-Drebel didn't want me to leave."

Mrs. Hernandez raised her thin black eyebrows at Della.

"Sorry, dude. I forgot to grab a pass."

"It's o-okay," Marigold said. "Everyone m-makes mistakes."

"Jade?" Mrs. Hernandez turned complete attention her way.

"This morrrning, at exactly 12:02 a.m., Sinbad locaaated Billy beneath Solly Bridge in the park. It was the saaame bridge you hid under, Marigold."

Marigold winced. "That's a-a scary place."

"Evidently, he was sittiiing close to that same drunk man and shivering."

"Sinbad needed me there to kick and chop, kick and chop." Della split the air with her hands, just for good measure. "Been there, done that."

Now, Mrs. Hernandez's voice took on an exasperated tone. "Please continue, Jade."

"Welll, Sinbad notified me that heee had located Billy, so III went to Solly Bridge and hypnoootized Billy, with a suggestion to fall asleep. It worrrked."

"That's good, very good." Mrs. Hernandez walked to the open window and made a tap, tap sound on the glass. Within seconds, Sinbad's face filled the space.

"Jade, it was quite advantageous, for all of us, that Billy was receptive to the hypnosis and fell asleep." Kate joined the principal, after she opened the window to pet the huge bird's head.

"Yesss, it was 'advantageous', Kate, duuue to my talent and my skill, to put Billy intooo a hypnotic trance, with a strong suggestion for sleeep." Marigold thought she heard Jade make a low growl.

"Jade, we all are thankful for your gift," Mrs. Hernandez said.

Marigold nodded. "Yes, w-we are so lucky y-you can do that."

Jade closed her eyes. "Sinbad picked Billy up with his beeeak and transported him to the barrrn, where Jusss was lying asleep, on a pile of haaay."

"Caw! Great work, Sinbad!" Sinbad pushed himself further through the open window, and Mrs. Hernandez kissed him on the head.

With her eyes still closed, Jade said, "I immeeediately informed Mo, who rushed to see The Proprietor and giiive him that information. I belieeeve he's still underground with The Propriiietor. "

"Wonderful, " Mrs. Hernandez said. Sinbad fruitlessly tried to shove his entire body through the space. "Sorry, baby. Not going to happen."

With a loud, "Caw!", Sinbad was off, making huge circles in the blue sky.

"What if B-Billy had woke up on the trip t-to the barn?" Marigold asked.

Kate said, "Remember, because Billy is not a Misfit, he would not have observed Sinbad. All he would have acknowledged was that he was being swept through the air, by some force, not his own."

"In other words," Della said with a kick, "Billy just would have thought he was somehow flying through the air like Superman!" She adjusted her black mask.

"Thankfullly, that did not occur." Jade pressed her eyes closed. "Right now, Billy is still sleeeping beside Jus on the barn's floorrr."

"We shall leave for the barn immediately after school." Mrs. Hernandez peered out the window. "I can see Sinbad about a mile away, most likely flying toward the barn."

"Y-You can see that?"

"Yes, Marigold. Remember that Mrs. Hernandez's gift is sight. Her vision is so excellent, other birds may be envious." Kate walked over to Marigold. "All I could perceive was a blue sky and several puffy, white clouds."

Della flipped right there in place. "In other words, dude, Mrs. Hernandez can see real good."

Marigold didn't want to tell Della that she had perfectly understood Kate and simply said, "W-Wow. That is f-fantastic, Mrs. Hernandez."

Mrs. Hernandez smiled. "Thank you. As I become more bird-like, I imagine I will see even better."

Marigold's thoughts switched to her sisters, Mrs. Toon and Ms Hernandez.

"Day by daaay, her sisters' affinity and involvement, in the birds' kingdom, is becoming stronger."

Suddenly, Mo ran in. "Mrs. Hernandez! I think we should leave now to go to the barn!"

Mrs. Hernandez sighed. "No, Mo. Let me review with you Jus's previous statement: 'School is important'. I happen to agree. Because of that, we shall leave for the barn after school."

"But J-Jus isn't here at sc-school."

Mrs. Hernandez explained, "Jus's job, as one of our leaders, requires him to be at the barn. I have given him an excused absence. He will catch up later, via the internet. "

Jade closed her eyes. "Ommm. Sinbad has arrived at the barn. Billy is still asleep on the hay and Jus, now awake, is sitting beside him."

"Thank you, Jade." Mrs. Hernandez walked back to her desk and sat down. "Please advise me if that should change."

Still with her eyes closed, Jade said, "Ommm. Willl do."

Mrs. Hernandez handed out passes. "Now, skadoodle to first period! Caw!"

Chapter 26

Marigold made her way to math class. Once there, she attempted to pay attention to what Mr. Nicholson was teaching. It wasn't long before she realized that wasn't going to happen. All she could think about was Jus, in the barn with Billy (who was hopefully going to stay asleep). Then after school, she would be pedaling away on her bike and following Kate and Jade to the barn, the place where Jus's method to help Billy would happen. Mo and Della would already be there, and Mrs. Hernandez would arrive by car. Their principal probably would get there before them, too.

Maybe Jus and Mrs. Hernandez thought school was important, but today? Today, even with the math teacher standing on the table and flashing his laser beam around the room? Today, when there was no chance she could concentrate on algebra formulas? Were the other Misfits able to think about whatever their teachers were trying to teach them? She doubted it. And Jus was allowed to skip school because he was a Misfit leader? In a daze, she traveled from class to class, thinking about her important mission to a barn tonight. It would be happening soon, but not soon enough, in her opinion.

At last! The final bell announced the end of school! Out the door, Marigold ran, without even stopping at her locker. Onto the bus, she bolted, and into a seat where she hoped Tasha would join her. So intent was she at watching for Tasha, bopping up the steps, she only half-listened to the words coming from the Droobs. But maybe they weren't saying negative things, since Billy wasn't at school today. Their leader was absent, and when he came back, would he be different? Would Bully Billy become Nice Billy? Could that really happen?

Finally, Tasha stepped slowly up the steps and slid down into the seat beside Marigold. She looked like she had been crying, and she stared down into her lap. She had been the last one to enter, and Mr. Carini cranked his big head around to yell, "Whats-a matter with you? I almost left without you-a!" Then he put the huge yellow machine into gear and roared off.

"A bad d-day?" Marigold asked.

Tasha pulled a tissue from her purse and blotted her eyes. "Yeah."

"What h-happened?" Marigold touched her new friend on the arm.

"It doesn't matter, cause it's not going to change." She blew her nose, wadded up the tissue, and stuffed it into her pocket.

"It m-matters to me." She guessed some bullies were alive and well, even without Billy there.

"Well, today-that Tyler?"

"Y-Yeah?"

"Today he said--" Tasha covered her face, with her shaking hands, and sobbed.

"I'm s-sorry about what that Droob said to you, r-real sorry."

Tasha looked her beautiful dark eyes up into Marigold's green ones. "He told me I ought to just kill myself. That Billy and everybody else agrees. That all I am-all I am-is filthy, black garbage, with big ears." She gasped for breath, and Marigold wrapped her in a big hug.

"B-Billy told me I should die before, in a n-note that the teacher read in front of-of the class. But I promise y-you, things are going to get b-better. I can't tell you h-how I know that, but they are. Y-You have to believe me."

"No, it won't. You better quit hugging me, though, cause Tyler is saying mean stuff and making fun of us. He is calling us the gooney, gay girls, and the other kids are laughing. They are saying other real mean things, words I can't repeat."

Marigold lowered her arms and turned to look behind them. "B-But Tyler is sitting clear in the very b-back--" She realized Tyler must not need Billy around to continue on with his meanness.

"I know. Sometimes my gift of hearing isn't a good thing. I hear everything, even coming from real far away."

Marigold again thought about Latasha's gift, and what an asset she'd be to the Misfits. When things settled down, she would mention it to Mrs. Hernandez, The Proprietor, and Jus-their Misfit leaders.

"Well, thanks for listening," Latasha said. The bus had arrived at her stop, and she stood to begin her walk toward the open door. "You're a good friend, because you really care; it's like you can put yourself in my place." Then she scurried down the bus's steps. Some Droobs, with Tyler in the front, followed.

Marigold popped up and walked forward to watch Latasha through the front window. She wanted to make sure she didn't get hurt again.

"Whats-a matter with you-a? Sit down!" Mr. Carini tilted his rear view mirror so he could see Marigold better.

"I'm w-watching my friend, l-like you ought to be! Don't want h-her getting hurt like last t-time."

"Mind your own-a business!"

"She is m-my business!" From what she could see, Latasha escaped uninjured and ran from the bus stop. Then like some crazy man, with road rage, the bus driver pulled out. He careened away, at such a great speed, Marigold fell onto the filthy floor-again.

In his rear view mirror, Marigold could see Mr. Carini's lips curl into a cruel sneer. "See what I mean-a? You are not-a in your seat? You get hurt-a!"

There were many loud cheers and giggles. Her getting yelled at, then crawling across the dirty floor to her seat and raising herself up again, was oh, so funny to the Droobs. Hilarious, even without Billy there. Well, at least Latasha had left unhurt, and Marigold hoped nothing bad happened on her run home.

In a few minutes, the bus arrived at her stop, and she was the first to scramble down the steps. She didn't allow herself to look at the crazy bus driver or listen to the kids' mean words. In a huge, bird's beak, the Droobs' ring- leader had been flown to a barn, where he now slept. Oh, if they only knew.

When Marigold unlocked the door and entered her house, she was surprised at how quiet it was. Her mom didn't greet her at the door with questions about how her day went. That made a lump form in her throat. What if her mom wasn't okay? That recent happening, regarding her mother's injury and near-death experience, was stuck in her brain like a very sharp needle; however, she knew Jake Smith was far, far away.

A snore from the recliner drew her attention there. Marigold smiled, knowing Jade had already been at work. Her mom was hypnotized, sleeping away, and none too soon. Just as Marigold turned to close the door, she saw Jade and Kate sitting on their bikes, in front of her house.

Marigold dumped her book bag and locked the door behind her. Off, she ran to the garage to get her red, rusty bike, and within minutes, she was pedaling behind the other two. The trip Jade and Kate led her on went up hills, down hills, through the woods, around the park, over the bridge, behind a row of houses, onto a bumpy, gravel road, and into the country. At last, Jade, then Kate, and finally Marigold stopped behind an outbuilding by a barn. Mrs. Hernandez's car and two other bikes were there. Marigold knew that meant everyone had arrived.

"Youuu are correct, Marigold," Jade said, while the three of them parked their bikes. Jusss, Mo with Della, Mrs. Hernaaandez, and now weee are here.

Marigold took in their surroundings. To those observing this barn from the road, they would think this was just an ordinary, faded, red barn. An uninhabited, gray farmhouse stood nearby. Anyone traveling by would have no idea what was about to occur inside that barn.

Jade pushed the barn's splintered red door to the side, and the three of them stepped inside. Marigold helped her slide it closed, once more, behind them. It smelled like sweet hay and of animals-cows and horses, who must have resided here, once upon a time.

"Welcome, mon," Jus said. Daylight slipped through cracks in the barn's siding, and Marigold squinted to locate him. When she finally saw him sitting next to Billy, who was lying on his side, she also located Mrs. Hernandez, Mo, and Della sitting on Billy's other side. There was not a sound, except for Mo's shuffling feet, sliding quickly back and forth in the hay.

"Mo!" Jus whispered. "Stop!"

"Sorry!" Mo said.

Mrs. Hernandez said, "First, I must report that everything has gone according to plan. Jade, your gift provided us with the results for which we had been hoping. Billy did fall into a deep sleep, right after Sinbad arrived, and he has remained asleep this entire time in the barn."

"J-Jade, I so appreciate what you did to g-get Billy here," Marigold said.

There was a chorus of whispered agreement from the others.

"I diiid not fly him here. You neeed to thank Sinbad for that."

Mrs. Hernendez quickly interjected, "Sinbad could not have accomplished what he did, without your gifts, Jade."

Jade said, "Thaaank you."

Mrs. Hernandez swished a shiny, black sleeve into the air. "Now, Jade, are you ready?"

"I ammm. When Billy awakens, he will be in a traaance. He will hear what we say, but he will not rememberrr us. Hopefully, whaaat we tell him will make an impact."

Kate said, "The trance of sleep will now be transferred to wakefulness, without the memory of our interactions with him."

"I think we got it, dude. We got what Jade said." Della made a chop, chop.

Kate interrupted with, "Your orchestration of this agenda is excellent, Jade. Thank you."

Jade nodded but continued her position of eyes closed, hands in front of chest, and humming.

Mo was now up and jogging in place. "So let's get started! I can hardly wait!"

Now Mrs. Hernandez raised both arms, and she looked like she was about to take flight. Marigold hoped she didn't make a loud, "Caw!" Instead, the principal said, "Mo! Stop! Sit down!"

"Sorry," he replied, sinking down into a heap. "Just anxious."

Jade stood in front of Billy and stated in a very clear voice, "Billy, whennn I snap my fingers, you will awaaaken. You will seee all of us sitting here, and you will listen to the words we saaay, but you will not reeemember who spoke to you or this place. You will not remember yourrr flight over or back. You will rememberrr, however, our suggestions to you, and you will act accordingly. Pleeease nod if you understand."

Although still sleeping on his side, Marigold could see Billy's head moving up and down.

"At the sound of myyy fingers snapping, you will awaaaken and sit up." Jade snapped her fingers, and Billy sat up, eyes wide open.

"Does he know we are sittin' here?" Jus whispered.

"Yes, heee knows, but he doesn't carrre."

"Okay, mon. Do your thing, Jade."

"Billy, you are in a saaafe place. We are gathered here to tryyy to help you. Pleeease nod if you understaaand."

Billy slowly raised his head up, down, and then his glassy eyes stared straight ahead.

"Weee will now take turns giving you suggestions regarding how youuu should begin acting. After each suggestion, if you understaaand, you will nod."

Again, Billy nodded.

"Billy, you neeed to stop showing off." After he nodded, Jade said, "Jus, would you pleeease suggest, and then design the order of speeeakers?"

"Yeah, mon. I can be doin' that." He cleared his throat and said, "Billy, you must stop encouragin' others to be mean."

When Billy nodded, Jus said, "Marigold?"

"B-Billy? You need t-to stop saying mean w-words."

He nodded.

"Mrs. Hernandez?" Jus gestured toward their principal.

"Caw! Billy, you have to stop getting in trouble and showing up in the office."

Again, his head went up, then down.

"Mo? Your turn, mon."

Mo slid his feet quickly back and forth, but this time nobody corrected him. "Billy, you have to stop tripping people in the halls and classrooms!"

Billy nodded.

"Della? Suggest, without kickin' or choppin', mon."

"Okay." Della sat still and said, "Billy-no more mean notes, dude."

Billy nodded and yawned. Marigold wondered if the sleep trance was still affecting him.

"Kate? It's bein' your turn."

Della interjected, "You need to tell him in simple words, dude. Don't talk like a dictionary."

Again, Mrs. Hernandez's arms waved above her head. "Della!"

"Okay, okay-" Della said.

"Movin' forward. Movin' forward. Kate?" Jus asked.

Kate slowed down her speech down, like she was speaking to a small child. "Your dad-was cruel-and-you-must-quit-trying-to-find him." She aimed a sarcastic smile at Della. "Simple enough, Della?"

Billy nodded.

"And finally, time to be finishin' up, Jade." Jus nodded at their resident hypnotist.

Jade lowered her hands and opened her eyes. "Ommm. Billy, you have listened to the worrrds spoken to you. You will reeemember and put them intooo effect. You will not remember this plaaace, or whooo suggested these changes of behavior to you. Pleeease nod if you understand."

He did.

"Goood. Now, when I snaaap my fingers, you will fall asleep. You will awaaaken, in your front yard, when I snap my fingers again. Youuu will not remember your trip here orrr home. Do you understaaand? Say yesss if you do."

Billy said in a loud, robotic voice, "Yes!"

"Sinbaad awaits." Jade snapped her fingers, and Billy fell back down onto the hay, a konked-out boy. "Mrs. Hernandez, will youuu please open the doorrr?"

Mrs. Hernandez stood and slowly slid the door wide open. Sinbad managed to squeeze his huge body through the space and grabbed Billy's red jacket in his beak, before carefully waddling his way back outside. With all the Misfits gathering at the open barn's door, Sinbad batted his great, black wings and was off into the sky, a red bundle swayed back and forth in his orange beak.

"Safe travels, my baby," Mrs. Hernandez sang, then blew a kiss into the air. Marigold was glad the bird wasn't bound, for the South Pacific, to some uninhabited island. She was happy Billy was going home, and she hoped he would apply the Misfits' words, so he didn't have to be removed.

Once Sinbad and his cargo were out of sight, the group joined in a round of applause.

"The fourth step of the plan is right now bein' accomplished, mon." Jus rubbed his tired eyes.

Marigold wondered what four steps had been accomplished, but she didn't have to wonder for long. Jade quickly explained:

"Step One: Sinbad fouuund Billy, and I hypnotized him to sleeep.

"Step Two: Sinnnbad delivered Billy, to thisss barn, where Jus awaited.

"Step Three: We arriiived, Billy was awakened, and weee gave him suggestions.

"Step Four: I hypnotized him back to sleeep, and Sinbad is nowww flying him home."

Marigold nodded. "O-Oh, okay. Thanks, Jade."

"And now, Step Five, mon. It is time for us to be headin' out," Jus said.

As they walked to their modes of transportation, and Mrs. Hernandez closed the barn's door, Marigold looked into the clouds. Who would ever believe what had just happened? The amazing things she had observed just kept getting bigger and better!

How had she ever been allowed to be part of these adventures? These Misfits had invited her, of all people, to join their group. These bullied people were recruited by The Proprietor, discovered their talents, and then taught her about her gift of empathy. Nope, nobody, unless they were a member of this group, would believe what had just occurred. Mrs. Hernandez, with a wave, roared by in her car.

Jade slung her leg over her bike and said, "You are riiight about that. Now, follow meee to Billy's house and then to yourrrs. I have two people tooo awaken."

"B-But can't you do that long-distance?"

"No, mon," Jus said, after releasing his bike's brake.

"Remember, proximity of a Misfit, to the person Jade is hypnotizing or releasing from hypnosis, is necessary," Kate explained. Then she began pedaling away on her shiny, blue bicycle.

"O-Oh, right." Marigold pedaled on her rusty red bike, as hard as she could, to follow Kate, Jus, and finally Jade. Mo, with Della on his handlebars, was far in front of them. Like two bouncing dots fading farther and farther from sight, that pair of speed and strength traveled ahead into the countryside.

Finally, with a bumpety-bump-bump, Jade, then Jus, next Kate, and finally Marigold came to a stop in front of the Smith house. Yep, there was Billy sleeping on his front lawn. Jade motioned them behind a row of shrubs bordering the Smith yard. They dismounted their bikes, and once in a huddle peeking through the branches, Jade snapped her fingers. Not only did Billy open his eyes; he also jumped up and ran to his front door. After it didn't open, he started pounding and pounding hard.

Mrs. Smith, with Lila, opened the door and screamed, "Billy! You're home! Where have you been?"

Billy swayed back and forth, like he was trying to regain his balance. "I was under Solly Bridge in the park."

"You have been under the bridge in the park? This whole time?"

"No. Not this whole time."

"Well, where else have you been?"

"I-I don't know."

She wrapped him in a hug. "Come in, my honey bun. We have missed you so much!"

Stepping through the door, Billy yelled, "Is Dad here? I couldn't find him. He had better be here-or else!" Then he ran inside, followed by his mom and sister, before the door closed.

Marigold exchanged concerned looks with the others.

"Uh-oh, dudes," Della said.

After climbing onto their bikes, they started pedaling toward Marigold's house.

Chapter 27

At her house, Marigold parked her bike in the garage and ran into the house. Just as she blinked the porch light on and off, her mom popped up in the recliner and stretched her arms out in front of her, then she made a loud yawn.

"Oh, my goodness, Marigold! What time is it?"

Marigold looked at her watch. "S-Six forty-eight."

Marsha Stroop stood and walked, to the kitchen, in a daze. "Six forty-eight? Why was I sleeping at six forty-eight? It's high time for supper! I am so sorry, sweetie-you must be starving!"

"Um, not too much, M-Mom." And she wasn't. All of the excitement, in the barn after school, had kind of squelched her appetite.

Mrs. Stroop began clattering dishes around in the kitchen. "Oh, but we have to eat, right? How about some microwaved dinners? I have one Indian and one Mexican."

Marigold walked into the kitchen. "O-Okay, I'll take Indian, if y-you don't care."

"Perfect. You know me, I could eat bean enchiladas every day."

"G-Good, and you know me, I l-love Indian Malai Kofta, those v-veggie balls, in that yummy s-sauce. Do you w-want almond milk or tea?" Marigold peeked into the refrigerator.

"Tea tonight, honey. Thanks for pouring drinks; you are such a big helper."

Marigold poured tea for her mom, milk for her, and put out forks. No need for plates with microwaved dinners. After both dinners had been cooked, and Marsha had lowered them onto the table, she said, "Marigold, I got paid today, and there are some surprises for you on your bed."

Marigold sat down and smiled, wondering what weird surprises her mom had gotten her. She told herself that no matter how crazy the gifts on her bed were, she would be appreciative. No matter what. After she had downed the Indian balls and rice, she drank the milk, put her glass into the dishwasher, and placed the empty, plastic dish into the recycling bin. Then she did the same for her mom.

"Thank you, Marigold Marsha Stroop. Can I go with you, to see the look on your face, when you see your surprises?" She stood up and clapped her hands.

"Of course, M-Mom." Marigold tried to hide the apprehension she felt. What if she didn't like the surprises? How was she going to hide that?

Back the two went to the closed door of her bedroom, and Marigold slowly turned the gray knob, reached inside, and flicked on the ceiling light. But what was this? What was on her bed? She scurried over and picked up two-yes, two-pairs of new jeans! Nice jeans. Beside the jeans were two T-shirts-one orange and one yellow-but an orange Nike and a yellow Adidas T-shirt! She grinned happily and hugged her mom. "Thank you s-so much!"

"You are welcome, but you need to wash them tonight, before you wear them tomorrow. Plus, the clothes you have on now are rather-" Marsha plugged her nose.

"I g-get it. I will w-wash and dry them all t-tonight." Again, the smile.

"Oh, I almost forgot! There are new socks in your top drawer. Check 'em out."

Marigold winced as she started to slowly pull out the drawer, knowing the socks were going to be orange or yellow, maybe ruffled or striped. But the clean, white socks folded there put her doubts to rest. "They're wh-white!"

"Of course, they're white. No colored socks should be worn with white, running shoes. Guess I know that, because I arrange flowers for a living. I'm good at coordinating things." Marigold slowly nodded. "I'm sure y-you are."

"Now I know you might want to wear your cute orange or yellow socks, but they would look, well, really uncool."

"Un-c-cool?"

"Yes, uncool. I don't know why you always wanted to wear those other clothes and socks. They don't look like what your friends are wearing. Do you want to get bullied? Do you want that Billy to encourage everybody to laugh at you, because of your crazy clothes?"

"Um n-no, Mom. I sure d-don't." For the second time, her mom had said she wanted her to wear regular clothes. What was happening? What had caused her, self-proclaimed Miss Fashionista, to change? She wanted to ask her but didn't, didn't want her to rethink her updated fashion choices.

She also wanted to add that Billy wasn't going to be a bully anymore, but she didn't say that either. That was confidential. Instead, she did laundry, homework, and prepared lunch snacks for the other Misfits-cauliflower with ranch and hot sauce sprinkled on top. Finally, she crawled under the covers to sleep.

In the morning, Marigold grabbed her newly laundered clothes and put them on, along with white socks and white shoes. It was cooler this morning, so she put on her yellow jacket with frayed sleeves, a jacket that was two sizes too small. At least, her red book bag would help cover it up.

"Sweetie, I don't want to hurt your feelings, but I will be watching you from the living room window from now on. I will no longer be in the front yard. After all, you aren't a baby, anymore. You can do it-be brave. You've got this." Then she put a flower hair clip in her daughter's hair.

Marigold felt her head spin, but she managed to peck her mom on the cheek. "I'll try, Mom."

Down to the bus stop she strolled, a big smile on her face. Today was going to be a much better day, with Billy no longer a bully. And with him no longer being mean and taunting others, well, his gang of Droobs might stop, as well.

Billy's shouting, "Hey! Gross Girl!" made that happy, hopeful feeling crumble to the cracking concrete at her feet.

The other Droobs, spitting their usual cruel words in her direction, proved to Marigold that nothing had changed. The familiar hate-words started filling the air.

"Hey, you think you look so cool wearing those clothes?"

"Well, you don't!"

"You are so ugly, somebody ought to throw you in a trash can!"

"That's probably where your clothes came from!"

"Yeah, you were probably dumpster-diving last night!"

"I know she did! Can't you smell the rotten food?" And Mike plugged his nose.

"Dweeb!"

Uh-oh, Marigold thought as the bus pulled up. She looked up into the sky and saw Sinbad flying sharp darts back and forth. Did he realize, like she, the hypnosis last night hadn't worked?

On the bus, she found her seat and hoped Tasha would arrive at the next stop. As the bus went past Marigold's house, Billy bellowed, "Hey Gross Girl! How come your crazy mom isn't in the front yard? Did my dad kill her last night?"

"Hope so!" Mike yelled.

But instead of feeling hurt and chewing at her fingernail, Marigold closed her eyes and wondered why Billy hadn't changed.

At the next stop, Tasha entered and sat beside Marigold; she stared out the window.

"Are you sad?" Marigold asked.

"Yes. The Droobs called me mean names at the bus stop and are saying awful things in the back of the bus right now. They keep saying I need to go back to the jungle, and somebody is telling everybody I should just die."

Marigold wished she could tell her that things were going to get better, but right now she wasn't so sure. Instead, she patted Tasha's arm and said, "S-Sorry." When she looked toward the front, there were Mr. Carini's mean eyes in the rear view mirror. Another bully, who was actually glaring at them?

As the bus stopped, and the kids clambered past Tasha and her, the cruel words continued verbally smacking both of them. And what was this? The bus driver was grinning? The bus driver was high-fiving some of the worst potty mouths? Really? Marigold couldn't help but believe he definitely was a bully and probably had been a bully since he was a kid.

She also bet Mr. Carini had been abused by his dad, or somebody, and was beyond help. If he acted like this on the bus, she couldn't even imagine how he behaved at home. Was he married? Did he hit his kids? His wife? Did he shout insults at them? Well, she didn't know the answers to those questions but figured he was beyond help-just like Officer Jake Smith had been.

Marigold marched down the bus's steps and waved good-bye to Tasha. She sure hoped her new friend would be okay today. Because of the support she had received from the Misfits, the bully's words had begun to roll off her like "water off a duck's back". She also knew Tasha needed help, and she had a gift, a great gift of hearing, and Marigold believed it would be a big asset to the Misfits.

After arriving at her locker and having Billy run by and slam her locker's door, almost crunching her hand in the process, she reopened it. But what was this? There was a new, black jacket hanging on the hook! Attached to it was a note that said, Enjoy! From Mrs. Toon. Mrs. Toon had given her a jacket? Mrs. Toon and Ms Henley had her back. Literally, they had-her-back.

She ran her fingers over its smoothness, held it to her nose and smelled the newness. She wondered how Mrs. Toon had known she needed a jacket? Had somebody by the name of Jade Chung, their telepathic goddess, told her?

Marigold heard the "Ommm," and Jade shuffled up to her, with a wink, and then glided away.

With a big smile, Marigold hung up her old jacket and placed the morning class's books in her book bag. Then she went jogging, down the hall and to the office, to see Mrs. Hernandez. When she entered, the secretary, Miss Pinlay, nodded, and she barreled in to see the principal. Mrs. Hernandez stood looking out her window, but she turned when she heard Marigold enter.

Slowly, the principal walked over to her desk and sat down. "Marigold, I have requested all homeroom teachers to direct the others to my office." She kneaded her forehead with her very long fingers.

Within minutes, Mo, Jade, Kate, Della, and Jus rushed into the office. Except for Jade, who obviously knew, they each wore a questioning look, probably wondering why they had been requested to come here to the office, first thing in the morning.

After Jus closed the door, they formed a half circle around Mrs. Hernandez's desk. Marigold thought you could have heard a paper clip drop. At the sound of tapping on the glass, the principal opened the window, and Sinbad stuck his head in through the space. After massaging the area between his eyes, she cawed, sat back down, and drummed her sharp fingernails on her desk.

"It has come to my attention that Billy Smith is back at school, and his behavior has not changed. If anything, his behavior has worsened," she said.

Jade opened her eyes. "It is truuue."

"Jade, have you investigated this occurrence and determined the probable reason why the hypnosis was not effective?" Kate asked.

"I dooo not know."

Marigold spoke up in a clear voice, "J-Jade, you already told us hypnosis d-doesn't work on everybody. It's not your f-fault."

"It doesn't worrrk on everybody, and I'm sorry."

"Hey, mon. No reason for bein' sorry. But tell me, has this ever been happenin' before?" Jus asked.

"Not thaaat I know of. As far as I know, myyy hypnosis has always worrrked. I dooo not understand why Billy Smith did not reeespond to the hypnosis and all of yourrr suggestions."

"It's because, dude, he can't be helped. Let me go knock him down in homeroom, and Sinbad can remove him." With a big flying kick, she almost knocked Mrs. Hernandez's lamp off her desk.

"Caw! Sit down, Della!"

She did. "Sorry."

Now Mo started running in circles. "Let me run and capture him! Bring him back here, where we can yell at him! Tell him he has to change-or else!"

"Mo? You need to be sittin' down, just like Della." Jus pointed a ringed, index finger at him.

"Okay, okay-just trying to help!" Mo pushed his crooked turban, back to the correct place on his head, and then he sat down.

Marigold said, "I-I think we need to m-meet tonight in The Contributing Room. W-We have to find another answer for helping B-Billy."

Mrs. Hernandez nodded. “I agree with Marigold, and I thank you for your empathetic suggestion. Let’s meet tonight, in The Contributing Room, and come up with Plan B. Now, time to get to class.”

The morning was the same-o, same-o for Marigold. Same rude words and taunts, but Marigold was oblivious to it. When she passed Tasha in the hall, she smiled at her, but Tasha made no response; instead, she just sadly continued on toward her next class.

At lunch, the Misfits were unusually quiet. Most ate, got yelled at by Coach Reynolds, and seemed to be thinking hard. Marigold figured they were all wondering what would be decided, regarding Billy, tonight. Jade, sitting on top of the table and humming, seemed lost in her other world; she didn’t eat.

During last period, when Marigold was looking out the window and watching Sinbad performing loop-de-loops in the sky, a way to help Billy change his behavior whooshed into her thoughts. Yep, that was it. She was sure, beyond a doubt, this was the answer! She couldn’t wait to tell the others, in The Contributing Room, that evening. On the bus trip home, Marigold was quiet. Tasha stared into space.

Following a supper of two microwaved Indian dinners and watching her mom fall asleep in her recliner, Marigold ran with the Misfits and slid down into The Meeting Room. After being joined by The

Proprietor, saying the oath; after having a great dinner of salads and desserts in The Dining Room, served by the Timmers; after jogging through The Kitchen, The Tropical Rain Forest Room,, and entering The Contributing Room; the Misfits finally sat in the same places they had two nights earlier.

Marigold, Mo, Jade, Della, and Kate sat on the couch, while Jus, Mrs. Hernandez, and The Proprietor perched high, on their thrones, in the front. Sinbad was lying on his back before Mrs. Hernandez. She cooed at him and ran her toes through his black, belly feathers.

"Caw! It is time to begin the meeting and decide upon a new plan, regarding Billy Smith. Once all suggestions have been offered, another vote will be taken. I now open the floor for suggestions," Mrs. Hernandez stated.

Mo jumped up and ran in place. Bouncing energetically up and down, he held a hand atop his turban this time,. "I suggest I run and catch him! Then Sinbad flies him to an island far away! A different island than where his dad is!"

"Suggestion noted. Now sit back down, please," Mrs. Hernandez stated. "Next?"

After Mo sat back down, Jade stood and said, "Ommm. I thiiink you should let me tryyy my hypnosis once more, and let Sinnnbad fly him back to the barn.

Weee can repeat what we did last night." She gracefully lowered herself back, onto the couch, and resumed her cross-legged position.

Now Della was kicking the air. "No, dude! You already had your chance! I need to run to his homeroom this morning and kick him down. I will so kick him down. Then I will drag him here to your office, Mrs. Hernandez. All the Misfits will yell at him, and I will do some chops on his ugly face."

Mrs. Hernandez frowned. "Della, you can sit down."

Della did an aerial in front of her throne. "But I'm Batgirl, dude! I am here to protect you and all the Misfits!"

The Proprietor started crying, and Mrs. Hernandez handed him a tissue. "Sorry, Mr. Proprietor. We will not carry out such a violent plan. Della, you need to hold your emotions in check. Did you take your medication today?"

"I don't need my medication. My schizophrenia is all better. I am Batgirl!"

"I don't think so. You take your meds tonight, or you don't meet with us again." Mrs. Hernandez stood up and elevated a bit into the air, her arms pointed straight over her head. "Caw! Caw! Caw!"

Everyone seemed taken aback, and Della quickly sat down. "Okay, but you are wrong."

Mrs. Hernandez floated back down onto her throne but aimed her black eyes in Della's direction.

Jus said, "Yes, mon, Della will be takin' her meds tonight and never be decidin' they are not needed." He cleared his throat. "Now, let us be continuin' with me." He stared at the ceiling. "Guess I am bein' without a suggestion, though. I thought the design, performed with you all last night, was the best I could be comin' up with. I pass, mon."

"So noted, Jus. Caw! I am of the same mind-set." She turned toward The Proprietor. "Do you have a suggestion?"

But The Proprietor was now crying loudly and shaking his head no.

"All right," she said, with a pat on his arm. "Kate or Marigold?"

Kate stood tall. "I believe this situation is without a positive resolution. Clearly, Billy Smith has proven himself unable to have his behavior altered. His actions are beyond help. We either agree to have him removed, or we must be willing to deal with the negative and cruel behavior he displays on a daily basis. It is important to realize the behavior he witnessed his father exhibit was indelibly ingrained into his psyche'. It will not be long, before he will display very violent actions toward other kids, his mother, his sister, and someday, his spouse and his children." She sat down.

Again came the sobs from The Proprietor, and Mrs. Hernandez handed him another tissue. Sinbad raised his huge body up and tried to press his face against the tiny crying leader, to nuzzle him with loving concern, but almost crushed him, in the process.

"Sinbad! Caw! Kind idea, but no!" Mrs. Hernandez yanked at a huge wing, and Sinbad lowered himself slowly back to the floor. He gave his keeper an irritated look-once he was "grounded".

Finally, Marigold stood with a straight back and unwavering eyes. Her voice was clear, as she stated, "I-I have been thinking very hard about a way to h-help Billy, so we don't have to remove h-him. I believe the s-solution I c-came up with is the answer."

Everyone turned their attention to her. "Continue," Mrs. Hernandez said. The Proprietor stopped crying, and Marigold thought he wore a hopeful look.

Clearing her throat, Marigold continued, "First of all, let m-me repeat what I already s-said. Jade, I-I do not think y-you did anything wrong. You d-did everything right."

Jade smiled at Marigold.

"And Jus, the d-design was perfect. What w-was wrong was the approach. W-We were too negative. When somebody tells me what n-not to do, I don't w-want to change; at least, not like when they t-tell me what I should do."

"Huh? What are you talking about, dude? What he needs is a kick and a chop," Della said.

"If I may interject," Mrs. Hernandez said, "Marigold is saying that while Billy is under hypnosis, we need to give him directions, but in a positive way. Am I correct, Marigold?"

"Y-Yes. Exactly."

"All the positives in the world aren't going to be changing him, dude." And Della was up chopping the air again. "You need me to annihilate him!"

Mrs. Hernandez pointed a sharp nail in Della's direction. She shouted, above the murmur of the Misfits and The Proprietor's blubbering, "Della, you may leave The Contributing Room now. See me in my office tomorrow morning, and if you have not taken your meds, if your behavior has not changed, you will be dismissed from our organization. Unless matters require extreme measures, as in the prior possible murder of Marsha Stroop, we do not resort to violence! You should know this! Go!"

Della dashed quickly to the door and was gone. Marigold was shocked. Della might be removed? Was that a possibility? What would happen to the Misfits and their secrets? The knowledge of this underground cavern, The Proprietor, the oath, Sinbad, and Mrs. Hernandez? Not to mention the Timmers? How about

Officer Smith's removal? Jade's gifts, as well as the others'? Wouldn't removing Della mean the entire Misfit organization would go down the tubes? She could not stop the tears spilling from her eyes, with the fear that this wonderful group of people, her very best friends, might never meet together ever, ever again.

Chapter 28

Jade leaned over and said in Marigold's ear, "Not to worrry. If Della's removal should occur, I will hypnotize her tooo forget everything-the secrets and this plaaace."

"O-Okay." But Marigold hoped Della took her meds and could remain a Misfit.

"I am not certain this positive process will alter Billy's behavior; however, I am willing to revisit the procedure in the barn." Kate nodded at Marigold.

Jus stated, "Then let us be puttin' it to a vote, mon. 'Yay' if you wish to meet again in the barn tomorrow night and be tryin' to suggest changes to Billy, with a more positive approach; 'Nay' if you want to be developin' a different plan, such as removin' him. Is anybody opposin' this way of votin'?"

Nobody objected, so Jus began, "As far as me, it's a 'yay'. Mrs. Hernandez?"

Mrs. Hernandez said, "A definite 'yay'!"

Jus said, "The Proprietor?"

The Proprietor looked at Marigold, and his smile beamed almost as brightly as his twinkling, light blue eyes. “Yay!” He put so much effort into his response, he almost knocked himself off his throne.

“That’s three ‘yays’, mon. Kate?”

“Although it goes against my realistic judgment, I still say, ‘yay’.”

“Jade?” Jus gestured in her direction.

“A definite yaaay. Marigold, thank youuu for a positive proposal.”

Marigold said, “Thank-y-you for sharing your gift.”

“Youuu are welcome.” Jade closed her eyes, and with hands in front of her, began humming.

“Mo? What is your vote bein’, mon?”

“I don’t think anything will change Billy, but I will vote ‘yay’!” He ran in circles, until Mrs. Hernandez cawed at him, and he plunked his butt back down.

“Well, mon, with Marigold bein’ a ‘yay’, of course, it is unanimous. Tomorrow, we shall be meetin’ and tryin’ to change Billy’s behavior, but with a positive approach this time. Same time, same place. I will be spendin’ the night again, with Billy, once Sinbad is locatin’ him and flyin’ him to the barn tonight.”

At that, Sinbad started beating his wings, soaring above their heads, and then vanishing through the opening in the sky. “Safe travels, my baby! Caw!” And

Mrs. Hernandez floated upward, until she was no longer visible.

"Jade, we will need you to be hypnotizin' Billy, prior to the flight, mon."

"Yesss, of course."

"Kate, Jade, and hopefully Della (dependin' on Mrs. Hernandez's decision) will be arrivin' at Marigold's house on bikes, right after school. Mo, can ya be ridin' fast and meetin' me in the barn, like before?"

"Yeah! I will be there real quick, and Della can ride on my handlebars, if she shapes up!"

"That is all good, mon. We will be meetin' in the barn, after school, tomorrow."

Marigold was concerned, again, that Jus's parents would be worried if he didn't come home tonight. She approached him, just as he was leaving through the door. "J-Jus?"

He turned. "Yeah, mon. You havin' a question about our agenda?"

"N-No. I'm just wondering if your m-mom or dad will worry if y-you don't come home tonight?"

"I am not bein' worried about that. Both of my parents are sittin' in jail in Jamaica for killin' somebody. I was flown here by an aunt, but since she died, I am livin' in a group home."

"A gr-group home?"

"Yeah, mon." Then he was off.

Marigold turned toward the others. "A-A group home? Why a group h-home? He should be in a f-foster home, or adopted!"

Kate said, "There are simply not enough foster homes or adopting parents to care for the hundreds of thousands of children in the United States, removed from their homes. Most have been removed, due to parents' drug use or for neglect of their offspring; there is often a combination of the two. Because of his older age, there is almost no chance he will be placed in a foster home.-or adopted. The court has deemed him a Ward of the State, and a group home is now his residence."

"P-Poor Jus."

With a sigh, Jade said, "Yesss. But at least heee has a roof over his head and food to eat, as long as he doesn't get in trouble forrr not going to his group home toniiight. He was reprimanded forrr not going there after his last sleeepover in the barn."

"O-Oh no!" Marigold raised her hands to her cheeks. "Then what will happen t-to him next?"

"The court will decide then!" Mo darted back and forth. "Probably, a lock-up!"

"Like a-a jail?" She recalled Billy's overnight placement, after he'd been removed in handcuffs.

"A jail for kids!" Mo said with a jump.

"Jus haaas his priorities for which 'Right' is at the very top. He knows the 'Riiight' thing to do is sleep in the barn. Now, lettt's journey home."

Back home, Marigold unlocked the door and found her mom still in the recliner, sleeping at 12:07 a.m.. After flicking the porch light and bedroom lamp on and off and retreating under her sunset comforter, she heard the recliner squeak. Then her mom's footsteps began approaching her bedroom door. After that, her door opened, there was a kiss on the forehead, and her bedroom door closed. Her mom took the aroma of lilacs with her. She didn't remember another thing, until her alarm sounded at six a.m.

After donning her blue jeans, yellow T-shirt, white socks and shoes, new black jacket, and kissing her mom good-bye, Marigold, a cinnamon roll in hand, was off to the bus stop. No mean words were thrown in her direction. Billy was not there, and Marigold wondered if he was back at the barn? Although he could be so mean, Marigold felt sorry for him. He had been abused for many years by his dad and had seen his dad hurt his mom. Now, that his very mean dad was gone, Billy missed him. Why? Well, just because Jake Smith was his dad. Yeah, Billy's big, tough act was only that-an act. Billy was really a sad, little boy. And the Droobs? Well, she supposed they all needed to be part of a group, because they couldn't be happy alone, even if that group was a very cruel one. Or maybe they were afraid of Billy.

Marigold let her thoughts come to a stop, when the bus arrived. Into her regular place she went; she threw her book bag onto the seat beside her, to save the seat for Tasha, and the bus roared away.

"Hi!" Marigold said to Tasha, once she had boarded and sat down beside her.

Tasha gave her a soft smile but didn't say anything. Marigold didn't pry; she already knew the feelings her friend was having. She just patted Tasha on the arm and wished she could say her life was going to get better, but she knew she couldn't say that. Not yet, anyway.

After she had switched books at her locker and was heading to homeroom, Ms. Henley jogged her brown, teacher's shoes up beside her. "Marigold, Mrs. Hernandez needs you in her office now."

"O-Okay." Marigold turned and trotted to see what Mrs. Hernandez had to say.

In the office, Della stood quietly, in front of their principal's desk. Mrs. Hernandez wore a small grin on her face. Suddenly, like a great tornado, in rushed Mo, followed moments later by Jade and Kate.

Mrs. Hernandez said, "Caw! Della assures me she took her meds and will continue in that pattern. From the behavior she is exhibiting, I believe her."

"Ommm." Jade scooted forward until she was inches from Mrs. Hernandez's desk. "I can assure youuu, she has taaaken her medicine."

"Yay!" Mo exclaimed with a jump. "Now, you can be part of the Misfits again!"

Della pulled the mask off her face and looked at each of them. "I can promise you that I will keep taking my medicine, dudes. I am real sorry."

"Well, that is good news, just the kind of news we wanted to hear." Mrs. Hernandez smiled even wider. "And I have some other good news for you. This morning, around 12:30 a.m., Sinbad located Billy when he walked, outside the house, to take the garbage to the alley. Sinbad informed Jade that he had him in a bird's eye view, our telepathic goddess arrived to hypnotize Billy, and Sinbad flew him to the barn. He is once again sleeping, on a big pile of hay, right next to Jus."

"Just where we want him to be!" Mo spun in a circle.

"All is going as we had hoped," Mrs. Hernandez said. "Jade told Mo, and he ran to tell The Proprietor, so he is in the loop. Today after school, Marigold, watch for Kate and Jade outside your home on their bikes Caw!"

"I-I will be watching for both of y-you."

Kate said, "It will be more expeditious, when you see us, to depart your home through the back door and retrieve your bike. Jade will hypnotize your mom prior to your exit."

Jade opened her eyes and stomped a foot. "Kaaate, it is not necessary for youuu to tell Marigold what I will beee doing."

Kate stomped a foot back at her. "Well, excuse me! I presumed your hypnosis was an expected action, as a result of inductive reasoning! You have used hypnosis on Marsha Stroop before; therefore, thinking inductively, it is only logical that you will be performing the same action tonight!"

"III already know whaaat inductive reasoning is, Kate!" Jade's dark eyes flashed.

"Kate is trying to educate us on something we already know Jade will be doing! It's all good!" Mo hippedy-hopped on one foot.

"I would do a kick in the air to emphasize Mo's words, dudes, but I won't." Della jumped in place instead.

"And that is very good, Della," Mrs. Hernandez said. "What we do need, is for you to ride on Mo's handlebars and go very quickly to the barn, right after school." She batted her arms swiftly at her sides.

"So, Mo, can I ride with you, like last night?" Again came Della's jumps.

"Yeah, man! That is good! I will get my bike and pick you up!"

"Awesome, Mo. Thanks." Della gently raised a foot into the air and made a slight kick-kick.

"So, are we all set? Any questions?" Mrs. Hernandez looked out the window at Sinbad, who had just arrived. Sinbad gave her a wink. The principal opened the window and made a loud, "Caw!".

"I thiiink we are ready for a dooo-over," Jade said. "Ommm."

"Then let's meet after school at the barn. Let us travel swiftly, without allowing anything to prevent our arrival, and let this attempt at behavior modification, through hypnosis, be successful." Kate gave the group a "thumb's-up".

"And you, Kaaate, don't need to beee--" Marigold could have sworn she actually heard a low growl sound deeply in Jade's throat again. Mrs. Hernandez stopped Jade with an out-thrust arm in her direction and a loud caw. Jade nodded and said, "Sorrry, Kate."

Kate smiled. "It's certainly acceptable, as well as understandable, when your frustration is aimed in my direction."

The group trooped out of the office together and scattered in different directions, heading toward first period. It was another very boring day for Marigold, and she was happy when the end of school arrived. She jogged, with renewed energy, out of Brentwood Middle School and onto the bus.

Chapter 29

Tasha dived into her place by Marigold on the bus. She immediately slammed her fists onto her ears and said, "Why don't they stop?"

Marigold thought about telling Tasha that they were just words, that she needed to ignore them, but knew it wouldn't help. She understood how awful and cutting the sharp words were. Instead, she whispered, "I am s-so sorry, Tasha," and she was. So very, very sorry this kind friend of hers had to endure such horrid cruelty.

Tasha nodded and gave her a small smile, so Marigold knew she had heard her words. Still, her friend kept her fists tightly covering her ears the whole rest of the trip to her bus stop.

When Tasha disembarked from the bus, Mr. Carini curled his lips downward and said, "Whats-a wrong with you? You gotta put your hands there, cause you got some kinda mental problem-a? Your hands are supposed to be down-a at your sides, you dumb idiot!"

Well, those words made Marigold shoot up, a frantic friend on a mission. She dashed her way to the bus driver's side and yelled, "Y-You stop! You st-stop now! Those w-words you just said? They were so m-mean!"

He turned to Marigold and hissed, "R-Really? Wh-What are you-you-a s-sayin, St-Stutter G-Girl?"

Once Tasha was safely off the bus and running home, her fists still covering her ears, Marigold quickly made it to her seat, before the bus jerked away, knocking her to the floor again. She refused to look at Mr. Carini and whatever mean expression he was flashing toward her in his rear view mirror.

After arriving home, Marigold kissed her mother hello-but really, good-night, since within a minute of spying Kate and Jade on their bikes out front, her mom gave a loud yawn and fell backwards onto the couch. Marigold locked the front door, ran quickly out the back door (which she locked) to the garage and her bicycle.

Down the street they pedaled, following the same route as the day before. Jade led the way, and Marigold marveled at the internal compass she must possess. She never made a wrong turn-well, none that she was aware of, anyway.

The trip seemed faster than the one yesterday, and soon they arrived at the outbuilding behind the barn. Mrs. Hernandez's car was parked behind Mo and Jus's bikes, and behind the car, went Jade's, Kate's, and finally Marigold's bikes.

Inside the barn today, Jus stood in front of the window. He must have nudged the faded red and white checked curtains apart a bit, since the space had more light than it had before. The same sweet smell of hay and animals enveloped Marigold's senses. Billy was lying on the barn floor and snoring away, just like before. Mo hopped, and Della kicked in place. Mrs. Hernandez stood tall; her arms were crossed over her chest. Jade lowered herself and sat cross-legged on the barn's floor. She hummed, clearly traveling to that "other world" in her mind. Marigold and Kate sat down on each side of her.

Jus said, "Whenever you are bein' ready, Jade."

Mo and Della sat down, followed by Mrs. Hernandez.

"Ommm." Jade stood and walked the short distance to where Billy was lying. She knelt down in front of him and said, "Billy, when I snap myyy fingers, you will awaaaken and sit up. If you understaaand, nod your head."

Billy nodded, and at the sound of Jade's fingers snapping, he sat up.

"Youuu will listen to the suggestions given by eeeach of us here, but you will not remember our faces, this plaaace, or your mode of transportation. If you understaaand, nod your head."

He did.

"The suggestions we are about to giiive you are meant to help youuu have a better life. You are to implement theeese ideas from this point onward. If you understand, say, 'yes'."

Billy said, "Yes."

"Good. Billyyy, open your eyes."

Billy's eyes popped open, and although they shifted from one Misfit to the next, they looked glassy again, and he did not seem to recognize them.

"Jus said, "Marigold, I am askin' you to start, mon."

"M-Me?"

"I agree with Jus," Mrs. Hernandez stated. "You are the one who came up with this new approach."

There were murmurs of agreement, from the other Misfits.

"Okay. B-Billy, you will begin saying k-kind words to those around y-you."

Jade said, "Billy, if you understaaand and will say kind words to people around you, pleeease nod."

Billy nodded.

Jus said, "Kate?"

"You shall decide that being a bully is detrimental to the lifestyle you wish to incorporate, from this monumental moment on and throughout your daily encounters, with all of those who cross your path."

"What are you saying? Give it to him in English, dude!" Della jumped up and began a kick, but she immediately sat back down, when Mrs. Hernandez leveled her with those black eyes.

"I apologize," Kate said. "Billy, it is important to show caring to everyone around you."

Jade smiled in Kate's direction. "Billy, if you understaaand and are willing tooo show caring to those around you, please say, 'yesss'."

"Yes," he said. He blinked his eyes and then stared straight ahead.

"Mo?" Jus pointed at the Misfit, with the gift of speed, who stood and jumped in place.

"Billy, you need to be telling your friends to be nice to everyone!"

"Billy? Will youuu tell your friends to be niiice to everyone? If so, please raaaise your left hand."

Up went his left hand, and Mo sat down.

"Okay, mon. It's bein' your turn, Della."

Marigold was amazed when Della sat in place and said, "Billy, being nonviolent is a good thing, dude. Keep your hands and feet to yourself."

"Billy, raaaise your right hand ifff you understand and will keep your hands and feeet to yourself."

Up went the right hand this time.

Jus said, "Okay. Mrs. Hernandez?"

"Caw! Billy Smith! You must stay in class and be a good student!"

"Thisss time, raise both hands if you will staaay in class and work hard to beee a good student."

Billy raised up both hands.

"And now, Jus, please take your turn. Caw!"

"Okay. Billy, you need to start bein' especially kind to your mother and sister, mon."

"Nod if you will beee especially kiiind to your mother and sissster, Billy."

Billy did.

Jade said, "Billy, youuu must begin taking care of yourrr health. Eat correctly and exerciiise. If you have heard and will begin doing this, say 'yes'."

"Yes."

"Well," Jus said, "I am thinkin' everyone has spoken and--"

Mrs. Hernandez's arms started flapping. "No! Not yet! The Proprietor sent his suggestion with Mo."

"Sorry, mon. Yes, Mo, please be tellin' Billy what The Proprietor would like him to do."

Mo jumped up. “Billy, you must begin, from this moment on, to love yourself! Regardless of what you have heard in the past, you are very special!”

Jade smiled. “Yesss, Billy. If you are willing to begin loving yourrrself, from this moment on, pleeease clap your hands.”

With a great sweep, Billy’s hands came together in one loud clap.

Jade’s eyes swept from person to person. “Are weee finished?”

Silence seemed to provide Jade with the answer that yes, all the Misfits had spoken and were, in fact, finished.

“Today, Jade, can you be givin’ a summary?” Jus asked.

“Certainly. Billy, you have heard and agreeed to the following suggestions:

One, you will say niiice words to everyone.

Two, you will show kindness tooo everyone.

Three, youuu will tell your friends to beee nice to others.

Four, you will keeep your hands and feet to yourself.

Five, you will staaay in class and beee a good student.

Six, youuu will be especially kiiind to your mother and sister.

Seven, you will beeegin healthy eating and exercising.

Eight, youuu will start loving yourrrself.

If you still understand whaaat I just repeated and willl begin acting in those waaays, please smile."

A forced, but very large smile, covered Billy's face.

"Okaaay, you already know the drill. When I snaaap my fingers, you will close your eyes and fall asleeep. You will not remember your flight here orrr back. You will not reeemember us or this place, and you will beginnn the process of following the suggestions youuu have heard and agreed to, once you waaake up. If you are agreeeable to this, please nod."

Billy nodded. Jade snapped her fingers. He closed his eyes and fell over onto his side. Mrs. Hernandez slid open the barn door, and in came Sinbad. He grabbed Billy's sweatshirt with his beak and tottered out the door. With a wild batting of wings, the large bird soared into the sky and into the late afternoon clouds, Billy swinging back and forth like a stork's baby bundle.

Quickly, the Misfits mounted their bikes and took off (Mo and Della in a mad flash), away from the barn, and Mrs. Hernandez roared ahead in her car. Marigold pumped her small legs with all her might. Suddenly, from out of the corner of her eye, she seemed to see a man watching them! A very familiar-looking man had peeked out, from behind a tall, evergreen tree, bordering the road!

"Was that? It couldn't be!" She slammed on her brakes and almost fell off the bike's wobbly seat. Then she used her feet to scoot backward to make sure, but the face she thought she had seen, was gone.

"No", she told herself, "it was just my imagination." She had been involved in so many unbelievable happenings, her mind was simply playing tricks on her. It was impossible that person could be here and watching them. No way. But she felt her stomach lurch harder than her bike's tires, once she began pedaling over a bump in the road. Obviously, the Misfits in front of her hadn't seen him; she had to have imagined it. But should she tell them? No, she knew they would just think she was seeing things, too.

Once Jade, Kate, Jus, and Marigold arrived at Billy's house, there he was lying in the grass again. After the four of them had crouched down behind the same long row of shrubs, Marigold watched Jade snap her fingers and heard her say, "Billy, awaaaken." Billy jumped up with a start, just as Lila and his mom ran out the front door.

"Where have you been, Billy? We have looked everywhere, and here you are! We have been so worried!" Meghan rushed over and gave her son a huge hug.

He shook his head, like he was trying to figure out how he had ended up in the grass, in front of his house-again. "I took out the trash real late. Guess I must've been tired and fell asleep here."

When Billy, his mom, and Lila started into the house, Marigold wondered if her ears were tricking her. Had Billy really said, "Need any help making supper, Mom? You must be real tired after your hunt for me. Sorry you both were worried!"

She knew Tasha would have known for certain, with her gift of hearing. Still, when Jade looked at her with a big grin on her face, Marigold understood she'd heard Billy correctly. But, she wondered, would it last? Would Billy really begin using all of the suggestions? Time would tell.

"Tiiime will tell," Jade said, once they had started riding toward Marigold's house. "Next, I will snap my fingers to awaaaken your mom, when youuu are under your sunset comforter."

Marigold swallowed hard. Jade knew she had a sunset comforter? Then she reminded herself, of course, Jade knew she had a sunset comforter. She probably knew how many times she had blinked her eyes that day.

Jade said: "28,725---no, 28,726 tiiimes so far---"

Marigold laughed the hardest she thought she had ever laughed before.

Once inside the house, Marigold clicked the porch light on and off, grabbed her book bag from off the floor, and scurried to her room-where she dove under her comforter. She pulled her math book from her bag and turned her bedroom lamp on. None too quickly, either, as Marsha Stroop was soon standing at the bedroom door. "Hi, Mom," Marigold said.

With a big yawn, Marigold's mom stretched her arms over her head. "Oh, my goodnesss---so tired. A lot of arranging flowers today, breaking my back so we can have clothes on our backs, a roof over our head, food on the table, all because--"

And Marigold, who was sprawling on her stomach under the comforter and pretending to be involved in her math book, rolled over onto her side and said, "B-Because you love me." Then her stomach growled loudly.

"Yes, I do." Her mom sat down onto the bed, while the smell of roses wafted across the bed. She ran her fingers through Marigold's hair.

"I love y-you too, Mom."

Marsha Stroop kissed her daughter on the head. "I know you do, darling. Now, was that a tummy I heard growling?"

With a wink, Marigold said, "Kind of h-hungry, I guess."

Marsha squealed, "I can't believe the time!" The clock beside the bed said 7:02 in big red numbers. "Guess I fell asleep because--"

"You broke y-your back at the flower shop today."

"Got that right, baby girl. Well, how about a frozen pizza and salad? Not too fancy, but fast."

"S-Sounds great, Mom."

Marigold figured her mom was still a bit groggy. She didn't bombard her with the normal number of questions, as they slammed down a veggie pizza, tasting a whole lot like chewy cardboard. Marigold didn't care about the pizza's texture, since she was happy to be sitting here at this table with her mother. She wondered if the hypnosis in the barn had worked, and would Billy be a different guy tomorrow?

She must have looked lost in thought, because her mother raised her fork from her bowl of salad and asked, "Are you okay, sweetie? You are just staring into space."

With a bunch of blinks (was Jade counting those, she thought with a grin), she forced herself back to reality. "I-I'm okay, Mom. Just f-fine." But she knew she wasn't really going to be okay until the next morning. Not until Billy demonstrated his new self, and she had proof that the hypnosis, along with the Misfits' suggestions, had worked.

"Well, good. Hey, would you mind helping me with the dishes? I think I need a nap. I have to get some more sleep to get ready for the energy it takes to arrange flowers tomorrow."

"M-Mom, you just go to bed. I c-can take care of the d-dishes."

"You can?" Another big yawn and arm stretch. "Well, thank you, sweet girl. I think I will take you up on that." She walked toward her bedroom, after saying, "Night, Marigold Marsha Stroop. I love you to the moon and back."

"I l-love you, too, Mom." As she filled the sink with sudsy water and washed the few dirty dishes, her mind traveled back to the events at the barn. She sure hoped the positive approach had worked with Billy, and that guy she thought she saw peeking out at them as they rode away? She hoped it had just been her imagination. Because if it hadn't been? Well, that was going to be bad. Real bad.

***

However, the next morning, when Marigold walked to the bus stop, she heard the awful shouts begin. There were the same rude words and raucous laughter. Obviously, the hypnosis had not worked, and nothing had changed! The closer she got, the louder grew the awfulness, and Billy was standing smack-dab in the middle of it. She looked up into the bright blue sky and saw Sinbad weaving his way about, before diving downward and flying just above her head. She could have sworn he winked and gave her a small smile, before darting up, up, up into the clouds! Wink? Smile? Did Sinbad just wink and smile at her? Why? Well, at least she knew that big bird was watching over her.

"What's the matter, Geek Girl? You looking up into the sky cause you can't look at us?" It was Mike.

"Scaredy Cat. Chicken Freak!" a girl named Tina joined in.

But what occurred next almost caused Marigold to fall over, smack, onto the sidewalk. Could this really be happening, or were her ears deceiving her?

"Be quiet, you guys. Don't be mean." And it was Billy Smith, who'd said those words! Billy was telling the Droobs to be nice? Marigold choked and stopped in place. It took a moment before she could even continue forward.

Mike mumbled, "What-What did you say, man? Don't think I heard you right."

Billy repeated the words, and the others stared at him with open mouths.

They also stopped dissing her. The Droobs were so quiet, and Marigold thought she now understood Sinbad's wink and smile.

"Thanks, Billy," she said. And what was this? He gave her a "thumb's- up"? Wow. She hated to make a premature presumption, but it appeared to her that their work, in the barn the night before, had been successful. Sinbad must have understood that was a fact; that was the reason for the smile and wink. Hooray! Yippee! Yaaaaay for the Misfits! Marigold felt like jumping up and down in place; and yet, she wondered how things were going to be on the bus. With so many Droobs present and encouraging in the back seats where Billy always sat, would he be strong enough to resist heading up the bully gang, once more?

Chapter 30

Onto the bus, Marigold climbed, telling herself to be ready for disappointment. Billy had been resistant to hypnotic suggestions before, so maybe this time didn't work either. She smiled, however, when no mean words were shouted from the back. Tasha even said, "The Droobs are being nice!"

Back in school, Marigold didn't stop at her locker; instead, she tore straight into Mrs. Hernandez's office, where the principal and Jade stood. "It worked! It w-worked! It-It worked!" Marigold hollered so loudly, Jade shuffled over and closed the office door.

"Weee know it worked." Jade smiled and gave Marigold a hug.

Mrs. Hernandez flapped her fringed black sleeves. "Caw! It worked, Miss Marigold Stroop, because of the positive approach, an approach you developed!"

Marigold could feel her cheeks flush. "W-Well, everyone helped--"

"Wee helped, but only because there was a plaaan to implement," Jade said.

"Great job, mon!" Jus yelled, when he exploded into the room. "Billy was just sayin' good mornin'!"

Following him, Kate, Mo, and Della dashed into the office, a series of rapidly firing fireworks. Their excited words caused Jade to shut the door again.

"I can't believe it! Billy just waved at me!" Mo ran in place.

"Caw! Caw! Yes, he has changed! He responded to the positive suggestions!"

Kate did a pirouette, a bit out of character for her. "I am feeling immense glee. I'm quite ecstatic."

Della made a kick, kick. "Well, dude, we can thank Marigold for coming up with changing Billy, in a positive way. Just know I am ready if you need me to-to-" She stopped at the look from their principal.

"Della! Did you take your meds this morning? Caw!"

Della stopped mid-kick. "Yeah, I took them this morning. See? I can control my kicking. I'm just saying, if you need me, I'm ready. I can so protect you."

"Okay," Mrs. Hernandez said. She opened the window, and Sinbad stuck in as much of his glistening, black self as he could. And yep, Marigold could see that he was winking and smiling again. Sinbad really could do those things!

"Heee only winks and smiiiles when he is verrry happy," Jade said.

Mrs. Hernandez added, "Well, I predict today is going to be a much better day for Billy, and for all of those he has bullied in the past. Hopefully, he gets the message to the rest of the Droobs that they need to behave appropriately, as well. Caw!"

When a knock sounded on the door, and Billy's face filled the glass, Mrs. Hernandez groaned. "Oh, no. Let him in, Jus."

Marigold feared the hypnosis had not lasted.

Billy sheepishly entered, and the principal asked, "In trouble again?"

"No, no, Mrs. Hernandez, I'm just here to tell you I'm sorry for always being in trouble and causing you problems. I promise I won't be getting any more referrals."

"Well, that's very good, Billy." Mrs. Hernandez flashed him a big smile.

Marigold questioned if he was wondering why all of them were crowded into this office, but this was answered when Billy said, "And the rest of you? Well, you'd better start being good and stop getting sent here. It's important to behave right and not be a troublemaker!" Then he hurried out of the office.

Once he was gone, there was a collective cheer of happiness and high fives among all of them standing there. Even Sinbad cawed so loudly, Marigold wondered why someone didn't run in from outside the office and see the humongous bird, who had partially invaded the room.

Jade closed the door and stated, "Nobody but we can seee or hear Sinbad, Marigooold."

"Oh, that's r-right."

"To class, to class," Mrs. Hernandez sang, anxiously flipping her hands in the air, like she was pushing baby birds out of the nest. She scribbled, then handed each of them a pink pass to homeroom. "Tonight, our regular meeting will occur. Now, go! Like Jus says, 'School is important'!" As she flapped her arms in the air, Sinbad backed out of the window and zipped his way up into the sky.

During homeroom and Marigold's other classes with Billy, the bullying was subdued. When a Droob began the verbal clobbering of her, Billy amazed Marigold by telling them to stop. The Droobs? Well, there was no doubt they were equally surprised. Marigold observed them stare, wide-eyed, at their once- great leader, Billy Smith. It was clear their world and knowing their place in their world, had changed. They were used to yelling mean words. What were they supposed to say now?

In addition to stifling his followers, Billy suddenly became an attentive student. Frequently raising his hand in response to questions and busily doing assignments, also appeared to surprise his teachers-surprise and delight them. In turn, Billy received much positive reinforcement from these teachers, and that made many big smiles fill his face.

During lunch time, Marigold tossed around her celery stuffed with peanut butter, pickles, and radishes (much to Mo's disappointment), and she eagerly accepted the food from the others. But when Mr. Reynolds stomped toward the table and aimed his knowing, angry eyes directly at her, she realized the truth of what she had seen yesterday. He had definitely been the gawking, "rubberneck" from behind that tree!

In his black workout suit and cool kicks, he arrived at their table and hissed, "Hello, Freak-os." And as Marigold looked into his crazed eyes, she became even more positive. Yep, if he were in a line-up, she'd definitely identify him as the stalker. Mr. Reynolds had seen them pedal away from the barn!

The other Misfits just kept munching away. Well, all of them except Jade, who quickly scooted away. Where is she headed, Marigold wondered.

"I am Coach Reynolds, and you will answer me when I say, 'hello'." His eyes were simmering, ashy gray coals.

"Not when you are callin' us Freak-os, mon." Jus didn't stop eating.

Marigold watched in horror, as Mr. Reynolds stomped over to Jus and raised him up into the air by his collar. "Are you disrespecting me? Want me to send you flying through the air, boy?"

Jus managed to say, with a very constricted throat, "I'm not a 'boy'. That's what they used to call slaves. Not a slave, and I'm sure not respectin' ya, mon." Jus's face had turned bright red.

"You listen to me, you devil-worshipers," the coach said, throwing Jus back onto the bench. He leaned over the table, the knuckles on his clenched fists turning white. "I know you are up to something real strange, because I followed you to that barn yesterday. You are doing some kind of witchcraft, and I can't even send you to the office, because our principal is probably the main witch. But you are mine! Mine! And you are going to suffer!"

Marigold decided the only thing looking angrier than Mr. Reynold's face was Mrs. Hernandez's, when she marched toward him on her tall, black, spiked heels. Jade shuffled along at her side.

He turned and glared at her. "You ugly witch," he said.

Marigold wondered if Mrs. Hernandez was going to "caw" and then attack him, with her very sharp fingernails, but was relieved when she didn't do either. Instead, she said, in a low, gruff voice, "Mr. Reynolds, you are suspended from teaching, beginning today, and continuing for two weeks, while investigation is performed. Go secure your belongings and depart these premises. Now!"

The coach stepped closer, his face mere inches from hers. "I have teachers' tenure. You can't do that, you insane satanic worshiper."

How she remained civil, Marigold didn't know. Instead of flapping her sleeves and diving at him, Mrs. Hernandez calmly said, "You can call me all the names you want; however, child abuse is a crime. Calling the noble kids at this table, 'freaks', is a crime. Lifting Jus up by his collar is a crime."

"Hey, you didn't hear me, didn't even see me!"

"Oh, I have my ways." She turned and winked at Jade.

"Yeah, you can see everything, because you're a satanic-worshiping witch! Just like everyone here!"

"Go! Now! Oh, did I add that your two weeks off are without pay?"

"You can't do that! Wait till I contact my lawyer!"

"I would be careful about doing that, but go ahead if you want all of your actions published on the front page of the 'Freemont Front Newspaper.' Caw!"

The look on his face shouted, "I want to kill you!" Then Billy Smith approached.

"Uh-oh," Marigold whispered. Was Billy going to defend his football coach?

"Hi, Billy. Good to see you, quarterback." Mr. Reynolds patted him on the back. "I'm going to be gone for a few days, but I'll be back. I'll be right back. You just keep eating protein and doing your push-ups, okay?"

"No, I'm quitting, Coach Reynolds."

Were Marigold's ears deceiving her? What had Billy just said?

Well, Mr. Reynolds must have been thinking the same thing, because he said, "What did-did you just say? I-thought-you-said--"

"I did. I'm quitting, coach. I can't play for a guy who acts like a middle school bully. No way. And I can't play for a crazy man."

"But Billy, I'm not--"

"Yeah, you are. You say mean words, and what you said about seeing me flying through the sky? Well, that's just nuts, Mr. Reynolds."

"Not yourrr imagination," Jade whispered in Marigold's ear.

"So I did s-see him behind that tree," Marigold whispered back.

"Oooh, yes, you certainly diiid."

"But Billy, I did. I really saw you-" Mr. Reynolds continued, and Marigold thought he sounded like he was actually whining. "And it's Coach Reynolds."

Billy stomped off, after he said, "Mr. Reynolds to me, man."

Mr. Reynolds turned toward the table, pointed at each of them individually, and said, "You-are-mine." Then, after trying to stare down Mrs. Hernandez (which didn't work), he turned, with a squeak of his fancy black gym shoes, and marched away. Mrs. Hernandez slumped down at the table.

"Oh n-no," Marigold said in a very low voice. "He s-saw us. All of us. Worst of-of all, he saw--."

"Yes. He saw Billy's flight." Mrs. Hernandez whispered, "We have much to address in The Contributing Room. Go there tonight, without stopping in The Meeting or The Dining Room."

The Misfits departed the cafeteria to finish the school day. Marigold knew all of them felt like she did. What are we going to do about Mr. Reynold's knowledge?

***

Tasha did not trudge onto the bus, like usual, but instead ran straight to her seat beside Marigold.

"Did you have a b-better day?" Marigold asked her.

"Yeah, a little bit better. They didn't say as many awful things to me. Weird."

Marigold wanted to tell Tasha about Billy's change, but she knew she couldn't share confidential information. Never ever. Within seconds, Billy charged onto the bus and stopped at their seats. Marigold readied herself for the familiar, verbal abuse Billy was so good at giving.

"Hi!" he said, smiling at Marigold, then at Tasha.

"H-Hi," Marigold said. She smiled back at him, because she was happy he had chosen to be nice. She also gave a silent kudos to Jade, with her major gift of hypnotic nudges.

"Hi?" Tasha responded, but Marigold detected apprehension in her voice. She probably wasn't real certain about Billy's friendliness.

When Billy walked toward the back, he turned and said, "I hope you both have a good evening!"

Tasha looked at Marigold with her big, brown eyes. "Did he just say what I think he said?"

"Y-Yes. That's what he s-said. Guess h-he must have decided to be n-nice."

"Wonder why--"

Marigold smirked. "Just glad h-he did."

Billy had reached the back of the bus, and even Marigold could hear all the Droobs welcoming him to their pack with roars of greeting and laughter. Oh brother, she thought-here it comes. She wasn't worried about the mean words that were going to be yelled at her, but she was majorly concerned about her new friend, who reacted to the words like knives were cutting her. Marigold sure understood.

And yep, the snake-venom words like, "Freak Yellow Girl", "Ugly Black Face", "Dweeb Creeps," etc., began filling the bus, accompanied by many cheers and applause. The bus driver even turned around and started churning his arm in the air, encouraging them to continue. His evil smile flashed in his rear view mirror, and Marigold knew that smile was aimed directly at Tasha and her. Mr. Carini continued the wicked smile, even while he drove the bus away from the school.

Then suddenly, there was silence from the back. What is going on, Marigold wondered? That's when Tasha whispered in her ear, "You aren't going to believe this."

Although Marigold thought she knew what Tasha was going to say, her friend continued, "Billy just told them to stop, that it wasn't nice to be mean to us."

"Wh-what?" Marigold feigned surprise. "He s-said that?"

"Yeah! I can't believe it!"

Marigold felt great happiness, glad that Billy was still following the program; glad for Tasha, her, and for all the kids Billy and the Droobs had bullied in the past, but she was also glad for Billy. She knew his life was going to be a whole lot better, if he was nice to other people-if he tried in school, was kind to his mom and sister, tried to be healthy, loved himself. All of that, together, was going to give him a lot more happiness. Billy was showing he could be saved and wasn't going to have to be removed to some remote island in the South Pacific Ocean, like his father had been.

Well, Billy's change in behavior demonstrated itself again, when he walked to the front of the bus and whispered in Mr. Carini's ear, right before Tasha stood to get off the bus. Then Billy told him, "Have a good evening," before he ran back to his seat.

Marigold looked over at her friend. "What did he say to M-Mr. Carini? What did h-he whisper in his ear?"

"Hold on to your seat, girlfriend. He told him to quit being mean. That it isn't nice being a bully."

"H-He did? He said that to Mr. C-Carini?"

Tasha nodded, with a big smile, and jogged ahead to go down the steps. Marigold stood up and watched her friend safely walk away from the bus stop . Thank goodness, she thought with a sigh of relief. But the bus driver? His glaring eyes were reflected in his rear view mirror.

***

"Welcome home, my honey bear," Marsha Stroop greeted her daughter when Marigold came through the front door. "I hope you had a good day." She was wearing a huge smile.

Why the huge, much bigger than normal, smile? Marigold wondered.

"Here, come out to the kitchen." Marigold's mom skittered ahead of her and put a bowl of macaroni and cheese, as well as a plate of veggie sausages, on the table.

"Early s-supper?"

"Yes, I hope you don't mind. You see, I have something to tell you--" Marsha Stroop sat down in a chair across from Marigold's and motioned that she should sit down. Marigold slowly lowered herself into her chair and looked into her mother's intense eyes. Her mom reached over, clutched her daughter's hands.

"Y-Yeah?" Marigold asked, wondering just what kind of drama her mother was going to share with her today. Her mom really had a strong grip.

"Marigold? You are getting to be a big girl."

"Yes? I-I know that."

"Well, honey, I have raised you by myself for eleven years, eleven of the happiest years of my life. Have I ever told you that before?"

"Uh huh. Th-Think so."

"Marigold, it's time I started doing fun stuff; I mean, doing some things for myself, things that make me happy."

"O-Okay..." Where was this going?

Her mom squeezed her hands tighter. (Ouch) "Guess what?"

"What?" She tried to release her hands, unsuccessfully, from her mom's grip.

"I have a date tonight!"

Uh oh. A date. Tonight. "W-Well, that's good, Mom."

"Really? You don't mind?"

"Um, n-no. Of c-course not. Are you g-going to be out late?" The question as to how Jade was going to perform her magic and hypnotize her mother, so she could return home without being discovered, stood center stage in her mind.

"You seem upset by this. Does it bother you? Are you afraid to be alone in the house tonight? Yes, I probably won't be home until late. Stuart--his name is Stuart--is going to take me out for supper, a movie, and then dancing!"

"Y-You are? You are g-going to be home l-late?"

Marsha Stroop stood up with a big clap, and Marigold was happy to have her let go of her cramping hand. "Yes, I am. Now, you will be just fine by yourself, sweetheart. You are a big girl." She reached over and tweaked her nose.

"R-Right. I-I know I am, Mom." Marigold smiled but wondered how she was going to get back before her mom returned; plus, how was Jade going to know not to hypnotize her mom, before she left on her date? Hopefully, Stuart would arrive and take her mom away, before Marigold needed to leave with the Misfits. That way, Jade wouldn't be able to hypnotize her mother, because of the proximity thing. But Marigold had to get home before her mom did.

"Just keep a phone close by and the doors locked, honey." Marsha looked out the living room window. "Oh, look! Here he is! And he's driving a bright red convertible! See you later, sweetheart!" She was out the door in a flash, leaving Marigold to lock it behind her and sit down to macaroni and cheese, sausage, and great concerns. Good her mom had left early, but when would Stuart bring her back home?

At dusk, Marigold stood outside her house, waiting for the Misfits to arrive. Her heart beat kabooma. kabooma, kaboom-kaboom-kaboom in her chest.

"I knowww," Jade said, approaching from the back of the house. "Your worries caaame through loud and clear. The big question isss whether or not weee can get you home prior to her arrival, and if we caaan't---then what?"

Marigold started biting her fingernail, as the other Misfits arrived. "R-Right. That could b-be a problem."

There were several nods of agreement from the others. Then together, they ran to the shed, slid down the slide, and landed on the soft blankets.

"Well, let's get to The Contributing Room, dudes," Della said with a kick, kick.

Marigold looked around. "Where is J-Jus?" In all her worries about returning home before her mom did, she hadn't noticed Jus was missing.

"Heee got delayed, but he will be meeeting us here."

The others joined Marigold with questioning looks at Jade. "Did h-he get in trouble for not coming home l-last night?" The fear of him sitting in some juvenile lock-up alarmed her.

"You shall find out sooon enough," Jade replied.

Chapter 31

"Weee must wait here a minute," Jade announced. There was a collective amount of arguing words, reiterating Mrs. Hernandez's statement that they were not to stop in The Meeting Room or The Dining Room, but go straight to The Contributing Room.

Jade said, "Hush! Thiiings have changed! You willl be finding out soon eeenough!"

Then with a great swoosh, Jus flew from the slide and into the room, accompanied by someone else right in front of him; a little someone else who stood up and looked with frightened eyes around her. "Where am I?" She wrapped her arms around her shaking body.

When Marigold realized who had landed right in front of Jus, she gave a gasp-then squealed, "Tasha!" She ran over and threw her arms about her friend.

"Marigold! I didn't know you would be here! What's going on? Where are we?"

Suddenly, The Proprietor slipped out from his door in the wall and hobbled over to Latasha. He analyzed her with his light blue eyes, stroked her cheek, and, as if giving approval, he gave a grunt-a very squeaky grunt. Then a smile. Marigold interpreted it as a way he showed he was glad Tasha was there. "I am The Proprietor. Welcome."

"Heee is happy she's here; it was his idea after alll."

"H-His idea?" Marigold asked.

Mrs. Hernandez floated down from an opening in the ceiling of The Meeting Room (Marigold didn't know an opening existed there), to the ground, and Sinbad flew in after her. Instead of landing, the bird made giant circles above their heads.

Tasha watched these happenings, with her head cranked upward at such an angle, she actually stumbled backwards and fell down. Mrs. Hernandez rushed over and grasped Latasha's hands, with her long fingers, then raised her up.

"Latasha Trine, I am so happy to meet you! Caw!"

Tasha's eyes appeared ready to pop from her head. "Aren't-Aren't you the principal?"

Mrs. Hernandez knelt down and looked directly into Tasha's beautiful brown eyes. "I am. I am also a leader in the Misfits, a group we are inviting you to join tonight, a group made up of those who have been bullied, but who choose to do 'Right, not Might'. The Proprietor received word of your gift from Jade, who learned about it through Marigold's thoughts."

"Wait. Somebody, named Jade, learned about me from Marigold's thoughts?" Tasha turned toward Marigold.

"Yes," Mrs. Hernandez continued. "Much for you to discover. After thorough investigation, The Proprietor decided you are needed to be a part of us, if you are willing. We so hope you are going to join us. Because we believe you will, you have been given the ability to see Sinbad, this magnificent bird; otherwise, you wouldn't see him. It is the reason Marigold was able to see him that first day of school, when she walked to the bus stop."

"It is?" Tasha asked and looked at Marigold. "You did?"

"Y-Yes, Marigold replied.

Well, Tasha was speechless, looking from person to person surrounding her, then said, "I-I-I don't know-" Her focus turned to the big bird soaring above. "I don't even know where we are! Who all of you are! And that-that monster bird?"

The Proprietor squeaked, "We first need to slow down and have our regular meeting, even if it delays us. This beautiful girl, with the gift of great hearing, must learn about us-before she makes her decision, regarding whether or not to be a part of the Misfits. Let me add, Tasha, we certainly hope you choose to become part of this wonderful group and share your gift."

"You do? You all were bullied? And you, Mrs. Hernandez, came from up there?" Tasha pointed to the space above their heads. "And that bird? That huge bird? I have never seen a bird that big and-and- Where are we? We came down a slide and landed here? I-I-"

Marigold had never heard her friend put so many words together at one time. She wrapped her in another big hug, then backed away, and said, "Trust me. I f-felt the same way, just days ago, and decided I d-didn't want to join these new friends, standing here. But I changed my m-mind, and if you decide to b-be a part of the Misfits, well, you will n-never, ever regret it. I promise y-you."

"Since you say I will like it, I will join," Tasha said. "You are the only person who has ever been a good friend to me, Marigold."

There was a great round of applause, from everyone in The Meeting Room.

"T-Tasha, you are about to have eight more g-good friends."

"Eight?" She scanned the group.

"Yes, eight m-more." Marigold said each name, "The Proprietor, Mrs. Hernandez, Jus, Mo, Kate, Della, Jade, and Sinbad the bird." While being introduced, each nodded, "high-fived" her, or raised his hand.

Sinbad batted his wings and cawed loudly. Those loud caws forced Tasha to cover her ears.

Mo ran in circles. "Let's get started, with our meeting, like The Proprietor said!"

Della flew through the air, making a major kick. "Mo is right, dudes!"

With a pointing finger toward Jade, Mrs. Hernandez said, "Do your thing."

Jade went over and opened the chest, removed the capes, and put one around each current Misfit. When they had been regally donned, Mrs. Hernandez held her hands out, and all joined into a circle. They said, "Ommm", together. Tasha held onto Marigold's hand, on one side, and Jade's, on the other.

Jus began, and everyone's voice (except for Tasha's, who didn't know the words yet), said,

"For Right,
Not Might
For the greater good
To all upon this planet earth
And for all who have met on these hallowed grounds
From Time Unknown
Until Time We Know."

Marigold figured they said it fast, because they were in a big hurry. Mrs. Hernandez motioned that they were to be seated; then, each Misfit took a turn standing up and telling Tasha about themselves. After they'd finished, Jus asked Tasha to please tell them about herself. She wavered to an upright position and stared, wide-eyed, at all of the others. After clearing her throat, she began.

"Um, my name is Latasha Trine, but I go by Tasha, and I don't really have much to say. There's nothing very important about me. I went to Crisson Elementary School, where there were only about three other minority kids in the whole school, so I-I got bullied all the time. Well, I got bullied, cause I was black and since I have big ears. Not just big ears--huge ears. But because I do, I have really good hearing. Anyway, I live with my dad and six brothers. My mom left us, after she found a boyfriend on the internet, and went to live with him in Alaska. That's all." She sat down, and everyone gave her a round of applause; Mrs. Hernandez scurried over to raise her up.

"Let us begin the initiation process!" The Proprietor shouted. He went on to tell Latasha how happy the Misfits were that she wanted to join them, and that her extreme auditory skills were greatly needed. He explained that her ability to hear was her wonderful gift.

After the ceremony had ended, and Tasha had become a member of the Misfits, Jade wrapped her in a gold cape. Tasha put on the biggest smile Marigold had ever seen her wear. It was even brighter than the shimmery gold cloth wrapped around her. Next, they all trooped over to The Contributing Room, after crawling into The Dining Room, traversing The Kitchen, and scampering through The Tropical Rain Forest Room. Latasha squeezed Marigold's arm intermittently, as they journeyed through the various rooms. She made squeals of amazement and surprise, especially when the Timmers ran excitedly in circles about The Tropical Rain Forest Room.

"Look!" she cried. "There are little, purple people!!"

Marigold, trying to keep up with the others and hurry Tasha along, said, "Yes! They are called T-Timmers."

"T-Timmers?"

"Yes, b-but without the stutter."

That made Latasha laugh loudly, a sound Marigold had never heard before.

Jade yelled back, "Sooon, we will explain to you all about the Timmers, the rooooms, and how the Misfits came to beee. We have so much tooo tell you, and you have so much to learrrn!!"

"Okaaay!" Tasha hollered back.

Marigold giggled at Tasha's response, imitating Jade.

"No neeed to copy me, Tasha!" Jade yelled from up ahead.

"Okaaay!" Tasha replied, and Marigold laughed harder.

"Pick up the pace, mon," Jus said from the rear.

Once they had arrived at The Contributing Room, Jus, Mrs. Hernandez, and The Proprietor sat on their thrones, and Sinbad hunkered down at Mrs. Hernandez's feet. She began the barefoot massage, then all the other Misfits sat on the couch facing them. Latasha's eyes were lost in the diamond-laden sky.

"Where are we?" Latasha asked. "What kind of a magical place is this?"

Marigold squeezed her friend's hand.

Mrs. Hernandez's small black eyes searched those on the couch. "We are here tonight for an extremely important purpose. Mr. Reynolds followed us to the barn last night and saw Billy flying through the sky, before witnessing the rest of us leaving the barn."

"Huh? What is she talking about?" Tasha whispered in Marigold's ear.

"Shhhh. You will sooon find out," Jade said.

Marigold touched her friend's arm.

"We will be takin' suggestions regarding what to be doin' about Mr. Reynolds seein' Billy flyin' through the air, and watchin' us leavin' the barn," Jus said.

"Whaaat do you suggest?" Jade asked.

"I am havin' no idea, mon."

"I think I need to run and find him!" Mo jumped up and down in place.

Well, that sent Della into a series of round off, back hand springs, across the room. "Dudes! I will join Mo and take him down! Take him right down!"

"Della!" Mrs. Hernandez was up flapping her arms. "Caw!"

"I took my meds. I won't hurt him, Mrs. Hernandez... unless you need me to." She lowered herself onto the couch, giving a little chop, chop.

Mrs. Hernandez sat back down and resumed the massage. "Okay, okay. But there must be another solution."

Kate stood. "It has become apparent, from day one of school, that Mr. Reynolds is a threat to what we are attempting to accomplish-through kindness and empathy (but also with realistic expectations)- inside and outside Brentwood Middle School. Perhaps his only consequence is to be removed. He has exhibited abuse, both physical and verbal." She sat back down.

The Proprietor began his sobs again. Mrs. Hernandez reached over and patted his shoulder, then she handed him a tissue from her pocket. "There, there-"

"C-Can't we just hypnotize h-him and tell him to start being n-nice, like what we did for B-Billy?"

Marigold had stood up, and all eyes were on her.

Kate shook her head. "No, that will not suffice. It is imperative Sinbad performs his duty of removal. Mr. Reynolds is a mature man, and, like Officer Smith, cannot be saved."

Again came the sobbing from The Proprietor and more tissues from Mrs. Hernandez. She said, "I agree with Marigold. The positive approach was effective with Billy. Caw!"

"I am agreein' with Marigold and Mrs. Hernandez, mon. The positive approach is always bein' the best approach," Jus interjected.

But that's when Tasha leaped up. "Do the Timmers ever enter this underground place, by going down the slide?"

"No. The Timmers never leave here. They are normally in The Dining Room, The Kitchen, or snoring in their hammocks, in The Tropical Rain Forest Room." The Proprietor had stood his short self up. "We will soon explain about the Timmers to you!"

Tasha tilted her head to the side.

"What is it?" Mrs. Hernandez asked.

"I hear snoring," Tasha said, "but something else."

Mrs. Hernandez said, "The snoring is probably from sleeping Timmers."

"S-Something else?" Marigold asked her friend.

"Yes, someone slid down into The Meeting Room. We are not alone."

"Oh no!" The Proprietor cried. "Not alone?"

Tasha tilted her head the other way. "No. Not alone. Someone is definitely coming this way-and coming very quickly."

Mrs. Hernandez started cawing loudly, and she furiously flapped her arms. Sinbad soared in giant circles. All of this made Tasha run into a corner.

"Was the door into The Dining Room left open?" Mrs. Hernandez asked mid-flap.

"I was last, mon, and yes, I left it open. We always leave it open!"

"Yes, we always leave it open because we have never been afraid of anyone coming in before!" Mo ran in quick circles.

Della was up and kicking. "Armed and ready, dudes. Armed and ready. My body is my weapon, your weapon, all of our weapon!"

Soon everyone was standing, and Sinbad careened above their heads.

Tasha shouted, "We need to leave now; the footsteps are getting very close!"

"There is bein' only one way out, mon." Jus pointed toward the door, through which they had entered. "We will be runnin' into whomever you are hearin'."

"Well, thankfully, Tasha and her gift of hearing has granted us adequate time to prepare ourselves," Kate said.

Marigold didn't know how they'd "prepare" themselves, but Jus yelled, "Misfits! You need to be hidin' with us behind our thrones, mon!" Marigold, Tasha, Jade, and Kate ran up behind the thrones and scrunched together with The Proprietor, Mrs. Hernandez, and Jus. Marigold watched Sinbad soar into the hole of the sky and was gone, and she wondered why Mrs. Hernandez didn't float back up through that space to join him.

"A captain neverrrr leaves her ship," Jade whispered. Marigold understood that since Mrs. Hernandez was one of the leaders, a captain, she would never leave them in danger.

"We are here to protect you! Never fear, dudes!" Della yelled, and Marigold knew Della and Mo were in a position to charge ahead and level the intruder, should he or she enter The Contributing Room.

Chapter 32

And what happened next, Marigold never could have predicted. Gunshots began firing into the air! As she peeked around the throne, into that golden-lit room, she saw a man charging into the space!

In his familiar voice, he yelled, "I'm here to get rid of all you satanic witches!" He fired off shots, from the huge gun, he was carrying. Pow! Pow! Pow!

Into The Contributing Room, Mr. Reynolds came, like a jungle cat searching for his prey. "Where are you? I know you are here, you Freak-os! You have ruined my career and sent my quarterback flying through the air! You are mine! Mine!" The rat-a-tat-tat series of bullets, exploding throughout the room, forced Tasha to cover her ears. Marigold trembled uncontrollably, and she was sure she wasn't the only Misfit shaking in fear.

That's when, with a loud "Heee-yiii!", Della went flipping through the room toward the killer. She connected with a kick to his head, almost knocking him onto the floor; then she attempted again. As she charged at him, her hands wildly chopping the air, Mr. Reynolds turned swiftly in her direction and fired off a shot. It missed. He reached into his pocket and began reloading his gun. During that pause, Mo charged out, on his very huge feet, and threw himself onto Mr. Reynold's back. Down the coach fell, losing his gun onto the floor. Della grabbed for the gun, missed, and it was once more in his hand.

As he jumped upright, he bellowed, "You are mine! Mine! I followed you here for one purpose-to get rid of all of you Freak-os!" The shots started peppering the room, and one grazed Della's arm.

"Owwwa!" she cried, grabbing her wounded limb. Blood dripped down and dotted the floor.

"H-He shot her! We have to s-save her!" Marigold said. She started out, but Jus pulled her back.

"If we go out now, mon, he'll be killin' all of us!"

"It has to be every one of us, together, but it needs to be at the right time," Mrs Hernandez said in a low voice.

The very wicked man continued, "Better watch out, Batgirl! The next shot is at your heart! Your evil, satanic heart!"

Della dropped and rolled away from him. She started crawling, with her bleeding arm, to approach him from the back. He didn't notice, because he had now focused on Mo and aimed the gun directly at him. "You big-footed, Middle Eastern killer! You remember what your cousins did on 9/11? Do you? Well, now it's your turn to die!"

When he fired a shot at him, Mo, with all of his swiftness, spun in a series of circles and escaped toward the wall. That's when Della charged from behind to knock Mr. Reynolds over again! He threw her off and rose to a standing position, a cruel sneer on his face.

Even though injured, Della clutched at her arm and rolled away. Mr. Reynolds took one step, then the next, toward the spot where she was curled, motionless, on her side. He aimed his gun at her head, and once he was about two feet away, Della stuck out a foot and tripped him. With a whimper, she shifted onto her back and closed her eyes. That's when Mo charged out with a battle cry! He threw all of his weight on top of that evil man.

"Now! Caw! Caw!" Mrs. Hernandez crowed, and all of those who had been hiding, charged forward! Mr. Reynolds lay groaning, on the floor, under Mo's weight. The other Misfits barreled forward, an army on an onslaught!

“Whaaat?!” Mr. Reynolds managed to get out.

The Misfits all joined Mo in covering the coach. Della, who must have had a sudden recovery, managed to crawl over and grab the gun, now lying a few feet away from his crushed hand.

“You evil freaks! You witches!” he sputtered, from under all of those, on top of his body.

“Sinbad!” Mrs. Hernandez called out, and the giant bird soared from above to those piled on the floor.

As the blood from Della’s wound pooled on the floor, she used all of her strength to say, “You can-can get off him. I have-I have-the gun.” Then she collapsed, and Jus left the top of the mountain of Misfits, to grab the weapon.

One by one, they each rolled off the pile, and Jus aimed the gun at the coach. Slowly, Mr. Reynolds stood up with a snarl, then started walking backward toward the door. “You think I’m afraid of you? Well, I’m not! You might have my gun, you satanic derelict, but there are plenty more where that came from! I will kill all of you! Just you wait and see!”

Mo picked up Della and cradled her in his arms. “I am off to the hospital!” He dashed out the door.

“Sinbaaad, time to fly!” Jade shouted.

Sinbad, in a great, dark flash, grabbed Mr. Reynolds by the collar and swooped him away, into that black sky. The coach dangled like a wriggling worm, from the giant bird's beak.

"What is haaap--pen--iiiing!" the coach hollered.

"Up, up, and away!" Mo yelled after him.

Mr. Reynold's voice faded farther and farther away, and Marigold could no longer hear him.

"What is he saying, Tasha?" The Proprietor asked, quite out of breath.

Tasha shook her head in disbelief. "You aren't going to believe this. He is saying that he will be back to shoot all of us! He said, 'I will kill all of you! You are still mine!'"

"I believe he said that," Kate said. "Like I stated before, Mr. Reynolds was beyond help and needed, obviously, to be removed."

Really? Even as he was being swept away, he was saying that he would be back to kill all of them? How insane was he? Marigold wondered.

"Oooh, he is verrry insane," Jade said to Marigold.

Marigold could only stare, into the diamond- laden sky above, and shake her head.

"I hope it was okaaay that I commanded Sinbaaad to remove him, that I made an almost-execuuutive decision."

"You read my thoughts, Jade, didn't you?" Mrs. Hernandez asked.

"I diiid."

"It was better than okay, Miss Jade. Caw! And I am figuring you read all of our thoughts, knowing that removal was the only appropriate consequence."

"Yesss. Even Marigold understood what Sinbaaad needed to do."

Marigold nodded. "I did. It m-made me sad, but it w-was the only answer."

Mrs. Hernandez said, "And The Proprietor?"

He wiped his eyes with the same tissue. "Yes, he was going to kill all of us. Even if you had managed to get him out of our sanctum and above ground, the police might never have believed that he'd almost killed us. They might have released him, and that would have provided him time to do away with all of us in the future. The very near future." Then he started sobbing again.

Jus said, "I am happy, mon, that we were all bein' in agreement."

"Where d-did Sinbad take him?" Marigold asked.

"To anotherrr remote island, somewhere in the Paciiific Ocean." Jade closed her eyes and folded her hands in front of her chest. "They are over Kaaansas right now. They should reeeach an uninhabited island, within a few hourrrs."

Mrs. Hernandez flapped her arms very energetically. "Thank you, Tasha, for joining us tonight. It was quite timely, since you saved our lives."

"I did?" Tasha asked.

Jus gave her a smile. "Yeah, you did. Because you were hearin' him, mon, it gave all of us time to be hidin'."

Kate interjected, "You certainly did. Had your auditory skills not detected his approach, Mr. Reynolds would have charged in and eliminated all of us. Instead, he was removed, as I had suggested."

"Thank you, Tasha!" Mrs. Hernandez cried out.

"Yes, thank you!" everyone's voice sounded in The Contributing Room.

Tasha was a recipient of many hugs and words of affirmation, and when they finally stopped, she said, "Thanks, guys."

"N-No, thank you for j-joining us," Marigold said.

"Now, if I might interject," The Proprietor said with a another swipe of his eyes with the tissue, "I do hope Della will be okay."

"Me, too, mon," Jus said. "She was losin' a lot of blood."

"I expect to see all of your faces in my office in the morning. I hope and pray I will have good news to share, regarding Della. Caw!" Then Mrs. Hernandez raised her arms over her head and floated up, up, up, until she was gone.

As Tasha watched that ascent, she fell over backward again. Marigold stuck out a hand to help her up.

"Well, mon, let's get started home." Jus led the way through the door, and they traveled through The Tropical Rain Forest (as the Timmers snored), The Kitchen, The Dining Room,and The Meeting Room, where Jade removed their capes and gently tucked them back inside the chest.

Tasha clutched onto Marigold's hand in the elevator ride, and on the walk back home, until they reached her house. Because her home was the closest to the shed, the Misfits bid her good-night first. She walked into her well lit house, and Marigold asked, "W-Won't her dad wonder where she w-was?"

"No," Jade said. "With thaaat house full of kids, Mr. Trine was probably not even aware sheee was gone."

"O-Okay," Marigold said. The rest of the trip was uneventful, until they reached her house, and there was a police car parked in the drive. Marigold, Jus, Jade, Mo, and Kate slipped their ways across the yard and crept to the side of the house. Her mother was standing in the front yard, waving her arms energetically, and talking to two officers.

"I don't know!" Marigold's mom screeched. "She was here when I left! Something has happened to her! I just know it!"

Oh no, Marigold thought. She took tiny steps toward her mom.

That's when Marsha Stroop noticed Marigold approaching her. "Oh! Oh! It's my darling Marigold!" She ran with open arms in her direction.

Wrapped within her mother's giant, tight scrunch, it was a bit before Marigold managed to get out, "Hi, M-Mom. Sorry you were w-worried."

Marsha's look suddenly changed from extreme joy at seeing her daughter had arrived home safely-to anger. Major anger. She held Marigold out, her eyes red from crying. "Where were you? Do you know how worried sick I have been? I have been scared to death! Scared somebody came into our house and took you away! Remember when that happened to me? I was afraid Officer Smith had broken in and driven you down to the river-to-to kill you, like he tried to kill me!"

Marigold opened her mouth to say, well, that wasn't going to happen, but instead said, "S-Sorry, Mom."

"You go into the house this minute! You are grounded--for-ev-er!"

One of the police officers said, "Just like Jake told us, you both are nuts."

And the other policeman said, "Wait! You think Officer Smith was going to kill you, lady?"

Marsha Stroop ignored the policemen and opened the front door, led Marigold inside, and slammed the door behind them. Then she turned the deadbolt lock. "You sit down! You sit right down on that couch!" Her shaking finger pointed at a worn, gray, couch cushion.

Marigold slumped down onto it. "Sorry, M-Mom."

"Sorry? Sorry? No, sorry doesn't make it! Where were you?"

"Wh-Where was I?"

Now Marsha had crossed her arms over her chest and was tapping her toe. "I believe that's what I just asked you."

"W-Well, um, I was just out t-taking a w-walk." Crossed fingers, right hand.

"What? Taking a walk? In the dark?" Her mom's face was beyond crimson.

"Y-Yes." What was she supposed to say? That she was out saving the world from crime? That her mom wouldn't be alive, if it hadn't been for the Misfits?

Marsha now began tapping the opposite toe. "You are grounded, so grounded. Do you hear me? You will stay in this house for-ev-er! No more walks!"

Marigold swallowed hard. "I can't e-even go to school?"

Her eyes narrowed. "Yes, you will go to school. But only school-that's it."

"O-Okay," Marigold said, but she wondered what she was going to do about the Misfits' meetings. Was she going to have to quit the group she loved so much? She slowly walked to her room.

All weekend, Marigold was grounded to her room. The only thing she looked forward to was Monday morning and joining the Misfits, at school, once more.

Chapter 33

Mrs. Hernandez closed the door after Jus, Tasha, Jade, Mo, Kate, and Marigold had entered her office Monday morning. She stood in front of the window and raised the glass, so Sinbad could stick his head inside.

When she turned around, she smiled and said, "It is my great pleasure to announce that Della is going to be fine. She lost a lot of blood, but she is now receiving transfusions and should be able to return home tomorrow."

"Yay!" the group let out with a simultaneous cheer. Sinbad cawed so loudly, Mrs. Hernandez had to shove his beak closed, because Tasha cried out in pain and covered her ears.

"Shh", their principal said, and Sinbad winked at her.

"Can we be goin' to the hospital and visitin' her now? I'm wonderin' if she'd like company, mon?" Jus asked.

"Sheee is sleeping now, but maybe toniiight. Ommm," Jade said, with eyes closed.

"Tonight let's meet at the hospital, instead of going underground," Mrs. Hernandez said.

Marigold bit her fingernail. "I c-can't go. My mom had a d-date and came home last night, before I-I got home. She had called the p-police, and they were there when w-we walked up. She grounded m-me for-ev-er. I can't l-leave the house-except for school."

Everyone looked concerned, except for Jade, who still had her eyes closed. "No problllem. I will hypnotiiize her like before. She will not know youuu left for the hospital."

Marigold frowned and stared at the floor.

"I am thinkin' Marigold doesn't want to be goin' against her mom's rules." Jus smiled at her.

Marigold nodded. "I-I don't. Plus, what h-happens when she goes on another date and g-gets home before me?"

"Just tell her you need to be with your 'new, little friends'!" Mo jumped up and down.

Jade said, "Thaaat may work. Your mom simply neeeds some time to coool off. The fact that youuu have 'new, little friends' is very important to her. After I telepathically suggested to her that youuu be allowed to wearrr the clothes you have on, sheee went with it."

"That's wh-why she was o-okay with these clothes?" Marigold ran her hands across her yellow Nike T-shirt and new jeans.

Jade nodded. "That, and beeecause she really only wants the best for youuu."

"O-Okay. I c-can try talking to her about being w-with all of you."

Jade winked. "It willl probably work. Now, Mrs. Hernandez, can you turn on Channel 67 LIVE?"

Mrs. Hernandez grabbed the remote, flicked on the TV in the corner, and clicked the channel button until she reached that station. The blond haired reporter, on the news show, said to a woman standing before a small brown house, "So, your husband, John Reynolds, never returned home last night?"

The tiny woman was emotionless when she said, "No, he didn't."

The reporter asked, "Do you have any idea where he might be?"

"No. And I don't care." She pressed her pale lips into a thin line.

"You don't care?"

"Here. Come with me." The camera followed Mrs. Reynolds through the tiny living room, down a hall, and into a room. There, it panned over a long table, completely covered with a line of assault weapons.

Clearly, the reporter was shocked as she said, "Are-Are all of those your-your husband's?"

"Yes, and there are more in the basement."

"More?"

"Yes, at least a hundred more, and he was also building a bomb down there-in the basement, I mean."

The reporter swallowed hard. "Did you tell the police?"

"Yeah, I told Officer Jake Smith, who was his best friend, but he didn't do anything. Jake also disappeared, you know." She stared at the row of weapons. "Guess I should have told a different policeman, somebody who would have cared. I just hope John and Jake are both far, far away."

Well, that statement was closer to the truth than Mrs. Reynolds could have ever known, Marigold thought. As she looked at the other Misfits, she believed they all were thinking the same thing.

Mrs. Reynolds continued, "I can't tell you how many times John held a gun to my head. Last night, he loaded one and told me he was off to kill a group of evil witches, and that I shouldn't wait up." Her face filled the screen. "And all of you out there? Lock your doors! My husband is armed and dangerous!"

The clearly shaken reporter faced the camera and said, "This is LIVE. Let's go to a commercial."

Mrs. Hernandez turned off the television and said, "Oh, my goodness. He was worse than I imagined. I wonder if even his wife was capable of knowing what Mr. Reynolds, coach here at Brentwood Middle School, was capable of doing."

"Me, too," Tasha said, and most agreed.

Most agreed, except for Kate. "I knew that, from the initiation of the process, the process when we determined whether or not he was salvageable. As you now have ascertained, he was not, and I was correct."

"Oooh, get off your high horse, Kaaate. Idiom meaning, quit acting liiike you are better than all of usss." Jade retreated to the back wall and hummed.

"Sorry. So sorry," Kate said.

"Well, it is time to go to first period." Mrs. Hernandez scribbled across pink passes and handed them out. "Go! Meet at the hospital lobby tonight after supper! Caw! I am off to let The Proprietor know Della will be fine."

"I can go!" Mo shouted to their principal, exiting through the door in the office wall.

"You shall go to class! Caw!" she cried back. "School is important!"

With the others, Marigold scrambled from the office and to class. That night, the Misfits would be going to see Della, their Batgirl, recovering at the hospital. Marigold made a hope against hope her mom would understand, and she'd let her go. She doubted that would happen, however.

Later in art class, Billy smiled when Marigold entered and said, "Hope you're having a good day, Mari. Mari is your new name, because I think you're so pretty, and you need a nickname. You know, something special from me to you." Then he winked.

Well, it took all Marigold possessed to continue onward and find her seat.

The substitute, Mrs. Crinel, searched across Mr. Reynold's desk and said, "I can't seem to find a seating chart. Mr. Reynolds must have left, without knowing he wouldn't be returning today. Can't find any lesson plans, either. Oh, dear. Well, just draw a picture of your favorite animal."

That was no-brainer for Marigold, and she sketched a big, black bird flying through white, puffy clouds. She smiled, remembering how only a week earlier, she had wanted to fly up into the sky and never come back. She now knew she didn't have to travel up, into the sky, to be with that big, black bird. Sinbad had flown down to be with her and all of the other Misfits. He came down to earth, a planet that she was very happy to be living on now. Living on, and also visiting underground, by traveling on a twirly-whirly slide.

My, how the Misfits had changed her life. The rest of art class was without any major happenings, except for Billy, turning around intermittently to give her a wink, wink and Marigold, trying to cover up her blushing cheeks with her hands.

***

At the kitchen table at 5:00 before a plate of hot dogs and green beans, Marigold said, "Mom, one of m-my Misfit friends, Della, is in the h-hospital. May I-I please walk with the other Misfits to Methodist Hope Hospital and s-see her after supper?"

"Why is she in the hospital?" It was clear from her cool tone, Marsha Stroop was still angry.

"She-um-got h-hurt."

"Hurt? How did she get hurt?" With her fork, Marsha stabbed at a green bean.

Marigold lowered her voice. "She got sh-sh--"

"Sh-?"

"Shot. She g-got shot."

Marsha Stroop leaped straight up. "Shot? She got shot?"

"Yes, but she's in the h-hospital and getting tr-transfusions."

"What? No! You may not go to the hospital! You will no longer run around with wild kids, who get shot by guns!" A shaking Marsha Stroop plopped herself back down into her chair. She shook her head, ran her fingers through her hair.

Sadly, Marigold knew she couldn't go, but Marsha Stroop reached over and took her hand in her own. "Still, I understand how much your new, little friends mean to you, sweetheart, and I believe they must be good kids, since you say they are."

Now, it was Marigold's turn to feel shaken. "H-Huh? What did y-you say?"

"Yes, you may go to the hospital and see Della, with your new little friends."

"I-I can?"

"Yes, you are no longer grounded. I want you to have friends, and these Misfits are special to you. Just be careful, okay?"

"O-Okay." Marigold stood on wobbly legs to walk over to the sink and rinse off her dishes. As she peered out of the window, whom should she see, but the Misfits standing in the back yard: Tasha, Mo, Kate, Jus, and Jade stood together, waving at her. Jade stepped closer to the glass and gave her a wink.

"What are you looking at?" Marigold's mom asked, joining her at the window. "Oh, look! It's your little friends!"

"Y-Yes, Mom. That's who it-it is, all right."

"Would they want to come in for a brownie?"

"Um, n-no, Mom. Thanks, b-but they are in a hurry to get to the h-hospital."

Her mother stood with arms akimbo, tapped her toe. "Well...I don't know."

Uh-oh, Marigold thought. Was her mom about to change her mind?

But that's when Marsha Stroop burst out with a laugh. A big laugh. "Just kidding! Get out there and join your friends, sweetie!" Then she kissed her on the cheek.

Marigold grabbed her jacket and charged out to join the Misfits-the Misfits, who were her very best friends, and who also thought she was pretty special. Off they went to the hospital to see Della, their resident Batgirl. She wondered what would be in store for them tomorrow? Whatever it was, Marigold knew it was going to be important. Very important. After all, saving the world from evilness with 'Right, not Might', ranked in that "very important" category.

THE END

Made in the USA
Columbia, SC
10 July 2022